A LIADEN UNIVERSE CONSTELLATION

D0707744

Received On:

MAR 14 2022

Ballard Branch

BAEN BOOKS
by SHARON LEE & STEVE MILLER
✧✧✧

THE LIADEN UNIVERSE®

THE FEY DUOLOGY

By SHARON LEE

To purchase any of these titles in e-book form, please go to www.baen.com.

A LIADEN UNIVERSE® CONSTELLATION
✧ Volume 5 ✧

SHARON LEE & STEVE MILLER

A Liaden Universe® Constellation Volume 5

A Baen Books Original

Baen Publishing Enterprises
P.O. Box 1403
Riverdale, NY 10471
www.baen.com

ISBN: 978-1-9821-2590-5

Cover art by Sam R. Kennedy

First printing, February 2022

Distributed by Simon & Schuster
1230 Avenue of the Americas
New York, NY 10020

Library of Congress Control Number: 2021051772

Printed in the United States of America

10 9 8 7 6 5 4 3 2 1

✦ Contents ✦

Story Copyrights

✦ ACKNOWLEDGMENTS ✦

Many thanks to the Mighty Tyop Hunters;
your efforts are appreciated!

Doreen Farrar, Drammar English, Kathryn Sullivan,
Julia Hart, Alice Hickcox, Sam DiPasquale,
Bex O., Evelyn Mellone

A LIADEN UNIVERSE® CONSTELLATION

✧ Volume 5 ✧

✧ Authors' Foreword ✧

WELCOME TO THE FIFTH Liaden Universe® Constellation, which reprints stories from many venues in one convenient volume!

With the publication of this volume of shorter works, the Liaden Universe® is now on the order of three million words strong.

Three million words. Thirty-three years (absent the decade when no one would publish our work). Twenty-three novels. Seventy-two shorter works.

Not bad, considering that we had initially sketched in seven novels—say 700,000 words, total.

But here's the thing. The more we wrote, the more we learned about the characters, the more worlds and cultures we visited in this expanding universe we had created—the more we *wanted* to know.

And here we are at a cool three mil, still writing, still wondering, still exploring.

Still having fun.

As we hope you'll have fun with the ten stories in this volume. All of these stories have previously appeared in other venues, so it's entirely possible that you'll see old friends in these pages. You may also make new friends—even surprising new friends.

Thank you for reading.

Enjoy.

Sharon Lee and Steve Miller
Cat Farm and Confusion Factory
March 2021

✧ Fortune's Favors ✧

FORTUNE'S FAVORS is two things. First, it's a discovery story for two characters who would eventually appear in a novel. Secondly, it's a check-in with characters we left just after they had taken a Momentous, not to say life-changing, Decision in a previous story—"Degrees of Separation."

✧✧✧

ONE

IT WAS TO THE GAYN'URLEZ HELL in lower Low Port that his feet finally brought him, over the objections of most of himself.

There were those who dismissed Low Port as a miserable pit of vicious humanity where lived predators and prey, the roles subject to reversal without notice.

Those contended that there was nothing of value in Low Port; that it was worth the life of any honorable person to even attempt to walk such streets.

They . . . were not wrong, those who lived in the comfort of Mid Port and the luxury of High, and who bothered to give Low Port half a thought down the course of a Standard Year.

They were *not* wrong.

But they lacked discrimination.

It was true that there were very many bad and dangerous streets inside the uneasy boundaries of Low Port, and then—

There were worse.

The gayn'Urlez Gaming Hell occupied the corner of two such thoroughfares, and the best that could be said of them is that they were... somewhat less unsafe than the Hell itself.

Mar Tyn eys'Ornstahl had made it a policy—insofar as he was able to make policy—not to enter gayn'Urlez, much less work there.

Today, his feet had trampled policy, and Mar Tyn only hoped that he would survive the experience.

So anxious was he for that outcome, in fact, that he took the extreme action of... arguing... with his feet.

On the very corner, directly across from the most dangerous Hell in Low Port, Mar Tyn—turned to the right.

His feet hesitated, then strode out promptly enough, even turning right at the next corner, with no prompting from him, toward the somewhat safer streets where he was at least known.

Another might have assumed victory, just there, but Mar Tyn had lived with his feet for many years. It thus came as no surprise when they failed to take his direction at the next corner, bearing left, rather than right, until they stopped once more across the street from Hell.

He sighed. That was how it was going to be, was it?

Best to get on with it, then.

• • •✧• • •

THE BARKEEP was a thick woman with cropped grey hair and a prosthetic eye. She gave him a glance as he approached and leaned her elbows on the bar.

"Got reg'lars on tonight," she told him, pleasant enough. "Two days down there's a bed open, if you want to reserve in advance. Reservation includes a drink tonight and a hour to study the layout. The House takes six."

Mar Tyn smiled at her over the bar.

"I'm not a pleasure-worker," he said, gently.

She frowned.

"What *are* you, then?"

"A Luck."

She might have laughed at him; he expected it. She might equally have accepted him at his word; most did. Who, after all, would claim to be a Luck, if they were not?

He did not expect her to be *angry* with him.

"A Luck! Are you brain-dead? Do you know what happened to the last Luck who worked here?"

He did not. Not actually. Not *specifically*. He could guess, though.

"Her winner beat her, and robbed her of her share?"

The barkeep looked dire.

"Her winner followed her home, beat her, raped her, murdered her, took the money, her child—and for good measure, fired the building."

She paused, and took a breath, ducking her head.

"They say she was lucky to the last—no one died in the fire."

Mar Tyn took a breath.

"Ahteya," he said.

That earned him another hard glare, the prosthetic eye glowing red.

"You knew her?"

"No. We—Lucks—we know . . . *of* each other, in a general way. I had heard that a Luck named Ahteya had been killed—" Rare enough; most who hired a Luck didn't care to court the *ill* luck that must come with such an act, though Lucks were still regularly beaten and robbed. Mar Tyn supposed that it was a matter of necessity. Violence was Low Port's primary answer to hunger and want, and it could be reasoned that a Luck whose gift did not protect them was *meant* to be robbed.

"I hadn't heard where she'd been working," he told the barkeep. "Or that she had a child."

"Well, now you know, and I hope the knowledge improves your day. You can leave."

"No," he said, with real regret—for her, and for him. "I can't."

Another red glare.

"*Can't?*"

"Despite appearances, I'm not a fool. When I saw where I had come to, I tried to walk away. With what success you see."

He produced an ironic bow.

"I believe the choice before us is—will you allow me to sign the book, or will I freelance?"

The color drained out of her face.

"You poach here and gayn'Urlez will break all of your bones. Slowly."

"I understand," he told her.

She sighed, then, hard and defeated.

"You're *certain*?" she asked.

"Rarely have I been more certain," he said, and added, for the wounded look in her natural eye, "I don't like it, either."

She reached beneath the bar.

"Here's the book, then; sign in. House's piece from your cut is twelve."

He glanced up from the page, pen in hand—"Not six?"

"Six is for whores; they comfort the losers, and convince them to try again, which is good for the House. If a Luck's good, they're bad for the House, 'cause their winner's going to go big."

"I'm good," he told her, which was neither a lie nor a boast. "The Lucky Cut is—?"

"Thirty-six."

"*Thirty-six*?"

Great gods, no wonder Ahteya's winner had wanted her share. Even after she had paid the House its twelve percent . . .

"House rules," the barkeep told him. "gayn'Urlez wants them to think before they hire. Better for the House, if they don't hire."

"Of course."

He signed, and sighed, and pushed the book back to her. She glanced at his name.

"All right, Mar Tyn. The House pays for your winner's drinks. You get a meal before you start work, and as much cold tea as you can stomach. I'll show you the back way out, too."

That last was truly kind. He wondered how well she had known Ahteya.

"Thank you."

"Stay alive, that's how you thank me," she snapped, glancing over his head at the clock.

"Let's get you to the kitchen for your supper. It's near time for the earlies to get in."

. . . . ◇ . . .

HIS SUPPER LONG EATEN, and his third cup of cold tea sitting, untouched, by his hand, Mar Tyn sat behind the small red table, within good view of both the door and the bar. His winner had not yet arrived, and he might have been inclined to wonder why his feet had brought him here, were it not for the certainty that he would find out soon enough.

He had, very occasionally, been delivered to this place or that, only to find that . . . something—perhaps the simple act of obeying the compulsion of his gift—had altered circumstances sufficiently that he was no longer required in that particular place and time. On every one of those occasions, however, he had felt . . . a release. His feet lost their wisdom halfway down a busy thoroughfare, or his sudden thought that it would be pleasant to have a cold treat resulted in his arrival at the ice vendor's stall.

This evening he felt no such release, and a trial thought—that it would be pleasant to go back to his room in the attic of Bendi's House of Joy—did not result in his standing up from behind the table, approaching the bar, and informing the 'keeper that he was quit.

Mar Tyn sighed.

No, his winner was taking her time, that was all. His gift *did* prefer to be beforetime in these matters. His part was to recruit his patience, and be vigilant.

He looked at his cup of tea, then around about him. There was something that was said on the streets—that *like called to like*, and here in gayn'Urlez Hell one could see ample evidence of that small truth.

Those who framed the residents of Low Port as brutes and less would need only to look through gayn'Urlez' door to be vindicated. Gambling was the primary draw—and those it drew ranged from the desperate, willing to do anything for a meal, to those who had the means to oblige them. Opposite his corner was another table, like his, clearly visible from both door and bar. The woman sitting there was the current local power to contend with. Her name was Lady voz'Laathi, and she held six entire blocks under her protection, with gayn'Urlez Hell being the center-point. Two bullies stood behind her, guns and knives on display, and those who dared approach the table did so with hunched shoulders and bowed heads.

As if she had felt his glance, the lady turned her head and met his eyes. For a moment, they regarded each other. The lady spoke over her shoulder and one of her two protectors stepped away from the table, and crossed the room.

Mar Tyn drew a deep breath. Surely, he thought, *surely* not . . .

"Luck," the man said, standing on the far side of the red table.

"Gun," he answered, politely.

"My lady asks you to look aside. She's got no need of your gift."

Mar Tyn bowed his head, pointedly averting his eyes.

"My regards to your lady. Please assure her that I am here on other business."

"I'll tell her that. She says, too, that you're on her ticket. Eat, drink, whatever you want. My lady's no enemy of Luck."

"I honor her," Mar Tyn said, not entirely without truth. There were those who would have had an audacious Luck shot for his incautious glances. "The House feeds me this evening."

"I'll tell her that, too," said the lady's Gun, and turned away, but not before he had dropped a coin to the tabletop.

Mar Tyn's reactions were Low Port quick. His hand flashed out, covering the bright thing while it was still spinning and pinning it flat to the table.

He glanced quickly around the room, careful to avoid the lady's eyes, though he could feel her attention on him. He pulled the coin to him, and slipped it away into a pocket. It was a valuable thing, and a dangerous one, and he wished it had not been given.

Well, but given it had been; and, once accepted, it couldn't be returned, unless he wished to risk offering the lady an insult that would certainly be Balanced with his life.

He took a breath.

That he had been given no chance to refuse the favor . . .

. . . that . . . was disturbing.

Mar Tyn closed his eyes, drew a deep breath, held it for the count of twelve—and exhaled.

There was no tremor from his gift, nor sizzle of anticipation in his blood.

He opened his eyes, and turned his head to make a study of the room behind the bar.

Try, he told himself, considering the greater room, and the crowd at the card table . . . *Try not to be a fool.*

The Luck's Table was set as far as possible from the games of chance. That was prudent; proximity *was* a factor in the working of his gift. He personally felt that he was not situated quite far *enough* from the games to avoid influence, if his gift was feeling playful— which, fortunately, it was not.

He did not, of course, say this to Sera gayn'Urlez when she came to his table, shortly after the Gun had left him.

"You're the Luck Vali signed in, are you?"

"Yes, Sera. Mar Tyn eys'Ornstahl, Sera."

"Why choose to come here?"

"Sera, forgive me; I did not *choose* to come here."

That earned him a grin, unexpected and attractive on a broad face with one short white scar high on each cheek.

"So, you've been here before?"

"Twice, Sera. Once, when I was a child, with my mentor. Again, when I was newly my own master."

"Not since?"

"No, Sera."

"Why not? Didn't earn enough?"

"Sera, I earned well that night. My winner was killed by a wolf pack, three paces from the door, and I swore that I would not help someone to their death again."

The frown was as fearsome as the grin had been attractive.

"I don't allow wolf packs on my corner, or on either street, for the length of the block."

Mar Tyn had heard about this policy, which was enforced by the lady at whom he had been bidden not to stare. Such enforcement benefited both, after all, and gayn'Urlez *did* sit at the center of the lady's base.

"Sera's brother was gayn'Urlez," he said. "When last I worked here."

Interest showed in her face.

"My brother died six years ago. You're older than you look."

In fact, he did look younger than his years, and had in addition come unusually young into the fullness of his gift. Which gayn'Urlez had no need to know.

He therefore inclined his head, acknowledging her observation.

"Vali told you the rules and the rates?"

"Yes, Sera."

"Questions?"

"I collect my commission, less the House's fee, from the floor boss?"

"That is correct. Your winner will also collect, minus the House's fee, from the floor boss." She paused, seeming to consider him.

"If you feel that you're in danger from your winner, or from anyone else on the floor, you have Vali send for me, understood?"

This was an unexpected courtesy. Mar Tyn inclined his head.

"Yes, Sera."

"Yes," she repeated, and sighed. "I'm in earnest, Luck eys'Ornstahl. Vali would have told you about Ahteya. I don't necessarily want Lucks operating out of my premises, but that doesn't mean I want them beat and killed for doing what they were hired to do."

"Thank you for your care," he said, since it seemed she expected a reply, and it was good policy to be polite to the host.

She stood another moment or two, studying him. He gave her all his face, feeling no twinge from his gift. His was to sit there, then, and wait, until waiting was over.

• • • ✧ • • •

THE ROOM HAD FILLED and the play had grown raucous before Mar Tyn felt a shiver along a particular set of nerves, and looked up to see a man approaching the Luck's Table. He wore a leather jacket of a certain style, though to Mar Tyn's eye he was no pilot. His face, like so many faces in Low Port, bore a scar—his just under the right eye, star-shaped, as if someone had thrust a broken bottle, edges first, at him.

"Luck for hire?" he demanded, voice rough, tone irritable.

"Ser, yes," Mar Tyn said.

"Stand lively, then! I've work for you tonight!"

Mar Tyn rose, looking over his prospective winner's shoulder to Vali at the bar. He caught her prosthetic eye, and she inclined her head, teeth indenting her lower lip.

"Gods, you're nothing but a kid! Do you think this is a joke?"

"No, Ser," Mar Tyn said truthfully. "I'm not so young as I seem."

"You can influence the *kazino*, can you?"

Well, no, not exactly, but there was no coherent way to explain how his gift operated to someone who did not also bear the gift. And this man did not want an explanation—not really. He wanted a guarantee that Mar Tyn would make him a big winner, which, Mar Tyn realized, considering the warmth of his blood, he would very likely do. Barring stupidity, of course. Not even Luck trumped stupidity.

So.

"Ser, the *kazino* is a specialty," he said, which was almost true. Wheels, machines, and devices were the easiest touch for his Luck. Cards were more difficult, and Sticks the most difficult of all. His win average for Sticks was fifty-eight percent, only a little over what native probability might achieve; while his success rate with the machines was very nearly seventy-three percent. Keplyr had found his affinity for *kazino* amazing. But Keplyr's gift had favored cards.

"All right, here."

The man grabbed his shoulder and pulled him to a stop by the *kazino* table.

"Get busy," he said, and leaned close, voice low and full of threat. "If I catch you slacking off, I'll break your fingers. You don't need your fingers to give me a win, do you?"

"No, Ser," Mar Tyn said quietly. "But pain will disturb my concentration."

"Then keep your mind on the job," snarled his soon-to-be winner. He reached into his jacket pocket and withdrew two quarter-cantra, which he gave to the croupier in exchange for a small handful of chips.

Mar Tyn closed his eyes, the better to see what his gift might tell him.

"Well?"

He answered without opening his eyes.

"Everything on red three."

· · ·✦· · ·

HIS WINNER HAD DONE WELL, though he did not seem pleased with either his success or Mar Tyn's obvious diligence on his behalf. He did not win all of the spins, of course; chance simply did not operate that way. However, he won very nearly three-quarters; and his losses were—save one—minor.

The big loss—Mar Tyn had felt it looming, and directed that a prudent bet be set on green eight. It wouldn't have done to cash out of the table entirely, not with the rolling waves of plenty he sensed hovering just beyond the loss. Besides, it put heart in the other players to see that even a man augmented by Luck was not immune to a setback, and he owed at least that much courtesy to the House.

So, he had directed that prudent placement, but his winner—his winner had not been drinking. Perhaps he was drunk with success; certainly he was arrogant.

In any case, he turned his head, met Mar Tyn's eye, and placed twice the requested amount on the square.

It could have been worse; at least the man had not let everything ride on the spin. Also, the loss had the happy outcome of demonstrating that Mar Tyn knew his business far better than the man who had engaged him.

After that, his winner placed his bets as directed by his Luck, though he did so with ill grace, and continued to win. The table lost players, and filled again, in the way of such things, until—two hours before the day-port bell forced even gayn'Urlez to close—the man abruptly swept all his winnings off the table, and carried them to the floor boss's station.

It was gayn'Urlez herself at the desk, which ought not have surprised him, Mar Tyn thought. She tallied the chips, did the conversion to coin, and counted out the whole amount.

That done, she paused, the money on full display until the winner stirred and growled, "Agreed."

"Excellent," she said. "We will now pay your just debts. Thirty-six percent to the Luck."

She counted it onto the desk before him, fingers firm.

"Agreed," said Mar Tyn in his turn, "and twelve percent to the House."

She smiled faintly.

"Indeed."

The appropriate amount was subtracted. He accepted the remainder and slid it away into various pockets.

"You are done here for this night, Master Luck," gayn'Baurlez said then. "The House can bear no more."

"Sera, yes. My thanks."

She did not even look at him, her fingers already busy with the remaining money.

"You will of course share a drink with me," she said to the winner. "On the House."

Mar Tyn was already through the bar's pass-through, on his way to the back exit, but he heard the winner clearly.

"No."

* * * ✧ * * *

HE RAN, his feet and the rest of himself of one accord.

Fleetness was a survival skill in Low Port, and Mar Tyn had thus far survived. Still, his winner, though heavier, had longer legs, and a great motivator in the money in Mar Tyn's pocket. If it came to an outright race, the larger man would overtake the smaller.

Happily, the race was not nearly so straightforward.

Mar Tyn's goal was not his attic room at Bendi's. No, he was flying full speed toward one of his bolt-holes, a cellar window left off the hook beneath a pawn shop in Litik Street. He was a bare two blocks from that slightly moldy point of safety, confident that he could reach it handily.

In fact, he had the pawn shop in view, and was veering to the left, aiming for the alley that unlatched window opened into . . .

When his feet betrayed him again.

He hurtled past the pawn shop, even as he flung out a hand to snatch the post at the corner of the building, intending to swing himself 'round and into the alley.

"Hey!" he heard a man shout behind him. "You! Luck! Stop!"

Dammit.

Mar Tyn took a hard breath—and let his feet take him.

· · ·✧· · ·

HIS WINNER caught him at the corner of Skench and Taemon, when a speeding and overburdened lorry lurched into the intersection as he started through. He missed his stride, staggered, threw himself to the right—and was lifted from his feet by a grip on his collar.

His winner tossed him, casually, into the wall of the building on the corner. Luckily, the wall was plas, not stone, and Mar Tyn bounced, ducking out of the way of his winner's fist.

The second punch connected, knocking him back into the wall. Mar Tyn used the slight give, and kicked out, hard and accurate. His winner yelled, doubled over—and Mar Tyn was gone, hurtling across the intersection, guided by feet or fear, it hardly mattered. He had no taste for being beaten, nor did he care to buy out of a beating by surrendering the evening's earnings. He had a far better use for—

His feet dashed down an alleyway, a dark tunnel with a light at the end.

A courtyard, he saw, and the gate standing, luckily, open. Much good it would do him. A deadend was still a dead end, and his winner would have him.

He saw it, as his feet threw him into the yard—a window, there on the second floor, showed a light.

He might get lucky, after all.

"The house, the house!" he shouted, as his feet sped him forward. "Thieves and brigands! Be aware!"

The grip this time was on his shoulder, and the wall he connected with was stone.

The light flared and fragmented; he twisted to the left, dodging the next blow, hearing his winner curse as his fist struck the wall, and the grip on his shoulder loosen.

He tore free, intending to run back through the gate, but his own feet tripped him, and he went down to the cobbles on one knee. His winner spun, face shadowed, light running like quicksilver along the edge of the blade as he raised it.

Mar Tyn took a breath and shouted.

"The house! Murder!"

. . . and dove to the cobbles between his winner's feet, rolling, knocking him off-balance.

He heard the metal cry out as the knife struck stone, its brilliance swallowed in the shadows, and lurched to his feet, turning this time toward the house, where more lights had come on. He heard shouting—and his collar was gripped.

He was thrown against the wall again, and held there as his winner slapped him hard, driving his head against the stone.

All the lights went out; he felt his jacket torn open, a hand exploring the pockets, heard a grunt of satisfaction, and release of the punishing grip that held him upright.

He slid to the cobbles, the light coming back, smeared and uncertain.

The first kick broke his arm, and he screamed, earning a second kick, in the ribs.

A distant noise broke on his befuddled ears, and a woman's voice, speaking with authority.

"Who is brawling in my yard? Her Nin bey'Pasra, you rogue! Have I not told you often enough to stay away from here?"

A shadow loomed in the smeary light, snatching his winner and spinning him about as if he were nothing more than a child's toy made from twisted rags.

A blow landed; his winner staggered, and it occurred to Mar Tyn that this was his final chance to live out the night.

Run, he told himself, but he had no strength to rise.

Instead, he lay there on the cobbles while a large red-haired woman, briskly efficient, dealt with Her Nin bey'Pasra, slapping him into the wall as an afterthought, stripping him of his jacket as he slumped; at last picking him up by scruff and seat, frog-marching him to the gate, and pitching him into the alley.

Metal clashed—perhaps, Mar Tyn thought muzzily, she had thrown him into the garbage cans.

The woman turned, grabbed the gate and pulled it to, leaning down as if to get a closer look at the latch.

Perhaps she swore; her voice was low, the words nonsensical. She pulled a piece of chain from somewhere in the shadows, and wrapped the latch, muttering the while.

Then she crossed the yard, and squatted next to Mar Tyn. He blinked up at her, the light making a conflagration of her hair.

"Can you rise?" she asked him.

"I believe so," he said, and found that, with her arm, he could, though he crashed to his knees when she withdrew that kind support.

"My head," he muttered, raising his good hand, only to have it caught and held in firm fingers.

"I see it," she said, and raised her voice, "Fireyn!"

He flinched.

"There is nothing to fear here," she told him, her large voice now soothing and soft. "You were lucky that our gate was open."

"And why was that?" came another voice, this one male.

"The latch was broken again," the woman answered him. "We are in need of a solution there."

"Tomorrow," said the man, kneeling beside her and looking into Mar Tyn's face.

"You may put yourself in our care," he said with a gentleness rarely given even to children. "You have come to the safest place in Low Port."

He smiled, wry in the smeary light.

"I understand that is not so very much to say, but, for now, at least, you are safe. My name is Don Eyr; this lady who succored you is Serana. Fireyn, who is coming to us now, is our medic. May we know your name?"

"Mar Tyn eys'Ornstahl," he managed, as the medic approached

him down a long tunnel edged with fire. He wanted only to close his eyes, and surrender to that kindly dark, but he owed them one more thing. They must be told of their peril.

"I am . . . " His breath was coming in short, painful gasps, but he forced the words out. "I am . . . Luck . . . "

The darkness reached out. He embraced it, sobbing. The last thing he heard before he was taken utterly was the man's voice, murmuring.

"Indeed, you are that."

INTERLUDES

MAR TYN WOKE TO A MULTITUDE OF ACHES, and opened his eyes upon a thin, fierce face. Two achingly straight scars traced a diagonal path down her right cheek, white against tan skin.

"Medic?" he whispered. There had been a medic—or at least, a medic on the way. He recalled that, particularly, for a medic in Low Port was a wonder of herself.

His observer dipped her chin in approval, and added, "Fireyn. Tell me your name."

"Mar Tyn cys'Ornstahl."

Another dip of the chin.

"Your right arm is broken; your ribs are accounted for. You have proven that your head is harder than our wall, so you need not make that experiment again. I used a first aid kit on the ribs, the head, and the arm, and injected you with an accelerant, which will speed healing. The arm is your worst remaining problem. You will need to wear a sling, even after your other wounds allow you to leave your bed."

He licked his lips.

"How long—" he began, but the darkness rushed up again, swallowing the thin, clever face, amid all of his sluggard thoughts.

• • •✧• • •

HE WOKE FEELING TIRED, and opened his eyes to a different face, not quite so thin, nor yet so fierce, with a clear golden complexion rarely found in Low Port. The features were regular; cheeks unscarred; eyes brown, and serious.

"Do you know me?" he asked. His Liaden bore an accent—tantalizingly unfamiliar.

"You are Don Eyr," Mar Tyn answered. "I recall your voice."

Don Eyr smiled.

"It was rather dark, wasn't it? You may be pleased to learn that Fireyn wishes you to rise, and walk, and afterward make a report of yourself. She will also be observing you with her instruments."

He tipped his head, and Mar Tyn followed the gesture, finding the medic standing at a tripod across the room.

The room—it was small, but very light. He turned his head, finding a window in the end wall; a clean window, through which the afternoon sun entered, brilliance intact.

"When?" Mar Tyn asked.

"Now," Fireyn said. "If you are able. If you are not able, then I will be informed."

He marked her accent this time, and noted the way she stood, balanced and alert. One of the Betrayed, then, which made sense, of her paleness, and the precision of the cuts that had formed her scars.

"What she means to say is that, if you are not able, she will immediately intensify your treatment," Don Eyr said, rising from the chair next to Mar Tyn's bed. "She was military, and believes in quick healing."

"A necessity, on a battlefield," Fireyn said.

And also on Low Port, thought Mar Tyn, putting the coverlet back with one hand. His right arm was in a sling, and he was wearing a knee-length robe.

Carefully, he put his feet over the side of the bed, situated them firmly—and rose.

He paused, but his head was quite steady, his balance secure. Looking up, he saw Don Eyr leaning against a wall, perhaps a dozen paces from the side of the bed.

Mar Tyn walked toward him, steps firm and unhurried.

Reaching Don Eyr, Mar Tyn bowed. Finding his balance still

stable, he turned and walked to the window, where he paused to look out.

Below him was the yard his feet had carried him to in his race against his winner. It was a tidy space, seen in decent daylight. He particularly noted the tiered shelving, filled with potted plants.

"I hope I brought no harm to your garden," he said, turning to face Don Eyr.

"Not a leaf was bent," the other man assured him.

"Good."

He walked back to Fireyn.

"I report myself able. Shall I go?"

He heard Don Eyr shift against the wall—but Fireyn was shaking her head.

"I fear you are guilty of under-reporting," she said, and glanced over his head.

"I recommend an additional round of therapy," she said, to Don Eyr, Mar Tyn understood.

"You are the medic," came the answer. "Friend Mar Tyn."

He turned.

"This choice is yours. I stipulate that the therapy is not without risk. I also stipulate that none of those under my keeping—or, indeed, myself—have taken harm from it. If you wish my recommendation, it is that you allow it. This house will stand for your safety, while you are vulnerable. If you do not care to risk so much, that is, of course, your decision. It is understood that you may have business elsewhere."

It was gently said, and Mar Tyn was somewhat astonished to find that he believed that he was safe in this house, in the care of Fireyn and Don Eyr. Which left only the question . . .

Do I, Mar Tyn inquired with interest of himself, *have business elsewhere?*

There came no restless fizzing in his blood. His feet were as rooted to the floor. He was, he realized, at peace, which was very nearly as dangerous as believing himself to be safe.

And yet . . . his feet had brought him here; his feet were content that he remain here.

He was curious to learn why.

He turned to Fireyn.

"Additional therapy," he said. "I accept."

TWO

HE WOKE FEELING HALE AND BRIGHT, and more well than he'd been in his life. Opening his eyes, he discovered himself alone. The chair beside the bed had a shirt—not his—draped carefully over the back, and a pair of pants—likewise not his—folded neatly on the seat. The boots on the floor by the chair were, indeed, his, though someone had cleaned them, and even produced the beginning of a shine.

Mar Tyn sighed. His blood was effervescent, and his feet were itching to move.

Apparently, he had business to tend to, and he'd best be about it quickly.

• • •✧• • •

HE HAD MANAGED THE SHIRT, the pants, the socks—even with the sling—but the boots had proved beyond him.

Sock-foot, then, he danced lightly out of the room, along a short hall and down a metal staircase. At the bottom, he turned right, down a longer hallway, and found himself in a kitchen, warm, bright, and smelling of baking.

There was a long table along the right-hand side of the room, much be-floured, and holding a large bowl, well swathed in toweling. Across the room, a light glowed red above what he took to be an oven, set into the heavy stone wall.

Despite the evidence of previous industry, the kitchen was at this moment empty.

Mar Tyn spied a teapot on a counter, holding court with a dozen mismatched cups. His feet assumed; he poured, bearing the brightly flowered cup with him to the window overlooking the courtyard, and got himself onto one of the two high stools there.

He waited, sipping tea; his feet at rest; his blood a-sizzle.

Footsteps in the hall heralded the arrival of Don Eyr, who bent his head, cordial and unsurprised, before crossing to the teapot, pouring, and returning to the window, slipping easily onto the second stool.

He said nothing, nor did Mar Tyn. Indeed, there was scarcely time enough for a companionable sip of tea before more footsteps sounded in the hall, overhasty, and desperate.

A girl burst into the kitchen, lamenting as she came.

"Oh, the bread! It will be ruined!"

She dashed to the worktable, snatching the towel from the bowl, shoulders tense—and loosening all at once, as she erupted into a flurry of purposeful action, a sharp punch down into the bowl before upending it and turning an elastic mass out onto the floured table. The bowl was set aside, as with her free hand she reached for a wide, flat blade...

"I wonder," Don Eyr said quietly from beside him, "what you did, just now."

Ah, thought Mar Tyn, and turned to face his host.

"Forgive my ignorance, but first I must know what happened, that went against your expectations."

Don Eyr glanced to the girl, who had divided her dough into two even portions, and was busily shaping the first with strong, sure fingers.

"The bread—the dough in the bowl, you see—it *ought* to have been ruined—*fallen*, as we have it. She left it too long at rise." He sipped his tea, and added:

"These matters are delicate, and... not always precise. Bread-making only pretends to be a science."

"Ah."

Mar Tyn sipped his tea, and met Don Eyr's eyes.

"I am a Luck. You say that this"—he used his chin to point at the busy worker—"is an art, and not a science. That there is some element of imprecision inherent in the event."

"Yes," said Don Eyr, "but in the case, she had left it beyond the point of recovery."

"You know your art, and I do not," Mar Tyn said gently. "I only say that, given what we have seen, there must have been some small probability that the bread would *not* be ruined, and my presence... gave that probability an extra weight."

Don Eyr sipped, eyes fixed on some point between the stools and the worktable.

"In fact," he said eventually, "you altered the future?"

Mar Tyn sighed.

"So it is said. It's the reason we're banned from Mid and High Ports, and why the Healers and *dramliz* spit on us."

Don Eyr frowned slightly, his eyes on the baker, who had finished shaping the second loaf. She transferred the pans to the shelf by the oven door, covered them with the cloth, and wiped her hands on her apron.

Mar Tyn took a careful breath, surprised to find an ache in his side, as if one of the ribs had not entirely healed.

"I will leave," he said softly. "An escort to the gate—"

"There's no need for haste," Don Eyr murmured. "Drink your tea."

The baker approached them; bowed.

"The loaves are shaped, Brother," she said to Don Eyr.

"So I see," he answered. "Mind you do not neglect them in their rising. You cannot count on good fortune twice."

Which was, Mar Tyn thought, finishing the last of his tea, very wise of him.

The baker blushed, and murmured, and turned to clean the worktable.

"I wonder," Don Eyr said, turning on his stool to face Mar Tyn, "if you will come and eat breakfast with myself and Serana." He raised one hand, fingers wide. "If you feel that you must go, I will not detain you, though I will ask for a moment to fetch those things which belong to you."

Mar Tyn paused, considering himself, and his condition.

His feet... were content. His stomach... was in need, noisily so.

He inclined his head.

"I would very much like to share a meal with you and Serana," he said.

He slid off the stool onto his quiet feet, and followed Don Eyr out of the kitchen.

* * * ⟡ * * *

THEY ASCENDED a short staircase to a room half a floor above the kitchen. A table set for three was under the open window. Mar Tyn glanced out over the courtyard, and realized that the light he had seen, the night his winner had caught him, had come exactly from this room.

He turned his attention to the larger apartment. A bureau stood against the wall next to the table, laden with dishes of biscuits, vegetables, and cheese; and a teapot, gently steaming.

Shelves lined the walls, overfull with books and tapes, and where there were not shelves, there were . . . pictures—flat-pics, hand-drawings, swirls of color . . .

Along the wall opposite the table was a screen, a double-lounge facing it. In the far corner, two more chairs sat companionably together in an angle of the shelves, a light suspended from the ceiling over both. A red-haired woman sat in one of the chairs, reading. There was a door in the wall directly behind her, almost invisible in the abundance of . . . *things.*

Mar Tyn's feet had taken him to larger rooms, and longer tables. But he had never been in so comfortable—so *welcoming*— a room. Indeed, by the standards of the rooms he most usually frequented, this cluttered chamber was . . . he groped for the word, and had only just achieved *luxurious* when the woman looked up from her book.

"Ah, here he comes, on his own two feet!" she said cordially, rising—and rising some more.

Her height was not so much of a surprise—she had cast the shadow of a giantess in the courtyard. No, what startled was her . . . fitness; this was not a woman who knew want, or who went often without her dinner. From her part in his rescue, he had assumed that she was a soldier, but he saw now that she was not. Fireyn— *there* was a soldier, from squared shoulders to flexed knees. This person—was upright, and strong, and—*proud*, thought Mar Tyn.

Just as Don Eyr was proud. And well fed.

As the baker of breads, in the kitchen below: well fed, strong. Embarrassed, but not abused.

"I strike him to silence," Serana noted, drily.

Mar Tyn bestirred himself and produced, having seen such things on tapes, a bow of gratitude.

"I mean no disrespect," he said. "I was overcome for a moment, recalling that I owe you my life."

"Glib," came the judgment from high up.

"But truthful," Don Eyr said, stepping to Mar Tyn's side.

"Serana, I make you known to Mar Tyn eys'Ornstahl, who is a Luck. Ser eys'Ornstahl, here is Captain Serana Benoit."

Well—a soldier after all?

Serana smiled down at him.

"My rank comes from worlds away, where I was one captain of many in the city guard. Security, not military."

Security, thought Mar Tyn, recalling her bent over the broken lock. *House* security. She would have questions for him. How not?

He took a breath and met her eyes—blue and bright. She smiled faintly.

"Come," she said, sweeping a large hand out, as if to show him the buffet and the table, "let us eat."

* * * ◇ * * *

IN GENERAL, Mar Tyn ate more regularly than many residents of Low Port—a benefit of his gift, which would have no use for him, if he were too weak to obey its whims.

The breakfast he was given at Don Eyr and Serana's table was beyond anything he had ever eaten; something other than mere food, so nuanced that he felt his head spin with the multiplicity of tastes and textures.

His attempt to eat sparingly was defeated by his host, who monitored his plate closely, and immediately replaced what he had eaten.

At last, though, he sat back, dizzy and replete, and looked up into Serana's gem-blue eyes.

She smiled at him, fondly, or so it seemed, and leaned back comfortably in her chair.

"Tell us," she said.

He sighed slightly, unwilling to face the inevitable results of having told them. But—he owed them no less than his life, and nothing but the truth would pay that debt.

Also—they had children in their care—he had heard their voices round the house and yard as he had eaten. Well-fed, strong, and prideful children, like the girl whose bread he had preserved. If the purpose that united this house was the protection of children—a purpose nearly unheard of, in Low Port...

The house needed to know about Lucks and the particular perils attending them—not only so that they might be more careful of who they let behind their protections, but to know the signs, should one of those in their care prove to be Lucky.

So, he sighed, but he told them—quietly and calmly, beginning with the day he found the woman he supposed to have been his mother lying on the floor of their basement room. He had thought her asleep, but she hadn't woken, not even when there came heavy footsteps and loud voices in the hallway.

That had been the first time his feet had moved him, away, *not* to the front of the house, where the voices were loudest, but down a back hallway, and into a pipe scarcely large enough to accommodate his small, skinny self, which, after some small time of crawling, led into a deserted, rubble-filled alleyway.

He had climbed out of the pipe, half turned back toward the place he had just quit—but his feet took him, and he walked for many blocks, up and down streets he had never seen before, until he came to Dreyling's Tea Shop.

His feet took him into the shop, and marched him to the backmost table. He hoisted himself into one of the two chairs—and waited, for what, he could not have said. No one took any note of him. He tried, once, to wriggle out of his chair and go away, but some force he did not understand kept him where he was.

Eventually, a man with grey streaking his dark hair, wearing fine and neatly patched clothing, joined him at the table, called for tea and a plate of crackers, and when they had come, asked what was his name.

He disposed of the years with Keplyr as mentor and master with a simple, "He took me in, and taught me how to survive my gift. He had lived a long time as a Luck in Low Port. It was his belief that his gift had called mine."

Keplyr's death—the stuff of nightmares that *still* woke him—he did not mention, only saying that, in time, he came to be his own master.

He spoke of the nature of his work, the particular risks found in gaming houses, and told the story of Ahteya as a caution for them, before finishing with his own misadventure, from which Captain Serana had so kindly extricated him.

"So," said that same Captain Serana, when finally he came to an end. "It seems to me that the first question we must ask is—*why.*"

Mar Tyn blinked at her.

Beside him, Don Eyr laughed softly, and rose, taking the teapot with him.

"Nothing occurs to you?" Serana prodded gently.

"Why," Mar Tyn said slowly, "so that you might save my life."

But Serana shook her head.

"You would have been safe at your first bolt-hole, but your feet bore you past," she pointed out. "Running on is what put you in danger."

Mar Tyn took a breath. He was not accustomed to questioning the motives of his gift, even after the instance was over. His chest was suddenly tight, and his breath somewhat short . . .

"Surely," Don Eyr said, returning to the table and leaning on the back of Serana's chair, "Aidlee's loaves were not worth so much."

The pressure in his chest dissolved in laughter.

"A shattered arm, and a broken head? No, I think we can agree there," he said, and looked again to Serana.

"Perhaps," he offered tentatively, "it was necessary that I alert the house that the gate was standing wide?"

Don Eyr and Serana exchanged a glance.

"Certainly," she said slowly, "it would have been no good thing, had some we can both name found us open. Yet . . . "

She looked again to Mar Tyn.

"There was no sign, after, that any had come back to complete their work, and been surprised to find the gate in force."

Mar Tyn moved his shoulders, uneasy once more.

"The fact that the gate had been relocked—the noise alone, when my winner caught me—might have changed intentions."

There was a light knock, and Don Eyr went away again, to the door. He returned with another teapot, newly steaming, and poured for all three before sitting down.

"Your *winner* . . ." Serana said, her mouth twisting with distaste. She took a sip from her cup, lips softening.

"We unfortunately know of your winner," Don Eyr said. "His name is Her Nin bey'Pasra. A very bad man. A thief, and also a murderer, many times over."

Mar Tyn nodded, unsurprised.

"I saw the jacket," he said. "There are those who take particular pleasure in damaging pilots, but they will take easier meat, if they must."

"Yes."

Serana sighed.

"I should have left him the jacket, perhaps . . ."

Don Eyr reached across the table, and put his hand over hers.

"It is done," he said, firm and quiet. "Serana. It is done."

"True," she said, and slipped her hand away, giving him a crooked smile.

She rose, then, and moved to the bureau. Opening a drawer, she removed a packet, which she brought back to the table, and placed before Mar Tyn.

"We will allow you to tell us," she said, sitting down and picking up her tea cup, "if that might be worth shattered ribs, a broken arm, and a cracked head."

The packet was sealed. Mar Tyn ran a thumbnail down the seam—and sat staring as the coins rolled and danced along the table.

Here was not only the Luck's portion from gayn'Urlez, he thought, but the winner's, as well.

"A considerable sum," Don Eyr murmured.

Mar Tyn took a breath.

A very considerable sum, as he was accustomed to count money. Was it worth a beating that had nearly killed him?

Maybe, he thought. Maybe not the money, particularly, but what the money might *buy* him?

Oh, yes.

. . . but there was . . . a problem.

He glanced down at the sling cradling his right arm.

"Where may I find Fireyn?" he asked.

"She has a short-term outside of the house," Serana said. "It is possible that we might be able to answer your question in her stead."

He nodded.

"I only wonder how much longer the arm must be restrained— and if," he added, as the next thought came to him, "if it *must be* restrained, or that is only *advisable*."

Serana laughed.

"Hear him! *Only* advisable! Fireyn would gut him where he sits."

"Perhaps not so much," Don Eyr protested, "though she would certainly avail herself of a teaching moment."

Mar Tyn considered them both, wondering if he might receive an answer, after their laughter had died.

"Ah, he glares. I ask pardon," Serana said. "I have myself made the error of inquiring of Fireyn if a certain protocol was necessary or *merely prudent*. And I will tell you that it is well I keep my hair thus short, for she would have surely snatched me bald."

"From this you learn that Fireyn's advice is immutable," Don Eyr said. "I am also able to tell you that she felt another three weeks would see you completely healed and whole."

Three weeks?

Mar Tyn looked at the coins on the table, seeing their worth in terms of his life.

"Might I . . ." he said slowly, "be given another dose of accelerant?"

Don Eyr shook his head.

"No more accelerant for you, my friend. It is not without cost, and you have had three doses." He held up a hand, first finger extended. "One, to keep you with us, for you were in a perilous condition, and more likely to die than to live."

Mar Tyn blinked, recalling Fireyn's wry assurance that his head had proved harder than the wall.

"The skull injury?" he asked.

"The ribs," Don Eyr said. "Several had broken; at least one compromised your lungs. Fireyn immediately saw how it was, used the first aid kit, and employed the accelerant."

Mar Tyn drew a breath and bowed his head.

"I understand. The other occasions?"

"After you had wakened the first time and fainted almost immediately."

Mar Tyn eyed him.

"I held conversation with Fireyn; she told me her name, and asked for mine."

Don Eyr smiled, sadly.

"That was not the first time."

Mar Tyn took a breath.

"And the third time you surely recall, as you agreed to the dose."

"That, yes," Mar Tyn admitted, and asked. "Was I still so ill?"

"No more than you are accustomed to being, I think. Fireyn, however, took into her calculations that Her Nin bey'Pasra is still alive, and inclines toward holding a grudge."

"That was prudent of her," Mar Tyn said slowly. "I wonder—how long have I *been* in your care?"

"Two weeks."

"So long as that?" Mar Tyn murmured, hardly surprised; scarcely dismayed.

He let his eyes rest on the money again. *His money.*

Plus, the winner's share.

Knowing what he now knew, he asked himself again: Was the money—the brighter future the money would assure him—*was* it worth a beating which, absent Luck, and Fireyn, would have meant his death?

No, certainly not . . . except, he had *not* died, because neither Luck nor Fireyn had been withheld from him.

That meant, then . . .

Well, and what *did* it mean?

"We have created more problems than we have solved," Serana remarked. "I regret that. Tell us what we might do, to ease your burden."

But Mar Tyn was thinking, now that Serana had put him on this unaccustomed path. His Luck had brought him here. Why? Why *here*? Why had he been so badly damaged? Why put him in debt to these people—a debt he could never repay—

Repay.

He touched the money with just the tips of the fingers of his good hand.

The house cared for children, who were constantly at risk in Low Port. There would be those who would see the prosperity of the house and seek to steal it, and make it their own—witness the broken gate lock. To maintain such an establishment, with proper security—these things did not come cheap. That they existed at all in Low Port was . . . almost beyond belief.

He looked up.

"This," he said, meeting Serana's eyes, since he did not think he could meet Don Eyr's. Serana was the hardheaded one, he thought.

The ruthless one.

He cleared his throat.

"This," he said again. "I believe this is yours."

Serana's eyes opened wide.

"No, my friend, that it is not! We are established here in Low Port, but we strive—we strive to do better. There are children in the house, whom we have taken it up to educate, and so we must stand as an example to them."

Involuntarily, he glanced to Don Eyr, who nodded, solemnly.

"Indeed, that is your money. Very nearly you gave your life for it. Is it that have you no use for it?"

Almost, he laughed.

"I have good use for it," he said, and sighed. "But I cannot use it, with my arm thus."

"Why?" asked Don Eyr.

Mar Tyn sighed.

"In the Low Port, there are three houses—guild houses, you may call them—which offer a measure of safety to those Lucks who can afford the buy-in, and the monthly dues."

He took a breath.

"From least to greatest, they are: the House of Chance, the House of Fortune, and Prosperity."

"And you have here . . . " Serana placed her fingertips lightly against the coins, "enough to buy into Prosperity."

It was a question born of honest ignorance, and he did not laugh at her.

"The only way to join Prosperity is to be born there," he said gently, and nodded at the riches on the table. "That, however, will buy me a place in the House of Fortune, and pay my dues for a year or two."

Serana frowned, and looked beyond him, to Don Eyr. Mar Tyn waited, and presently, her eyes came back to him.

"These are princely prices, for Low Port."

"Yes. It is why most of us are freelances."

"But tell me why you cannot go inside of this hour and buy yourself safety. If it is for the need of a guard, perhaps one of us may accompany you."

"As it happens, it is for this." He rocked his arm in its sling. "I will be asked if I am accident-prone. That would make me a bad risk for the House."

"I see," Don Eyr frowned. "They must, of course, tend to their profit."

There was no answer to that, and Mar Tyn made none, merely frowning down at the table, and trying to work out the moves.

"What would you have us do?" Serana asked.

He stirred, and looked up at her.

"I have lodgings," he said. "But I cannot have such a sum with me, there, or on the streets."

"But, that is easy!" Serana said, looking over his head to meet Don Eyr's eyes. "We can hold it in the safe."

"Yes," he agreed. "That is no trouble at all."

A safe. Who possessed such a thing? Well. Carmintine the

pawnbroker would very likely hold this dragon's hoard for him, as she already held the greater balance of his money. She would, of course, charge him interest. With such a sum, that would be no small expense, and he was still left with the problem of transporting it through the streets.

No, best to leave it where it was.

"You understand," Serana said softly, "that there *are* children in the house, and they are our priority."

"Therefore your money is lucky," Don Eyr said, "for it will receive our same protection, though it is of far less value."

Mar Tyn stared at him, but he seemed to be serious.

"I will be pleased to leave my money under the protection of your house," he said slowly. "What interest will you charge?"

Serana half laughed.

"What a place this is!" she exclaimed. "We will hold your money for love, my friend. Or, if you will have your Balance, we will hold it in payment for having brought more trouble into your life."

"After *saving* my life," Mar Tyn added, but there seemed to be no arguing with her, and he was suddenly aware of a small twitching in the soles of his feet.

"I feel that I must go," he said, looking between them. "Now."

Don Eyr rose immediately.

"Allow me to help you with your boots," he said.

THREE

HIS FEET took him home.

Which was to say, to the customer entrance of Bendi's House of Joy. He tried to bring his meager influence to bear; to force his purposeful march past the front and round to the back of the house, the delivery door, and the stairs to the attic room where he slept, which he was let to have so that his Luck would shield the house.

Of course, his preference counted for nothing.

Cray was on the front door, a man big even for a Terran, and who thought more quickly with his fists than his head.

Still, they had never fallen out, nor had much to do with each other, beyond a nod, and a murmured greeting.

Today, however, Cray saw him approaching, and shifted to stand in the center of the door, muscled arms crossed over powerful chest.

"Go away," he said.

Mar Tyn stopped just out of grabbing distance.

"I need to see Bendi."

"Go away," Cray repeated, and Mar Tyn was wondering if his feet were so eager that they would try a dart around the big man, and through the door.

Possibly, he would be fast enough, even with the odd balance lent by the sling.

It was not put to the test, however, for here came Bendi out of the house, to stand beside Cray, fists on her hips, and her face flushed so dark that the ragged gash along the left side of her face stood out like ivory.

"You! Find a cush job somewhere else, did you, Luck? See what's happened to *me* while you were gone! I've got three hurt, and a broken water pipe, because *you* couldn't be bothered to pay your rent! Do you think I'm letting you back in here now?"

"I—" began Mar Tyn, but Bendi had noticed the sling.

She stiffened, her fists fell to her sides.

"*Get out*," she snarled.

"Bendi—"

"Get out! Your Luck's broken, hasn't it? Get away from me and mine before you bring down worse upon us!"

"I'll go," Mar Tyn said, understanding that this was not an argument he could win. "Only let me get my clothes from upstairs, and the money I had asked you to hold—"

"The money went to repair the pipe," she interrupted, "and I know better than to let broken Luck into my house. Go away, *now*, or Cray will kill you."

That, Mar Tyn thought, was possible. Bendi was beyond angry; she was terrified. Terrified that his broken Luck would visit more grief on her house.

He was inclined to mourn the money he had given to bind her trust, and his other shirt—nearly new! But . . . he had money, he reminded himself. He could buy another shirt.

So, he went away, his feet walking him to the right, down the long block of fallen-in buildings, and right again, round the corner, and up the alley that ran between Bendi's house and the grab-a-bite next door. That was where the bolt-door was, and there—there stood Jonsie, Bendi's partner and sometimes worker, holding a sack, which he held out as Mar Tyn came near.

"Your stuff," he said, even the Low Port patois bearing the accent of his native speech. "Nothing to do for the coins, I'm feared; long days them're spent."

"I'm grateful," Mar Tyn said, taking the sack. There was a slight rattle, which would be his sewing kit—all he had left of Keplyr—and the weight suggested that Jonsie had rousted out his second pair of pants, as well as his extra socks and small clothes.

"'S'all right," said Jonsie. "Jes' don't be seen, gawn out. Bad for both of us, that."

"Yes," Mar Tyn said fervently.

His feet turned him around, back to the mouth of the alley, and up the street, away from all of Bendi's doors.

* * * ⬧ * * *

THE SACK MADE WALKING . . . awkward.

Not that people carrying sacks were anything unusual in Low Port. In his particular case, however, he had only one good arm to use for defense—and it was occupied with the sack. He supposed he might simply push the thing into the arms of anyone who tried to take it, and make good his escape when they fainted in astonishment.

A small tremor of nerves disturbed him at the thought of giving away his clothes, even as a tactic for survival. He could, he reminded himself again, buy more clothes. *Better* clothes, though he always tried to promptly mend any tears, and to wash himself and his clothing, regularly. That was Keplyr's training, Keplyr having been Mid House, before he came of age a Luck, and his clan of respectable Healers cast him out into Low Port.

As it happened, no one tried for Mar Tyn's sack, and he turned into Litik Street where the pawnshop was located with something like a spring in his step—

His feet faltered—and stopped moving altogether.

There was smoke in the air, and a crowd down toward the middle of the street, where the pawnshop was located. The pawnshop, where he leased space in Carmintine's safe, for his money—his savings. His *considerable* savings, which had been very nearly enough to buy himself a place in Chance...

He walked, carefully, through the smoke that got thicker the nearer he came, until he was on the edge of the crowd staring at the burnt ruin of Carmintine's shop.

There was something going on at the front of the crowd that he was too short to see. With a sigh, he carefully slipped into the mass of bodies, and squirmed forward.

It was slow going, and surprisingly painful, as his not-yet-healed arm in its sling bumped against solid bodies—and the solid bodies pushed back, or, at best, did not yield.

Finally, though, he made it to the front edge of the crowd, and there was Carmintine, sooty and grey from head to boot soles, and four others who were known on the streets as enforcers for hire. It would appear that Carmintine had just finished paying them to stand as guards on the gutted shop, and keep away those who might risk burnt fingers for the silver and gemstones they might find among the ash.

Such protections did not come cheap, and Carmintine had hired a good team that stayed bought, once they had accepted their money—at least until the first payment was missed.

Mar Tyn slipped back into the crowd, and, once beyond it, turned away. There was no use trying to speak to Carmintine now, with her livelihood gone to ash, and the hungry crowd pressing 'round. He would try again later, maybe, but he thought he knew what would happen, if he asked after the money the pawnbroker had been holding for him.

He paused in the street, changed his grip on the sack, and started away back up the street, when he heard his name called.

Glancing to the side, he saw Pelfit the Gossip in her rickety roost, waving urgently at him. He thought he would ignore the summons, then thought better of it, just before his feet turned him toward her.

"Yes?" he said, when he had arrived and all she did was look at his arm in its sling, and the sleeve of his jacket pinned up out of the way.

She dragged her eyes up to his face, and held out one unsteady, bony hand.

"Word on the street, Mar Tyn Luck."

Pelfit's ears were large. If not intelligent, she was at least shrewd, and more often than not her gossip was worth the price.

Mar Tyn set his sack down between his feet, reached awkwardly into a jacket pocket and pulled out the packet of bread and jam that Don Eyr had insisted he take with him.

"Fresh bread," he said, "and berry spread."

Her hand darted, and the neat packet was gone, vanished into layers of rags.

"Word on the street," she said again. "A dozen days now I've heard it. Mar Tyn's Luck is broken, and he's a danger to all who know him."

Mar Tyn frowned. That sort of Word could be got out on the street easily enough, a matter of whispering into the ear of this Gossip and that one, with a protein bar slipped into a receptive hand as proof of the news ...

"Word on the street," Pelfit said again, her hand extended.

He considered her.

"If you would tell me that Bendi's house has taken hurt, and the pawnbroker burned out, I have those Words, I thank you."

She sighed, her hand falling away.

"That's everything, then," she said slowly, and turned away from him. She did not wish him well.

Of course not. She'd already taken a risk, speaking to a man who wore his broken Luck plainly visible in a sling.

Mar Tyn took a breath, picked up his sack, and waited a heartbeat, to see if his feet would move him.

When they did not, he walked away up the street, taking care how he went, until he turned down a short dim alley, and slipped into a niche in the crumbling stone wall.

When he was satisfied that no one had followed him, he proceeded down the alley, until he came to a set of metal stairs, which he climbed until he reached a ledge of that same crumbling stone, that made the beginning of a graceful arch across the alley—and ended not quite halfway across.

He settled himself carefully in the shadow against the wall, made certain he could see the alley below in both directions, and set himself to think.

Mar Tyn the Luck was a danger, to himself and all who knew him.

That was a warning. A warning that Mar Tyn was being hunted, and those who knew him would do best for themselves by thrusting him away.

It was . . . interesting, in its way, that *he* had been given a warning. That sort of courtesy was reserved for the disagreements that might fall between Lady voz'Laathi and her rivals. Not merely a warning, but an invitation to choose sides in an upcoming war.

Mere Lucks did not go to war, though some were *brought* to war by those who sought to insure their victory.

No.

His blood ran cold, with nothing of his gift in it; merely his own reasoned certainty.

Ware, Mar Tyn Luck, whose friends will suffer.

The small mischiefs at Bendi's house; the greater one at the pawnshop—those had been . . . surety. Proof that whoever had put that Word out was in earnest.

Deadly earnest.

And, further . . .

He closed his eyes.

The warning was not *for him*.

It was for his friends—Bendi, Carmintine.

Don Eyr. Serana. The children.

The bakery, with its broken gate latch.

The bakery, where Her Nin bey'Pasra had lost his winnings—and his jacket of honor, too.

Someone—the likeliest being Her Nin bey'Pasra—was going to war against the bakery. He was calling for allies, who would share in the profits gained, which would include the children, so carefully kept, so proud, and so soft.

Mar Tyn's mouth dried. He thrust himself clumsily to his feet, the elbow of his slinged arm banging against the wall and sending a thrill of pain through his bones.

He waited, panting, until his vision cleared, then began to pick his way across the rubble, back to the top of the metal stairs.

He must return to the bakery, at once.

FOUR

FOR A WONDER, his feet remained obedient to his will, walking his chosen route at a prudent pace. He therefore arrived at the bakery as he chose to do—at the front door. His decision was influenced by the certainty that Serana would have long ago managed the difficulty with the lock on the back gate, and that whoever kept the front door would have instructions on whether he was to be admitted.

What he would do, if the house would not admit him—he hadn't . . . quite . . . worked out.

But, as it happened, he need not have wasted any thought on that question.

He had barely gotten his foot on the lower step when the door sprung open and Fireyn leapt down to grab him 'round the waist, hoisting him and carrying him up the rest of the flight. A second of her kind, also bearing the scars of those who had been Betrayed, stood in the doorway, gun not quite showing; sharp eyes parsing the street.

He swung out as they reached him, clearing the way for their entrance; and swung back behind them, pulling the door closed.

Locks were engaged. Mar Tyn heard them snap and sing into

place even as Fireyn set him on his feet in the hallway, and looked down at him, eyes squinted—an expression on her scarred face that he could not, precisely, read.

"Are you hurt?" she snapped.

"No. Not hurt. Is Don Eyr to house? Serana? I have news."

"They are teaching. We heard the whisper on the street. We were afraid, that you had heard it too late."

Mar Tyn sighed and sagged against the wall.

"Aidlee!" Fireyn raised her voice slightly, and there came a stirring down the hall in answer.

The girl who had not lost her breads appeared, wiping her hands on an apron. Fireyn nudged him forward.

"Ser eys'Ornstahl wants some tea, and a quiet place to sit until Don Eyr's class is over."

"Yes," said the girl, and smiled at him. "This way, Ser. You may rest in the book room. I will bring a tray."

• • • ✧ • • •

THE TRAY had held not only tea, but several fist-sized rolls which Aidlee named cheese breads. She filled his cup, asked him if he wanted anything else, and when he said that he was very well fixed, told him that he might find her in the kitchen if he went left down the hall from the doorway to the book room.

She left him then, and he sat in the chair she had shown him to, and drank his tea in small, appreciative sips. Such good tea, that pleased the nose as the cup was lifted, and the tongue as the sip was taken.

He closed his eyes and savored that small wonder, and when he had done, he put the cup back on the tray, stood up and looked around him.

Book room, he thought, and it was so—an entire room full of books. Upstairs, in the quiet room where he had shared breakfast with Serana and Don Eyr—he had thought *that* room held a wealth of books. But here . . .

It was not much larger than the upstairs room, but of more regular proportions. Several long tables marched down the center, bracketed by benches. Each table held four notepads—two at the top of the table, and two at the foot. At the wall nearest the door was a small table, supporting a computer. Light strips along the ceiling made the place bright, in the absence of windows.

Mar Tyn went to the nearest shelf and began to read the titles.

He had not made much progress before he heard the door open behind him.

He turned as Don Eyr entered, a white cap on his head, and an apron over all. His eyes looked tired, but he smiled when he saw he had Mar Tyn's attention, and came quickly to his side.

"We were worried," he said, grabbing Mar Tyn's good arm in both of his hands. "I am glad that you came back to us."

"You may not be glad, very soon. Have you heard the Word on the street?"

Don Eyr frowned.

"It is said that Mar Tyn the Luck is lucky no more, and has become a danger to his friends."

"Yes!" said Mar Tyn. "I ought not to have come back, only—"

Only, his money, enough to buy his way to Fortune, and, belatedly, the thought that, after all, his gift had not played him false.

First, though, to be certain.

"I had not thought to ask before—who is your protector?"

"Our protector?" Don Eyr shook his head. "We protect ourselves, here."

"That will not do," Mar Tyn said. "Not in this. They—Her Nin bey'Pasra, is my belief—has put out a call for allies. He has declared war on this place—on you, on Serana, and everyone you mean to keep safe here. He will see all you have built destroyed. You cannot stand against him alone. Here—"

He had realized on his way back—realized at last why his gift had guided him here that night; understood why he had been given no opportunity to refuse...

He reached into his pocket, and brought the thing out.

"Here!" he said again, and opened his fist to show Lady voz'Laathi's token.

Don Eyr glanced at his palm; his shoulders moved in a silent sigh even as the door worked and Serana strode into the book room.

"What have we, a tableau?" she asked, stopping behind Don Eyr's shoulder, and glancing down at Mar Tyn's palm.

"Our Lady of Benevolence," she said, softly. "She is not so well-named, that one."

She raised her eyes and met Mar Tyn's glance.

"Are you one of hers, my friend?"

"I am not, but you ought to make haste to become so!" he said sharply.

He should have waited for Serana, he thought, wildly. Serana, who was ruthless, and practical—and who would surely grasp the weapon that he had brought to her hand . . .

"Now, why, I wonder?" she asked, still in that soft tone.

"Because Her Nin bey'Pasra calls openly for allies on the streets. He means to break the bakery, Serana, and destroy it all!"

She said nothing, merely continuing to wait politely, her eyes fixed on his face.

Mar Tyn took a breath, found he had no more words, spun and slapped the coin on the table.

"Use it," he said, harshly.

"Of a certainty, we will treat it as it deserves," Serana told him.

She reached out and gripped his shoulder. "You are concerned for us. It says much, and we love you the more for it. Tell me, what will *you* do?"

"I?" He stared, at a loss for a moment, though he had thought of that, thought it straight through. He would—he would . . .

Oh, yes.

"I will take my money, that you hold for me, and buy myself safety."

"This is intriguing," Don Eyr said. "But I beg you will rethink that plan, if only for the moment. Ail Den and Cisco have been keeping the streets under eye, and there are loiterers where usually there are none. They are not yet an army, but they would be able to visit a great deal of trouble upon a one-armed man, especially if he were slowed by the weight of so much money."

Mar Tyn looked at him bleakly.

"I cannot stay here."

"Because you will bring bad luck down on our house?"

It was said gently; without mockery. Mar Tyn drew a hard breath.

"There is no such thing as *bad luck*," he said straightly. "There is no such thing as *good luck*. There is only Luck, which is an . . . energy. A field. Some of us are focal points for the field, but make no mistake, *it* uses *us*. Lucks who attempt to force their gift die more quickly than those of us who are receptive, and hold ourselves ready to act in defense of our lives."

If we are allowed so much, he added silently, Keplyr's death flickering behind his eyelids.

"My gift sent me to gayn'Urlez's Hell; it drew Lady voz'Laathi's coin to me, and granted my winner what would be a fortune even in Mid Port. Luck led me here, to this place, to you, and those you protect, with this token of the lady's protection. To preserve you and your works. You had asked me *why here*? *This* is the answer. It would not have served so well, had I been killed, because you might not have found the token in my pocket, or known it for what it was."

He took a breath, looked from Serana's face to Don Eyr's.

"I beg you, do not cast this aside."

Serana looked at Don Eyr. Don Eyr looked at Serana.

They both looked back at Mar Tyn.

"It is a kindness," Don Eyr said gently. "I—we—accept that you offer us this from the fullness of your heart. We are grateful, for your regard, and for your courage, which brought you back, knowing your danger."

"You worry that we are soft, and easy to crack," Serana said then. "But you have not considered—perhaps you do not know!—that we have kept our place here for nearly four years. This is not the first time a mob has attempted to break us. We are not complacent, but we are, I think, not in as much danger as you believe us to be. Stay and stand with us. Will your gift allow it?"

He considered himself—feet at rest, blood a little quick, but without the sizzle of the field manifest. Truth told, he was doubtful that he *could* leave, if it came to that . . .

"My gift . . . insists upon it," he said, wryly.

FIVE

THE STREETS fought for them.

He had not realized—had not been part of the life of the bakery long enough to ... *see it*.

The bakery's influence did not stop at its reinforced stone walls. And it was a bigger place, of itself, than he had understood: a huge stone square, which Fireyn had told him had once been a barracks and military offices. One such office had a large window onto Crakle Street, which was now a shop that sold bread, and other foods, which the ... *neighbors* purchased with coin, or barter, or labor. Children who lived on those surrounding streets attended classes with the children who lived inside. Adults also came for classes, for meetings, for sparring sessions.

Serana and Cisco taught courses in self-defense. Fireyn taught strategy and first aid.

All taught a curriculum of self-esteem, and ... ethics.

Ethics ...

Mar Tyn had tried the word on his tongue in Don Eyr's hearing, and had been given a book tape for his trouble. He'd tucked it into his pocket, promising to read it after the current event was done.

For, despite the startling fact that its protectors were more than four adults and the children themselves, the war was going ... not well for the bakery.

To be fair, neither were matters proceeding as quickly as Her Nin bey'Pasra and his allies doubtless wished.

Which was probably why they decided to bring fire into it.

The first thing they gave to the flames was the Gossip Roost at the corner of Toom Street. It was only made from cardboard and plas— and burned too fast to serve as a rallying point. Nor was anyone hurt, since the Gossip himself had taken shelter inside the bakery.

When news of his loss reached him, he had sighed, and sat, tight-lipped and silent, glaring at nothing in particular, until one of the older children came to him with a notepad.

"Bai Sly, help me sketch what the Roost looked like," the child said earnestly. "How big was it? Were there any drawers or cupboards?"

"That is so, when this is over, we can rebuild quickly," Cisco said to Mar Tyn, when they stopped at the kitchen for jelly-bread to have with them, in case they should become hungry during their shift as door guards.

"Rebuild," Mar Tyn repeated, as they moved to take over their post from Don Eyr and Ail Den.

"Yes."

"What if the invaders win?"

"They won't." Cisco threw him a grin. "If this plays like the other attacks, what's going to happen is they'll get bored in a couple days, when they find out we're not as easy as they thought we'd be, and start fighting among themselves."

They turned into the hallway that led to the side-door post.

"Why don't they fire the street?" asked Mar Tyn.

There were signs of fire on every street in Low Port. Not all—or even most—had been set by bullies intent on smoking out their prey. But such tactics weren't unknown.

"They may try to fire the street," Don Eyr said as they reached the door. "But they will have a hard time of it."

"Why?"

"Fireyn and Dale"—Dale was the other one of the Betrayed attached to the bakery—"produced a flame retardant, and all the neighborhood helped to coat the buildings."

"Most of the buildings," said Cisco. "A couple are still vulnerable, like the Gossip Roost, but most aren't."

He stepped forward.

"The Watch changes. Go get something to eat, and some rest."

"It has been quiet," Don Eyr said, and produced a weary smile. "The Watch changes, brothers."

He and Ail Den passed up the hall. There was a small *boom*, which was the far door closing behind them.

* * * ✧ * * *

THE RIOT ARRIVED exactly two hours after Mar Tyn and Cisco had taken over the door.

Dozens of bullies came storming down the street, throwing stones, breaking doors, engaging with the defenders. Knives and pipes were in evidence, employed by both sides. There were no guns—not yet . . .

Cisco swore, and pulled a comm from his pocket, stepping back to call Serana.

Mar Tyn stood his post, breath caught in horror. It came to him that the allies had gotten bored already and this rolling wave of destruction was Her Nin bey'Pasra's way of keeping them to his cause.

He sighed, then, relieved to be safe behind closed doors, rather than scrambling for cover inside the erupting mayhem—and swore aloud.

His feet—his feet were moving, and there were locks on the door, locks a one-armed man could not manipulate, even if he did know the codes.

He thrust his good hand out, bracing himself against the wall, but his feet kept walking, inexorably, toward the locked door.

There was a snap, and a flicker, as if Low Port's spotty power grid had achieved one of its frequent overloads.

Mar Tyn put his good hand out to grip the handle—and pulled the door open.

His feet marched him out into the riot. He pulled the door closed. Behind him, he heard Cisco yell.

* * * ◇ * * *

HIS FEET TURNED LEFT, determinedly moving into the teeth of the riot. He was, Mar Tyn thought dispassionately, going to die. He was going to be torn into pieces, like Keplyr had been, trying to use his Luck—and who had known better than Keplyr that Luck was *no one's* to use!—trying to *use his Luck* to turn aside a mob raging down on a band of Mid-Porters, who had crossed the line with no purpose other than to bring food to the hungry.

He dodged a knife halfheartedly thrust at his belly, ducked away from a blow that would have knocked his head from his shoulders—all without a break in stride. In fact, he had gotten past the worst of the confusion and fighting before the expected hand closed 'round his collar and he was jerked backward, into a thin space between two houses.

"You!" Her Nin bey'Pasra shook him like a mongrel with a rat. "Where's my money?"

"I don't have it, Ser." The sound of his own voice astonished him. He sounded utterly calm and unafraid.

A hard slap across his mouth; his head hit the plas wall. He stood, head turned half-aside, waiting for the next blow.

Which did not come.

"Do you want to live, Luck?" snarled his captor.

What game was this? Mar Tyn turned his head slightly, watching the other out of the side of his eye.

"I want to live," he said flatly.

"Then earn your life from me!"

Another blow—and the world went black.

· · ·✧· · ·

PAIN BROUGHT HIM BACK to consciousness. He was lying in the dirt, his head throbbing, and Her Nin bey'Pasra looming above him, smiling.

Mar Tyn closed his eyes, seeing his own doom in that smile.

"Look at me! Unless you've decided you no longer want to live."

He opened his eyes and stared into the smile, which seemed to please the man.

"Give me victory in this war, Luck, and I will let you live."

A terrifying promise. Let to live, in Low Port, with all his limbs broken? Or with or a knife wound to the gut?

Still . . .

"I will try what I may do," he said, which was not a lie, and added, "Ser."

Teeth glinted.

"Try," his winner advised. "Try hard."

The shift of balance warned him; he rolled, but he could not avoid the boot that came against his weak arm in its sling. Lightning flared through his head, and he screamed.

Curling around his damaged arm, he heard Her Nin bey'Pasra speak again.

"Give me the delm of flour and all of his treasures, or you *will* know pain, Luck."

"Now, *try!*"

There came the sound of steps, retreating, of a door being heavily slammed into place and the song of a lock being engaged.

Mar Tyn lay in the dirt, and wondered if, after all, there was such a thing as bad luck.

· · ·✧· · ·

HE MAY HAVE PASSED OUT AGAIN. He woke to a touch. A touch from a soft, very cold hand, against his cheek.

Carefully, he opened his eyes.

A small, exceedingly dirty child was kneeling next to him. Her hair was a dusty snarl, bruises and cuts clearly visible between the rents in her rags.

"Hello," he said, very softly, feeling Luck burning in his blood.

She continued to stare at him out of light eyes surrounded by black bruises.

"You are like my mother was," she said, her voice gritty and low. "I can see the colors all around you."

He took a breath, deep and careful, and slowly, without taking his eyes from hers, he uncoiled until he was flat on his back.

"Was your mother Ahteya?" he asked her softly.

She closed her eyes, and turned her face away.

Mar Tyn waited, his bones on fire.

The child turned back to him, desperation in the gaunt, scratched face.

"I can fix it," she said.

"Fix what?"

"This," she said, and leaned forward, putting her two small hands against his newly shattered arm.

Pain—no. Something far more exalted than mere pain flowed into him from the two cold points of her hands. He couldn't scream; he had no breath; and it continued, this strange, clear, not-pain; his arm was encased in it, and he imagined he could feel the broken bones grinding back into place.

Above him, the child whimpered, and he tried to tell her not to hurt herself, but he had no voice, until—

She lifted her hands away, and sat back on her heels. Tears made streaks of mud down her face. There was a sound, and she snapped around, gasping, but whatever—whoever—it was passed by their sturdy locked door.

Mar Tyn remained where he was, feeling nearly transparent, now that both pain and anti-pain had left him. Carefully, he raised his recently re-broken arm, turned it this way, that way; flexed his fingers.

Everything operated precisely as it should.

A Healer, he thought. *The child is a Healer.*

Awkwardly, he rolled into a seated position, and put two good arms around his knees. The child turned to face him again, and he saw that she was shivering.

He reached into his pocket and pulled out the packet of bread and jam, worse for its recent use, but certainly still edible.

"Eat," he said, offering it to her on the palm of his hand.

She stared at it; he saw her wavering on the edge of refusing, but one grubby hand snatched out, as if of its own accord, and she was unwrapping the treat.

"He'll be back," she whispered. "He'll beat me, unless I make the bakery unlucky. I can't make the bakery unlucky—can you?"

"No," he said softly, watching her cram the bread into her mouth. "I can't. There is no such thing as good luck or bad luck. There is only Luck."

She swallowed, somewhat stickily, and he wished he had water for her.

"He says I'm a Luck," she said. "A bad and *stupid* Luck."

"He knows nothing. What is your name?"

"Aazali."

"Aazali, my name is Mar Tyn, and I *am* a Luck, as your mother was. Thank you for healing my arm. I will take you away, and I swear to you, on my mentor's honor, that Her Nin bey'Pasra will never beat you again."

She looked up at him.

"You can promise this?"

He paused, listening to his blood.

"I can," he said, with absolute certainty. "I will take you to a safe place, to rest and to heal." That first, and most importantly. The rest of what must happen—that could wait until she was safe with Don Eyr and Serana.

"Where will you take me?" she asked him. She had stopped shivering, he saw. That was good.

"I will take you to the bakery. Will you come?"

"When the bakery falls and he finds me there, he'll kill me," she said matter-of-factly.

"The bakery is not going to fall," Mar Tyn said, certain again, as he was so rarely certain.

She considered him for a long moment.

"He killed my mother," she said.

"I know. He will not have you."

Another pause, as if she were looking very nearly at those colors she claimed to see spiraling around him.

"I'll come," she said at last.

"Good."

He rose, effortlessly, to his feet. She rose less easily, and wavered where she stood.

"It will be best," he said, "if I carry you."

Another ageless stare from those bruised light eyes.

"Yes," she said.

He bent and took her into his arms. She weighed nothing.

"Arms around my neck," he told her. "Head down. Eyes closed."

She did as he asked. Her hair scratched his chin.

He took a breath, standing quiet, and felt his feet begin to move.

"We go," he said, as they marched toward the door. "Hold firm."

There came a snap, and a fizzle, as if Low Port's spotty power grid had achieved one of its frequent overloads.

Ahead of them, the door sagged on its hinges.

Mar Tyn extended a hand and pushed it out of his way.

• • • ✧ • • •

THE RIOT HAD DISSOLVED into isolated pockets of violence along the street—and what looked to be a full-fledged brawl across from the bakery.

Mar Tyn's feet walked steadily and with assurance down the

littered street, detouring around rocks, and bodies, and other debris. The child in his arms scarcely seemed to breathe.

He had the side door of the bakery in his eye before the shout he had been expecting came from behind. His feet did not falter; he walked, not even looking aside.

"I'll kill you both!" Her Nin bey'Pasra roared. Heavy footsteps thundered from behind.

Ahead, the bakery door burst open. Fireyn had a gun in her hand, and her face was terrible to see. Cisco held the door, also showing a gun, and Don Eyr was scarcely behind him, shouting.

Mar Tyn's feet deigned at last to run. A shot sounded from behind, a second, and a thud, as if a sack of rocks had hit the street. His foot struck a rock, and he stumbled, throwing himself forward, into Don Eyr's arms.

The three of them pulled back into the safety of the hallway, Fireyn leaping in behind.

Cisco slammed the door.

"Done?" he asked.

"Done and dead," she answered.

"What happened?" Don Eyr asked nearer at hand. He straightened slowly, one hand on Mar Tyn's shoulder, one hand on Aazali's narrow back.

"I'll tell you everything," Mar Tyn said. "But first—the child."

"Yes," Don Eyr said. "First—the child."

SIX

THE STREETS WERE RECOVERED from the war; the rubble had been cleared away, the Gossip Roost rebuilt. Repairs had been made as needed. Classes had resumed.

Aazali sen'Pero and Mar Tyn eys'Ornstahl—well fed, well washed, well dressed—stood in the large parlor, with Don Eyr, and Serana, and Fireyn.

"You should have a third," Serana said, not for the first time, "to guard your back."

It was prudent, but Mar Tyn's feet, rebels that they were, would have none of it.

"Myself, and Aazali," he said. "We cannot arrive as an armed delegation. Mid Port wouldn't understand."

Don Eyr stirred, and sighed, and spread his hands, meeting Serana's eyes with a small smile.

"He is correct, my love; accept it."

She sighed, her answering smile wry.

"In fact, I am overprotective."

"We share the fault," Fireyn said. She turned a stern eye on him. "Mar Tyn. You will be *prudent*."

He smiled at her with new-learned tenderness.

"Now, how can I promise that?"

Almost, she smiled in turn. Almost.

"Do what you might, then," she said.

"I will."

Serana dropped to one knee and opened her arms.

"My child, remember us. If you have need, come. You will always have a place with us."

"Thank you," Aazali said, and threw herself into the large embrace. "I might stay here," she whispered, but Serana put her at arm's length and shook her head.

"We cannot train you, and training you *must* have, for your own protection and that of your friends. If, when you are trained, you choose to come back to us, we will have you, gladly."

"Yes," said Aazali. They had, after all, been over this, many times.

She turned, then, to hug Don Eyr, then Fireyn, and at last came back to his side, slipping her small warm hand into his.

"Mar Tyn," she said, looking up into his face with grey eyes still shadowed from all she had endured. "It is time for us to go."

SEVEN

SOME HOURS LATER, and they were in Mid Port. Thus far, no one had taken notice of them, neatly dressed and cleanly as they were. Mar Tyn was at one with his feet, as they walked into the pretty court, with its flowers and fountains, and the house just there, as if waiting for them.

Aazali's grip on his hand tightened on his as they climbed the stairs.

"Mar Tyn," she said, when they had finished the flight, and stood before the polished wooden door. "Mar Tyn, what if they don't want me?"

This was not a new question, either, but he did not fault her for asking again.

"They would be fools, not to want you," he said patiently. "If it happens that they *are* fools, we will return to the bakery, and make another plan."

"Yes," she breathed, and he raised his free hand to touch the bell pad.

Three notes sounded, muted by the door.

They waited.

The door opened, revealing a halfling with wide blue eyes and curling yellow hair. Doubtless, his face was pleasing enough when he smiled. But he was not smiling. He barely glanced at Aazali, his attention was all for Mar Tyn, or, rather, whatever he saw just beyond Mar Tyn's shoulder, which plainly pleased him not at all.

"We want none of your sort here," he said shortly. "Go, before the hall master comes."

It might, Mar Tyn thought, have been kindness, of its sort. He chose to believe so.

"You want none of my sort," he agreed. "But this child is one of yours, Healer, and the Hall holds an obligation to train her."

The boy's frown grew marked.

"Tainted . . . " he began—and spun as a shadow flickered behind him, and a plump woman, her pale red hair pulled into a long tail behind her head, stepped to his side.

"I will take care of these gentles, Tin Non," she said.

"Yes, Healer." The doorkeeper bowed and left them.

Mar Tyn met the Healer's pale blue eyes. She was, he thought, with a small shock, no older than he was. Surely, this was not the hall master.

"Tin Non gives you good advice," she told him. "You should be gone before the hall master arrives. We have perhaps twelve minutes."

With that she turned to the child standing very still beside him, her grip bruising his fingers.

She bent, her eyes on the child—and abruptly went to her knees, as if what she saw there were too much to bear, standing.

"So young," Mar Tyn heard her whisper, before she extended a plump hand.

"My name is Dyoli," she said softly. "May I know yours?"

"Aazali," the child said, ignoring the outstretched hand. "I am Aazali sen'Pero. And this is *my friend*, Mar Tyn eys'Ornstahl."

There was a small pause, during which the Healer slanted her eyes at him, before returning her attention to Aazali.

"I see that he is your good friend," she said, softly. "He is very brave to bring you here, placing himself so much at risk. I see that you honor him. I honor him, too."

She paused, as if she were scrutinizing something visible to only herself.

"We in this Hall will take care of you," she said, after a moment.

"Serana said you would train me," Aazali answered.

Healer Dyoli bowed her head.

"We will do that, also. But first, we will take care of you," she said softly, and offered her hand again. "Will you come with me?"

The child stiffened, her fingers tightening. Mar Tyn dropped to his heels, so that all of their faces were level.

"Aazali, this is what we had talked about," he said gently. "This is the *best* outcome to our plan."

"Yes," she said, then, and of a sudden threw herself around his neck.

"Stay safe," she said, her voice breaking on a sob. "Mar Tyn, *promise* me."

"Child, as safe as I may. You know that is everything I can promise."

"Yes," she said again, and he felt her whole body shudder as she sighed.

She moved her head, and kissed his cheek, then pushed against his shoulder.

He let her go, and watched as she stepped forward and at last took the Healer's hand.

"Thank you," she said, subdued, but willing.

"Thank you, Sister," the Healer answered, rising slowly. "I will do my best to be worthy of you."

Mar Tyn rose, as well, and cleared his throat. She looked to him.

"I have," he said, reaching toward an inner pocket. "Funds for the child's keep. Her mother is dead. She has no clan, no kin."

The Healer frowned, glanced past his shoulder, then looked into his face.

"The Hall will keep her, and I will myself take her under my care. You—use your money to secure your fortune, Mar Tyn eys'Ornstahl. I . . . feel, *very strongly*, that you ought to do so."

He blinked at her, momentarily wordless, but there—it was said that some Healers saw ahead in time.

"Thank you," he said. "I will take your advice."

She glanced behind her suddenly, the long tail of her hair swinging, and stepped back into the hallway, drawing Aazali with her.

"The hall master. Go, quickly! Stay as safe as you are able, Mar Tyn."

The door closed, and he turned, at one with his feet—down the stairs, and out of the courtyard, into the wide street, walking brisk and light, away from Mid Port—back to Low Port and his fortune.

✧ Opportunity to Seize ✧

OPPORTUNITY TO SEIZE is a multiple novel outtake. Honest, we tried to fit it into two books before we admitted defeat, and pulled it. But, in our humble opinions, it was too good not to share.

✧✧✧

SUREBLEAK

Dudley Avenue and Farley Lane

IT MIGHT HAVE BEEN thunder that waked Daav.

If so, it waked *only* him. His bedmates slumbered on, Kamele's head on Aelliana's shoulder; a pleasant picture, which he tarried a moment to admire before slipping out from beneath the blankets.

His pants came easily to hand, and he pulled them on before turning toward the window. A line of light showed at the edge of the drawn shade; he eased it up a fraction and gazed upon a street filled with shadows, along which street lights glowed. Above, the sky showed the faintest streaks of peach and cream.

Well, then, possibly it had only thundered in his dreams. It would not have been the first time.

He let the shade fall back, looking again to the bed, and the pair sleeping there. Given the advancing hour, he really ought to wake them. Surely they had tried Kareen's patience—and her hospitality— far enough. He and Aelliana had stopped yesterday for a morning visit, to make themselves known to one who deserved the truth from them, and expecting—on his side—to have been summarily dismissed.

Instead, they had proceeded to monopolize Kamele all day and night, nor had she been an unwilling participant.

In retrospect, it could hardly have been otherwise. After so much time apart, and so many adventures, in which Aelliana's physical presence, and his own abrupt youthening, were not the least strange—of *course* it would take hours—days!—to catch themselves up. It had been his error, to expect that Kamele would meet them coldly. His *grievous* error, unworthy of the man who had been Kamele Waitley's *onagrata* for twenty Standards.

Well, and he had his error shown to him, vigorously, and they three had filled in the broad outlines of their lives since last they'd been together. That, at least. His sister had been forbearing, perhaps even kind—witness the discreet series of trays sent up to the scholar's rooms, and the lack of a call to Prime.

To tell truth, neither he nor Aelliana had planned a bed visit, nor, he was persuaded, had Kamele. Yet, when the moment came, it had been recognized by all, and accepted as inevitable.

So—a touch, and another, a press, a stroke; knowing kisses shared between familiar lovers—and the bed, all three aflame. And after they had rested, once again, comfortable and comforting, before sliding into shared sleep . . .

To wake with a new day barely dawning, and the particular business he and Aelliana had at the port yet to be accomplished. Not that there had been a deadline attached to that business, other than their mutual desire to become properly established as pilots, and certified to fly.

He considered the bed, and the choices before him: To wake them, or not to wake them? Surely, whichever it came to, it would be *them*; he was done with sneaking away from Kamele while she slept.

As he stood contemplating his best course, there came a discreet knock at the door, which was very likely their eviction notice, solving the problem for them all.

Running his hands over his short-cropped hair, he crossed the room and opened the door, expecting to see his sister, properly chilly in her irritation.

Instead, there was another tray on the table beside the door, a multitude of small covered plates clustered on it, with a steaming teapot, and a carafe of morning wine nestled next to a small vase holding three small dark red flowers.

Well.

He picked up the tray, brought it into the room, and put it on the table by the window.

Daav, Aelliana murmured inside his head, *has Kareen had enough of us?*

Very much the contrary, he told her. *True affection is honored, and we are invited to make merry.*

We have *made merry,* Aelliana pointed out.

Ah, but have we been merry thrice? he asked, focusing deliberately on the vase and its contents.

There was a flicker of . . . something from Aelliana. Perhaps it was astonishment.

Kareen sent that?

So I suppose, as it was Kareen who urged us to call and make our bows. She must feel a certain proprietary interest. And she does appear genuinely fond of Kamele.

She is . . . much changed, Aelliana offered eventually.

I am told that age mellows, he answered. *Not that I would know, of course.*

Of course, his lifemate said politely. *If you have done fussing with the tray, you might come and help me wake Kamele.*

Daav smiled, and bowed gently to the three bold flowers in their vase.

Certainly, he said. *After all, one would scarcely wish to disoblige one's sister.*

. . . ⋄ . . .

LATER, HAVING OBLIGED KAREEN most thoroughly, they tardily addressed breakfast, each telling over the tasks of the advancing day.

"We have two ships to inspect, so that we may vigorously debate the merits of each," Aelliana said, sipping the last of her tea.

Kamele tipped her head to one side. She was still damp from the shower, and droplets glittered like gemstones strung through her pale hair.

"Will you set up as small traders?" she asked.

"As couriers," Aelliana said. "We are quite unsuited to be traders, I fear."

"And it must be said," Daav added, "that the potential of randomized danger draws her, like a moth to flame."

"Very true," Aelliana said gravely. "Besides, you know, if I fail to fall into enough scrapes from which I must be extracted, Daav becomes bored, which I am certain you agree is something to be avoided."

Kamele laughed.

"When he's bored, he takes things apart," she said, giving Aelliana a comradely nod, "as you know. You'd definitely want to avoid that, on a spaceship."

"Unkind!" Daav protested. "I always put them back together again!"

He put his empty cup on the table, met Kamele's eye, and lifted a shoulder in a rueful half shrug. "Nearly always."

She laughed again.

"Do you plan an immediate lift?"

"Not quite immediately," Aelliana said. "The debating of merits may take some time. Also, we must be tested for new licenses."

Kamele frowned, and glanced to Daav.

"Theo tells me that a master pilot's license never expires."

"Very true, but in the particular case, it is—*more expedient*, let us say—to obtain a new license under a new name than to undertake an explanation of my current estate to either the Pilots Guild or to the Scouts."

"The delm is adamant," Aelliana added. "We must qualify on our current abilities, and the tickets we fly on must be true."

"No falsifying sources," Kamele said wisely, and was rewarded with a wide smile.

"Exactly so."

"And you?" Daav said. "Are you entirely fixed on resigning your position at Delgado?"

"Yes. I'll be sending my letter this week. I expect Admin will be delighted. I've been more of a thorn in their side than a rose in their crown, lately."

"I wonder..." Aelliana said, and hesitated, casting Kamele a conscious look. "I fear that I am about to meddle."

Kamele met her eyes blandly.

"Well, I'm certainly not used to *that*."

Aelliana inclined her head gravely.

"Indeed, how could you be? Now that you have been warned, I proceed—Kamele, *must* you resign?"

"What else should I do? Go back to Delgado and be compliant?"

"Oh, no; that would be too dreadful! I was only thinking that—*of course*, you will wish to use your expertise to build Surebleak an educational system. Surebleak, though, is short of funds, and likewise short of scholars trained in the traditional way. How if you allowed Delgado to participate in the project? Would not a satellite school on a planet which is poised to enter the universal conversation increase Admin's *melant'i*, and the whole worth of the university?"

"Especially," Daav murmured, "if they could assign some of their more...noncompliant scholars to the project?"

Kamele stared...*toward* him, though what she was seeing was her thoughts. It was an expression he knew well.

Our work here is done, van'chela, he said to Aelliana.

We may trust so. And only think what a gaggle of Delgadan scholars might do with Surebleak.

Imagination balks, he assured her.

Bah.

Kamele blinked back to the room.

"I take your point," she said to Aelliana. "This is an opportunity."

"Precisely so," Aelliana said with a smile. She glanced toward the window, now showing a street filled up with the full light of day.

"I fear that we must take leave of you now, to pursue our own opportunity."

She stood, and Daav did.

"Of course," Kamele said, rising with them. "Visit again, when you're able. At least"—she cast a stern eye over Daav—"you might write."

He bowed his head in contrition.

"At the very least," he said softly.

"Now, *that* was effective," Aelliana said approvingly. "I will have to copy your style."

"Be sure to let me know how it turns out," Kamele said. "Now, quickly, another kiss from each of you—and go! We all have opportunity to seize!"

✧ Shout of Honor ✧

ORIGINALLY MEANT to be part of a novel, this story grew in scope until it needed its own freestanding title and presentation. Yxtrang Ambassador Vepal and Commander Sanchez appeared together briefly. Here, they have the opportunity to expand their acquaintance, and work together to solve a most vexing mystery.

✧✧✧

ONE

THEY CAME INTO INAGO for news, and supplies, and other such items of interest that a way station might be expected to offer. Vepal had chosen this particular way station because it was in a more populated sector and enjoyed a level of traffic that the ports they usually chose did not.

Traffic, then, he had expected.

He had simply not expected *so much* traffic.

Nor that so much of it would be . . . martial . . . in nature.

Some might have leapt to the conclusion that Inago was under attack. Commander Vepal's trained eye immediately discerned the lack of lines, the lack of order in committed approaches. Oh, there was *station* order, this ship to *such* berth on *that* heading—but nothing like military discipline, or thinking, here.

But if not an attack, then—what brought so many soldiers and fighting ships to Inago Prime, surely among the least warlike location in this section of space?

His board pinged receipt of a communication originating at the station. Not, according to the wrapper, from station admin—they were too far out, yet, for the station master's attention. No, this message originated inside the station, sent from a private source.

Intrigued, Vepal opened the packet.

Perdition Enterprises is hiring soldiers, pilots, techs, and specialists for assignments starting immediately! All may apply—papers or paper-free; lone guns to entire units. Soldiers and specialists must have own kit. Working units will be retained intact, if possible. All contracts with Perdition Enterprises. PE provides transportation, target, mission goals, and timeline. Generous bonuses for early completion! NDA required. Come to Core Conference, station center, any hour, any day. Recruiters standing by.

The message began to repeat, and Vepal killed it.

"Are we looking for employment?" Pilot Erthax asked, and waited just a breath too long before adding, "Sir."

Vepal considered him.

"I've been going over the mission's funding. Temp Headquarters used to omit only one of our five stipends per Cycle. Of the last five due, we have received . . . three.

"This lack of funding decreases our efficiency and our scope," Vepal went on, talking quietly, gaze on his screen. "It might be . . . to the benefit of the mission to find what this Perdition Enterprises considers reasonable recompense for the skills of a pilot. If there is a signing bonus, as well . . . "

Though he kept his eyes scrupulously on his screen, Vepal's peripheral vision was good enough that he saw Erthax's hard dark face flush, and his mouth tighten.

"Yes," he continued. "You make a good point, Pilot. We should definitely find what assignments are on offer, and of what duration. It seems to me that we have become soft in our small unit here. A stint in the field might be what is required."

He was . . . not joking. Jokes were made between comrades. No, he was deliberately egging Erthax on, out of temper and dislike.

Which, he thought, with some chagrin, proved his point. They *had* become soft of discipline. *He* had become soft, for it was true that the troop was the reflection of command. And a commander who would taunt one of his own soldiers . . . ought to offer himself to the High Command for a field tour at reduced rank.

Which, interestingly enough, was what Perdition Enterprises offered.

Vepal frowned at his screen. It was outside of his authority to enlist in a military action, even if Perdition Enterprises included Yxtrang among those it found acceptable. Papers or paper-free, was it? Legitimate, licensed soldiers fighting beside pirates, renegades— and Yxtrang?

Still, there was opportunity here. The point of his mission was to discover, per the continuing orders from Headquarters, the proper entity for those of the Troop who had survived the collapse of the old universe to offer their allegiance, and their skills.

It seemed . . . unlikely that Perdition Enterprises was that entity, but it was not . . . *entirely* unlikely that they might have information about such an entity.

For almost the first time since he had rediscovered their continuing orders, lost for hundreds of Cycles, Vepal felt a stirring of hope, that this was not entirely the mission of a fool.

· · ·✧· · ·

THE ANSWER to his request for an interview with a recruiter upon their arrival on Inago, was—an application.

A form letter asked that he complete the application and send it ahead so that an appointment with an appropriate recruiter could be made. There was also a brief and uninformative blurb, from which he learned that Perdition Enterprises was in the business of brokering military and quasi-military assignments. There was no information about those in command, the owners or directors. The planet upon which Perdition Enterprises was registered was—not Waymart. Not quite Waymart.

It was, however, registered, licensed, and approved by the Better

Business Bureau of Gilstommer, which, as Vepal understood it, was to corporate entities precisely what Waymart was to ships.

So, the application.

He applied as "Vepal Small Troop," listing their personnel as one senior officer with advanced piloting and command skills, one line pilot, and one line soldier, detailing the skills shared among the troop, save those specific to Explorers. In a section headed "Other Assets," he noted that the troop maintained its own vessel, lightly armed and armored, suitable for reconnaissance or courier. He admitted that their treasury was small, and added that each member carried a complete and well-maintained kit.

Put thus, they looked a sad case, indeed, and he hesitated overlong, wondering if he ought to expand their worth. It was his purpose to gain an interview to learn about these *immediate assignments*, and to put particular questions of his own.

In the end, however, he sent in the nearly truthful application.

And, to his very great surprise, a communication from Perdition Enterprises met them at the dock, naming an hour not too far distant for Commander Vepal to meet with Recruiter pen'Chouka, in the Core Conference Center, Room 9A.

Vepal considered the name, which suggested that the recruiting agent was . . . Liaden. It was well to consider beforehand, how a Liaden might react, confronted with an Yxtrang, even a certified and guaranteed safe Yxtrang.

Still—Perdition Enterprises encouraged all to apply—papers or paper-free, eh? Surely Recruiting Agent pen'Chouka had seen worse than a well-behaved Yxtrang commander, respectfully reporting for his interview in dress uniform, with only small arm and grace blade on the belt, his honor-marks old and faded, and grey showing in his hair.

He had been instructed to appear unaccompanied before Recruiting Agent pen'Chouka, which Ochin would not like. The central belief of the Rifle's life was that Commander Vepal ought always to be accompanied by an escort appropriate to his rank—an honor guard at least!—or by the escort available, which would be Ochin Rifle.

Vepal hesitated. He didn't like to disappoint his Rifle, who was a simple man, and loyal, as Erthax was not. Still, the request was not unreasonable—was, in fact, prudent, and efficient. Evaluate command first, as the face and mind of the troop. If the commander passed inspection, then he would be called back, with his troop, for a second evaluation, if the first interview proved not to be sufficient.

On the way in to the station, he had attempted further research on Perdition Enterprises, but beyond the information contained in the brief blurb provided by the company itself, and a great deal of chatter on the social nets regarding a large hire-on at Inago, with guaranteed good pay, he found nothing.

It was somewhat worrisome that there was nothing in the chatter from those who had *been* hired; maybe the nondisclosure agreement prevented such. Again, that would be ... not unreasonable.

And the only way to discover anything more substantial, apparently, was to attend Recruiting Agent pen'Chouka. Commander Vepal glanced at the time display, and at the route to Room 9A in the Core Conference Area outlined on his screen.

Time to leave.

He inspected himself once more in the mirror, seeing that everything was soldierly. Satisfied, he picked up his hat and left their dock, stopping first to issue specific orders to Erthax and Ochin, and to state the time by which he ought to have returned, or contacted the ship with an amended hour of arrival.

* * * ✧ * * *

"COMMANDER VEPAL, welcome."

Recruiting Agent pen'Chouka was, indeed, Liaden, dressed in what might be the off-duty uniform of a common Troop—leather vest over a close-necked shirt, with long, tight sleeves. Nothing to snag, nothing to flutter, nothing to call attention. As the recruiter rose to meet him, Vepal was also able to see the small arm on the right side of his belt, and the dagger on the left, before the day-pouch.

"Recruiting Agent, I thank you," Vepal said, wondering if the man would dare a proper salute.

He did not. Merely, he inclined very slightly from the waist, and on straightening, moved a hand to show Vepal the other person, similarly dressed, who had also risen.

"My associate, Agent ter'Menth, who has been asked to sit in on this interview."

It was not said who had made this request; quite possibly a senior officer, if Perdition Enterprises was, in fact, modeled on military organization. Certainly, had their places been reversed, Vepal would have produced at the least a soft show of strength for a soldier of an enemy race.

"Please," said Recruiting Agent pen'Chouka, "let us sit and discuss the matter before us. Commander, may I offer you refreshment?"

The room was small and bare, holding the recruiting agent's desk, with a large screen set to one side, angled so that he might see the information displayed there, but the applicant could not. A portable data pad sat near the recruiter's right hand—and that was all and everything, save the chairs they sat on—inside the boundaries of the room.

Refreshment would therefore need to be called in, adding to the time it would take him to find out what Perdition Enterprises was recruiting for, and also introducing the risk that the refreshment would be . . . impure.

"Thank you," he said, which even a Liaden would recognize as politely civilized, "but no."

"Certainly," said Recruiter pen'Chouka, equitably, "let us immediately to business."

He glanced at the large screen.

"May I say, we were gratified to receive your application, Commander? Of course we will have room for such a *small troop* as you propose. We anticipate no difficulties."

Vepal trusted that his face remained soldierly. They had him travel half-way across the station to a private meeting only to accept his troop's application without discussion? A chill swept down his spine, not unlike the sensation he had when he sensed an ambush.

"I hadn't realized that our troop was so well known among the wide field of fighters," he said carefully, watching the recruiter's face, which, Liaden-wise, told him nothing.

"Oh," he said, with what might have been a small smile at the corner of the mouth, "your reputation proceeds you, sir; I assure you."

"In that case," Vepal said, still treading carefully, "you will know that I cannot commit without having some information regarding the scope of the mission. Our group has other obligations..."

"Of course it does," said the recruiter soothingly. He picked up the data pad and offered it to Vepal.

"You will have all of the information you require, Commander. Simply sign the nondisclosure agreement, and—"

Vepal did not extend a hand to receive the screen. Instead, he directed a piercing glance at the recruiter's face, lips parted, and allowing a little tooth to be seen, while he considered the implications of nondisclosure agreements. He knew of such things, but it had been his impression that they were brought into the negotiations after a certain level of basic trust had been established. To offer the thing up to be signed immediately, before any attempt at trust-building...

"Some basic information would be welcome," he said, austerely. "I cannot commit resources simply because Perdition Enterprises finds our reputation admirable."

Recruiting Agent pen'Chouka placed the pad on the table by Vepal's folded hands, and inclined his head.

"Basic information—of course! Perdition Enterprises is a combat broker. In short, we bring grievances together with forces appropriate to resolving them. I will tell you, Commander Vepal, that we are presently recruiting for a large-scale event; very complex. I believe that you, as others before you, will find our compensation package to be very good, and the bonus structure generous. I hardly need say that, for such a troop as yours, there is room for negotiation."

"What is the projected duration of this event?" he asked, but Recruiting Agent pen'Chouka held up his hands, showing empty palms.

"Sign the agreement, Commander, and all the information I have is yours."

Vepal sat very still, considering his options.

"Commander, may I ask a question?" the other recruiter—ter'Menth—spoke for the first time, her voice light, and her Terran bearing not the slightest accent.

He looked to her, keeping her partner in peripheral vision.

"You may ask," he said, watching her eyes.

This one was a killer, he thought. Doubtless the other was, too, but this one made no effort to hide herself behind affable politeness, as if Vepal were Terran, easily soothed by smiles and soft words.

Recruiting Agent ter'Menth inclined her head.

"I thank you. I wonder—indeed, we had *all* wondered, immediately we saw your application, and your docking packet—is it possible that you speak for . . . a force larger than the small troop which travels with you? Perdition is prepared to be generous, even beyond our A-level contract, if you have a proposal in mind. You are, in fact, the answer to a conundrum we had not hoped to solve."

"I do not understand you," Vepal said, which was not entirely untruthful. "Please speak plainly, Recruiter."

She smiled, showing the teeth, as might a soldier who wished to establish precedence.

"Since you ask so gently," she began, and stopped in order to look at her partner, who had made a small noise, perhaps of denial.

"I take full responsibility," she said, and after a long moment, he bowed his head.

She turned back to Vepal.

"I will be plain," she said. "The scope of the project before us is such that we thought of contacting Yxtrang Command with an offer. We found no clear way to do so, and those sent to intercept your ambassadorial team failed, so far as we know, to arrive. Thus, we turned to our secondary plan, with reluctance. However, now that *you* have brought the ambassadorial team to *us*, perhaps you might assist us in approaching the High Command at . . . at Temp Headquarters with an offer."

He stared at her, and suddenly there was nothing more that he wanted from his life than to leave this room, alive.

"I may be able to assist," he said, slowly. "But in order to do so, I will need to know the details of your offer. I will tell you that the High Commanders are...unlikely to sign a nondisclosure agreement."

She smiled again, seeming genuinely amused.

"Of course we do not intend to deal with the High Command as we treat with mere mercenary soldiers and bully squads. What we propose is to offer the High Command a contract."

"A—*contract*," he repeated, the word sounding ominous in his head. "For what purpose?"

She leaned forward, her elbows on the table, and gazed up into his face.

"We wish to contract the services of a full Conquest Corps to destroy a target of our choosing."

TWO

HE HAD ESCAPED, with his life, and a very small additional amount of information. Recruiting Agent ter'Menth had not bothered to pretend that what she gave him was in any way useful. On his side, he pretended that what she offered was something that the High Commanders might wish to consider.

What he did not say was that the High Commanders would not accept a contract. The Troop were not *soldiers for hire*; they were *the Troop*. Created to take the war to an unbeatable enemy. Created to stand rear guard so that the civilians the Troop, from its position of bred superiority, protected, might escape with their lives, and find safety...elsewhere.

Sadly, his innate superiority had not been sufficient to disentangle him completely from Perdition Enterprises. Recruiting Agent ter'Menth expected an answer. She expected, in fact, that he would return to his ship and forthwith send a courier-beam to High Command, laying before them the wonders of this contract, which included rich looting, and the opportunity for more, like, contracts.

He was—not quite—so foolish as to do anything like. But what he must do, and quickly, was to leave this port, with his small troop intact.

Despite that goal burning brightly in his mind, he did not immediately return to dock, ship, and troop. He was in no fit condition to return to his command. Even Ochin would see that there was something amiss. He needed time to settle himself, to make a plan for removing them safely from the reach of Perdition Enterprises.

So, he called the ship, amended his arrival time, and was now seated at a back table at an eating and drinking establishment called, according to the sign over the door, The Headless Yxtrang. It could hardly be more fitting. He ordered beer and a soy-cheese handwich. He wanted neither, but the order would secure the table for an hour.

And give him a chance to think.

The existence of the Yxtrang Ambassador to the Outworlds was known among a certain set of persons with a need to know—the Liaden Scouts, the Portmasters Guild, the Pilots Guild.

Perdition Enterprises, being a broker of war, would naturally make it their business to likewise know such things.

A team had been sent to him, but never arrived, so ter'Menth had said. Was that a fact? If so, what had happened to that team? Had it defected? Been captured? Been diverted to another assignment?

Had—

"Ambassador Vepal," a clear, memorable voice said, carrying inflections of both surprise and—pleasure? "You may remember me, sir, from Seebrit Station."

He raised his head to meet black eyes set in a strong, lean face.

"Commander Sanchez."

He stood, out of respect for her rank, and for the scar that adorned her right cheek. Many have known the caress of the war blade, though few survive it. That JinJee Sanchez was one of those few—pleased him in a way that he could not have explained. She was a warrior, and intelligent; an equal, which he had in neither Ochin nor Erthax.

"I remember you, Commander, and I am pleased to see you well."

There, that was polite and civilized.

Sanchez smiled like to the smile that passed between old comrades, chance-met off the field.

"I am glad to see you well—and to see you again. May I join you?"

Join him? Ah, she meant to sit at his table, and share time over the meal.

"I would welcome your presence," he told her truthfully.

She sat across from him, her shoulder to the room, while he resumed the seat that gave him the wider view. Among comrades, this would indicate that he was point in this place and time. It was gratifying, that she allowed him this honor.

Gratifying—and strangely troubling.

"I will have what this, my comrade, is having," Sanchez was telling the waiter. "All to go onto the Paladins account."

He blinked, was about to protest that he was able to feed himself—and subsided at the bare shake of her head.

"Allow me to discharge the remainder of my debt to your good nature," she said, gravely.

"If you feel such a debt exists," he told her. "I do not."

"Another display of good nature!" she said, with a certain lightness to her voice.

Her handwich and beer appeared on the table before her. She nodded without taking her eyes from Vepal's face.

"I wonder to find you here," she said. "Did you come for the job fair?"

"I came to find information to assist me in my duty," he told her. "The . . . job fair was a surprise."

"Ah." She picked up her beer and had a swallow. "Then you have not been to the recruiting office."

"I've just come from the recruiting office," he said, following her lead. The beer was good, he noted with surprise.

"I went yesterday," she said, "on behalf of the Paladins. Will you tell me your impressions?"

He hesitated and she held up a hand.

"I don't ask you to violate the NDA, of course."

"I did not sign the form," he said.

Black eyebrows rose in interest.

"Oh, you didn't..." she said softly.

She put her elbows on the table, and leaned closer.

"Now, I am *very* interested in whatever you choose to tell me," she said.

He considered her strong face, finding honor there. She was a warrior—yes; and a fighter.

But she was not a killer.

There were details which he could not share. But there were other matters on which, he thought, he *must* speak, comrade-to-comrade, if only to help order his own thoughts.

It crossed his mind that she might have been sent from the recruiting officers, to test him. It was possible, after all, that JinJee Sanchez had signed the nondisclosure agreement, and was thus on assignment.

He picked up the mug and swallowed beer in a leisurely manner, to give himself time to think.

Even if she was constrained by orders, he decided, there were certain matters he must share with her. To do otherwise would be to further besmirch his own tattered honor.

He put the mug back on the table, and raised his eyes to meet hers.

"I am ... dismayed by the insistence that the nondisclosure agreement must be signed before *any* information is given out. It would seem easy enough to provide specific information regarding payments and bonuses, for instance, as an incentive to sign the agreement and learn more."

She was nodding.

"They are too careful. It makes one wonder *why*, does it not? As you say, the publication of even an *average* pay scale would speedily fix the interest of some. It might be argued that they have had poor advice in how to best go forward, but the solicitations they are sending out along the merc channels promise *competitive* and even *merc scale* recompense."

She held up one hand, hefting her mug with the other.

"Mind you, *merc scale* is fair nonsense, as any merc can tell you. But it demonstrates a willingness to entice."

He considered her.

"Did you sign the NDA?" he asked bluntly.

"I have not," she said, and gave him a bland look. "I await my co-commander before proceeding, and had merely visited the recruiting office to ensure the Paladins a place in queue."

She lifted her mug and drank, deeply.

"Another?" she asked, when she had put the empty on the table; she nodded at his mug, which he raised and drained likewise.

"Another—yes; though I will buy this round, so that we sit together as true comrades."

"Neither beholden to the other?" she asked.

"Yes."

She inclined her head.

"I agree."

He called for the drinks. When they arrived, he looked again to JinJee Sanchez.

"When will your co-commander arrive?" he asked.

She smiled.

"When he is needed. I hope that he will *not* be needed, if I may speak frankly between comrades."

"The Paladins have no need of employment?"

"Whenever was there a mercenary troop who did not need employment? In fact, we were on our way to a hiring hall when the advertisement for this job fair crossed our comm-lines. We thought to save ourselves some weeks of travel, with only a minor adjustment of course. And, it was not immediately obvious from the tenor of the advertisement that this was not a merc-sponsored event."

"Now that you have seen it—"

"Now that I have seen it, there is no question that the mercs do not endorse Perdition Enterprises, nor do our competitors, or our sisters."

"So, this would be a new organization, seeking to establish themselves?"

"New, they certainly are, but if they seek to establish themselves *credibly*, they have chosen an odd course."

She glanced down at her plate and picked up the handwich.

"Eat, Comrade! Who knows when we will have anything other than field rations again!"

He obeyed, admiring the neat efficiency she brought to the task.

"What is odd about their course?" he asked. "Besides a tendency toward secrecy?"

"In the normal way of things, this new enterprise would have among its founding membership some few from other, more established, organizations. They would take good care to advertise the names of these founders, so that those they seek to hire, or to bring into the new structure, will feel that it is built upon the strong shoulders and experience of known professionals."

She pointed at him with her half-eaten handwich.

"Perdition Enterprises does not advertise its founders, which ought to be its greatest strength, until they have excelled in the field for half a dozen missions, and proven their own merit."

"And their backers?" Vepal asked. "I searched, but it was by necessity shallow and quick . . . "

"No, do not expend another ounce of your energy looking for their backers!" she said earnestly. "We have searched, wide, deep, and long, as my staff researcher styles it. If there are backers, they very much wish to remain out of sight, and in this one thing, says Research Officer Aritz, who does not part with such praise lightly— they are masters."

Vepal frowned.

"No backers, no founders. It's as if they *want to* be in the shadows."

"That would seem to be their preference, but they must put themselves into the light in order to recruit the troops necessary for their mission."

"Which is also a secret."

She smiled.

"Exactly."

Silence fell then as they finished their meal.

When both were done, the plates set aside, and another round of beer ordered, Vepal looked again to his comrade.

"Despite all these things, will you commit to this mission?" he asked. "Without knowing what it is?"

He did not believe it of her, yet—this supposed co-commander, who might appear from among her troop at her word, so he was certain—what reason had she to remain here, especially when her troop sought work?

"No, I do not think that I will," she said, her eyes thoughtful. "At least, I hope it will not go that far. I am . . . squeamish of my honor, and I would prefer not to put it in peril. If there is no other way, though . . ." Her voice trailed off, and she considered the tabletop intently.

Vepal stilled, watching her think—and seeing the moment she made her decision.

"I will tell you," she said, with a nod. "I remain here because, after I met with the recruiters to ensure the place of the Paladins in queue, I was troubled by these things you and I have just discussed. That being so, I contacted an old comrade who makes it her business to know the secrets of others, hoping that she knew all and everything about Perdition Enterprises, and would therefore put my fears to rest."

She shook her head.

"She was also stymied, and she asked me if I would assist her in gathering information, for the usual fees. I agreed."

"You wish to find out who they are?"

"That—yes. There are many mercs already tangled in this— whatever it is—they having signed the NDA and been recruited. I talked to two commanders who have done so, and I will tell you, Comrade—they are not easily frightened. But I spoke to frightened mercs. *Frightened* mercs who saw no way out of what they had done, and who would not utter one word of what they had agreed to, their pay, or their assignment.

"This made me even more curious, and increased my concern threefold. What sort of hold does Perdition Enterprises have over its recruits? So—*that* I wish also to solve."

"But who are they building forces against?" Vepal asked. "Knowing the name of the target—"

"Yes!" she said, putting warm fingers briefly on his wrist. "Yes.

The answer to that question, my friend, could not only unlock the mysteries we have discussed, but it might well make us rich!"

· · ·✧· · ·

"HOW LONG?" Erthax asked. "Sir."

"We will accept the full station-week available to this docking," Vepal told him, and added, "Do you have more questions, Pilot?" in a tone that strongly suggested it would be best for Erthax's health if he failed of having any more questions for the remainder of his life.

For once, Erthax took the point.

"Sir. No, sir," he said, promptly.

He then produced a reasonably sharp salute, turned briskly on his heel and left the common room. Vepal did not sigh, but merely turned to Ochin, standing patiently by the bench where his evening meal sat untouched.

"Orders, Commander?"

"You are at liberty—eat, rest, amuse yourself. Visit the small bars, if you will, and find the temper of the station. Whatever you do, you will come to me at fifth hour, in my quarters. We will discuss schedules during our time at dock. Come prepared with a list of necessary tasks which you are qualified to perform."

There was a small pause, which one might expect, given that the orders required some initiative on the part of the Rifle.

Ochin saluted.

"Sir. Yes, sir."

Vepal returned the salute, and left the common area.

In his quarters, he sat at the theoretically shielded, private comm deck. Sanchez had agreed with his analysis, that the recruitment team would expect—would be waiting for him—to send a message. If he wished to learn more about those who thought that the Troop was for hire—if he wished, as he did, to assist Sanchez and her associate to whom all secrets, save this one, were open—there was no other course, but to send a message. Security wrap, absolutely. In fact, he thought, tapping the unit up, he might as well send two messages. It was time he knew for certain whether Firge remained in a position to aid him—or if she had, as he feared, been dispatched to Duty's Reward.

The first message, then, to the Finance Officer, citing the missing payments, and demanding that the shortfall be made up, immediately. He wrapped it in as many security codes as were available to him, and hit *send* with rather more enthusiasm than a sober message concerning an employment contract on offer might be expected to excite. The watchers at Perdition Enterprises needn't know that, of course.

The second message—not to Firge, no. If she still lived, he would not for his own life endanger her. No, the second message to the Records Officer, requesting an updated roster of High Commanders, and their seconds.

That, too, traveled in a thick security wrapping.

Vepal sat for a few minutes longer, weighing whether three messages might be seen as excessive, and to whom he might address another.

In the end, he judged the two he had sent sufficient, powered off the comm deck, and sought his bed.

THREE

PERDITION ENTERPRISES had spies all over the station; that hardly needed to be said. They'd probably tapped in to the station's own sensors—he would have if he was in their position, after all.

Vepal of course remained at dock, awaiting the replies to his high-security messages. He made certain that his activities were public and easy to document. He availed himself of the station database, as he had done at every port since the start of the mission, sifting for hints that might point to those peoples who were worthy to accept their knives . . . or who would have mercy sufficient to save them, who had made enemies of all this universe.

He went, variously, under escort, and his own recognizance. While the ship required maintenance, he considered it advisable to allow Ochin and Erthax generous leave time, as they were, each in their way, a boon to the mission.

Men talked freely around the Rifle, discounting him despite his stature, his modest facial decoration, and his uniform. Perhaps they assumed that he had no Trade or Terran, though he was perfectly fluent in each, at his commander's order, there being nothing much else to do during their long hunt, save polish the bright work—and study. For that matter, he also had Liaden. Anyone who traveled long among the stars was bound also to have *some* Liaden to get by. For safety.

Ochin, though, went further than that. Ochin had a small collection of *melant'i* plays, an accidental discovery at a Terran station where a some down-on-the-luck spaceman had traded them at pawn for cash or some more practical item. Erthax being nearly Liaden in his interpretation of rank, Ochin Rifle was a wolf deprived of his pack. At times, Ochin wished for companionship and turned to the plays for society. Vepal had seen him reading plays, on occasion, between required reading of regs and of rifle lore.

On Inago, Ochin spent some of his money on packaged sweet-foods, others on entertainments he might also return to the ship with—the High Command not having supplied the vessel with much in the way of games or desserts. He spent some of his time in the low-key places dispensing soft drinks, near-beers, and lighter inebriants along with machine amusements, clearly as much on shore leave as any. Sitting in dark corners was a habit of some years; he practiced his languages by listening and recalling. Occasionally, he'd be joined by a merc looking to be quiet and to sit not quite alone at the bar, where suits brought by would-be bedmates, paid and unpaid, sometimes made it difficult to drink in peace.

So Ochin brought back tidbits of gossip: who had been shorted by their last employer; who had gotten theirs back, with interest; who slept together, and who were partnered—entertainment, lightly gotten, and lightly dispensed. These tidbits were shared with the Commander and Erthax, of course, if they felt to him to have weight or import, or held in reserve by him to compare with his plays if they were worthy of extra consideration. Several of his table-side stories were not only recent but notable—and potentiality verifiable—those he'd share when he was sure of them.

Pilot Erthax enlisted in contests of small skills: darts, footraces, and the like, though he withheld himself from both drinking games and gambling—which Vepal admitted surprised him. He had been bolder on other stations, before he'd become so challenging to command.

The pilot's information tended to detail mischief and darker deeds: who had stolen a comrade's favorite blade, and in retribution for what imagined or genuine slight; who enjoyed the commander's favor; who was on his last probation—and for what cause . . .

What neither heard was news of the mission, though occasionally one or another would mention that commander this-or-that had gotten his price, and signed in blood, as the inevitable phrasing went, on the Liaden's dotted line.

Vepal's own impression was that there was a certain tension with regard to those signings. The wisdom among the common troops was that, while the promised payments might seem very fine on paper, the recruiting agents were, in large measure, Liaden, and the contract surely so. There would be a clause, a comma, or phrase in that document somewhere, so fretted the common troop, which would, in the end, rob them of their pay.

Occasionally, one would speculate upon the identity of the target, but those idle wonderings were, according to both Ochin and Erthax, and by Vepal's own observation, shut down forcefully with a snarled, "Ain't sapposa talk on that. Commander says, no chatter! Next wise wonderer gets their head bust, 'member it!" from a sergeant or an elder-in-troop—and the conversation would momentarily pause before veering off onto the safer topics of sex—prior or desired—or battles fought long ago.

* * * ✧ * * *

JINJEE SANCHEZ continued to await the arrival of her co-commander, which event she anticipated loudly whenever she and Vepal met, which was surprisingly often.

Commander Sanchez had many associates on station, and she called on them all, frequently attended, at her express invitation, by Vepal.

"Commander Vepal awaits clearance from his commanders at

Temp Headquarters," she told those acquaintances. "When he is given leave to sign the NDA, then will we all be kindred in arms. Now is not too soon to learn each other."

To Vepal's surprise, this argument carried force. None of the commanders he met in this way displayed any particular dismay at meeting an Yxtrang commander, though all of those who had signed the NDA, without exception, showed a tight-lipped distress, and a uniform refusal to talk about Perdition Enterprises' plans, even in the most general of terms.

When no one to whom she was personally known was available to receive her, JinJee called upon those she knew by reputation—the details of those reputations being supplied by her colleague, the commander of all secrets. On those days, she and Vepal would meet afterward, to share a beer, and often a meal, while she briefed him on what she had learned.

This shift, she arrived with a grin on her face, fingers up to bespeak two beers even as she slid onto the seat across from him. They were again at The Headless Yxtrang, by far their favorite meet-place, though by no means the only one.

"Have you news from your co-commander?" he asked her, that being the most likely public reason for such overt delight.

"No! The bastard sends no word past *urgent business*! I will sell tickets to his public skinning, when he finally sets boots on this station."

The beers arrived. They raised the glasses in one gesture and each took a hearty swallow.

Vepal put his glass down.

"But something has happened to please you," he said.

"Oh, yes, very much; but will it please *you*, is what I ask myself!"

"Does that matter?" he asked, watching her eyes sparkle.

"Improbably, it does, as it involves you most particularly."

"Then you had better tell me," he said. "If my honor is at risk, I must make answer."

"Now, there is where you give me cause for concern!" she said, but laughing as she spoke. She raised her glass and had another swallow.

Vepal, seeing how it was with her, brought two fingers into the air, even as he drained his own glass.

"I will tell you," she said, when the second beers had arrived, and the empties taken away. She put her elbows on the table, and leaned close. He did as well, bending until their heads nearly touched.

"Our frequent meetings have come to the attention of my command, who I doubt you hold in much esteem, given your introduction to many of them."

"The unit is the reflection of the commander," he murmured. "They had forgotten themselves, but recalled quickly enough, when you came among them."

She paused, head tipped, as if struck by this.

"You give me hope, then, that you will find my news as diverting as I do. The more incorrigible of my command have started a pool, Comrade, wagering on the shift and the hour in which we two shall . . . seek out a more private venue, for, let us say, a most intimate meeting."

It took him a moment to understand her, and when he did, he feared that she would feel the heat of the blood rushing into his face.

She shifted, and put her fingers on his wrist—cool fingers against his heated flesh.

"I have offended," she said. "Forgive me, Comrade. Among us it is . . . an indication of acceptance, and in this case, I confess, somewhat of pride, that their commander might conquer an Yxtrang."

He cleared his throat.

"You have not offended," he managed, hearing the growl in his voice, and hoping that she put it down to his obvious embarrassment. "It is done . . . differently among us. Wagers are made on . . . displays of skill and matches of strengths."

A small pause; briefly, she pressed his wrist, then withdrew her fingers.

"Not so much different, then," she said lightly, and leaned back into the seat, reaching for her glass. "If I call for two of today's special, will you share a meal with me?"

He straightened, settling his shoulders against the back of the bench, and met her eyes—raptor bright and fearless. The knot in his stomach loosened.

"I would be proud to share a meal with such a comrade," he said.

• • • ✧ • • •

"SIR."

Erthax rose from the command chair and saluted as Vepal came onto the bridge, itself surprising enough that he checked his progress.

"Permission to speak, sir," Erthax said.

Vepal considered saying no, which really was unworthy, before granting permission with the wave of a hand.

"An open message from Recruiter ter'Menth arrived while you were gone, sir, demanding that you attend her at the Core Conference Center at your first free moment. Only give her name at the desk, and she will see you immediately."

The intent of the message was, Vepal strongly suspected, phrased by Erthax in order to give maximum offense. That aside, the message—or one very like it—was not unexpected. One might quibble that a mere recruiter had insufficient rank to order a commander to her, but he was prepared to overlook the slight to what a Liaden would term his *melant'i*, specifically because he wanted no one of Perdition Enterprises to set boots on his decks. A meeting at the conference center therefore suited him well.

"Is there more?" he asked Erthax.

"That is the whole of it," the pilot admitted. "The original is on-screen, if you wish."

"No, I have no need. Archive it. I go."

There was a stir at the hatchway. Vepal turned his head to see Ochin, dressed for duty.

"Escort, sir?"

Clearly Erthax had shared the news of the message with his underling, if only to demonstrate how low the ambassador had fallen to obey an open summons made by a mere flunky, and a Liaden flunky at that.

Vepal might have simply said no, but it was his habit to show the Rifle his reasoning, when possible, so that he might perform his duty the better.

"Not for this. The recruiter is Liaden, and might think that we are escalating a situation which, by the tenor of her message, she already considers difficult."

He saw Ochin consider and reject that reasoning, but the Rifle made no argument. Naturally not. He merely saluted, and stepped to one side, clearing Vepal's path to the hatch.

"Sir."

• • •✧• • •

THE SOUND OF THE HATCH CLOSING had not quite faded away when the Rifle looked at the Pilot, and the Pilot glanced briefly down at his board.

"All right," he said, as if the other had said it aloud. "Go watch your Liaden plays. I'll escort at a distance since he always sees you, anyway. Lock down until he's back."

• • •✧• • •

AS IT HAPPENED, Vepal had not been required to ask for ter'Menth at the command desk; the recruiter was sitting in one of the chairs in the common room, and rose promptly when he entered.

"Commander, how good of you to come so quickly," she said, teeth showing behind her smile.

"Your message carried some urgency," he answered, smiling in kind. "Naturally, I came as soon as I was aware."

"You honor me," she told him, which he took leave to doubt. "Come, there is an empty room just here . . ."

She bowed him in ahead of her to another small cubicle such as the one where he had first met her. He took the chair nearest the door, as he had on that first occasion, while she passed behind the desk, and arranged herself there.

She did not glance at the screen; perhaps it was blank; perhaps she had no need.

"I regret that I must ask," she said, folding her hands on the desktop before her, "however, those whom I report to are becoming . . . restless."

"I understand," he assured her. "Ask without offense."

She inclined her head.

"We wonder when you might hear from the High Command at Temp Headquarters. Interest in bringing a conquest corps into our expedition remains keen, but there are schedules to maintain, and, as we are both aware, there is only so long that a project of this scope can be kept quiet."

He had, Vepal thought, expected this question. They were after all nearing the end of their week's berthing, and there had been no response—to either of his queries.

"I cannot predict with any accuracy when the commanders may choose to speak," he told her, which was the utter truth. "Understand, not only have Perdition Enterprises asked them to commit on the—your pardon—sketchiest of details, but the request for commitment is, of itself, unique. You will know from dealing with your own command structure that a new situation must be examined from all sides. It might, perhaps, speed their deliberations, if more details were made available to them."

"I understand you, I think," she said, blandly. "Like you, I am constrained by the orders of my superiors. I will therefore take your request to them."

"I'm grateful," he told her.

She moved a hand, perhaps sweeping away his gratitude—or perhaps, he told his rising temper, it meant some other thing altogether, and was nothing near an insult. He did best to let it pass.

"I see you about often with Commander Sanchez of the Paladin mercenary unit. I wonder—forgive me if I am forward—how you come to know her."

Vepal felt the hairs on the back of his neck rise. Had they come now to the real reason for this interview? Still, there was nothing, as far as he could parse the matter—nothing at all wrong with telling the truth.

He therefore did just that: the arrival of the Paladins at the speakeasy on Seebrit Station while Vepal and his small troop were at mess; the threats, the subsequent arrival of Commander Sanchez, and the quick restoration of peace and order.

"We met again, by chance, later that evening, and took the opportunity to talk, as commanders will between themselves. We found ourselves to be in agreement on several topics of importance to us both, and, I believe, we were each dismayed when our separate duties required that we part. I was surprised, but pleased, to find her—a comrade, as it were—here among all of these worthy strangers."

He paused, and gave ter'Menth a nod.

"She has been useful to me. Sanchez knows many commanders, and has introduced me to them. If these soldiers will eventually be fighting shoulder to shoulder with Yxtrang, it is better for all that they learn to know an Yxtrang."

"I see. A most beneficial relationship. And, yet, she confines herself to the commanders of mercenaries, even those previously unknown to her. I wonder that she has not continued her work among our other recruits, who might also benefit from her acquaintance, and yours."

This, thought Vepal, was an odd turn of direction, but candor continued to seem his best course.

"I believe she does not wish to intrude herself, having no acquaintance among those to ease her way as she eases mine."

"Doubtless you are correct," ter'Menth said, and rose, her hands flat on her desk. "Perhaps I shall make it my business to mend that situation for her."

It was said as blandly as any other thing she had said to him, yet Vepal was suddenly certain that the manner of that meeting would be to JinJee's peril.

He trusted that his face did not betray his unease as he rose and bowed slightly from the waist before he left the interview room.

FOUR

VEPAL GAINED THE BUSINESS concourse through the airlock open wide enough to march a parade through and walked in the vague direction of their docking, his pace brisk, but not over-hasty. As he walked, he reviewed the meeting with Recruiter ter'Menth, and failed to find less reason for the concern that still taxed him.

There had been nothing overtly *said*—ter'Menth, after all, was Liaden—but the manner of what had *been* said, and what had *not* been said, especially that last, almost absent-sounding comment—

Perhaps I should make it my business to mend that situation for her.

Of course, Recruiter ter'Menth, who was, in his opinion, no mere recruiter, nor had ever intended him to suppose her so—Recruiter ter'Menth most naturally had warriors at her beck. Not merely because there were those who had signed the NDA form, and were therefore subject to the orders of Perdition Enterprises, transmitted through their appointed operatives, but simply because Recruiter ter'Menth was the sort who would be certain to arm herself, as a matter of course.

JinJee Sanchez, now: interminably awaiting her co-commander, making her calls, asking her questions. It might, Vepal thought—it might very well make sense for Recruiter ter'Menth—or, rather say, Perdition Enterprises—to make an example, for the good of discipline. Through her own efforts, JinJee was well known on station. The Paladins were not the least counted among those mercenary units on-station; no easy targets, commander or unit.

Vepal entered a lift, and directed it to the food hub. No surprises there, for any who had happened to follow him; the food hub was a favorite destination of his, even when he was not scheduled to meet JinJee.

He stepped off the lift and crossed immediately to the comm-bank, keeping good watch as he called the ship, relaying to Ochin that he was delayed, and would call again when he was on approach to their docking.

That done, he slipped back into the crowd, still keeping a close watch for followers.

He was fortunate in his hour, one of the food hub's busiest. It would not be easy to trail a single man—even a large and distinctive man—through such a crush.

He was also fortunate that the Paladins were housed quite near to the food hub. He might arrive quickly to speak with JinJee regarding the potential threats to the security of herself and her troop.

Of course, there was no need to track him in order to bring mischief down upon the Paladins. ter'Menth knew as well as he where they camped. Vepal's hope lay in the . . . probability that it would take time for any orders ter'Menth issued to be received and acted upon.

He hoped he was wrong, and that his error would become a very good joke between JinJee and himself, down a long future.

In the meantime, he would watch her back, as she watched his.

* * *✧* * *

RECRUITING Agent ter'Menth returned to the common room as a very tall soldier in grays reached the receptionist's desk, and stated in an odd accent, "I want to see Recruiting Agent ter'Menth."

"Do you have an appointment?" the receptionist asked.

"I do not, but the recruiting agent will want to see me, and to hear what I say."

The receptionist was not, of course, a fool, and even if so, his orders contained the fact that ter'Menth was the single contact-point for Yxtrang. Still, there was some value in maintaining the proprieties, especially as this particular Yxtrang was new to the common recruitment area.

"May I tell Recruiting Agent ter'Menth your name and rank?" the receptionist asked calmly.

ter'Menth saw the Yxtrang soldier stiffen; apparently he considered the question impertinent. In the next instant, however, he had gathered himself into hand, and produced a very credible bow.

"I am Erthax Pilot, of Vepal's Small Troop."

Ah, thought ter'Menth, this might in fact be something interesting. She stepped forward, claiming the receptionist's attention with a wave.

"Here is the recruiting agent, now," the receptionist said, obedient to the cue. He stood up and bowed to ter'Menth's honor.

Pilot Erthax hesitated a moment, possibly at a loss for an appropriate form. ter'Menth inclined slightly from the waist, which he took up immediately, reproducing her bow precisely, which a Liaden would see as having declared them equals. Rather than lesson him sternly, she took it as a sign that he had not been fully briefed by his commander, so she smiled, showing the teeth a little.

"Pilot Erthax," she said smoothly. "I had not anticipated your arrival. It happens, however, that I am at leisure, and eager to hear what you have to say to me. If you will follow, there is a room just down here where we may be private."

She moved her hand, showing him the direction, and waited until he had stepped around the receptionist's desk, and followed her from the hall.

· · ·✧· · ·

AT ANOTHER TIME the place might have been used for a trade show; what it did now was hold many troops in close quarters. Vepal's ID card as a commander of troops allowed him entry to the area, JinJee being yet true to her open-camp philosophy.

The Paladins had been mustered for inspection, and they made a brave showing, Vepal thought, pausing at the edge of the impromptu parade ground. Leathers and weapons gleamed in the station light. Shoulders back, faces soldierly, eyes front, the troops stood motionless, scarcely seeming to breathe, as their commander made her leisurely way up and down the lines.

If her troop was brave, JinJee Sanchez was proud—a commander's commander, conducting a meticulous inspection. She paused before one troop, frowning down at his boots. Spoke, too low for Vepal to hear—a private matter, between commander and soldier. The man's fair face colored to a bright red, but he replied with dignity, eyes front. She spoke again, and his *Yes, Commander!* rang over the field, as she moved on to the next, hands behind her back, face grave and thoughtful.

Vepal stood at the sidelines at parade rest, and waited for duty to be done.

· · ·✧· · ·

PILOT ERTHAX sat on the edge of the chair, back straight, both feet on the floor. A pilot on the edge of action, in fact. Agent ter'Menth allowed him to remain so, while she played at tidying things away on the blank screen before her. He was, she thought, rather more patient than she had supposed he would be, though his control over his expression was not nearly so fine as Vepal's. Still, it was to be expected; that command should be the ideal to which all lesser troops must aspire.

"So," she said, without, yet, fully looking at him, "you are come behind your commander's back, to make your own arrangement with Perdition Enterprises?"

There was a moment of charged silence. She heard him take a hard breath.

"You would have me to be without honor," he said, "but you have not yet heard what I have to say."

"Then speak," she said, meeting his eyes squarely. "I will listen until—ah, until I grow bored, does that seem just to you? When I am bored, I will call your commander and desire him to take you into his care."

Interestingly, he laughed, a soft, disdainful sound.

"That is fair, recruiter of soldiers. I will speak quickly, not to risk you growing bored by the sound of my voice."

Another breath, as if to prepare himself for a long speech, which he began, keeping his gaze locked with hers.

"Commander Vepal does not have the ear of the High Command. He is *malkonstituita*—scorned, impotent. A laughingstock, as I think the phrase may go. If you wish to deal with the High Command, and I think you do, you will need someone whose messages they read, and whose advice they listen to."

"And this would be you?"

He did not move his eyes from hers.

"Yes."

"I seem to recall that Commander Vepal is an ambassador between the Yxtrang and the whole rest of the universe," she said, watching him closely.

He laughed again.

"Oh, he is that! He is a Hero, and a fool, and because he is the first, he cannot be executed for the second. So, he was given a title, and a mission, and sent away, High Command hoping that the universe would kill him, sooner than late. Me, they set to watch him, and to report his actions. If you want to send a message to the High Command, Recruiting Agent, you need me."

It did seem as though the pilot was telling the truth. However...

"I recall that Commander Vepal sent two high-security messages from this station, bound for Temp Headquarters."

"He did, yes. They were decoys. I have the texts here."

He reached to the pouch on his belt, and pulled out two thin sheets of hard copy.

"All of his messages are copied to my files," he told her, putting the papers on the desk before her.

She glanced down, but of course could not read them.

"I will need to have these translated, but for the moment, let us suppose that you will tell me what they say."

"Yes."

He tapped the first page.

"This addresses the Finance Officer on the matter of short payments to our expedition." He glanced up at her, and smiled, teeth very apparent.

"You see that he has no standing. The Troop does not cheat the Troop."

"I am informed," she said, truthfully. "And this next one?"

"That is to the Records Officer, inquiring after the current roster of High Commanders."

"So it may be that he strives to do what he was asked," said ter'Menth, "but merely wishes to ensure that he addresses the correct authority."

"Possibly. But he might have also sent a high-security message to the Secretary of Council, who would have distributed it to the High Command."

"I see. So, stipulate that Commander Vepal is stalling, and is not dealing with honor. What do *you* want?"

Another toothy smile.

"I want to help you. I will send your message to the Secretary of Council."

"So kind," she said, blandly. "And in return for this, you will want—what?"

"A command," he said promptly, which did not surprise her, "the ship I pilot—" Here he paused, as if coming to agreement with himself. "And Vepal."

Certainly, it was a bargain she could make, with very little chance of damage to herself or the mission. She inclined her head.

"I accept your assistance and your terms," she told him. "Payment upon receipt of a reply from High Command."

"I agree," he said.

"Good. You may use the sealed unit in this facility to send your message. I will give you the text."

His look of extreme satisfaction faded a little.

"Better it is sent from the ship, with the proper equipment."

"No, I insist that you use our equipment. Forgive me, but this ship of yours seems not in the least secure. *My* equipment does not leak."

He thought a moment, then thrust his chin forward.

"Yes," he said. "I am ready now."

"Excellent," she said. "Allow me to call my expert, so that there will be no misunderstanding regarding the message, and then we two will repair to the comm center."

• • • ◇ • • •

INSPECTION ENDED, and the Paladins were dismissed. JinJee Sanchez strolled over to him. Vepal was aware of many eyes on her—*on them*—and recalled the troop's wager. His ears burned, but he kept his face soldierly, and his demeanor everything that a commander should display before a valued colleague.

"Vepal," she said, reaching his side. "I am happy to see you." She paused, searching his face, and put her hand on his arm.

"What is wrong?"

He glanced around at the multitude of bright, interested eyes, not all of which dropped modestly when his gaze crossed theirs.

"Possibly nothing is wrong," he said, returning his attention to her scarred, strong face. "But I would like to discuss the matter with you . . . in a more private setting."

That may have been mis-phrased; he heard one of those nearest repeat . . . *a more private setting* and turn sharply to her mate. JinJee heard, surely, the corner of her mouth lifted in a half smile.

"I will be pleased to be private with you," she said, her voice pitched to be heard by the farthest soldier. Vepal wished he could share her amusement, but the worry that had brought him here was stronger than when he had left Recruiter ter'Menth.

"Come," he said brusquely, and turned back in the direction of the food hub, JinJee at his side. "To our regular table, I think."

She walked beside him, smile deepening at the sound of stealthy footsteps behind them.

"Did you wager as well?" Vepal asked her, with some bitterness.

She shot an amused glance up into his face.

"I, wager? For shame, Comrade. You know as well as I do that commanders must withhold themselves from such public displays."

She paused briefly, and added, as one being fair, "Of course, nothing prevents one from wagering with oneself. Does it?"

He was, for a moment, diverted—and a moment was everything that they needed.

There were six of them, in leather, guns belted, blades out.

"Keep 'im occupied; we'll take her," was the growled order, barely heard over the thunder of their boots on decking and a shout that was perhaps meant to freeze him with terror.

Vepal roared, to show them how it was done, and swept out an arm, knocking the nearest of his three against the wall, where he struck with a boom, and slid to the deck, head lolling, knife fallen from lax fingers.

The second made the error of leading with her knife. He broke her wrist, took the blade away, and thrust her, too, against the wall. She struck with a cry, and also slid to the deck, no more than dazed, by Vepal's estimation, but with the fight gone out of her.

The third—but the third was abruptly removed from his consideration by a merc in gleaming leathers, who disarmed the attacker handily, snaked an arm around his neck, and brought him to his knees on the deck.

Vepal spun, but JinJee's attackers were in like case, scattered like so many fallen batons on the deck. Several of the Paladins moved among them, retrieving weapons and applying restraints.

"This one's awake, Commander," said the soldier who had taken Vepal's third. She gave him a conscious look.

"Sorry to spoil your fun, sir."

He considered her, found the humor at the edge of her face, and gave her a nod.

"Not at all," he said courteously. "It would have been rude to keep them all for myself."

The shadow humor blossomed into a grin, and she hauled her prisoner 'round on his knees as Commander Sanchez arrived to look down upon him.

"Orburt Vinkleer," she said.

He grinned, showing a gap between his teeth.

"Hi, JinJee. Lookin' fine."

She did not return the compliment.

"Did you mean to attack myself and Commander Vepal, or are you merely drunk?"

"Orders," he said, his grin widening. "Just followin' orders, zackly like a bought 'n' paid for merc."

"Whose orders?"

His grin became a laugh.

"Why would I tell you that?"

"Why wouldn't you? A solid client roster must be to your benefit, as you seek . . . legitimate work."

"Signed the NDA, didn't I?"

"Did you? Will your commander be angry, that you failed in your mission?" She glanced about them, before returning to Orburt Vinkleer.

"At least, I assume that this was not the outcome you envisioned."

"Just showing what happens to them who don't sign on nor get out. Little demonstration for the other hanger-ons."

"Ah, I see." She considered the man, and suddenly snapped out. "What is the target?"

"Like to know, wouldn't cha?"

"In fact, I would; wouldn't you?"

He made as if to shrug, an action his restraints made difficult.

"S'long's they pay me, I don't care who we hit."

"Of course not," JinJee said politely. "Very well, Orburt. My soldiers will escort you to your quarters. Try anything like this again, and you will be returned in a body bag. This may be a game to you, but we are professionals."

She nodded at the soldier holding the prisoner.

"Get them out of here," she said. "No need to be gentle."

"Yes, Commander," said the soldier, and yanked Orburt Vinkleer to his feet.

Others moved, grabbing the downed fighters and throwing them ungently into field carries. Vepal and JinJee watched them out of sight, he very much aware of the four Paladins flanking them, at a respectful distance, and also of the glow along his nerves, the feeling of power rising in his muscles—the first signs of the euphoria. The little skirmish had been enough to waken biology, but not enough to finish it.

He took a breath. He was an Explorer. He was in command of biology.

Teeth set, he bowed his head, and spread his hands.

"My apologies," he said to JinJee. "I came to warn you of this possibility."

She considered him, silent, her expression speculative. It came to him suddenly that the possibility that he had come specifically to guide her into this trap fell well within the bounds of logic. He took a breath, and met her eye.

"I did not," he said, "think that anything would happen so—soon."

"I see," she said, and gave him a nod.

"I would like to hear what it was you were going to tell me before we were interrupted," she said, then. "I wonder if you will join me in my quarters?"

For him, this was a test, Vepal thought. For JinJee, it was an extra measure of security.

He nodded, feeling the telltale shiver in his blood. Taking another breath, he refused the euphoria of battle. He was civilized; he was rational. There was nothing, any longer, for him to fight.

"I'll be pleased to attend you in your quarters, Comrade."

• • • ✧ • •

"THE COMMANDER has not returned," Ochin Rifle stated. He did not say the rest of it, could not say the rest of it, as Erthax outranked him. But it was plain for any of the Troop to hear, unvoiced as it was.

Erthax had failed. He had failed his duty to the ship and to the commander.

He, however, Erthax thought, was not a Rifle. He was a pilot; his wits were quick, and his ability to spin a tale far superior to anything that the Rifle might produce. The Rifle was limited to statements of fact, no matter how damning. Erthax was able to be . . . *creative*.

"The Commander has not returned," he agreed. "He saw me, and he was very much displeased. He ordered me back to the ship. We are to lock down until he arrives, which he will do when, in his sole judgment, it is time to do so."

Ochin frowned.

"You were clumsy," he said—a reinterpretation of what Erthax had told him. Not fact.

"You think the commander is so inept he wouldn't have seen me?" he answered, certain that it would be hours before Ochin could untwist himself from *that*.

"You were clumsy, because you did not convince him to have you, even when you were both already out." Ochin pulled himself up, and looked directly into Erthax's eyes.

"I have followed so myself—twice. Both times, he took me, rather than to have me walk the docks alone."

The implication was plain: a mere Rifle had accomplished this, that a pilot had not.

Erthax held onto his temper, which was already frayed. He needed the Rifle, if not to stand with him, than at least to not stand against him.

"You are correct," he said moderately. "I did not try very hard to keep to him, once he had sent me away. My pride was touched, I think."

Ochin did not say what he thought of pride, if, indeed, a mere Rifle might be equipped to contemplate the concept.

"Now that I am here, shamed or not," Erthax continued, "our part is to follow his orders. We should lock down until he arrives."

"Yes," Ochin said after a moment. "That is all that we can do. Now."

There was a pause before he added:

"You should know that in fact the commander called, *before* you returned. The decks are uncertain. We are to remain locked down until he comes back. He will call again when he is on this level, to give us the order to open."

Erthax took a very careful breath. So close to being discovered, then.

"We will obey," he said.

FIVE

HER QUARTERS . . . surprised.

Vepal had expected a soldier's cell, much like his own, on ship, or perhaps a little larger, like his permanent quarters at Temp Headquarters.

He had not . . . imagined that there would be pale cloth draped 'round walls and ceiling, nor a carpet far richer in pattern and in color than any other he had seen on-station.

Muscles aching, he stood at parade rest, watching her cross the room to a small auto-kitchen, and turn to look at him.

"Will you have something to quench the dust of—we can scarcely call it a battle, I think. Perhaps skirmish?"

"Thank you," he said stiffly. "No."

"I see."

She came back, stopping within what had become a comfortable speaking distance between them.

"I suppose that you will refuse a chair, too, until you tell me. So, then, Comrade—tell me."

He bowed, slight and stiff.

"I returned to my ship this evening and learned that Recruiting Agent ter'Menth had called during my absence, demanding that I come to her at my earliest convenience. I went immediately."

He paused to review a distancing exercise, and continued.

"She asked when I might expect an answer from High Command. I made an excuse, and also a bid for more information, which was turned aside. She then came to what seemed to be her core purpose.

"She said that I was often seen in the company of Commander Sanchez, and wondered how we had come to know each other. I told her the circumstances of our first meeting, and added that you were useful both to me and to Perdition Enterprises. By introducing me to merc command, you were creating an opportunity for we who will hopefully soon be united in a glorious mission to gain the measure of our comrades."

He could feel himself shivering with need. If he didn't engage in physical exercise soon, he would collapse in an ignominious heap of cramped muscles. JinJee might then amuse herself by having him delivered to her command's common area, where he might be mocked by all.

"Recruiter ter'Menth made note that you called only on mercs, and not on those who were . . . other. I suggested perhaps that you did not wish to intrude upon them, having no acquaintance among them to ease your way, as you eased mine. It seemed apt enough when I said it, but it appeared to me that it gave her thoughts an odd trajectory. She said, 'Perhaps I shall make it my business to mend that situation for her.' It made me . . . uneasy, and I came to lay the matter before you, even though I half-believed I was being foolish."

"And now we have learned that you were not foolish at all, and that Recruiting Agent ter'Menth likes to make mischief when she grows bored. Unfortunately, if her goal was to widen my acquaintance, she chose badly—I am *well* acquainted with Commodore Vinkleer. Now."

She crossed her arms over her chest, and sent him a stern look, such as a commander might bend upon a trainee who had failed to enumerate *all* of his weapons.

"I will leave you now," Vepal stated.

"No," she said. "*Now*, you will tell me what ails you, Comrade. Were you struck? If so, you must come with me to our medic. Vinkleer's rabble have been known to doctor their blades, and those who don't never clean them. The chance of infection is not trivial."

"No, I—I must go," he said. He was shivering in earnest now. How he was to achieve his ship in this state, he hardly knew. Yet, to betray himself before JinJee...

"No, you must not," she said, command voice snapping hard enough to allow him to gain some control. "You are plainly ill. You will sit down. I will call the medic to—"

"No!"

It was a roar. JinJee raised an eyebrow.

"I—no medic," he managed. "Please. It is—only biology."

A second eyebrow rose.

"How so?"

"The skirmish, as you so aptly put it," he said. "It was long enough to trigger a—a release of... specialized hormones. However, it was neither long enough nor violent enough to burn them. If I do not act—soon—my muscles will cramp and I will be unable..."

"What is the antidote?" she snapped.

"Physical release. Perhaps I might spar with one of the troop. Or—"

"The punching bag," she said, in a tone of enlightenment. "I understand."

She smiled then, and stepped closer to him.

"I offer, Comrade, physical release. Will you accept?"

He had no choice; he would never make it across the docks. JinJee was able, as he had just seen demonstrated, and he was not out of control; he had never been one for the full battle frenzy.

"Yes," he told JinJee Sanchez, "I accept."

* * * ◇ * * *

HE WOKE ALL AT ONCE, which was his habit, and took stock, eyes closed, which was also his habit.

A tantalizingly familiar scent enveloped him; the scent of JinJee Sanchez, that was, entwined with others, less familiar. The surface he lay on was firm, but not so firm as his pallet on-ship. Against his left side was pressed a long warmth, which shifted even as he noted its presence.

He recalled—last night's attack, the unfortunate triggering of the battle frenzy; JinJee's offer of physical release.

. . . a release which had not at all been what he had expected, though . . . effective, nevertheless.

Very effective.

"You are awake, Comrade?" Her voice was much as always, and he smiled, at other memories.

"I am awake, Comrade," he replied. He hesitated, and added, "Thank you."

"I do not believe," said JinJee Sanchez, shifting so forcefully that he opened his eyes, and looked up into her face, as she leaned over him, the lean muscles of her torso on full display, "that I wish to enter into a protracted conversation of who is more grateful to whom. We both benefited, and I am neither thankful nor sorry."

Black raptor's eyes; the mark of the war blade's kiss a potent reminder of her strength. He felt the stirrings of last night's passions, in which the action they had engaged upon had seemed something more than the mere comfortable coupling of comrades.

"What are you, then?" he asked her, even as he wondered after his own emotions.

"I am *pleased*," JinJee said, with a long smile. She threw back the blanket which had covered them both, exposing him in full display.

"Also," she said, gripping him in one strong hand while she met his eyes boldly, "I am eager, as I see that you are. Shall we, again?"

He lifted one hand to her scar, the other to her breast, and smiled into her bold, warrior's eyes.

"Yes," he said. "Let us, again."

* * * ✧ * * *

THEY CAME ARM AND ARM into the Paladin's mess, amid shouting and applause. Attuned to her movements, Vepal paused with her, looking over the pandemonium until it had quieted. Only then did they continue to the commander's table, where a second chair had been hastily placed, and a second place laid.

They being among her command, Vepal waited to take the second chair until she was seated.

A soldier guided a serving tray to their table. A steaming cup of brown liquid was set before JinJee before the server looked to him, his hand fluttering between pots and carafes.

"Your pleasure, sir? We have coffeetoot, Terran tea, citrus juice, berry juice, water."

"Coffeetoot," Vepal told him, and while it was being poured, JinJee asked, "Who won?"

"McGyver and Hayashi split, ma'am."

JinJee put her cup on the table.

"Take them each my compliments," she said, "and collect the five percent for the medical fund."

"Hayashi put in already, ma'am. Sergeant Pillay's gone to collect from Mac."

"All in hand, then," JinJee said. "We'll serve ourselves, Thaydo, thank you."

"Yes, ma'am. Sir."

The soldier saluted and left them.

"There is," JinJee said, continuing the discussion they had begun in her quarters, "safety in numbers. While none of us are safe from ambush, you and your small troop, my friend, are considerably more at risk than I, or any of mine. We can double up, offer you guard—"

"We hardly present a menace, all three walking the deck together," he finished for her, and added, privately, *even supposing that Erthax would not wait that one telling heartbeat before leaping to his commander's defense.*

Which surely no one but a fool would suppose. Still—

"We have already purchased Recruiter ter'Menth's interest," he pointed out.

"You make my point for me," she answered, and looked up from her meal.

"Understand, I do not wish to absorb you. Your command will remain your command. My command will remain mine. We will be allies, which we have already shown ourselves to be, merely cementing our position."

"I will think on it," he said. "There is a thing that Liadens say, about putting all the wine in one cellar . . . "

She laughed, and shook her head.

"Indeed, indeed. However, if we are basing decisions upon

Liaden proverbs, it is also said that an ally is better than a cantra-piece."

Vepal laid his fork down, and met her eyes.

"These Liadens are very talkative."

Another laugh, this one softer.

"That does seem to be so. Well! You will think, and I will await the outcome of your thought. In the meantime, the Paladins will double-up in the common areas. We will no longer put our trust in the station's perimeter alarms."

"You don't ask my permission for these things," he said, "or my agreement."

"No," she agreed, calmly, "I don't."

He drank off the last of his coffeetoot, and pushed back from the table.

"I to my ship, for now," he said, standing.

JinJee also stood, and extended her hand. He took it, and they exchanged a brief pressure. The room had grown very quiet.

"Until again," JinJee said loud enough to reach every ear.

"Until again," he responded, and bowed slightly over their joined hands before slipping free and leaving her, amidst silence.

The moment he cleared the mess hall door, cheering broke out, and a chant which seemed to be only her name: "JinJEE JinJEE JINJEE!" Followed by a roar.

Vepal smiled.

After all, what more was there to add?

* * * ✧ * * *

HE WAS NOT SO FORTUNATE in his hour this shift; the food hub was all but deserted, and he was perfectly visible to the small figure who moved casually, or so it seemed, to intersect his course.

He could perhaps have lost her; his stride was twice as long as hers. But that would have been pointless, besides showing an unwillingness to be forthcoming and cooperative.

Vepal slowed his pace.

"Good day to you, Recruiting Agent ter'Menth."

"And to you, Commander Vepal. I am pleased to see that you suffered no ill effects."

He looked down at her, but her face was averted.

"Ill effects," he repeated. "From what should I have suffered ill effects?"

Recruiter ter'Menth was not put off her stride in the least. The look she cast up into his face might be said to express amusement.

"Doubtless the affair was so trivial it escaped your notice," she said. "I speak of the report of an altercation between certain operatives of the Vinkleer Cooperative and yourself and Commander Sanchez."

"Oh," Vepal said, still slightly puzzled, "that."

"Indeed. *That.* An unfortunate event, to be sure. However, I was pleased to note that all sides worked together to reach a mutually satisfactory solution. One only hopes that Commander Sanchez's co-commander arrives soon, so that we may welcome her and her company entirely into our ranks."

"I believe she anticipates his arrival daily."

"Yes, so I have heard. Repeatedly. Well! It was, as I said, good to meet you, Commander, and to see you in such robust good health. I will leave you here, and bid you good day."

"Good day," Vepal said, and paused for a moment to watch the Liaden depart, and the manner of it. She walked light; she walked alert; and for all her lack of size she walked as if she owned Inago Station and every life on it.

Which was, Vepal thought, resuming his own stride, a rather disquieting thought, at the least.

SIX

VEPAL WOKE, and lay, eyes closed, and body relaxed, questing after that which had wakened him.

Even as he did so, it came again: a small exhalation, as of air being released, or throttled.

Air. Being throttled.

It had come, he thought. Erthax had received his order to end the mission. It was ironic, perhaps, that it came now.

He took a deep breath, filling his lungs, recalling the breather he had placed in his command locker, years ago, upon taking his first measure of Erthax.

He rolled off his cot, dropped silently to the floor, extended a long arm, placed his fingertips against the lock...and a moment later the breather was around his neck, ready for use.

The hiss of whistling air came again, which was unnecessary. The air could have been evacuated from this compartment, very quickly, if not noiselessly, via the control panel in the main hall. There was no need to come to his very quarters, to release the air manually. Erthax certainly knew that. But Erthax didn't want him to die quickly, Vepal thought. Oh, no; Erthax wanted him to know what was happening. Erthax wanted to toy with him, as if he were *kojagun*—prey—rather than a true soldier of the Troop.

Oh, foolish.

Vepal rose to his feet, his blood warming agreeably.

One short stride brought him to the door. He pressed against the wall, making himself as small a target as possible, and triggered the release.

The door opened, which surprised him. Even a man drunk on revenge might think to destabilize the relative pressures sufficiently to seal the door.

He thrust his foot in the track so that the door would not close, swung out—

"I yield!" Ochin Rifle whispered, urgently. "Commander..."

Vepal blinked, grabbed the Rifle by the collar and hauled him inside, releasing the door as he did so.

"Explain yourself!" he snapped.

Ochin saluted, standing at attention.

"Sir. Pilot Erthax received a communication, sir. From High Command. Security wrap, and the Secretary's seal. I saw it, and I saw that he did not call you. Sir. Therefore, I stepped aside, where I could watch the Pilot, though I could not read the screens. He read the message, then rose and went to quarters. Sir. I thought—you should know."

Vepal considered him. The Rifle was a truthful man—how could he be otherwise? Though this tale did much, he realized, to call his simplicity into question. Whether it was a fabrication or the truth, the Rifle's actions had been extraordinary.

And if the whole tale had been given him by Erthax to tell out again to Vepal? But what would be the purpose of that?

"At ease," he told Ochin.

He went to his private console, and opened the message queue. The last message there was from station, reminding them that they would be required to depart, or move their docking inside of the next twenty-six Standard Hours, or face fines.

"This message," he said over his shoulder to Ochin, "when did it arrive?"

"Thirty-three minutes ago, Sir."

So. He had known of Erthax's private account, but he had considered it best to pretend ignorance. And, if indeed this were merely an acknowledgment of a previously filed report—but no. Council high-security wrap, and sealed with the Secretary's codes. This had been no mere ack. This was worth accessing, though Erthax would know that his line was no longer secure, nor his operations secret.

On that thought, he brought up the ship plan, finding himself and Ochin in his quarters, and Erthax—

But there was no third heat signature in Erthax's quarters, nor anywhere else in the ship. Vepal took a deep breath.

The time for subtlety and subterfuge was over.

He was inside of the Pilot's private queue in a matter of moments. High Command's query was brief: an extraordinary message had been received under Erthax's codes, but sent from an unauthorized source. Had Erthax been compromised? Was this message from him? An explanation by return secure pinbeam was . . . demanded. If, in fact, the message was from Erthax, more details were solicited.

There was no ack in the sent queue. And Erthax was not on the ship.

The matter, Vepal thought, was plain. Erthax had made his bargain with Perdition Enterprises. He had gone to meet his contact, to wrest more detail from them—no, he corrected himself, from *her*. Recruiting Agent ter'Menth, of course, who liked to make mischief when she was bored. He wondered what she had agreed to give Erthax for sending this message—and abruptly straightened, for the answer was obvious, and he must act quickly, on behalf of his own command.

Vepal spun toward the Rifle, standing yet patiently at attention. Ochin Rifle, loyal to his commander—to *his* commander, Vepal saw now; not merely to command.

"You will carry a message to Commander JinJee Sanchez of the Paladin Mercenary Unit," he said sharply. "You will take your kit, and field pack. After delivering the message, you will place yourself under Commander Sanchez's orders. Go, now, and make ready."

"Commander—" Ochin said, astonishing yet again.

Vepal stood forward, and put his hand on the Rifle's shoulder.

"It was well done, that small hiss of air to wake me. I am pleased with your ingenuity and forethought. A message not to be discovered in the files! You will obey your orders, and you will serve Commander Sanchez as if she were myself. You will at all times protect her as if you are protecting myself and our mission. You are on detached duty; Erthax is no longer in your chain of command; you will not engage with him if you see him. I will recall you when conditions allow."

He removed his hand.

"Go now, and make ready."

Ochin did not like his orders. Very nearly, Ochin protested, a second time, but in the end, he was a Rifle, and Vepal his commander. He saluted, and left, to make ready.

Vepal penned a brief message for JinJee: Here was Ochin Rifle to receive the training Vepal had discussed with her. He trusted she would find him an apt student.

That done, he dressed and armed himself, and went to meet Ochin at the lock.

* * * ✧ * * *

VEPAL OPENED ONE EYE and considered the main board, with its one bright yellow telltale.

Someone had opened the outer lock.

He opened the other eye and lazily spun the pilot's chair until it faced the open hatchway, and the main hall beyond. His hands were laced over his belt, elbows resting carelessly on the arm controls, and his legs were thrust out before him, crossed at the ankles. The very picture of indolence, with nothing soldierly about him.

A shadow moved at the end of the hall, and here at last came his tardy pilot, walking very lightly—and freezing in surprise to see the hatch unsealed, and Vepal beyond it.

"Well met, Pilot!" Vepal said, showing his teeth in a wide grin. "Come in! I've been waiting to talk with you."

Erthax visibly shook himself and came forward, his tread wary now, and his eyes glinting.

"Commander," he said, sharp enough to fall outside of the line of insolence, and produced a perfunctory salute.

"Pilot." Vepal didn't bother to return the salute. "Was Recruiting Agent ter'Menth forthcoming?"

Erthax did not bother to pretend.

"I have enough for Command," he said, with a sort of sneering certainty.

"Rich pillage?" asked Vepal.

"Yes; and more. A world vulnerable to attack, though occupied by mercenary forces. The Troop stands to gain weapons and matériel, and to rid itself of a considerable number of trained opponents, in one hammer-strike."

Vepal frowned. Such a target *would* appeal to Command. And a mixed invasion force meant that the cost of acquiring these benefits might be attractively low. Command would understand those things very well. As for the contract, Vepal thought—what was a contract to the Troop, to bind them when it was time to strike?

"Coordinates?" he suggested.

"Not yet," Erthax said. "This will be enough."

He grinned again, teeth flashing.

"She gave you to me."

Vepal moved a lazy hand.

"Your price. Naturally. My life, and the Rifle's, and a ship to command. She *did* give you a command?"

"I will have it as soon as the High Commanders send their agreement, and I sign the contract for them." He paused. "I need the Rifle, of course. But you, Commander—you, I do *not* need."

"Recruiting Agent ter'Menth may still have questions for me," Vepal pointed out, watching Erthax's hands.

"Then, she will need to ask them of me," the Pilot said, and there was the gun, in the left hand, arm swinging up—

Vepal punched the control under his elbow; the chair spun hard to the left, as he threw himself to the right.

* * * ⟡ * * *

COMMANDER SANCHEZ considered the note, and again considered the soldier who had delivered it. Ochin Rifle, as he named himself. He held himself well, though there was an edge. His orders, so he had told her, received from the commander himself, had been to deliver the note, and to place himself at her word.

He had obeyed his orders, had Ochin Rifle. Plainly, JinJee thought, looking into his eyes, he did not *like* his orders, but he wasn't, after all, required to like his orders, no more than any other soldier.

"In your opinion," she said now, "is Commander Vepal in danger of his life?"

There was a slight hesitancy, before a fist rose to strike the opposite shoulder.

"Commander. Yes, Commander. In my opinion."

"Thank you. Keep with me, Rifle. Abercrombie, Singh, Henshaw, Pike, Latvala—to me, please. We're going for a walk. Sergeant Pillay!"

"Ma'am!"

"Seal up, Sergeant. Disable noncertified personnel seeking to enter our area. Commander Vepal is certified. If he arrives, hold him lightly, and with all respect for his rank—but hold him."

"Yes, ma'am," Pillay said with enthusiasm. He snapped off a very pretty salute, possibly to soothe Ochin Rifle's feelings, and turned, already shouting out the squad list, and protocols.

JinJee shook her head. They'd been at dock too long. They'd all been at dock too long; and it was a major miracle that none of the assembled mercs and pirates hadn't started a war yet, out of simple boredom.

"All right," she said to her squad. "We're going to recover Commander Vepal and give him safe escort to Paladin space. Eyes sharp. With good luck we'll intercept him on his way to us. With bad luck, we'll need to extract him from a Situation, in which case, he could be wounded, even badly wounded. Medic Latvala, stay sharp."

"Yes, ma'am," Latvala answered, sounding positively eager.

JinJee shook her head.

"Let's go."

. . . ✧ . . .

ERTHAX HAD KNOWN NOTHING beyond what he had initially reported; Vepal had made certain of that. Grisly work, not proper soldiering, but necessary. Once he was sure that there was nothing else, he had used Erthax's own grace blade to end the business, and disposed of the remains before he composed the message to High Command, wrapped in Erthax's codes, and sent from his console.

"Treachery," read the message. "Account terminated. Vepal."

These duties complete, he picked up his field kit and exited the ship, making for the food hub, and beyond.

Of course, he could not remain with the Paladins; he must seem to those who watched him to be going about his usual affairs. Tomorrow, for instance, he would need to find a more appropriate docking for the ship. This off-shift, however . . .

This shift, he wanted, very much, to talk to a comrade, to someone who understood command and the duties of command. He wanted to be in a proper camp, surrounded by proper soldiers, who knew about duty and loyalty, and the price of betrayal.

Also, Erthax's information. JinJee would need it, for herself, and to send on to her colleague, the master of all secrets.

He took the lift to the food hub, which would be very nearly deserted at this station-hour.

But, it was not deserted. He was confronted by a crowd as he exited the lift—and felt a spike of sheer joy at the prospect of a clean fight.

Then he recognized the tallest in the crowd, even as Ochin Rifle called out.

"Commander Vepal, sir!"

"At ease, Rifle," he said, as a less-tall figure separated from the group, and JinJee Sanchez put her hand on his arm.

"All is well, Comrade?" she murmured, for his ears alone.

"Maybe not so well," he answered, just as softly. "We need to talk. I place myself under your protection for this shift and perhaps the next. If you will allow, Commander."

Her fingers tightened on his arm, and she turned, bringing him with her.

"Not only do I allow, I insist," she replied, and raised her voice to address her soldiers.

"We have achieved our goal; and now we return to camp. Singh and Henshaw, take the rear; Abercrombie and Pike on point. Latvala and Rifle, flank us."

She released his arm and brought her weapon out, and Vepal did the same.

"Yes," she said, and gave him a feral grin. "We go."

SEVEN

TWO DAYS LATER, an unassuming lieutenant, or so it would seem, walked into camp during evening mess, presenting credentials which caused her to be conducted without delay to the table where Commanders Sanchez and Vepal were dining together, as had become their wont, and, at JinJee's lightly raised hand, was forthwith given a third chair, a plate, and, at the lieutenant's rather breathless request, a pot of coffeetoot.

"Vepal," JinJee said as the junior officer poured and drank a cup of 'toot straight down. "This is Lieutenant Cheladin. She's attached to this mission with the Lyr Cats. She has no manners, as you can see, but she is often entertaining. Chelly . . ."

The lieutenant glanced up, and put her cup gently on the table.

"I apologize for my lack of couth," she said, her voice soft and drawling. "I really did need that, JinJee. Thank you for your forbearance."

"Not at all; I am used to you." JinJee glanced to Vepal. "We took training together," she explained, and looked back to the lieutenant.

"I only worry about the impression you make upon my comrade; he is accustomed to a more rigorous style." She extended a hand and touched Vepal's sleeve.

"Here is Commander Vepal, Chelly. He and his aide Ochin form an auxiliary with us. Nolan is his sergeant, should you have need."

"You don't say! I'd thought Ezra had retired years ago!"

She turned to Vepal.

"Nolan was born a sergeant, sir; you'll get nothing but the best from him. Not that you need me to tell you that."

Vepal inclined his head.

"I have already been much comforted by the sergeant's care," he said blandly, and Lieutenant Cheladin grinned.

"Of course you have," she said.

The serving tray arrived at that juncture, and the lieutenant busied herself with choosing foodstuffs.

Vepal, under the guise of giving attention to his own meal, considered the side of JinJee's face.

He had come to know her well; easily well enough to see the worry through the mask of amused tolerance she bent upon her creche-mate as she filled her plate and addressed it with gusto.

"I am of two minds," JinJee said, after the lieutenant had paused long enough to pour and drain another cup of 'toot. "*Do* I want to know why you are here, Chelly?"

The lieutenant sighed, her shoulders softening, and neatly crossed her knife and fork over the negligible remains of her meal.

"No," she said, meeting JinJee's eyes.

"Splendid," JinJee responded. "Then do not tell me."

She raised her hand, and here came the aide to gather up all their plates and offer dessert, which, surprisingly, Lieutenant Cheladin declined.

"Let us go for a turn about the camp," JinJee said, pushing back from the table and rising. "I don't think you've seen the new configuration."

"Is this *another* new configuration?" asked her comrade. "By which I mean, the fourth?"

"Such a retentive memory—the fourth, yes. We must keep sharp, you know."

"Then, I'm agog to see the new configuration. I was amazed you managed to get three varies out of this space. Four leaves me speechless."

"As if such a thing were possible," JinJee said amiably. They had reached the door of the mess, which was opened for them by an attentive soldier.

JinJee exited first, followed by Vepal, then the lieutenant, in strict order of rank. Once outside, JinJee turned to the left, and Vepal to the right, where his small command made camp, and where Ochin Rifle stood expectantly at guard by the flagged perimeter.

"No," JinJee said softly. "Vepal, please accompany us."

So, this *was* something more than an old friend at liberty.

Vepal hesitated, glanced at his loyal troop, felt his companions take in his glance.

"I'm seen as remiss if I have no guard," Vepal said with a sigh. "Clearly, two mercenary officers are insufficient honor to my rank."

"I see," JinJee said. "He has been much alone of late, hasn't he? Let him be our honor guard, then."

The ambassador summoned his man.

"Five paces behind, Ochin Rifle. Guard us carefully, as befits a combined command."

Ochin saluted very smartly. "Yes, Commander Ambassador. A combined command."

Vepal fell in at JinJee's right hand, the suddenly sober Cheladin on her left, and they moved out.

"Advance troops were being selected last night," she said, softly, but not making any effort to obscure her words. "They've got to prep their equipment and command structure. They haven't boarded yet. We've got a tracer on them."

"We'd heard Liad was the target; Clan Korval the sponsor," JinJee said.

"I'd heard that one," Chelly said.

"Vepal disagrees with that target, by the way."

"And so?"

Vepal sighed, shook his head vaguely. "These are not warlike people, this Korval, except when pushed. They do not seek trouble. Clan Korval is not on the attack against Liad."

Chelly nodded. "I'll put my coin with the commander's—so then, not Liad."

"Have you anything more likely?"

"I did have a thought. Surebleak might not yet be secure."

There was a small pause, before JinJee murmured.

"In fact, that is Clan Korval's new home world?"

"That's right," Cheladin said.

JinJee waved a hand, taking in, so Vepal surmised, the entire space station, and all the soldiers on it.

"All of this, to dispose of a single Liaden clan?" she said. "They must be formidable."

"They are," said Cheladin. "But they're not necessarily the target. Or maybe only peripherally the target."

"What else, then?" asked JinJee.

"Mercs," said Cheladin succinctly.

"Clan Korval has hired forces? Perdition Enterprises, or whoever is behind it, sees this as a threat to their own agenda?"

"Clan Korval's situation," said the lieutenant, "is unique. I will send files—nothing that Research Officer Aritz couldn't locate in six minutes, and compile in an hour, but I happen to have it all to hand.

"The short form: Korval is exiled from Liad for crimes against the planet. They relocated to Surebleak with, I gather, a strictly limited show of remorse, and a ready plan. Recall, too, that it was Korval that took command of the forces on Lytaxin when the mercs there were blindsided, and they handed the Fourteenth a thundering loss. There's a fondness for Clan Korval among certain of our brethren, some of whom subsequently assisted in the so-called crime against Liad— under proper contracts, the terms of which were scrupulously kept.

"Also, Clan Korval has chosen for its new base a planet rife with opportunity, in a sector previously thought closed. I've heard that there's a new Merc Intake Center with Recruit Depot planned; they have a sufficiency of uninhabited land in interesting sizes and shapes, as well as a challenging climate."

Vepal bowed slightly in agreement. "This matches my information."

"Rich plunder," said JinJee quietly. "Either the mercs or Clan Korval would not be quite tempting enough. Two such targets in one location, however..."

"Becomes irresistible, to a certain type of client."

"Speaking only for myself," JinJee said, "I would give a very great deal to know who is the client."

"Working on it," Cheladin said.

"Warnings have been sent," JinJee said. "Of course."

"Well," Cheladin said, and failed to admit to that case.

JinJee paused, and turned to face her creche-mate.

"Warnings have *not* been sent?"

"We're trying to get the word out, as a hint," Cheladin said, sounding suddenly weary. "I lost a courier—whoever Perdition Enterprises is has the station under tight patrol. I'm afraid we lack our own pinbeams at the moment due to our civilian docking arrangements, and we dare not assume station pinbeams are secure."

JinJee took a quiet breath; and another.

"Which," Cheladin said quickly, "is why I'm here. Actually."

"Go on," JinJee said.

"You'll recall that my team, laggards and thrill-seekers as they are, and thinking themselves above their brethren in arms, on arrival sought for themselves quarters on the civil and residential side of the station."

"I recall this, of course," JinJee murmured.

"Yes. And you will also recall that I, as officer in charge, made it my business to seek out station society, particularly the station master and the board of governors. Inago being situated as it is, and reasonably busy even when not hosting a hiring fair of epic proportion, begin to find, let us say, the peculiar strains placed upon the station by the presence of the fair to be stretching their expertise.

"Happily, I was in a position to offer the station the use of my laggard team, most of whom, as you know, are quite knowledgeable, once they allow themselves to be roused to work."

"Has there been an increase of . . . system stresses, on the civilian side?" JinJee asked politely.

"Sadly, there have, and though my team has become interested in the emerging problems, it was suggested that they might need reinforcements. I thought of you."

"I think," JinJee said quietly, "that it is time for my co-commander to have found us an easy security job on Panore, or perhaps one of the seaside worlds at Canova. We'll be striking camp and moving out tomorrow. I will, myself, call at the recruiting office and formally remove the Paladins from the list. Vepal—how would you?"

Before he could answer, Cheladin spoke again.

"That . . . may not be possible any more, JinJee."

"When I have heard complaint from Recruiting Agent ter'Menth herself that she grows bored with my malingering? I think she would be very glad to see our backs."

A chime sounded, very softly. The lieutenant reached to her belt, raised a communicator to her ear.

"Cheladin," she said quietly, and, on a different note—"Got it. Take precautions."

She clipped the comm back onto her belt, and—said nothing, her gaze seemingly on something beyond the station's horizon, or years in the past.

JinJee placed a careful hand on her friend's arm.

"What happened?"

"An altercation, between forces known and unknown. Two of the Lyr Cats were attacked and injured pretty badly. Preliminary report is they were cornered near the airlock to the civil side, and made it through to aid on that side—but now the airlock's been taken hostage and held, by someone. No firefight, but edged weapons and deadly intent."

JinJee raised an eyebrow.

"We're not visible yet; have to wait for portmaster's response."

JinJee nodded at that, her reply unheard as station hazard klaxons sounded urgently, the red and blue flashes of the warning lights signifying a pressurization problem. Behind them, to their right, curtains of metal slid with a rumble from side walls, and dropped from ceilings with tremendous force, leaving behind them pressure changes and echoes. Rather than an open concourse they stood now in a long hall with small access doors topped by more blinking lights.

The vocal warning in Trade followed quickly: "Airlock issue Deck Seven. Follow standard protocols, Lock Three on emergency seal. Avoid this area. All region airlocks on emergency full seal now. Section airlocks by authorized poll cards only. Refrain from crossing air boundaries until further notice."

There was cussing in several languages as the group heard the news.

"We're on the wrong side of these doors to get back to our command, aren't we?" JinJee asked as everyone checked their weapons. Behind them, Ochin turned in a crouch, on guard, gun in hand, as more distant rumbles and clanks shook the floor, and the station locked down hard.

Chelly unclipped her handheld, pulling up a map.

"There may be a way to get through!"

EIGHT

THE LARGE ACCESS DOORS to cross boundary openings were sealed and locked but the doors to the manual stairways were not: Cheladin confirmed that the one across the corridor from the one Ochin experimentally opened was also accessible.

"We can go up or down," she muttered, "but not through!"

Cheladin's fingers ran over the face of the device as she tried another idea, cussed, worked on.

"The stairway lights, Ambassador, are on the battery. Subsystems may not be as well guarded."

"Thank you, Rifle, I hadn't considered that . . ."

"Do you think all the units are cut off? Or is this a Perdition operation?" JinJee glanced back and forth between the doors held open by Ochin and the lieutenant.

Cheladin pulled another comm from a pocket, punched that into operation—

"Cheladin," she said, "Update. We're on the wrong side, um, here; can you give me directions to anything open?"—and read off the corridor and level markers above the door she leaned against.

"You, too? Check with anyone who'll talk to you, we're going to have to be patient or hike..."

The lieutenant's face showed her worry—

"Station master is going full storm on this, looks like."

Vepal nodded agreement to JinJee, asking both, "Priority? My ship is far enough out on the docking rim to send a pinbeam if you have the coords and trust me to have them. If we need to storm a barricade we may lack the weapons and staffing."

"Wait—I'm getting possible routes—one's up the stairs your man has open—" She showed him the screen. "There are routes in red, those are closed. There are routes with blue stars—those are pollways. There's one that's gray—status not known—that's up three decks and should lead to both merc and business sections."

Agreement was instant, with Ochin perforce taking the lead, jumping three stairs at a time with remarkable ease and quiet, gun tucked away on favor of agility. The officers followed, Cheladin mounting the stairs with comm in one hand and gun in the other, the officers using hand grips to speed their way. The stairs were part of an air transport system, grids and grills open.

The sound above of a door slamming, and busy feet; Ochin froze, glancing down to Vepal for guidance.

JinJee signaled pause, and Vepal did too. Ochin took the time to pull a knife from his leg pocket.

No more sound came to them. Had someone been testing a door to see that it would open, or going through one?

Cheladin stretched, hands touching here and there about her person before pulling a tiny item from her belt, considering, and putting it back...

"Gods of guns, who'd think we'd be having this much trouble because of a Liaden no one knows? No record of her in any merc contract histories, none of her organization. It'd be one thing if it *was* Korval invading Liad—might be some sense there. But what's to trust this crew, or their contracts? And Korval's no pushover. Korval's not a pushover even for *his* people," she said, nodding toward Vepal. "Did your High Command go for an alliance?"

Ochin laughed from his spot higher on the stairway, startling the officers.

JinJee raised her eyebrows and looked toward Vepal, who spread his hands wide, palm up, shrugging Terran fashion.

"Please, Rifle," she said, "your thoughts, if the ambassador permits."

"Indeed," said Vepal, "we are intrigued."

"I think," said Ochin, tucking his laugh away and showing a serious face indeed, "that such a strategic mistake is not likely from the High Command. The lieutenant mentions the defeat of the Fourteenth by Tree-and-Dragon.

"After, they routed an enemy on Liad, using their own battleships, Scout ships, and local forces led by Korval's own leaders. Surely they are not without strength, and resource, this Korval."

Ochin paused, head cocked as if listening, then went on.

"This does seem a potential reason for Liaden revenge against Korval."

He paused, gained surety.

"I think, too, that the High Command must know, if even *I* do, that the Clutch are allies of Korval. Did you not know that Korval's very headquarters building from Liad was delivered, in one piece, building and infamous tree, by a Clutch vessel cut from an asteroid?"

He paused, listened to silence yet again, went on.

"The Clutch have weapons no one can stand against. Troop lore tells us of ships of monstrous size appearing at will inside defense rings and absorbing the energy of the strongest beams, and of an invasion where songs sung by five Clutch soldiers brought down walls and destroyed weapons held by Troops. It is said that if a

Clutch begins to sing it is safest to throw your weapon far away before it blows up in your hands."

Ochin turned, looked meaningfully at Vepal.

"The Troop knows, mouth to mouth across the years, that Temp Headquarters itself, within a ring of five defensive moons, could not prevent the landing of a dozen Clutch vessels at Prime Base itself."

Vepal blanched. So much for security and the secrets of command!

Ochin plowed ahead.

"Will the High Command forget this?" He looked them straightly in the eyes then, a man secure in his thoughts.

"For that matter, there are mercenaries here, who fought... for Korval. A man I spoke to, a Life Sergeant of the Lyr Cats, talked of being on the world called Surebleak when the Tree came down out of space in a rock bigger than Surebleak's biggest city, to be installed at the top of a hill defending the city. So, Command probably knows."

Ochin laughed gently.

"It would be madness to take on this fight, unless it was all for one last shout of honor. We cannot be that desperate, the Troop. Our High Command should not listen to such an offer, for sake of history. Nor should any. I have read many of the *melant'i* plays and seen cites of the history behind them. Attack a world where Korval *is* the line of command and is backed by mercs in place and has these Clutch as allies? Only if the plan is to sing Honor's Song while being destroyed. That I believe, but this is not my decision."

Then a sigh, and he continued more quietly.

"In the plays, there is this: what some might call revenge the Liadens call Balance, and this sounds to me like an attempt at that— why not make the mercenaries who fought for Korval fight against them? Why *not* have the Scouts who fought for Korval destroyed fighting mercenaries. Why *not* weaken all of them, this Surebleak, this Korval... so that those sitting on Liad can laugh and sweep up what is left without damage to themselves?

"In the most important Liaden plays—friends would fight friends and allies fight allies, all to illustrate proper behavior. And

here? If the High Command could be drawn in and the Clutch
destroy Temp Headquarters, Liad would be victorious and without
enemies."

He was quiet then, Ochin, fully delivered of his thoughts.

"Rifle? May I quote you in this summation? Or use the
recording?"

Ochin glanced sharply downward, but Cheladin was without a
trace of humor on her face.

"If the ambassador permits. My thoughts are merely those of a
Rifle . . . "

Vepal nodded at Cheladin.

"You may quote my second-in-command, who is Ochin, Master
Rifle."

If Ochin drew in a breath at being so named it was drowned in
a distant rumble. Above, distant echoes, as if someone ran two or
three decks overhead, and perhaps a very slight mumble of voices.

"Forward," said JinJee, which meant up, of course, with Ochin
in the lead. "Quietly!"

NINE

INAGO WAS A WELL-RUN STATION, smelling far less of
plastics and paints than most; nonetheless as they climbed the stairs
there was a slightly pungent odor. Ochin in the lead was first to see
its source, which was a small man working at the door of the next
slide hatch, one landing up, crouching. There was at least one other
there, hand in sleeve all that showed.

Ochin held back and Cheladin was beside him, taking in the
same sight. She nodded and ghosted downward.

Ochin thought if he had been doing careful work on a sealed
door and caught sight of a man with open blade approaching
stealthily he might take pause, or take alarm. Best not to have either.

The knife then went away.

Cheladin returned, nodding and whispering . . . "Make just a
little noise, we go up!"

"Yes," he said in Terran, "I will."

With Cheladin a step behind, Ochin continued upward, allowing his boots to scuff a step, and then another, as she did the same. A turn of the steep stairs and by then there were five visible on the landing, several with guard hands close to holstered guns, the one working, now with an assistant, and another still in half shadow, all of them dressed in the uniforms favored by Perdition Enterprises.

"Hello," Cheladin said. "Can we all get through here, do you think?" She and Ochin moved forward into the light. "We have two Commanders..."

Consternation, then a voice from the shadows: "Who is here?"

From below came the ambassador's firm voice:

"Vepal and Sanchez, Agent ter'Menth. Have you also been caught out on the wrong side?"

"Come ahead," said the agent, "we believe we make progress. This station administration could use some reordering, could it not?"

· · · ◇ · · ·

THE LANDING WAS CROWDED now, the walls giving back the noise of work going forth on the door as well as people too close together in a small area. Vepal recognized Recruiting Agent pen'Chouka, among those gathered, as well as ter'Menth.

Introductions included only the principals, with Cheladin as an administrative officer, the others being pointed to as Rifle, tech specialist, staff. Progress had been made, after all—the specialist had a knack and certain specialized tools permitting door access, and in the end it took that and Ochin's extra muscle to help force the thing, there being no pressure differential between the sides to speak of.

Agent ter'Menth spoke as the hatch was secured.

"Shall we find you at the Paladin's camp, Ambassador? Do you not have another staffer, your pilot? I had left a message . . . for you, a reminder, at your ship but have had no reply . . ."

Vepal loomed close, straight lipped.

"Another pilot on staff, Agent? Oh, the former line pilot. I had forgotten. I will need to amend my troop listing with you, for I am my own pilot now."

Agent ter'Menth's eyes went wide, but she recovered quickly.

"Do you say so? Has he been stolen away by one of the units we've signed here, then?"

"His location is of no moment, Agent. He is no longer of my unit."

Uncharacteristically, grim emotion played across her face before that expression went bland—or decisive—and the querying voice gave way to an artificially light tone.

"Well then, we may all—no, let us speak privately. The others may move forward. If we step this way for a moment..."

The agent bent close to the specialist, who was gathering tools. She spoke rapidly in quiet Liaden and then to the other agent, waving at them peremptorily as if shooing them on, then in Trade, saying, "Walk together so that you may explain to any of the station personnel..."

"Please, Commander Sanchez, excuse us for this moment—we shall catch up with you shortly."

JinJee looked unhappy at this, but nodded, with Cheladin staying well back.

"Commander Vepal," Ochin began, but Vepal signed for silence as the agent gave another round of rapid instruction in Liaden to her minions.

"Commander!"

Vepal turned on Ochin, then.

"Master Rifle, you have your orders. We shall be along shortly!"

Vepal and ter'Menth both leaned somewhat in the direction of the hall when motion caught Vepal's eye.

The agent may also have seen the motion; her shoulder rose, her left arm reached, her mouth tensed as if she was going to say something, but all stopped at once as the motion was followed by the distinctive cough of three pellet gun shots, and the rustle of the agent, ear bloody and throat glistening red, falling lifeless to the floor.

By the time Vepal finished his turn two other Liadens were dead, the others thrown to the floor and held under threat of weapons.

Ochin's face was grimly pale as he spoke to Vepal in the quiet aftermath, breathy with rage.

"Sir, she'd commanded our execution and promised yours. I have protected the combined command, sir, as ordered."

Breathing was the only sound for a moment, and then the air system picked up a notch.

"We are defended, as ordered," Cheladin remarked, pulling the comm to her face. "I will report this to the station, immediately."

· · · ✧ · · ·

CHELADIN BROUGHT TEA from the dispenser for Vepal; he stood by JinJee, taking comfort from her presence. They had called the station for assistance and assistance had arrived.

Ochin was under arrest. The others were witnesses or material witnesses, and possibly uncharged co-conspirators, but at the moment they were all locked in together while the station master and her staff "checked the records" to decide what to do.

For Ochin, wearing the silly restraints insisted upon by the station staff, she brought a foamed double hotchoc. Ochin being seated at the table before a view screen, she sat next to him, and said, "Have you found it?"

"Exactly as I told them. Act three, scene three, *Of dea'Feen's Necessity*, by pel'Gorda."

"Show me."

He awkwardly touched the control, and—a little too loudly by the way JinJee shrank at the rapid Liaden dialogue—the action continued.

Surely Cheladin knew Liaden, but the Rifle translated along with the recording: "So take them down the hall, and kill them quickly around the corner, while I take the treacherous one this way, and he will know his throat is cut."

Vepal winced, JinJee grimaced, Cheladin blew out a deep breath.

"She *said* that?"

"Yes, she was being amused, it seemed to me, to rush us all to death using a famous line from a most famous play. I could not ignore such an obvious threat! My orders . . . "

"Oh, jeez!"

That was Cheladin, watching as the play continued— "Bloodthirsty bunch, were they?"

Ochin turned the sound down on the video play, finally.

"Balance was involved. Revenge, you see, revenge with malice and"—he fought languages for a moment—"perhaps expert cunning. More than that, cunning with prideful cruelty. I've known someone like that, but he is gone."

Cheladin turned to them, JinJee and Vepal together.

"What do you think?"

JinJee shrugged, looked toward Vepal, came to the table.

"I've seen people like that myself, but this is frightening as much as enlightening. If this is an example of Balance done properly I'm not in favor of being involved with any of it."

"I would be pleased not to deal with these people," said Vepal, with sudden energy, coming to the table and nearly backhanding the screen. "Not the ones who want this."

He turned to JinJee, earnest.

"These people—Perdition and those who foment such things— they deserve enemies who are strong and who are forceful and who are ... aware that there are bounds of action. That is what the Troop was meant to ensure, that cruelty would not win every time. That's why we were born and came through from the old universe to found Temp Headquarters."

Into the pause came noise from the hall outside, likely another escort to take the prisoner somewhere else. There'd been a holding cell, there'd been another holding cell, a division of the Liaden survivors from the mercs, and then there'd been a hearing in front of a tired woman with three tired confederates asking the same questions ...

And there'd been experts who'd spoken to the remaining Liadens. Things had taken longer than they ought to have, what with the station dealing with a hurried exodus of dozens of ships, with the several near riots when some who'd signed the NDAs discovered that there was no kill-fee for the operation crashing without warning, that Perdition Enterprises had no more behind it than the willful conniving of a failing scheme throwing the last of their money at an operation meant to justify centuries of sabotage, intrigue, and deception.

Ochin touched the controls, freezing the screen on the image of a satisfied man sipping tea, victorious. Two-handed, Ochin raised the cup of hotchoc and sipped.

The door slid open, with a low sound of a crowd waiting outside. A woman walked in, closing the door, waving a card and wand.

She approached the only one wearing restraints.

"You're Ochin? The man who made the speech we're all hearing?"

He stood.

"That's Master Rifle Ochin, of Vepal's Small Troop?"

"Yes," he said. "Master Rifle Ochin. I understand I have been quoted."

"Yes, you have. Which one is Vepal?"

The ambassador stood tall then, and came forward.

"You, sir, are to take charge of Master Rifle Ochin during the remainder of his visit to this station. You've got one station-day to arrange ... "

She stopped, took a crumpled sheet of hard copy from her pocket.

"Here it is. You've got one station-day to arrange your necessities and get on your way. Master Rifle Ochin has the same. Station master says you, Master Rifle Ochin, aren't to brandish, threaten, or be involved in any fighting. We'll deliver your weapons to ship side when you're on the way out.

"Other than that, all of you are free to go. Station master and the security committee have reviewed camera and sound recordings of the incident where the deceased ordered her crew to illegally force open the door and then ordered them to kill your group, one and all—the Liaden was quite clear that this was meant to be carried out immediately, by stealth, and without provocation from your side."

The woman looked at her hard copy again, and saluted Ochin Master Rifle.

"You sir, are exonerated of any charges of murder, manslaughter, or wrongful death in this situation as you were acting in self-defense as well as under orders to protect command. If the future returns you to Inago Prime you will be welcomed. Thank you for helping preserve peace on this station."

Apparently she'd run out of things to crib from hard-copy notes, so she tucked the page away and smiled at the group.

"You are all free to go, if you can get past the folks waiting to thank Mr. Ochin. We'll give you a couple minutes to see if some of them will go away, or you can go out the back door, if you like."

Vepal looked to JinJee—

"One station-day!"

As the messenger left they could hear the shout of honor from the waiting Paladins: "Ochin, Ochin, Ochin, Vepal, Ochin, Ochin, Ochin, Vepal!"

Ochin looked down at the restraints still wrapped around his wrists, took a deep breath, and with a sharp motion pulled them apart, leaving his arms free to move, and wristlets dangling.

"We can go now, Commander," Ochin said firmly. "I am ready."

TEN

THEY'D LEFT THROUGH THE FRONT DOOR, giving Master Rifle Ochin an opportunity to be celebrated by those wise enough not to blame the unmasking of a scheme with the failure of the scheme's promises to be true.

Not all of those interested in Ochin were waiting to congratulate him on his release for doing proper duty. Some, already plotters, were willing to plot again, or at least to blame.

Those people, hoodwinked as much by their failure to perform due diligence as by the deceased, were still at the bar and certain that they'd been sold out of the richest pay credits of their lives by a know-nothing newbie with too fast a gun hand.

The station master pointed out there were no more accessible funds in Perdition accounts held on station. The two associated Perdition ships, locked tight as they were, were being held for inspection by a Scout and a Merc technical team still to be assembled—and thus not available to be auctioned off for any of the debt, real or imagined, that those who'd signed the NDA claimed. In other words, no recourse.

While the bars were going straight cash or backed credit only the headaches got worse as the braver—or more foolhardy—of the former Perdition allies shared what they'd agreed to, discovering over and over again that they'd contracted to accept the same thing—shares of a planetary treasury, for example, where the shares added up to multiple hundreds of percents. . . .

For his part, Vepal was pleased enough to let Ochin take credit for what was, after all, the accident of their meeting ter'Menth's crew. He could but salute the purity of the Rifle's understanding of his orders.

Still, still he might need to talk to Ochin, who'd felt the need to apologize to him, twice, for shooting without warning, for—Well there, the battlefield had come upon them unbidden if not entirely unexpected, and Ochin, long away from an active front, had fallen back on his Rifle's training to take the most important target first. It had shaken Vepal, in the end, to discover his lapse and see the result, and now keeping Ochin . . . he would talk to him.

Of their day's grace before leaving, the first hour was spent returning to the Paladin's bivouac, the way made more difficult by the churning in the hall of the several corps rushing for their ships before station's demand for payment and even back-payment became burdensome.

Chelly left them, her people and the station's—backed with the addition of a contingent of Paladin specialists—taking full command of the rapid dispersal of the unemployed mercs to points elsewhere. Chelly having gone in the interim from Lieutenant Cheladin to Lieutenant Commander Cheladin of Admin, she'd personally overseen the removal of Vinkleer's crew along with the implements they'd meant to use to take over the station once the expeditionary forces had gone. Altogether, ter'Menth's ambitions had been immense!

Vepal and JinJee sat side by side at a hasty snack thrown together to honor Ochin, the pair smiling on the troops and quaffing careful amounts of beer while reports flowed in on the progress of the station's shedding of Perdition's effects. JinJee wisely pointed out to the Master Rifle that among the mercs was a tradition of drinking a hero into such drunkenness that might not be to the best interest of Ochin's head, nor the needs of safety. Ochin, accustomed to the ambassador's gentle hand with his crew, took that suggestion seriously, carefully losing track of his beers after a sip or two so that many of the Paladins might happily recall giving the hero yet another cup.

Vepal found himself studying JinJee's face from time to time, and smiling, and found her at times smiling at him though naught had been said. She even dipped her head at one point, giving a small laugh that turned into a willful smile.

"We're too old to be smitten, you know. But damn if it doesn't feel that way to me."

Vepal nodded, pleased to know that he was not alone in feeling emotions roiling along that were far from the emotions a commander ought to be feeling, to be filled with thoughts far from those a commander with an imminent departure ought to be thinking.

They laughed together, raised glasses to each other, and looked out among the troops as JinJee shared a note on her comm from Chelly—

"Lyr Cats assembled for lift-out; they'll be going to Surebleak and will be carrying my report to the new merc sector headquarters there. I'll ask them to share portions with the Scouts, Ochin's report in particular, if you agree."

Vepal thought, handing the device back to JinJee.

"They will be told that they were targeted for invasion?"

He watched her face, pleased to see her expression firm with thought. She was, perhaps, a work of art, even her willingness to share her considerations with one who'd been accidentally met during a brawl.

"If they don't already know that some see them as vulnerable, don't you think they should? It isn't like they've got Clutch living on planet, is it? Best that the Scouts, and Korval, know—but Korval must know their danger!"

He gave a very short nod of assent, seeing the eyes of various of her troops surveying the pair of them. They were good soldiers, if most of them were undergrown. . . .

JinJee smiled, too—

"They admire you, you know," she said wryly, "and they admire and like your Rifle. I can't think what the change of people's attitudes might be when they discover that the Yxtrang ambassador stepped into a merc problem bordering on critical mass and defused it with the application of considered force."

Vepal shook his head, barely suppressing his laugh.

"But that is not what happened, JinJee. We merely—"

"You merely acted in good faith at all points in this mess, which is more than can be said for several commanders I needn't mention. Well, one, yes, I will—Orburt Vinkleer and the Vinkleer Cooperative are still under guard by the station, and the story of your first meeting is going to be wrapped up in their trying to corner the Lyr Cat medical team and steal them for their own corps. Vinkleer may survive here—the station civilians will not want his blood specifically on their hands—but they may pass him along to the mercs. I am not sure he will survive in that case, my friend, since he will make a very thorough lesson by not living out the Standard.

"But there, no doubt about Vepal and Vepal's Small Troop. You were on the right side from the start. Cautious about ter'Menth, willing to let me take care of Vinkleer's goons without killing them outright—Chelly's telling people, and Chelly's going to end up on the committee the station's putting together to have a hearing on him. You won't be here, but my soldiers have already given evidence on that little fracas and it may well be that Vinkleer will be simply stripped of everything by the mercs. If the station doesn't space him for fomenting insurrection and endangering the integrity of the air system he may be seen more as a pawn than an actor in all of this. 'Course there's hardly a way to get an unbiased hearing at this point, since everyone knows he was the first to sign with Perdition and was acting as their bully squad."

Vepal listened, not only to hear her point but to hear her speak. Well, yes, the High Command had not been sending their regular and booster vaccinations, nor the money on time nor . . . perhaps his hormones and commander-sense were out of kilter after all this time on detached duty. He was not prone, now, to be sorry for it and the unexpected joy of this late adventure.

"Friend of mine, what will you do?"

Vepal sighed, JinJee again having reached the same point in his thought processes as he, no matter through what means.

"The station tells me they are not charging us for our stay but they wish us to go as soon as we may, in case there is luck involved. Given that, I hesitate to discuss these happenings at length with the High Command until I have more to offer than to tell them that a spy has been decommissioned and that their proposed ally has been demonstrated as a fraud. I am too sane to believe that decision was properly routed through all the High Command. I'm afraid that Ochin's summation is apt—perhaps I should simply make him my Aide and let his Rifle go!—but there, I wish not to abandon my mission, and I wish not to abandon the hope of dealing properly with the universe according to our First Orders."

JinJee nodded, leaning in, and said, "Wishes are not acts, as we both well know. I will be taking the bulk of my command to Werthing, where I own a quarter share of a small training reserve. We will have a short break there, to refresh ourselves—space station life is not the best for keeping in shape and on target."

She paused, smiled almost shyly.

"You are welcome to set Werthing as a destination if you will. I will give you the code; do not fail to understand your welcome."

He brightened at the thought, felt himself flush with the visibility of his eagerness. It took an act of will to master his urge to say yes and turn that into a regretful shake of head.

"Perhaps I will add that to the list of future destinations, depending on our other travels and communications. First I think I will take my ship to Omenski, since I have need of refreshing myself as pilot. There is a service order of peace-seekers there; they permit ambassadors and mediators a place to stay in pursuit of peace—I have been there before and find a certain measure of accord with them—and it is an easy Jump from there, I see, to this Surebleak."

JinJee's eyes widened.

"You'd go to Korval?"

"I am, after all, looking for a point of action to offer to the High Command, an embraceable change point, since at least some of the commanders seem disinclined to continue with our recent floundering. Korval is not averse to dealing with the members of the Troop, nor with any group that offers honorable alliance. Perhaps they will know a path forward if they are not themselves the ally I need."

He smiled wanly.

"The service order I speak of at Omenski? They have a beautiful campus on a lake, a serene place where meditation is favored, and life is unhurried. My plan is to hurry there, take full consideration of my situation and that of Ochin, perhaps to study, briefly, on the possibilities before me, as well as the ways of Liaden tea, which I may need if I am to deal with this Tree-and-Dragon. Then, before speaking to the High Command, I *will* speak to Korval."

JinJee nodded and gave a deep nod which was nearly a bow.

"Well considered, my friend."

Someone called for her attention, then pointed.

"See this, here, JinJee, look at this!"

—And she held up her hand to delay that a moment, reached out and touched his arm gently.

"Your plan has merit. If your meditation shows you that you need a new path, my friend, you can come to me on Werthing, or wherever I am. We can perhaps . . . "

The call for her attention grew louder, and Vepal stood as she did. The press of leave-taking upon them, he dared to take her hand in his and squeeze it tightly, and to feel the brave squeeze she gave his in return.

"Yes," he said, "perhaps we can. I would be honored to see you again."

✧ Command Decision ✧

THIS STORY WAS ORIGINALLY WRITTEN for (and appeared in) a themed anthology edited by Michael A. Ventrella called Release the Virgins, *and it is authored by Steve since Sharon had a different story she wished to tell in the same book. In it the author plays with a smattering of science oddities as well as a character inspired by a Liaden fan.*

✧✧✧✧

"**DALTREY'S STILL WAITING** in holding orbit. Wants to know why we haven't solved this yet! If the CMEs clear up he figures they can be down in thirty hours or so."

The intel officer, Lizardi, spoke low, just in case someone had a mic working nearby. She and her companion leaned against a rail fence at the top of a steep slope, observing.

Bjarni, the ad hoc planetary specialist—by dint of being the only member of the unit to have been on-world before—nodded.

"I had a note, too. Says Righteous Bispham's making noises re contract specs. Daltrey still wants to be there to turn the Nameless over to the Bispham, and the Bispham wants to Name them before they act. Silly damn . . . "

"Local custom," she said, with more than a little asperity.

After a pause: "You know, I think Daltrey's hoping to get out. If he gave me terms I'd buy him out. I think we could keep it together just fine."

The specialist nodded. Everyone always says they want a chance to be the boss.

"Any luck?" she asked after a moment of silence.

Bjarni took a deep breath, recalled his mission. His sensitive nose tried, but disappointed.

The planet smelled green when it didn't stink of sulfur from the open wounds of the tectonics. The seacoasts and islands smelled green with the giant seasonal rafts of seaweed spicing the tricky winds; the brief plains had smelled green with the waves of grasses ... and now the mountains smelled green of the great bristling tar-spotted pine analogues and the moss-walled rocks of the upswept basalt.

Years since he'd first smelled it as a traveling student. This time— he'd had a sunny tour so far instead of a war, landing ships aground and mired in swamp after taking damage from the stellar storms that had grounded both sides as far as the mercenary units went. They'd managed to get their hovercraft out of the landing ship, but were on the wrong side of the mountain when those comms went haywire and some of them crisped, grounding them the second time.

Elsewhere around the planet the green scent might be overridden with the scent of blood, of burning fields, of weapons cobbled out of machines meant for peace, the ozone of overworked electronics and overlay. This mountain had none of those, being as comfortably rural as a rustic guided tour.

The scent he really sought, the one that had intoxicated him on his private visit to InAJam as a youthful wandering philosophy student, was the cusp of green fungi. He'd been entranced by InAJam; he had some of the language and loved it, and more, he loved the food and admired the people. He even dreamed about the place. The most frequent dream was about the ripple he'd seen, when the fragrance of the carpet growths intensified and the colors changed as the spores of one generation fell on the neighboring growths from another, changing them.

"I smell something," Major Lizardi said, but her nose still had a hard time separating the wood flavoring from the aroma of overcooked meat, as he'd seen at dinner the night before. She blamed that on growing up on Surebleak, and if she survived long enough she'd eventually get a taste for finer things, but she'd likely not be able to smell a ripple in action.

He pointed then to the small sand pile and said, "Cat!"

She wrinkled her nose then, and said, "Not that!"

Bjarni's nose tried again, and he turned to his companion, shaking his head Terran-style, adding the laconic, "No," emphasized with a sigh, "not that either. Not from this direction, anyway."

"They're out there somewhere! They can't let this ripple go unnamed!"

She, of course, had never seen a ripple and while his experience was slight, hers was from training vid and poorly prepared sleep learning. On the other hand she was right—the New Decade was to be declared within the next three days, and the local beliefs required any ripple coinciding with a new year to be celebrated and named and feted.

The politics of that new decade had brought the mercs into play; but who expected the centerpiece of the event to be stolen away so that the planet might be without their most important export for years? He grimaced thinking of the loss to the gastronomes of the galaxy if the untouched initiates didn't come together somewhere by the appointed time.

One of the things Daltrey did right was letting the officers chance the food—their local cooks fed him very well and the others enough. While Lizardi tried the fungi, she wasn't a fan, like he was. He'd tried to introduce some of the others, explaining that they were not in fact eating cat, as numerous as *they* were around, but a variation of shroom with touches of this and that protein and . . . and it wasn't proper meat from hoof or vat, and they grumped about it, going with bar rations and instant soups. Bjarni reveled in all of InAJam, especially the food.

Which was why Bjarni was out beyond the lines on an alien mountainside with the intel officer, sniffing the winds of morning, hoping to sense a sign of the missing religionists or their rogue captors. That was what *she* was searching for. Something to tell Daltrey, some hint of how they'd win this thing, after all.

They stared down the green sides a while longer on this, the sacred side of the hill, looking toward the most distant and all but invisible sea, before turning toward the awkward pod camp in the lee of their downed hovercraft beside the idyllic lake.

• • • ✧ • • •

THE OTHER SIDE OF THE MOUNTAIN felt crowded. Soldiers guarded busily, as if they were able to do something real while waiting to be rescued, a rescue depending on one side or the other winning so that they might be either ransomed or lifted from this place by a working ship. Too, there were pilgrims, wandering through, offering food and oddities on their way up the mountain.

Bjarni smiled at a couple trying to sell him a carved bird, touching hand to forehead and speaking the local language and telling them, "I have too many already. How would I feed more?"

They laughed, touched hands to forehead in response, a real smile coming back.

"The locals act like they know you," Lizardi said before they parted. "Are these regulars?"

Shake of the head. "They may be—there are a few I've seen before—but I think there's a special smile, almost a family expression, you get after you've sat at meals here, when you speak the language."

She shrugged. "Might be it. It feels like they all recognize you."

He shrugged back. "I feel at home here, Major. I guess it shows."

The continent they were on was basically flat, with three folds of hills that rose to these mountains, the central high point of the continent where most of the people loved the flat lands.

Here, the lake, on a high plateau with one last taller hill swathed in vines and berry brambles behind it, overlooking their camp site. That last hill also held a religious refuge, a temple occupied by a few fanatics who could sometimes be seen standing, watching the plants grow, else soothing them with water and fish meal. Pilgrims came and went, bringing food for the most pious and taking away whatever they might learn on the hillside.

The pilgrims were also anticipating the High Ripple—something that came once every fifty Standards or so, and which coincided this time with the Decade. The signs had been good that this was the year the six variants would all prove good to spore and mix.

Below their plateau, which was occupied by the few ground-side forces of Daltrey's Daggers, was another reached by a barely tended road, home of a small town. From that town was a spiderweb of paths and rough roads leading in all directions, and below that were a series of hills and lakes leading to a plain. The daily pilgrims came that way, past the soldiers, and up into the sacred.

What exactly the sacred was for the locals Bjarni wasn't sure. To him it was the whole of the planet—a single month roaming about as a student on memtrek between course years had convinced him that he wanted to retire here. The war so far hadn't unconvinced him.

He'd written papers about his student experience. He'd mentioned the ripple, standing on a deck and watching the ground cover slowly go from one shade of green to another over a few hours as seasons changed, as the dominant fungi's spores spread themselves into the mat of greenery underlying all. When his home ship's fortunes waned and it was auctioned away from the family—they really should have listened to him!—he'd ended up destitute rather than a student, stuck on the other side of the galaxy, saved by a merc recruiter's happy offer of employment.

To this day, a dozen years plus on active duty and another three between calls, he thought of himself as exactly what he was—an administrator par excellence, a logistical technician making the force able to fight when it wanted to, with records impeccable and practical to keep everything in order, who happened to work as a merc. Intel Major Lizardi had ferreted out his InAJam connections and brought him on board for this tour.

In his pod Bjarni went over the latest news, of which there wasn't much—the mercs on either side hadn't got permission to put the action on hold while the fighting infrastructure got put back together. Instead Daltrey's orbital office sent multiple instances of the same command with the hopes that someone would pay attention, and the Bandoliers did the same for their side. Neither side knew the whereabouts of a certain important group of people and neither side wanted to give too much information the other side could use. No one even knew what they looked like!

"The young people" was the phrase that kept being used, the Nameless!

Bjarni'd watched the wording of communiqués, watched what weather reports they could get, and handled the ongoing inventorying and replenishment lists—not much else to do!—and waited for dinner. He wasn't sorry when he left his databases for the day, trudging down to dinner in the makeshift mess hall with the late-dusk skies already colored with the twisty bands of reds and yellows, purples and greens, as the auroras flared anew—or judging by the comm techs, continued to flare. He'd picked up a small parade of cats along the way, as he so often did here, and they walked him delicately to the mess hall, and were still there in the full dark to walk him back to his pod under the intricate flowing colors of the night.

* * * ✧ * * *

HE HADN'T LET ANY CATS IN, but something woke him from his vague dream of shrouded faces, piercing eyes, and the sounds of local rhythms. A sound? An aroma?

Bjarni sniffed, catching nothing but ordinary scents, but he knew he'd sensed something! The dream? Could he have been smelling this in his sleep? Could something have leaked in from outdoors?

He walked to the door, glanced into the night to see the aurora, muted to slight shimmers.

He sniffed once, hard.

No joy. No joy. He'd know; that he was sure. He'd smell when the ripple came through, know that the initiates had done the deed and melded the newest food, or failed. He'd also recall those eyes!

* * * ✧ * * *

IN THE LATE AFTERNOON next day Bjarni broke from his logistical and admin duties, and walked away from the busyness of camp, unsurprised to find the sharp-faced Lizardi out as well, standing by her pod as if waiting for him. The planet felt good to be on, even if there was war and destruction elsewhere, and being out in it a necessity turned pleasure.

Bjarni nodded at the major, and she back, and they proceeded wordlessly.

They passed by the guards on the well-trodden path leading toward the temple. The rules were clear—they were not to approach the temple without invite—and none from that structure had bothered even to survey the medical camp or its denizens. Other locals had come from the town below, seen that the strangers were settled well, and gone, some to the temple and some back down, in what was a constant stream of locals.

It had taken the guards awhile to get used to the prohibition on detaining all the pilgrims who wandered through camp: it was a given that someone dressed for pilgrimage was indeed a pilgrim. It was written: pilgrims do not engage in warfare.

The compromise Daltrey had reached with his counterparts in the local forces and the other side was that people—the pilgrims themselves—need not be searched. Could not be searched.

The baskets and packs they had might be searched, but not individuals; and for that matter standing orders said no shooting of wildlife, and especially no shooting, eating, or killing of cats. The cat thing didn't bother him, and the good behavior of the unarmed pilgrims made them as much curiosity as problem.

It was a confused war, far from Daltrey's Daggers' finest hour. They'd signed on to help defend one side's Decadal Ritual from interruption only to discover that this wasn't a simple binary argument but a long-brewing fight among a dozen different groups, most showing changeable allegiance. And that Decadal Ritual? If it was a failure, there'd be crop shortages or worse, and the rulers got to find new jobs—or new heads.

This time, instead of looking down, they looked up. There were birdish creatures hovering and swooping, among which a dozen drones might have hidden had not rules demanded that no such be flown. The temple was a stark white structure with red lines painted seemingly at random across walls; in the lowering afternoon light it was quite beautiful.

A bustle behind them then, steps nearby. Bjarni felt a twinge in one nostril. Fine spice, fine shroom somewhere close.

Alert now, Bjarni twisted where he stood. He recognized the sounds and the style of a walking caravan, people from the flatlands. This particular caravan was swathed each in voluminous robes quilted from the robes of ancestors which had been quilted from robes of ancestors which had been quilted before them.

They carried baskets, all sixteen of them, and they were roped together as proper pilgrims were, basket to basket as one line and person to person as another, walking—here at least—with a low chant. Cats walked with them purposefully, staying close, it appeared, to particular pilgrims, and careful not to impede the march.

Along with the chant there came another twinge. His nostrils flared, and then he realized the it was probably the aromas of the pilgrims' breakfasts or lunch. The song got louder as he moved in their direction—not because he was closer but as if they were gaining in volume as they closed in on their temple above.

Bjarni finally heard some of the words, which were a hymn to the sky with its star that brought the rain. Of course it did—such things were as basic as the aggregation of mass into hydrogen and into star, thence gravity leading to spheres collecting hydrogen and thus to atmosphere, atmosphere and solar energies to weather, weather, gravity, and energy leading to life.

As the pilgrims closed on the pair the steady up-slope breeze broke, so now a dozen scents mingled, all of food worthy of the gods. The locals, poor by galactic standards, ate as well as fat cats and potentates elsewhere. It was an easy world to live on, epicurean food literally underfoot much of the year. This caravan carried a fortune in fragile food.

The leader was a woman of middle years, as tall as he or the intel officer, carrying a basket. Bjarni had seen her the day before, and, he thought, days before that as they skirted the enclave, she often the last of them, stopping from time to time to sweep the trail this way or that, or attend to a branch needing repair from their passing. In a real war zone you'd have thought she was looking for sensors!

Today the woman was in front and she eyed Bjarni with care. He had the visible weapon, after all, even if he didn't offer the same demeanor as the camp guards. The middle of the line of travel drew his attention. They moved at a different gait and rhythm—their own and not the leader's, despite the pilgrim ties. Their baskets were smaller than the other travelers.

Also, the air was full now of the scent of shroom, from somewhere, the breeze muddling the source.

Bjarni stood as if rooted, watching, caught a glance from that group—

"Inspect!"

Surprised, he looked to Lizardi, who had a palm up indicating the group should stop.

"Spotted something?"

"Not me," she said, "but you're all aquiver!"

"Inspect, now!" This time she raised her voice, placing herself in front of them with both hands raised for emphasis.

Her peremptory demand acknowledged, came a ritual lining up of the group; one by one men and women alike opened their hand-woven baskets and stood back six paces from the potential contagion of the foreigners. The cats, however, stayed each and every one behind the baskets they'd walked with, and the chant went on—not by all of the walkers but by a group in the center of the pack—the most devout, perhaps.

The major raised a hand and from the camp came several sentries on a dead run.

Inspection of the locals wasn't usually his job; his job was compliance with an astounding number of rules and regulations. He was in charge of the proper on-time filing of notices, invoices, analyses, and reports as generated by a mercenary unit working on a fringe planet, barely a hundred years this side of being interdicted for Problematic Practices.

In the center of the line, the singers were six youngsters, not farmhands by his guess. They tried to hide in the cowls of their robes as they stood away from their baskets, but they did no good job of it. Still, they kept up their chant, with at least two dozen cats arrayed about them.

Lizardi gestured in their direction and looked at him pointedly as the fluent expert among them. The caravan leader stirred a little, as did several of the others. In an antagonistic population he might have been concerned.

The chant continued. His nose caught nuance of fungi, cooked and uncooked, and he felt a rising awareness, almost an arousal as might happen with the very finest of the fungi-concentrates.

He closed with that section of line, and the volume went up again, though they turned somewhat away from him—at least five of them did. The sixth sang something different in the song, something he couldn't quite make out as the hoods muffled words as well as faces.

Walking between the people and their burdens, he saw these baskets each had what he'd now expected, fungi being carried to the mountain. These were not piled high like the other baskets, but were mere handfuls, redolent of the highest quality.

Bjarni mimed throwing hoods back, saying in the dialect, "You may show your faces to the sun, may you not?"

Around him a rush of the cats, flawlessly groomed, crowding him as he was nearly an arm's length from the shortest singer. He waded through carefully and—they'd not listened yet.

While the other five singers sang the chant louder, this one sang softer. He looked into the face and saw the eyes of blue green, his breath catching. He thought, too, that the robed visage was as startled as he. Now he mimed with more force the throwing back of hoods.

As one, they did, revealing beauty. Strong faces, unlined, alert, singing—he was within touching distance now, the song loud, this one with intense eyes singing off-key a little—no, singing special words to him!

"We knew you would be here, we knew it was you, we knew you would find us, we knew that you could. We are we . . . we grasp the *ĉampinjono!*"

There was a commotion at the end of the line. A sentry stood in front of the leader, not holding her but standing between her and these six. The cats still milled about . . .

The six sang on, loosening further the travel robes, showing exquisite garments beneath.

The singing stopped.

Looking in his face, the beauty in front of him said, "We have the husks, we have a duty. This day should be *the* day, friend, this day should start the ripple!"

"You will do this for us all. You have the touch! I saw your face in a vision, I knew it!"

Bjarni whirled, raised his voice.

"Major, this group. This—force—they walked through our lines in the guise of mere pilgrims. These six must be freed! They must get to the temple now!"

It took her a moment to comprehend the bright-colored outfits beneath the robes—and the sentries bore down upon the others with professional interest.

"Mud and blood," she said without heat, seeing those arrayed before her. "Mud and blood times fifty!"

The beautiful one looked into his face and tugged at the ceremonial ropes attaching all together. "These have a magic about them. We cannot fight—if they ran we would have to run with them! We need these bindings taken off!"

Bjarni looked to the major, waved at the initiates. "We must get them to their temple—they tell us it is today. They must have their ritual today!"

He dared to hold the hand of the initiate with the amazing eyes and showed the rope with an extra metallic thread within to Lizardi.

"We have to get this off of them!"

"I don't know the language, Bjarni. You tell them."

Bjarni turned toward the woman who had been leader, now disarmed.

"*Liberigi La Virgulojn!*" he said, repeating it in Trade for all to hear. "Release the virgins!"

• • • ✧ • • •

"ARE YOU COMING?"

Lizardi shook her head, waving at the barely controlled confusion about them.

"I can't. I'm going to organize this"—here she laughed—"and then, I have to tell Daltrey he and his friend will have to miss the party. I'm on the spot—command decision and all that."

That quickly he'd been led by the freed virgins and two keepers up the mountainside to the blindingly white buildings where several dozen acolytes cheered their appearance and rushed to preparation. The chant resumed, and grew steadily in volume as passing pilgrims collected to add their voices.

Bjarni was given over-robes to wear, and brought to a thin stone seat, where a pair of attendants appeared, bringing him a bowl of water from a stone pool shimmering in the afternoon light, that he might wash his hands in preparation to witness . . . what?

He sat running over his reading in his head—obviously parts of the rituals were not usually shared with commoners and strangers.

He'd not been expecting the disrobing of initiates, nor the use of the pool as a kind of game of ritual cleansing while their bags and cats sat nearby.

The clean and naked virgins leapt from the waters of the sacred pool with no hesitation, charging among the cats to grab handfuls of the colorful fungus from their baskets and then full of excitement rushed to their bower, holding hands and chattering as they flung themselves within.

The coreligionists outside began to sing louder, and two found drums.

Laughter rose from the bower and became passionate, and more such laughter rang out over the mountainside, nearly smothered by the chants.

The drumming and singing went on until there was yet another burst of passion. The shadows on the long lawn lengthened and now the inside of the bower lit up as column after column collected the setting sun's rays and directed them within.

There was singing from within, a shout of cheer. Shortly after the six initiates emerged, one robed in red, one in yellow, one in green, one in blue, one in orange, and the last in purple, each collecting their baskets and the escort of cats.

They came as a group to him, Bjarni, and he stood.

"We, we get to stay here tonight," the one in purple said. "We are not done yet!"

The others laughed in agreement, quick glances stolen among themselves.

"The other part is not done yet, either. We need to collate these *ĉampinjono*, and we wish you, Bjarni, to help. Walk with us."

Walking was not easy—the cats were back, weaving between feet, prancing with tails held high, as if they too were part of the secrets here, they too—here!

They walked to the small apron of green beside the temple—from here they looked down the mountainsides that led to the hills that led to the flat lands, the camp and town behind the temple, unseen.

"Hold your hands together, thus!"

The one in purple made a wide bowl of his hands.

Bjarni followed suit, watching as the youths suppressed smiles, the solemnity growing on every face.

"Hold as that. We shall each place *ĉampinjono* upon your hands. These are not poison!"

Bjarni smiled—yes, many of the mercs had been warned not to eat random plants from this place—but these, these he could smell already!

The virgins—or perhaps the not-virgins—crowded around, discussing in quiet voices, each taking two of the stringy fungi from their baskets and holding them above Bjarni's hands. It was hard for him not snatch one, to bury his face in one, to eat it raw. Overpowering—

"When we drop these in your hands you must squeeze your hands together, squeeze tightly, and hold them. It may be a moment, it may be ten; warm them but do not look. When they sing you may open your hands and free them. Do you understand?"

He looked from face to face, all beautiful in their own way, all serious, all eager.

He nodded.

That was the moment they rushed to him. Treasure fell into his hands, the *ĉampinjono*; that was the moment he closed his eyes and squeezed. The fungi moved within his hands, as if they lived—but of course they lived! His hands did feel warm and warmer. Sing?

He opened his eyes, seeking direction. The initiates crowded each other, repeating for each other what they'd done for him.

Now his hands felt more movement, and a vibration, heat. From within his grasped hands came a weird sighing and then a clear birdlike singsong, heard through the chanting still going on. He closed his eyes, sure he could smell the most wonderful scent in the universe—the chirping increased!

Startled, he opened his hands to find not birds but flat rust-golden flakes, vibrating, expanding until they filled his hands to overflowing.

"You may blow them away now, Bjarni. *Release the virgins!*"

He did that and saw that each of the initiates was doing the same—opening hands and releasing these . . .

As the flakes hit the carpet of green a great sighing went up. The green turned gold here and there, the spot at his feet and in front of him sighed louder. The rusty gold spread a hand width, two, three, five, the length of his body . . . the green appearing to flee before it now, the sigh getting louder until the lawn was singing and the colors rushed out into the world, rushing down mountainside at breakneck speed, the world full of the undercurrent of sound, the familiar aroma fascinating, exactly that from his dream.

The six approached then, each rubbing their hands across his, smiling together at the slight gold shimmer of spore-stuff that all seven now shared fingertip to wrist.

There was an awkward moment then, as the initiates looked one from another.

The one with the eyes looked at him, perhaps sternly.

"This ripple is Bjarni's Ripple, now and forever. By morning it will be so around the world. You have freed us to revivify the *ĉampinjono*—and we will remember always the lesson you brought! It will be said for every ripple!"

"*Release the virgins!*"

✧ Dark Secrets ✧

AN ANTHOLOGY EDITOR came to us with a request for a "Liaden and really Liaden-style" story. After some consideration, we went out to a far corner of the universe, and happened upon the star-crossed partners Kilsymthe and yo'Dira, who were about to be in oh-so-very-much trouble.

✧✧✧

THEY CAME INTO VENZI STATION trailing pirates—and riding the redline on a guaranteed delivery, which was far worse.

They were known at Venzi—a scant blessing, so Simon thought, but then, given the current situation, he'd take every small positive thrown their way. At least they'd be allowed to rig to station and maybe even dock, if they could get there.

Caerli was first board, and flying like a madwoman. You'd think it was a gift she'd been given—at least to the point of the pursuit, there being nothing the ex-Scout loved better than to push her own personal piloting envelope.

The nearness of the deadline—neither one of them appreciated that, and it definitely added an extra bit of derring-do to Caerli's flying. His partner had a fond relationship with money. She'd felt the loss of the early delivery bonus keen as if she'd lost a finger. If it came round that they lost the whole fee, it would be a strike to her heart.

Come to it, he wasn't certain in his own mind how they were going to get on, if they lost the payout for this job. Might squeak themselfs into some local work to build the ship's 'count back up to safe levels. That was if there wasn't a fine to pay. Which . . . given Venzi Senior Station Master Tey, there was bound to be a fine to pay.

If they got a fine on top of a loss, Simon thought grimly, they were grounded—plain fact. Despite the station master, Venzi wasn't the worst ring to be grounded on, first reason being there wasn't no actual *ground* . . . but not being cleared to fly—that'd put Caerli 'round the hard bend in local space before a station-day was done, and himself running to keep up.

'Course, he told himself, there wasn't no sense looking so far ahead. Things might work out on their side, yet.

Pirate had range on 'em, after all. Even granting that Caerli could wring miracles from the board, they still might get hull-shredded with no backup to hand.

And wasn't that a cheering thought.

"We *are not*," snapped Caerli yo'Dira, "going to be hull-shredded."

"Dash every hope I got all at once, why not?" Simon answered, glancing at the screens.

"I'm seeing two missiles with our names on 'em, heading dead on," he said, just giving her the info.

She didn't bother to answer. Thin fingers flew over the board; the screens grayed. Simon's gut insisted that the ship had twisted around them, even as the screens showed real space all about. The instruments reported that they'd Jumped out and in again between one breath and the next.

The pursuing missiles were seventeen seconds further behind them, that being what Caerli's playing of the Ace had bought them, but it was still going to be close—too close, and if—

The universe twisted again, and this time when the screens came back, they were crossing Venzi's shield perimeter. Not the way Jump engines were supposed to be treated, nor the way physics was supposed to be dared. Station warnaways blared across all channels. The missiles, being dumber even than the crack team of Kilsymthe and yo'Dira, didn't answer, and a few heartbeats later the defense system defended the station, just like it was made to do, and there weren't any missiles, anymore.

The pirates, no surprise, were gone like they'd never been.

"*GelVoken*," came blaring across all-band. "You will be guided into a Section Eight dock. Lock in and await escort to the station master's office."

The comm light snapped off without waiting for a reply—well. Wasn't any reason to wait for a confirm, was there?

"We were not," Caerli stated, her voice raspy and not quite steady, "hull-shredded."

"That's right," he said, soothing her, 'cause the rush of dancing between life and death pretty often left her shaky. "We didn't get hull-shredded. Good work. I'm thinking Master Tey's gonna give us a citation for that, don't you?"

Caerli all at once collapsed back into her chair.

"Of course," she said. "Whyever else would she send an escort?"

. . .✧. . .

"YOU TWO." The station master glared from Simon to Caerli and closed her eyes.

"You two, *again*."

There was that to be said for being known at a particular port or station, Simon admitted to himself: no need to waste a lot of time bringing somebody new up to speed. Station Master Tey, now, she knew exactly who they were.

And she didn't much like them, individually or as a team. Didn't like them *being* a team, for that matter, which happened in more ports than it ought, Terrans and Liadens flying together not always a popular choice with admins.

"I guess you had a good and compelling reason for endangering Venzi Station?" Tey asked, sarcasm heavy.

Like they'd deliberately gone looking for a pirate to lead into station, thought Simon with a flicker of irritation. It was understood that a station master had a natural partiality for her station, but that didn't mean the rest of the universe considered it at all interesting.

"We have a commission to Venzi Station," Caerli said softly, reasonably. "We came out of Jump at the Kelestone Light boundary. They were waiting for us, thus we immediately Jumped for Estero—"

That was the story, but she'd short-Jumped there, dropping out well before charted Jump-end to take advantage of one of those asterisked endnotes in the ven'Tura Tables, which always creeped him, and one day Caerli was gonna miss her number and they'd fall outta Jump-space into the maw of a sun, or the center of a planet. Not that he worried about such things, much.

"We were clear when we came out," Caerli continued, glossing the abort. "Thus, we Jumped for Venzi."

The aborted Jump—that's what'd cost them the early delivery. Still, can't come into a station trailing pirates. Surest way known to pilot-kind to make the station master mad at you.

Case in point.

"You're telling me they were waiting for you at Venzi entry?"

The station master frowned, not liking that notion at all. Which proved she was a good station master, despite the personal lapse of taste that failed to find Kilsymthe and yo'Dira adorable.

Caerli shook her head.

"Station Master, the Jump-point was clear. They came in on our tail when we committed to an approach."

Tey liked *that* even less. Pirates lurking along the station approaches was way past serious. Most pirates weren't organized— or numerous—enough to hold a station hostage, though it'd been tried and done. Astrid Verity's Freebooters had held the lanes at Squalme Station for three Standards before TerraTrade hired Canter's Corpsmen to eradicate the problem. Which they'd done, at the cost of near-eradication their ownselves. Mostly, though, your garden-variety pirate didn't have the skill set—or the attention span—for that kind of long-term commitment.

And, in their particular case, there was an easier culprit, right handy.

"So, your package is interesting to somebody, is it?" asked Station Master Tey. "*Real* interesting, looks like to me."

Simon's stomach fell straight into his boots. He opened his mouth, though their ongoing agreement was that Caerli talked to

Tey, whenever they could manage it. The gods of lost stars knew what he might've been about to say, but it came moot as Caerli tilted slightly forward, her whole body conveying respect.

"We have guaranteed delivery, Station Master, and the hour fast approaches."

"More fools you, then," snapped Tey.

"Station Master." Caerli adjusted her posture slightly, mixing a smidgen of humble in with the respect. "With all respect, Station Master, if we do not receive the delivery fee, we will be reduced to a cold-pad on station's budget until we may get a rescue from guild or clan."

Simon blinked. It wasn't what either of 'em did, normally, sharing out Kilsymthe and yo'Dira personal bidness with station masters and that sort of person. Nor was Caerli in the habit of admitting she was low on funds.

Then, he saw the calculation behind that startling bit of candor. Station Master Tey saw it, too, and her mouth pursed up like her beer was sour.

Delay the delivery and she'd have Kilsymthe and yo'Dira on her station to deal with every shift until they got lucky—say, forever—or somebody—could be even Tey herself—came to the snapping point and did something maybe, a little, regrettable. Let the delivery meet the deadline, and Kilsymthe and yo'Dira would go away and leave her and her station in peace. More or less.

"All right," she snarled. "Get outta my sight."

Caerli bowed gently, which only made Station Master Tey look more sour.

"Spit it out," she snapped.

"Yes. One only wonders, Station Master, if we are free to pursue our own business. We had hoped for a speedy departure."

The station master looked at her hard, and Simon could almost see her measuring how much trouble she could still cause them, without being stuck with them forever.

"Make your delivery." There was a pause while she searched the office ceiling with her eyes, and then included them together with a wave of the hand.

"You're on probation and locked to station," she said finally. A glance at both of them, made with a grimace. "It'll be a hot-pad, never fear, but locked to my orders. Admin'll move as fast as practicable, but I want the pair of you where I can find you, in the likely circumstance that questions arise."

Questions about what, she didn't say, and neither of them sought clarity. Instead, in the interest of getting paid, they bowed—and left the station master's office.

· · ·⬧· · ·

THEY MADE THE DELIVERY VENUE—Aberman's Drinkery, which sounded considerably more upscale than it was—before the wire fell on the deadline, and only that. Caerli went first, with Simon lagging a step behind. His hands, trained for detail and fine work, worried the pay tab.

One long step and he was beside her at the table's edge, packet extended on the palms of his hands, so the man sitting there, scowling, could see it plain.

The *resevio* snorted.

"Took your time," he said, making no move to take possession.

"Yessir," Simon said, "scenic route."

The other man snorted again, and snatched the packet down to the table. He put a hand on it, and glared from Simon to Caerli.

"Will there be a return packet?" Simon asked politely.

"If there is, I can hire me a courier who respects a deadline, an' neither don't take the tab off like it was his to do."

Simon's face heated, but he said nothing.

Caerli bowed slightly.

"If there is nothing more, we depart," she said, and turned on a heel. Simon followed her out into the station hall, and kept to her side as she crossed to a clumsy corner, where two storefronts didn't quite match up, leaving a thin, triangular cubby. At her nod, he slipped into the slim cover first—that was standard operations, him being taller'n her. Caerli snugged in against him, tight and maybe even distracting, save he had a burning question at the front of his mind.

"What're we doing here?"

"Waiting," she answered.

He sighed, and for lack of anything else to do, being squished flat into the corner like he was, he scanned the bit of hall in his line of sight, which included the entrance to Aberman's Drinkery.

It was a back hall, so there wasn't a lot of traffic, though the Drinkery clearly had its adherents. A couple security types strolled in, arm-in-arm, like they was reg'lars, followed pretty soon by a man in mechanic's coveralls, and two women in librarian's robes.

A repair gurney lumbered noisily down the track laid in the center of the hall; three mercs in uniform swung 'round it, walking fast, vanishing before he could read their colors.

The repair rig crawled out of sight, and the hall was empty so far as he could see for the space of four heartbeats.

Three people—two wearing formal jumpsuits, one carrying a lock-case—hove into view. The two formals entered the bar, the third, in full station security rig, shock-stick on her belt, took up position outside the door in one of the classic poses.

"They're never after the *resevio*?" Simon whispered.

"Wait," Caerli said again, which was fine for her, being in front and her backbone not like to meld with a girder.

He hadn't quite become an integral part of the station's structure before the Drinkery's door opened from within, and here came one of the security team who'd gone in prior to the jumpsuits, their own cheery *resevio* walking between him and his partner, one hand cuffed to each. The jumpsuits followed, one still carrying the lock-case. They turned right, the officer who had been guarding the hall falling in behind, passing quite near to the uncomfortable little angle where Kilsymthe and yo'Dira stood concealed. The *resevio's* expression was slack, which was probably due to the pacifier collar lying flat 'round his collarbone.

The little procession passed out of Simon's range, and he sighed out a breath. Caerli stayed where she was, pressing him even tighter into the corner, which he didn't think was possible. He didn't argue her instincts, though, having seen Caerli's instincts at work on numerous occasions in the past.

Finally, she moved, and he did, slowly separating his backbone from the wall. He joined her in the open hallway, and turned with her toward Section Eight Docking, *GelVoken*, and some small certain amount of safety.

• • •✧• • •

SIMON WENT TO THE BRIDGE, pulling out the pay tab and feeding it to the reader. There was a hesitation long enough for him to suspect that Admin was monitoring their comm, then the green light lit. Accepted and paid. He sighed in pure relief, then headed for the galley.

Caerli'd already drawn two mugs of 'mite and set them on the table. Simon slid into the chair across from her.

"*Resevio's* gonna think we led Admin to him," he said, after he'd had a swallow from his mug. "That's gonna be good for bidness."

"No," said Caerli, and: "The tab?"

"Accepted and paid," he assured her. "'Course, speaking of bidness, we pretty much got zero chance to pick up a commission to see us off Venzi. I'd hoped to bolster the treasury a bit."

"No," Caerli said again. "Master Tey wants us off her station. It would also please her if we never returned to her station."

"Ain't *her* station," Simon objected, but his heart wasn't really in it. "Unnerstan, I'm inclined to her mind in this. If I never set foot on Venzi Station again in this lifetime, that'll be fine by me. Oughta at least give it an avoid for the next couple Standards. Let her have time to cool her jets." He swallowed 'mite. "Or retire."

"That is well so far as it goes—but you are correct that it would be far better if the ship was not forced to fly empty."

Simon shook his head, stood up and carried his empty mug and hers to the washer.

He turned and leaned a hip against the edge of the counter, crossing his arms over his chest.

"Be inneresting to know what we was carrying that pirates was so eager to liberate."

"By now, Station Master Tey will surely have the contents of the packet on her desk. Perhaps she will take your call."

"I'll wait an' read about it in the newsfeed. 'Less she calls us in on account of questions having arose."

"That is of course possible," Caerli said politely, her gaze fixed on a point in Jump-space just beyond the edge of the table.

"You don't think they were after the packet," Simon said, with one of the flares of surety that never failed to get him into trouble.

She sighed, and shook her head at that little spot in the void.

"If it was the packet they were after, they would have attempted to board. They fired upon us with earnest intent. Had we not been managed to cross into Venzi's space, we risked destruction, and the packet with us."

"They didn't fire 'til last prayers," Simon pointed out. "Coulda been a case o'being certain the packet didn't get to our man at the Drinkery. They'd've rather had the packet off of us, but it'd come down to hard choices."

Caerli moved her shoulders in a fluid Liaden shrug—*yes/no/maybe*, that meant.

Simon shifted against the counter. Caerli uncertain wasn't what he liked best to see.

"It is . . . too complicated," she said slowly. "If the client needed the packet lost, and herself clearly blameless for its disappearance, there were still less expensive means of arranging the loss. Piracy is a chancy venture with far more risk of failure than success. After all . . ."

Her voice drifted off.

Simon waited until he had counted to one hundred forty-four, then prompted, "After all?"

She started, and looked up at him, her abstraction melting into one of her occasional droll looks.

"After all, we might have won through, and the packet reach the *resevio*'s hands."

Simon sighed.

"Screwed up again, have we?"

Caerli shook her head, Terran-wise.

"Had they given us the script, we might have done better for them."

Simon grinned.

"True enough."

His grin faded.

"Caerli."

"Yes."

"They knew where we was going, the pirates."

She sighed.

"So it seems."

"They were *after* us, then, and if not the packet, then—what?" he asked. "*GelVoken*?"

Caerli said nothing, and Simon felt another flicker of surety.

"*Us*?" he said quietly, which wasn't so much of a joke as could be. They'd done some things—not necessarily *wrong*, but not exactly right, neither. For the ship, they said, citing spacer laws of survival, and it'd been true enough. Still, exception could've been took. Revenge might seem to be in order. It was...possible—*just* possible—that one of their victims had sworn an Affidavit 'gainst them, and offered a bounty.

Bounty hunters, though...Simon considered. Bounty hunters were straightforward creatures, who disliked complications just as much as Caerli did. An operation that had them chase a courier through Jump-space—they hadn't, so Simon sincerely believed, ticked off anybody with the means to set a bounty *that* high.

Before they'd become a team—well, he'd traded grey; it was how he'd almost lost *GelVoken* at Tybalt. *Would've* lost 'er, if one Caerli yo'Dira hadn't come by and taken an interest in what was none o'her affair...

Caerli...Well, he didn't know all Caerli's history, but, after all this time, he knew *her*. She wasn't utterly straight—she loved money too much for that—but she was conservative in the matter of adding new enemies to her string. By listening to what she hadn't said in addition to what she had, he'd arrived at the understanding that her leaving of the Scouts hadn't been her idea, had maybe been in the way of discipline. Still, that'd been close on to ten Standards back, Kilsymthe and yo'Dira having been formed all of seven Standards ago.

"We must do a search of bounties declared and Affidavits sworn," Caerli said. "After we have rested."

There was nothing but good sense to that. They were both worn out with adrenaline and long hours at the board.

"Right," he said. "Captain declares all crew on double-downtime, starting immediately."

"Yes," said Caerli, rising. "And if the station master calls?"

Simon looked black.

"Station master calls, she can leave a message."

· · · ✧ · · ·

SIMON'S DOOR was still closed when Caerli ghosted down the hall to the galley, some few hours later. She, who had training that Simon did not, had accessed the so-called Rainbow technique to ensure a deep, healing sleep, rising refreshed and focused in under a quarter of a shift. Simon would sleep yet for several hours. Adrenaline burned through his reserves quickly; the strain of the pursuit had already exhausted him, before they came to the necessity of coping with Station Master Tey and her little intrigues.

Caerli carried a cup of tea and a protein cookie with her onto the bridge, and settled into the co-pilot's chair, as was proper. *GelVoken* was Simon's ship, after all, however much he might credit her with returning it to him. They were operating partners, but not co-owners.

Perhaps she ought not to have accepted his offer of a partnership, but she determined that she was going to reform, to leave her previous life, and start afresh. It had seemed she was owed that, were Balance the natural state of the universe—the ideal on which the whole of Liaden civilization was predicated.

She had been desperate, she thought; certainly, she had not been naive. Even then, she had known that the natural state of the universe was chaos.

Even then, she had known that one could not outrun the past, no matter how able a pilot one was.

She slowly ate her cookie, considering how best to proceed.

Easiest for all, if An Dol contacted her. Sadly, An Dol had liked to play games, and if she was tempted to think that had changed over the years, she had only to remember two missiles in the screens, dead on and gaining. It was barely possible they were live with no warhead, to prove a point. Exactly what he might have done, before, except the last time they'd met, he had sworn he was through playing games.

The last of the protein cookie went in a crunch as she considered the likelihood of that.

No, An Dol still played games.

That being so, he would expect *her* to find *him*.

Caerli sighed and drank her tea. Truly, she was in no mood for games, nor in being forced back into An Dol's service—which, belatedly, made her wonder what it was he wanted her *for*. He had ruined her as a Scout, seen her discharged without honor, so she was no use to him in the old way. She had rebelled when he would use her as a drudge—and for years, he had . . . one might say *allowed* her . . . to remain at liberty.

That he came looking for her now . . . there must be something new afoot; something for which her skill set was uniquely fitted.

Well. There was an unsettling thought.

She closed her eyes and partook of the benefits of another calming exercise.

Whatever An Dol wanted, it was imperative that he be kept away from Simon.

Simon possessed a varied set of skills and strengths, peculiar to a man who had split his young life between space and bronk-herding. His grey-trading had root in the habits of his planetside father and uncle. Simon could track a bronk on hard high plains, kill a witchbird with his bare hands, and skin a chardog with his belt knife—or so he claimed. Whether or not these particular claims were true—and she did not see why they should not be—Simon's abilities were impressive, and occasionally startling. What he did not have was a true appreciation of the subtlety a highborn rogue Liaden might employ to grasp power, or to expand it.

Which meant that her counter was inside An Dol's orbit. Little as she relished it, she would need to go onto Venzi Station, and play seek-and-be-stealthy with An Dol.

Before she allowed misdeeds and *melant'i* of the past to claim her, however, she would embrace one more opportunity to act with honor.

She leaned to the board. A series of quick finger-taps on the board opened her personal files. Another hundred faultless keystrokes and she had done all that was needful. She purged the files, sat back in her chair, and reviewed her options.

Truth, she thought; she had none.

Best, then, to get on with it.

She rose, placed her ship key on the board where Simon would be certain to see it, and left the bridge, mug in hand.

The mug, she left in the washer in the galley, before proceeding down the hall to her quarters, where she armed herself, and shrugged into her Jump-pilot's jacket.

Thus armored against An Dol's sense of play, she left *GelVoken* by the service hatch, and made certain it sealed behind her.

* * * ✧ * * *

CAERLI WAS UP BEFORE HIM, which neither exceeded his expectations, nor hurt his feelings. Simon stopped in the galley to draw a mug o'mite, and moved down to the bridge, which was where he'd find her, certain enough. A thought had come to him while he'd been drifting up toward wakefulness. Might be they could check for small cargo on the salvage and surplus side. *GelVoken* could take a mini-pod; didn't often 'cause neither him nor Caerli was a born trader, but the option was there. An' if they were just hauling to another yard of like character, there wasn't no trading involved. Flat fee and not likely to be much of it, but ship's bank was low enough he'd—

The bridge was empty.

Simon blinked, and for no reason at all his stomach clenched. So, Caerli was still resting—or resting again. No reg against that, was—

It was then that he saw the ship key in the share tray between the two boards, and the message light blinking yellow.

He stepped up to the board, accepted the message with a touch, and stood looking down at a short list of files and account codes, balances appended, which was Caerli's private money, every one of 'em bearing his name as 'counts holder. At the end of that list was a note, cold as if they'd been strangers, traveling together by chance.

Captain Kilsymthe. I resign my berth, effective immediately. Caerli yo'Dira, Pilot.

He was shivering. He noted the fact like he was reading it off the screens. His fingers moved, bringing up the call log, finding it empty.

Just gone for a ramble out on the station, then. She did that. Done it many times.

Hadn't ever before found it necessary to leave her ship key behind her, or roll every single bit of her private money over to him. Not to mention leaving resignation letters just a little bit colder'n deep space.

Simon closed his eyes.

Something bad was happening, that was what. And before it got any worse, he had to find Caerli.

. . . . ◇ . . . .

IT WAS . . . unsettling, how easily the rules of An Dol's play came back to her. He had cast her as the supplicant, the seeker—*the lesser*, to whom he would reveal himself in the fullness of time and grant her succor—it would be succor, for An Dol played with live weapons. Had she not successfully eluded his missiles, An Dol would have seen that her abilities had atrophied, and that it would have been an error to trust any longer in her survival skills.

That she had played her second Ace, ensuring the survival of *GelVoken*, Simon, and herself proved that she was still worthy of him—and now the game went to a higher level. She could expect ambushes and assassins before An Dol revealed himself to her.

Best, if she found him before he was ready to step forward. It would annoy him, and An Dol made mistakes when he was annoyed.

She paused in the shadow of a cargo hauler, surveying the dockside and considering where he might be.

One might think he could be anywhere, and Venzi Station large enough for a man who wished it, to stay hidden for years.

Only, An Dol did not wish to be hidden; he merely wished not to be found until he had made his point and had his fill of fun.

So, then, he would be near *GelVoken*'s docking, but not in

Section Eight itself. Not that An Dol wasn't bold enough to hide himself on the station master's own dockside, merely that, for this game, it would not suit his purpose.

For it must be assumed that his purpose, in part, was to remind her, forcibly, that she was his inferior. He would see her hurt before he stepped forward to rescue her from worse.

Dockside would certainly suit him, much more than the civilized, and patrolled, core rings. A certain *sort* of dockside, certainly; the station's equivalent of a lawless zone—a low port— The Ballast, so it was referred to on Venzi Station.

Assuredly, An Dol would bide his time, awaiting her in The Ballast.

• • • ⟡ • • •

SIMON PAUSED at the edge of their docking area, looking around, for a hint, a clue—for Caerli walking down-dock toward him, arms 'round the waists of a brace o'port dollies.

Woman didn't leave her life's blood to her partner because she was gonna surprise him with a party, he told himself, and looked around some more.

Caerli was cautious; she was stealthy, and if she didn't wanna be found, well—there was a one in a million chance that the likes of Simon Kilsymthe would find her. On the other hand, one in a million was still odds. He wasn't beat yet.

He found the place where she'd paused for a bit, thinking out her next move, maybe. And he found that one heel—her left—had rested in a bit of drink-smudge, so that when she took her first step onto the public way, a sticky little crescent was pressed to the decking, and there, just at the proper length for Caerli's short, determined stride, was another, and beyond that one, a third . . .

The crescents faded finally, but by then, he had a direction, sensing rather than seeing where her feet had tread, and he hurried on.

Damn it, if Caerli had it in mind to take on The Ballast by way of letting off a little steam, he surely wanted to be in on the fun.

• • • ⟡ • • •

SHE'D NULLIFIED two attackers on her way across The Ballast, and frightened off a third. It was unfortunate that the second of her two attackers had some skill as a knife-fighter. He had touched her, and though she had wrapped it, she became aware of shadows gathering in her wake as she moved toward her goal; the honest citizens of The Ballast, that was who followed her now, scenting blood, and easy prey.

She kept her attention forward, seemingly oblivious, until one of her hangers-on took the bait, and darted forward, making a feint toward her pocket.

She spun, knife out. The would-be pickpocket raised her hands and backed away.

"Peace, now, Pilot. Cain't lay blame for a fair attempt."

"Your next attempt will be your last," Caerli said, matter-of-fact, and making sure her voice carried to the others, waiting at some distance. "I'm on business and I will not be interrupted."

"Certain, Pilot; certain. Ana fine shift to ya."

The pickpocket faded back into the pack of watchers; the watchers thinned away and were, to eyes less sharp than Caerli's, gone . . .

She turned and continued on her way. Not long now, by her estimation.

· · ·✧· · ·

THE BALLAST occupied a trapezoid section of less than premium space between the backup power coils and the emergency gyros. The door you wanted from Section Eight Docking was near the narrow end of the section, which was mostly transfer slots, and grab-a-bites, and fun houses. Simon did a quick tour of the possibles, put a couple of questions, and found Caerli not at all.

Onward, then, he thought, into the deep and dangerous side. He sighed. He wished he'd known Caerli'd been in this tone o'mind; hadn't seemed to be the case when they'd parted company, each to get their own rest. 'Course, Caerli was private—and there was still the question of her putting all her most valuables under his name. Sure, The Ballast was rough, but it wasn't anything like Caerli to consider she wouldn't survive a little bit o' exercise 'mong the station-bound.

· · ·✧· · ·

IT WAS NOTHING MORE than a hunch that turned her steps toward the repair hall. At the last, it always came down to hunches, with An Dol. If she was right, she'd soon enough have confirmation.

She was right.

They came boiling out of the dark storefronts ahead of her, and more, from the cross-corridor she had just passed. Others came out of the deep shadows at the side walls. A melding, Caerli saw, as she spun lazily on one heel, taking in the fullness of them. A dozen—fifteen, perhaps—the five in spacer's motley putting themselves forward, letting her see their faces. Of them, she thought she recognized the woman whose bald head was tattooed with a world's wonder of flowers, and possibly the man with the silver sash round his ample middle; the other three spacers were strangers: the rest of the mob were Ballasters, hugging the shadows, holding weapons that at other times were slot-drivers, span-hammers, and punch-blades.

Fifteen, five trained in An Dol's particular school of survival.

It occurred to her that An Dol wanted her dead, after all; that he had drawn her to him so that he might witness her ending in person.

Well. Fifteen against one, was it? From An Dol's perspective, it might be a compliment.

The least she could do was to show her appreciation.

She kicked, diving for the floor, hitting with her left shoulder and rolling.

One of her throwing knives found a nesting place in the breast of the tattooed woman; the second in the eye of a Ballaster who had darted in, hammer raised. Her gun was in her hand, and she managed three quick shots into the crowd before she was engulfed and it was fists, and feet, and knives.

· · ·✧· · ·

IT WAS THE SHOUTING that drew him into a run. One sight of the melee and he knew it could only be Caerli in the middle of it all. There were bodies on the decking here and there—dead, or nearly so, silent acks to his notion that this was no ordinary rumble, but Caerli fighting for her life, no regard for grace.

And expecting to lose.

Never in all the long years they'd been together had he known

Caerli yo'Dira fighting to lose. Woman fought the odds like they was personal, and he'd long ago lost count of the times she won over them, by willpower and cussedness.

Simon paused on the edge of the bidness, taking stock, testing the angles, wondering if it were better to start shooting, hoping they'd scatter, or—

"Why, what have we here?" A voice murmured in his ear. "This is most unexpected."

Simon spun, gun out and right in the face of a Liaden man dressed neatly in leathers, and a wide, Terran-style grin on his face.

"It is the partner, is it not?" he said, paying so little attention to Simon's gun that he had a moment's belief that there was no gun in his hand at all.

"Simon Kilsymthe," he growled, and jerked his head toward the melee. "If you can call that off, do it."

"I can," the Liaden said, his brows pulling slightly together. "The question, I believe, is—will I? And, do you know, I think I might. For considerations."

"What considerations?"

"Surrender your gun and yourself to me, now."

"And I'd do that—why?"

"Because if you do not, Jezzi, who stands behind you, will take your gun, and I will allow nature to take its course with respect to your partner, and my former associate."

He risked a glance to the side, catching a glimpse of Caerli. She looked bad, and if she got out of this mess alive, she'd flay him for doing what he was about to do. He looked forward to that, but in the meantime, this being a Liaden he was dealing with, he had to secure both sides of the promise.

"I give you my gun, you'll call off the fight," he said.

"I will call off the fight, if you give me your gun. That is correct."

Simon reversed the gun and extended it, butt front.

A hand snaked over his shoulder and took possession. The Liaden stepped away from Simon. Simon turned to face the riot.

From his belt, the Liaden withdrew a flare gun. He pointed it to the girders above, and fired.

Sparks filled the hallway, riding an ear-punishing *boom*.

"Freeze or fall!" a voice shouted, over the echoes. "Freeze or fall!"

The sound of safeties being snapped off numerous pellet guns was almost as loud as the boom.

In the center hallway, the melee sorted itself into some kind of order. Those who could rose, some leaning on the nearest shoulder. As if obeying some unheard command, they pulled away from the battered figure, bent and kneeling. She was panting, and there was blood on her face, her left arm hanging bad.

Slowly, she raised her head, and Simon saw her recognize the Liaden with a grim resignation he'd never before seen on Caerli's face.

"So, An Dol," she called, her voice hoarse. "Will you finish it yourself?"

"That had been the original plan," the Liaden—An Dol—said, cheerfully matter-of-fact. "But someone has entered a side bet, and thus made the game more diverting. You have a reprieve, Captain yo'Dira. Your partner stakes his life for yours."

Simon saw her blink; she moved her head carefully, and her eyes met his.

"Simon," she said. "You idiot."

* * * ◇ * * *

"YOU WILL SCARCELY CREDIT IT, I know, Captain Kilsymthe," the Liaden named An Dol said chattily, "but our so-dear Captain yo'Dira had been an associate of mine."

He wanted Simon to ask him for details, but Simon was smarter than that, at least. He said nothing, and hoped he managed to look a little bored.

Before the silence stretched too long, An Dol continued, not seeming to mind Simon's lack of curiosity.

"She was a Scout, you know, working for the Archivist's office. Her duty was to gather Old Tech and either destroy it, or tag it for retrieval and destruction. Sadly, she found herself in want of cash, so she sold a piece—quite an insignificant piece—to one of my agents. Well, you know how it is with honor, do you not, Captain Kilsymthe? Once broken, never mended. It was easier the second time, and even easier the third. By the fourth sale, I don't believe she even needed the money, and by the time the Scouts discovered her breach and discharged her, finding Old Tech for me was second nature to her. She was for a time among my crew; she really is very skilled at finding the caches of old machines, and is an able technician, besides. Matters proceeded in an orderly fashion, satisfactory to all for a number of Standards.

"Then, there was a mishap—perhaps a Scout was killed. It may, in fact, have been a team of Scouts. Regrettable, but it seems Captain yo'Dira knew them, and did not agree with my necessity. She left me soon after, and I—I let her go, because I knew I could find her again, should I ever want to do so."

Caerli was sitting on a stool next to Simon. She'd been patched up, rough, with a first aid kit. She hadn't said a word since greeting her partner. If he didn't know better, he'd've said she was asleep.

Now, she raised her head.

"What do you want, An Dol? If you've decided to kill me, do it, and let Pilot Kilsymthe return to his life."

An Dol laughed.

"You have undoubtedly taken several blows to the head, so I will not berate you for stupidity. How shall I let Pilot Kilsymthe go, when he has seen me, and will shortly know of my workings? Indeed, the more I consider this new situation, the more I like it. The two of you are known on Venzi as troublemakers. It will make the scenario more believable, if both of you are in it together."

"What scenario?" asked Simon, to save Caerli the trouble.

"Why, the scenario where Captain yo'Dira smuggled a disrupter onto Venzi Station, and she and her partner, after contacting the station master with demands, and being, as I imagine they will be, rebuffed, decide to demonstrate the strength of their position. Which they will do—sadly forgetting to take themselves to a place of safety beforehand."

He paused, frowning slightly.

"What is the Terran phrase? Ah. Screwups to the last."

Simon was opening his mouth to ask what a disrupter was, but Caerli's raw voice cut him off.

"You're going to disrupt a section of this ring? Which section?"

An Dol smiled, and it came to Simon right about then that the man wasn't sane.

"Why, I think The Ballast will do nicely, don't you? We shall demonstrate, and rid Venzi of a trouble spot, all in one throw. Balance shall be maintained."

"And then?" demanded Caerli.

"Then? Why, we shall perhaps need to stage a second demonstration; we are prepared to do so. I am determined to have this station. We need a base from which to operate, and there are several like-minded teams who would join us here."

Simon's stomach was not happy. Crazy or not, An Dol had ambition. *This* pirate wasn't just going to occupy station *space*, he was going to occupy *the station*.

He looked at Caerli, hoping to see some sign that she thought An Dol's little scheme was doomed to fail.

He saw the exact opposite.

· · ·✧· · ·

IT WAS AN ELEGANT LITTLE MACHINE, Simon thought, hardly any bigger than his head, and at that seeming too small to catastrophically shut down all systems in The Ballast.

Be a bad death, too, which Simon wasn't looking forward to.

"Now," said An Dol. "Captain yo'Dira, you will call the station master and deliver your lines. In the event that you should consider an ad lib, I offer you this."

The gun was buried nose-deep in Simon's side, and An Dol was behind him. If Caerli deviated, he'd be gut-shot, which would, Simon couldn't help noting, be a quicker, cleaner death than the rest of The Ballast was going to get. Caerli being Caerli, she might well think herself entitled to make that choice for him. Which, being honest, and their places switched, he might think the same.

Caerli gave him a long, unreadable stare, then turned to the comm screen and fed in the station master's call-code.

"You!" Station Master Tey growled. "Where are you? I been trying to find you the last half-shift."

"I have been busy, Station Master. Forgive me if we have presented an inconvenience to you."

"An inconvenience? You might say that. Do you know what was in that packet you brought onto my station?"

Caerli tipped her head slightly to the left.

"An Old Tech tile rack," she said.

Tey took a hard breath.

"You knew that, and you still brought it here?"

"I did not know when we accepted the commission. I have only belatedly deduced what it must have been."

"And you're calling me because of your powers of deduction?"

"No, Station Master." Caerli took a deep breath, and Simon sighed out the one he'd been holding. "I am calling to report an emergency situation."

The phrasing, that's what gave An Dol a distraction, a hesitation in his eyes—just the smallest possible hesitation, but that was all Simon needed. He sidestepped, ducked, and swung, knocking the gun arm high, belt knife leaping to his other hand.

One strike, straight to the heart, just like he was putting down a rogue bronk.

The dying fingers tightened on the trigger; the gun discharged; and Caerli leaned into the screen, speaking rapidly.

"Station Master, Venzi has been invaded by pirates, and is in mortal danger. You must immediately dispatch security teams to all sensitive controls. You are looking for devices—possibly Old Tech, possibly of modern make—set to disrupt critical station systems. We are in The Ballast with one such Old Tech machine. I am going to attempt to defuse it. If I fail, Venzi will lose this section."

Station Master Tey was staring.

"What ship?" she asked.

"*Chandivel*, out of Liad. Station Master, time is possibly short."

"Yes. Get to work, Pilot."

The screen went blank, and Caerli spun toward the device, stepping over An Dol's dead body.

"Well done, Simon," she said briskly. "Please access The Ballast's internal comm and announce an evacuation."

· · · ◇ · · ·

WELL, there was bounty money, which came to them, and left over a tidy sum, even after the fines had been deducted—the fine for bringing Old Tech onto Venzi, and the other one, for bringing pirates.

There was salvage, too, one twelfth of the value of *Chandivel*, which plumped up the ship's account to levels last seen by Simon when he was a boy and his ma *GelVoken*'s captain.

Simon had reversed Caerli's gifts, of course, and made her a third-part owner of *GelVoken*, even before all the funds were in. Someone that invested in him and his deserved a little for herself, too.

Also, they was free to go, with an invite from Station Master Tey not to visit again soon, which they promised, best they could.

"Comes to me," Simon said, when they was on their way to Venzi Jump-point. "I never did thank you for nearly getting me gut-shot."

"Co-pilot's duty," Caerli said, which was true enough.

"You got any other dark secrets in your past likely to come 'round and make us into targets?" he asked.

There was a small silence, and he looked over to find Caerli watching her screens with a fair degree of concentration.

"In fact, I am made clanless for my indiscretions," she said, quietly. "That need not concern you. There is nothing else, except— you know, Simon, the usual sort of thing."

Right.

"Well," said Simon, "just so long as that's clear."

✧ A Visit to the Galaxy Ballroom ✧

*A **CLOSER LOOK** at the repercussions faced by pilots and Scouts who have gravitated to Surebleak in Korval's wake. We'd shown a few of those pilots close to Korval making their decisions, but here we have someone new to the dilemma of loyalty in an age of change.*

✧✧✧

SCOUT LINA YO'BINGIM inhaled, tasting the sharp, cold air, feeling a phantom flutter against her cheek. She blinked up at the gray sky, at snow—snow! She paid off the cabbie, soft flakes melting against her face.

She liked the fresh smell of the snow, but she had not come here to linger in quiet appreciation on the street. No, her purpose was to have a good time, while enthusiastically expending energy.

Scout Lina yo'Bingim, off-duty for the next twenty-four hours, turned away from the curb, and walked determinedly toward the building with the message lit up in bright pink and yellow lights:

WELCOME TO THE GALAXY BALLROOM

According to her information, she would find Scouts and pilots and mercenaries inside. She would find dancing, and gaming, and drinking, and—bowli ball.

She had specifically come for the bowli ball.

Inside the bar was everything one might expect of a rowdy emporium on a deep-space route: twenty-three kinds of beer and ale instabrewed on the premises; both top-line and bottom-tier liquor, but none in between; and wine in quantity. A modest line of smokes was also on offer, for those who sought peace.

Peace was not what Lina had come for.

Ten Standard Days ago, she had been on Liad, and looking forward with warm anticipation to Festival, at Solcintra. It had been a very difficult year; she deserved the Festival and she had intended to take full benefit from all of the festivities open to her.

Nine Standard Days ago, she had been called in to her commander's office—and given a mission.

She was to transport the Council-appointed Administrative Arbiter of Scouts, one Chola as'Barta, to Surebleak in the Daiellen Sector with "all haste." She was detached from her usual duties to this mission, with Chola as'Barta her immediate superior and supervisor.

She was assigned *Bentokoristo*, she being one of six to have trained on it—a new ship sporting a not-quite-experimental enhanced drive, and an upgraded weapons system.

That was the sole piece of good news; *Bentokoristo* was beautiful to fly. But no matter how fast the ship was, she was not fast enough to get to Surebleak and back again in time for the Festival at Solcintra, even if Lina flew like a Scout—which was not, after all, an option.

Admin as'Barta was . . . not a Scout. Lina was therefore constrained to put together a series of Jumps which would get them from Solcintra to Surebleak with a minimum of downtime, and which would not strain the resources of a man who counted five trips to the gaming salons in Liad's orbit as being an experienced space traveler. Admin as'Barta must, the commander insisted, arrive in fit condition, able to immediately embark upon his mission. The Administrator had been appointed to find what had occasioned the schism of the Scouts on Surebleak, creating the foolish situation of two Scout organizations—the Liaden Scouts, and the so-called Surebleak Scouts.

Nine Standard Days, the trip had taken, coddling Admin as'Barta.

For his part, he ignored her advice to move onto Surebleak time before they arrived, and periodically infringed on her rest shifts to try to talk the politics of the fissioning Scouts. He'd asked her why she thought the break had occurred, and her reply—"pilot's choice"—had satisfied him not at all.

And, there, he *wasn't* a Scout, he was a Council appointee, selected for his supposed "connections" in the piloting sphere. It was unlikely he'd known anyone who had died at Nev'Lorn, nor was he aware of the treachery that had led to the battle there.

"But how," he had demanded, as they waited for dinner to warm, "could a Liaden, born and bred to excellence in all things, having achieved a place in life through being a Scout—how could any such person turn their back on Liad and all that Liad offers? Liadens have the advantage of the Code and delms for guidance!"

"The same reason, Admin. A pilot flies the best course they may with the information to hand. A pilot operates in the moment, with the delm light-years away and the Code irrelevant to the case."

"Have you found the Code irrelevant on many occasions, Pilot?"

He held up a hand, forestalling a reply she had not intended to make.

"Consider your answer carefully. I will be needing an assistant after I am approved as permanent Director of Scout Operations on Surebleak. Once I have spoken to ter'Meulen, and this foolish matter has been regularized, there will be many rewarding administrative tasks available to a discerning Scout who may wish promotion and increased *melant'i*."

At that point, the chime sounded for dinner being hot and ready, and Lina had deftly avoided the topic of promotion to as'Barta's assistant. As to the "foolish matter" of the schism—if it was *Clonak ter'Meulen* with whom the Admin was to liaise, then the matter would be settled by teatime. One could, if one wished, wonder why the most devious Scout currently serving hadn't fixed the "foolish matter" already, but that was merely a waste of time. Clonak always had his reasons, though they be ever so inobvious.

At last, they had made Surebleak, and she was granted leave—twenty-four hours free of Admin as'Barta!—but not before she had been instructed as to proper behavior even on her own time.

"Do not fraternize with the locals, Scout. Beware of any attempts to make you divulge your mission. I am told that there are places where proper Scouts meet. You will confine yourself to those venues."

Repairing to the small room she had been granted, Lina called up the screen and considered her options.

Given the connection to Clan Korval and their likely inclusion of the vague and detested "locals," she decided not to attempt the Emerald Casino. The entertainments advertised at Audrey's House of Joy tempted, but again, there would likely be "locals" present.

Best Bowli Ball Court on Surebleak! the next advertisement promised, and Lina grinned. She did consider the "local" angle, but reasoned such an emporium more likely to attract Scouts than Admin's loose "locals."

Lina therefore called a cab, and very shortly she was entering the Galaxy Ballroom.

She stopped at the counter to buy a ticket—not, alas, a token for a private Festival bower, or a key to an all-night playroom—but admission as a contestant in one bout of "real bowli ball action!", which would at least warm her blood and satisfy her need for action, if not her wistful libido.

She excused her way past several inebriated mercs, one a red-haired master sergeant who briefly thought she'd come for him alone, but then he recognized the jacket and insignia and bowed a polite, "Efning, Pilot!" at her hopefully. "Come back if you need a winner!"

He'd managed to grab a table and was large enough that it was mostly hidden behind him. "I got two chairs, prezzels, a warm heart—and I just been paid!"

She gathered that he did have a warm heart—her empathy rating was just below that qualifying as a small talent—but she'd been considering a real workout, and soon.

She smiled, and her hand flung an equally polite *busy here* in his direction as she moved into the darkness, seeking that proper bowli-ball deck, with transparent walls and resilient ceiling, an excellent air system, and opponents worthy of her.

Half-dozen languages brushed past her ears; the potent scent of alcohol mixed with the additional odors of many dozens of people exuding sweat and energy in the dimness.

Ahead, she heard a distant thud, and another, a round of cheers and laughter, a high voice calling, "I'll still take two to one on the blue boots!"

Scout skill to the fore, Lina yo'Bingim slid between two hefty mercs on their sudden way to the john as yes—there!

There were four players on the deck, their time almost up. She stopped to watch the play.

One player stood out. He was doing too many dives to stay in the game much longer; in the mirrored ceiling, she could see him rolling to his feet with an awkward re-step to gain his balance. She could tell that he was hurting—it didn't take her high empathy rating or her training in body language across three cultures to see that.

She pushed forward, the better to see the clock.

Ah, that was the key. He had only seconds to hit his mark ... and finish, at least.

The ball came at him again; he kneed it roughly; it went higher than his other knee, which had likely not been his intent, but he made a good recovery by striking it with his elbow, the ball's own kinetics giving it an off-centered boost in the direction of the oldest fellow on the deck, who nonchalantly elbowed it on to a third person who—

Blangblangblang!

The bell rang; the third and fourth in the action dove for the ball together and came up laughing, bobbling the thing back and forth as it tried to spend the energy gained from the last burst of action. The spectators cheered, money changed hands, and the transparent door to the deck was opened as the next players moved forward.

The MC spoke purposefully into the mic. "Next up we have a five-group, came in together, and then ..."

The player who had overexerted himself stumbled as he left the court, was steadied briefly by another of the combatants with an over-wide grin . . . and collapsed on the spot, nose bleeding.

"I'm a medic," one of the group entering the court yelled, and one of his companions added, "Field medics, here, let us through!"

That quickly, the downed player was off the floor, and the next group of players as well. The Master of Ceremonies looked around, eyes bright, and spoke into the mic.

"Hold up your tickets, show your cards! We'll do a quick single-match to give the next group time to get back!"

Lina's arm reached high—yellow ticket, solo . . .

The MC saw her, waved her toward the deck door and pointed at another yellow—

"Come on up, Pilots! Now or never; we got group play booked 'til after midnight!"

They met on the court, her opponent near her own age, a pilot, and, she saw with pleasure, a Scout. He wore light-duty clothes, no rank marks visible, save the wings on his collar; his face was open, and a hint of a smile showing.

He would do, thought Lina, and returned the smile.

"Well, Pilot?" she challenged him. "Shall we?"

He took a moment to survey her—she saw his eyes catch on the wings adorning her own collar, before he bowed, Scout to Scout.

"Pilot, we shall!"

"All right!" the MC called. "Let's get the ball rolling! Twelve-minute match—what'll it be?" he asked, turning to them. "Liaden training rules, Scout standard rules, open court rules?"

"Scout standard?" she asked her opponent, and got a flicker of fingers in agreement.

"I am Lina," she said, stripping off her jacket and giving it into the MC's ready hand.

"Kelby," he answered, also relinquishing his jacket.

"Check the equipment, Pilots, you got thirty-three seconds."

Kelby received the ball first to check. Lina ran a quick Rainbow, for focus, and looked about her.

"Spot!" she called, pointing, as Kelby called out, "Here also!"

The MC waved; a younger with a mop rushed onto court and dealt with the spot of sweat, and the other, of blood.

"Right!" the MC shouted into his mic. "Up here we got Kelby and Lina, pickup match, twelve minutes, Scout standard!"

The crowd cheered, briefly.

The MC turned to them.

"Any private challenge; any bet between the two of you?"

Kelby looked at her, hands raised, face glowing as if he'd already been playing five minutes...

Lina bent forward, as eager as he to get the match started, whispering:

"Loser buys both breakfast?"

A grin showed in brief appreciation; she saw interest in his eyes.

He bowed, formally, accepting the challenge of an equal, and repeated the stakes to the MC, who outright laughed.

"All right, soldiers and pilots! Scouts and citizens! These two know how the game is played! Got a little private bet going—loser buys breakfast for both!"

The cheering this time was fuller, longer; the bell went *blangblangblang*; the MC slammed the bowli ball into the circle between them, and dove for the safety of the transparent observer's booth.

• • •✧• • •

THE DECK WAS BETTER than Lina had anticipated. The floor gave a firm, even footing without being loud; it was resilient rather than bouncy. She and Kelby had almost overrun each other on the launch, but the spin favored Lina. She twisted to catch and flick the busy ball high off a wall behind Kelby.

From within, the walls were slightly smoky and even ball-streaked, but her first corner fling proved they were in good condition.

The first several minutes were given to testing—the facility, the ball, each other. The ball was regulation, with a tricky underspin. Every fifth or sixth time it hit, the ball added rather than subtracted and the amplified spin could push it along the wall or out of a grasping hand.

The match being timed rather than one-and-out, they both survived learning the ball's eccentricities—Lina first when the ball tore itself from her hand to bounce down her wrist and into her chest, much to the delight of the crowd, and Kelby who'd timed a leap-and-grab perfectly, displaying both great style and interesting physique, only to have the ball hang for a half-second longer than anticipated, before flinging itself across the surface of the wall like a hurrying caterpillar.

The bell *blanged* caution at six minutes; distracted, Kelby had to do a three-hit, elbow, shoulder, palm to get the ball where he wanted it for his next throw. Between them, they'd been upping the tempo, and both still taking time to observe each other's moves and strengths.

Yes, Lina thought; he'll do *nicely*, as he turned from the recover and threw unexpectedly over his shoulder with his back to her—a good view—nearly rooting her to the spot with the trick move. She deflected the ball with her ankle before it hit the floor, portions of the betting crowd apparently doubtful that she'd managed it, and then had to dive and kick with the other foot, but this was one of *her* tricks, angling the ball high off the wall, against the ceiling, and onto another wall, the ball under-spinning, leaving Kelby little choice but to do a dive of his own and juggle the ball until he mastered the tempo sufficiently to get his footwork back in sync.

"One each, here at the center stage!" called the MC. "Get your bets in, watch the action! Winner gets a free breakfast 'cause the loser's going to pay! Thrills and chills here—Hey! Didja see that recover?"

Lina took the next throw with her left hand and did a quick launch; Kelby barely had time to catch and do the same. For several moments, they traded the ball at throat level—flick, flick, flick—eyes on the ball, the throat, the face, slowly coming closer, faster ...

Their eyes locked briefly as they trusted the motion, then they began backing away as they continued the same throw-and-catch at least a dozen more times. He changed it up: took the ball left-handed and swung back and around once before launching vertically so Lina had to move closer to catch it.

It was her turn to vary, her throw bouncing off a sidewall so she could catch it, and she did that twice again, moving toward a corner, making him retreat to stay in front of her. Then an underhanded lob toward the leg he'd just raised and . . .

A roll! He landed hard, snatched the ball, the roll bringing him very close before the ball was released, and he used the wall for the save, the angle bouncing the ball from wall to ceiling.

It was the ceiling that almost defeated her, Lina managing to just get to the bounce that extended to the other side of Kelby, who was still rising. The ball was in overdrive. Lina lunged, got a hand on it, and then tangled in Kelby's legs, the ball bouncing overhead, with the crowd roaring.

Kelby lunged from his spot in the tangle, keeping the ball up, and she did the same, on one knee, as he reached through her arms and swung to keep it higher, the continued nearness a surprise, the joint effort promising.

The crowd was cheering wildly, some counting, and the "four, three, two, one . . ." ended with the *blangblangblang* of the closing bell.

Lina smothered the ball, hand on her shoulder to keep it still while Kelby's hand was also on her shoulder, and a laughing MC made his way onto the deck . . .

"Looks like we gotta live heat here! Even score! Guess the pilots here'll hafta figure out who pays for breakfast some other way, hey?"

He reached cautiously for the ball, with Kelby and Lina not quite smoothly working it from between them into his hand.

"I tell you what," he said into the mic, working the still-merry crowd. "This ball's had quite a workout—it's still buzzing and so am I! Big cheer for Lina and Kelby!"

The crowd obliged as the MC helped the two of them finish detangling, and the mop-up crew came in to make all seemly for the next group.

"You're good," Lina told Kelby as they hurried out, jackets in hand.

He bowed on the move, hand rising to sign, *So are you.*

"I'm just in today," she said, when they paused by the door to pull on their jackets. "Please, Pilot, lead on!"

* * * ✧ * * *

LINA RETURNED TO PORT with an hour still to run on her leave. The room she had been assigned was scarcely more than a pilot's ready room: a cot, some shelves, and a screen.

Kelby's rooms were multiple and tidy, the small kitchen, small bath, and small living area with both a couch and a bed far wider than a cot.

As it came about, she had paid for breakfast at Reski's, a mere three hundred paces from his rooms—perfectly equitable, as he had paid the taxi, shared his wine and worthy snacks, and not the least, his bed.

This room—well. If she were to be on Surebleak longer than three nights, she would have to find something else.

But that was for later. For now, her condition was considerably improved.

She'd had a romp far better than an impromptu Festival meeting, and had already accumulated a favorite morning café, taxi company, and bowli ball court, not to mention having Scout Lieutenant Kelby chel'Vona Clan Nosko's personal and work comm codes in her pocket.

Came the sound of steps in the hall, followed by imperious knocking and the querulous voice of her direct superior.

"Open now, yo'Bingim!"

For a heartbeat, she considered ignoring the command, her leave with yet an hour to run.

"yo'Bingim!"

She growled softly, and stepped to the door, opening with hairbrush in one hand and in the other, her wings.

Administrator as'Barta stood in the door, a pilot Lina had never seen before behind him—she was not a Scout.

"So you returned after making your contact, did you? I had word that you were off in the wilds beyond the city last night."

Lines of anger bracketed his mouth.

Mastering her own spurt of anger, Lina bowed a brief welcome to her superior, and made no answer regarding her whereabouts while on leave.

"Should you like to come in, Administrator?"

"No, I should not, yo'Bingim. Give me the key cards for our ship—all that are in your possession."

"All," Lina repeated, unsnapping her pouch even as she turned toward her jacket, hung on the back of a chair.

"You will not need your jacket," as'Barta snapped.

"A pilot keeps keys to hand, sir. You had wanted all in my possession."

She slipped her hand into the discreet inner pocket and removed the first set of keys, and the second set from her pouch. Those she brought to the door, and held toward the Administrator, who fell back a step and waved peremptorily at the stranger pilot.

"Pilot sig'Sted receives the keys."

The pilot stepped forward to do so, her eyes averted. Lina frowned at the logo on the breast of her jacket. vee'Mastin Lines, she saw. Administrator as'Barta's vaunted "connections with the piloting sphere" included owning half of vee'Mastin Lines.

Lina's fingers tightened on the keys, and she pulled them slightly back.

"I will surrender these to a Scout," she said. "vee'Mastin Lines has no cause to hold the keys to a Scout ship."

"You will surrender those keys when and to whom I direct you!" snarled as'Barta. "Give them to her!"

"No," said Lina, and put both sets of keys into her pouch.

"Insubordination! I will see you stripped of rank, and license."

"I will surrender the keys of a Scout ship to a Scout," Lina returned. "You have hundreds of Scouts at your beck, Administrator. Call one here."

He moved, suddenly, surprisingly, kicking at her knee. She jumped back, avoiding the clumsy blow—and the door closed with a snap that meant the outside lock had been engaged.

Lina crossed the room to her screen, and called the duty desk.

"This is Lina yo'Bingim. I need to schedule an appointment with the base commander, immediately," she said.

There was a pause.

"Lina yo'Bingim, you are already on the commander's hearing list," the duty desk officer said. "Administrative Arbiter of Scouts as'Barta has filed a complaint, and placed your license under lock. The hearing is scheduled in two hours. You will be escorted to the meeting room."

. . . ✧ . . .

ESCORT had been two Scout security officers. They had checked her weapon, locked it, and allowed her to return it to its place in her jacket. Ship keys were not mentioned; the first set was in her jacket, the second set in her pouch—standard procedure. Lina walked between her escorts calmly, eager to lay the situation out before a Scout, who knew the regs, and who would understand her objection to turning over the keys to a Scout ship to a passenger line pilot.

Her escort triggered the release on a door, and she walked into the conference room between them.

Before her was a conference table. Behind the conference table was Admin as'Barta, a hard-faced Scout captain—and the passenger line pilot to whom she had refused to give *Bentokoristo*'s keys.

There were no chairs on her side of the table.

Lina drew a hard breath.

"Why is there a civilian at this Scout hearing?" she asked.

"It is not your place to ask questions here," snapped Admin as'Barta.

The Scout captain frowned.

"I will answer. It is a reasonable question of protocol, and an unusual situation."

He inclined his head slightly.

"Pilot sig'Sted is Administrator as'Barta's advising pilot. As the difficulties the Administrator has come to solve are Scout-based, it is considered best that the Administrator's team be outside of the Scout hierarchy."

"The disciplinary hearing is now called to order," Admin said briefly. "This procedure is being recorded and will become part of your permanent records."

He glanced down at his tablet and began speaking in her direction without making eye contact. As he spoke, he ran his fingers down the tablet, apparently checking tick-boxes as he hit each point.

"Last evening I had dinner with Pilot sig'Sted, a mature pilot well known to me. Her *melant'i* is without stain, and I trust her implicitly in all matters of piloting."

Pilot sig'Sted, seated next to him, had the grace to look embarrassed.

Lina put her hands behind her back, and broadened her stance, waiting.

"I described to Pilot sig'Sted the irregular and exhausting journey produced by Scout yo'Bingim on my behalf. Pilot sig'Sted gave it as her professional opinion that the pilot in charge had been hasty and foolhardy, had made questionable and potentially dangerous choices of route, and subjected me to unnecessary hardship."

He paused to glance up, but did not meet Lina's eyes.

"Based on this information, I immediately moved to have Scout yo'Bingim's license revoked until she has taken remedial piloting classes and recertifies at every level."

Lina looked at the Scout Captain.

He avoided her eyes.

"I am," she said, "a Scout pilot. That is the equivalent of a *master pilot*. I—"

"You do yourself no good by being uncooperative," Admin as'Barta stated.

The Scout Captain said nothing.

Lina bit her lip.

"In addition to her piloting errors, and willful disrespect for my person, my *melant'i*, and my office, it has become clear that Lina yo'Bingim is an agent of the false Scouts. No sooner had we landed, she filed for leave, and met with an agent attached to the command structure of the very group which I am here to correct and bring back into alignment with the proper Liaden Scouts.

"In short, Lina yo'Bingim is working against my office, my mission, and myself. She is working to undermine and destroy the Liaden Scouts! Revoking her license to fly scarcely begins to address the problem. She must be struck from the lists of Liaden Scouts. In this, she will finally serve my office and my mission, by standing as an example of what happens to those who work against the proper order and the Code."

"Scout Captain—" Lina began.

"Be silent," Admin as'Barta snapped.

She glared at him, felt her escort shift closer from the sides, and closed her eyes briefly, accessing the rainbow, for calmness.

"You may retain your place in the Scouts, though at a much reduced rank," Admin as'Barta said, then. "Tell me what information you shared with this agent of the schismatic officer ter'Meulen."

She took a breath.

"He named his ship; I named mine. We shared our class years and first flight dates. We counted the bruises we had from the bowli ball match we had played, and laughed because there, too, we had tied. I did not tell him the name of my superior; he did not tell me the name of his, though ter'Meulen—"

She looked again to the Scout Captain, who did not meet her eye.

"ter'Meulen," she continued, facing the Admin again, "was head of pilot security for the Scouts—for the *Liaden* Scouts—for decades. He is no enemy of yours. If it is *ter'Meulen* who has authored this breach, then you must look for the fault in our own ranks."

Admin as'Barta sat back, satisfied. He turned to the Scout Captain.

"You hear her. She must be cast out."

"Yes," the Scout Captain said. "I hear her. The paperwork will be completed this afternoon."

"Captain," Lina said urgently. "The keys to the Scout ship I piloted here—*Bentokoristo*. There are only six trained to fly her..."

"That is no longer your concern, Lina yo'Bingim," he told her, and held out his hand.

"The keys, if you please."

Relief almost undid her. At least, in this, he would be proper. The Scout ship would be relinquished to a Scout.

She reached into her jacket, into her pouch, approached the table and placed the keys in his hand.

"Escort, take Lina yo'Bingim to her quarters. Hold yourselves ready to escort her out of this facility, once the paperwork is complete. Dismissed."

* * * ✧ * * *

SHE WAS A SCOUT; everything she needed or wanted was in her jacket. Her license . . . she drew it out, slid it into the slot—and caught it when it was forcibly spat out—rejected.

Thoughtfully, she considered Admin as'Barta, the Council of Clans, and the assumptions surrounding this mission to reunite the Scouts.

She then considered Clonak ter'Meulen, whom she had known, slightly. A Scout sublime, Clonak ter'Meulen, and one who cared for his pilots above all other things.

What could have happened, to make Clonak ter'Meulen break away from the Scouts he had loved?

The door to her cubicle opened. Her escort said, "It is time."

They handed her a stick—her records, they said. They walked her to the door, and outside, into the port. They left her standing on cold 'crete at the edge of the street, and went back inside.

Lina yo'Bingim inhaled sharply, tasting the sharp, cold air, feeling the phantom flutter of a snowflake against her cheek.

Across the way, she saw the bright green of a call-box. She crossed to it, fingering the slip of paper with Kelby chel'Vona's numbers on it out of her belt.

He answered at once, sounding pleased to hear from her so soon.

"I find we have an acquaintance in common," she said, after they had been pleased with each other. "Clonak ter'Meulen."

"Yes, of course. Everyone knows Clonak, so I've always heard it."

"I, too," she said. "He never let a pilot reside in peril. I wonder if you could bring me to him?"

"Certainly, but—why?"

"One of the things I recall Clonak saying—his fondness for Terran quotations, you know. He had used to quite often say that *It's better to be part of the solution than part of the problem*.

"I want to talk to him about becoming part of the solution."

✧ The Gate That Locks the Tree ✧
A Minor Melant'i Play for Snow Season

THIS STORY allows us glimpses of ongoing themes that have been hard to put into the main thread of the current novel arc. Korval's tree, the cats Korval brought with them, and what's going on "back home" on Liad all called out to us; and of course the taxi driver has been offstage for far too long.

✧ ✧ ✧ ✧

DRAMATIS PERSONAE
Being the List of Players

Vertu Dysan, a taxi driver
Cheever McFarland, Boss Conrad's right hand man
The Tree, a multiple exile
Tommy, a taxi driver
Jemmie, a co-owner
Vertu dea'San, former Delm of Wylan
Yulie Shaper, a farmer
Mary, his spouse
Anna, a kid
Rascal, her dog

Toragin del'Pemridj, a woman who believes in promises
blue-and-red driver, a cabbie who has run through his luck
Chelada, a mother
Talizea, a friend of cats
Miri, her mother
Val Con, her father
Jeeves, a butler
Boss Gotta, a metaphor
Nelirikk, a soldier
Jarome, a cabbie revealed

ACT ONE
Scene One

In the House of the Taxi Driver
Enter Vertu and Cheever

VERTU DYSAN rose with her lover, both too aware of the coming day's necessities.

Schedules for the week upcoming did not favor long morning comfort, and the wan bluish light of the port was still brighter than the meek dawning of the day-star. An extra hug at the door then, through his bulky coat.

"I'll bring dinner," Cheever said. "No sense going out in the snow."

"More snow?" Vertu said, stepping back and looking up at him. He grinned.

"Weatherman says there's a squall line moving in." He shrugged his big shoulders. "Hey, it's Surebleak *and* it's winter. Snow's on the menu."

"I will have something warmer than snow for my late meal, please."

"I'll see what I can do. You drive careful, 'kay?"

It was what he said at every parting—*drive careful*—as if she, the taxi driver, was the one who walked in peril.

Still, it warmed her, her Terran lover's tenderness for her, and she smiled, reaching high on her toes to touch his cheek.

"I will be careful. You be careful, also."

"Where's the fun in that?"—again, the usual answer, the half grin, the serious eyes.

And then he was gone, the door opening and closing so quickly barely a wisp of cold air snuck into the little hallway.

Vertu glanced out the side window, to see him, striding away toward the port. Cheever McFarland, Boss Conrad's Right Hand, had a breakfast meeting waiting on him at the Emerald Casino.

She turned away from the window. Her ride was due in half an hour. Time enough to drink her coffee—a taste acquired from Cheever, like she had acquired Surebleak's particular vernacular from Jemmie, and the daily round of her fares.

Cup in hand, she crossed the planned front room library, a challenge still unfilled. The house would grow in time, that she knew, and soon she would unshutter the windows, let light in, and add bookcases and storage—if this was to be her home, she would make it so.

Up the stairs she went, to the bedroom, and pulled on her warmest sweater, with its snow-shedding properties, and walked to the window, sipping from her cup.

She would eat breakfast at Flourpower slightly later, and as the day brightened she saw that Korval's Tree stood a little short against the still perceptible stars...perhaps they would catch that predicted-but-not-yet-arrived squall line, after all.

The bedroom was on the third level of a skinny building in the Hearstrings turf—*her* house, where she had rented a room during her first days of exile, and which she had only recently purchased. The window gave a clear view of the Port Road, and the hill it climbed out of the city. Vertu sipped her coffee and wondered if she was the only one in the city who told the mood of the world by the color the giant at the crest of that long hill showed to first light, and the height. It was more than just height, though—some days the Tree looked fuller, bushier, more open.

Maybe bad weather weighed on the branches. Maybe the Tree

purposefully shielded those under it, showing more leaf or less, leaf top or leaf bottom as required. Perhaps she should ask Cheever some mythical morning when neither of them was pressed for time.

The upstairs echoed a little now as she hurried toward and down the stairs, for the view of the Tree had nearly hypnotized her, as it sometimes did, as if the Tree felt her gaze and returned it. And why should the Tree not recognize her, as she it? In her fancy, it did, two exiles, making their ways on a strange new world. Why should they not acknowledge each other? For her side, she'd known it the whole of her life, first on Liad where she'd grown up and become Vertu dea'San, Delm of Clan Wylan, or Wylan Herself.

The name on the contract for the purchase of the house, *that* was Vertu Dysan.

She did not bow to Liad anymore; the Tree and its people were here, and she had long since decided that if any one of Clan Wylan wished to speak to her, they could come here, to Surebleak, and meet with Surebleak Port's new Business of the Year co-owner.

It was a quiet house she had, certainly not a rival to Clan Wylan—she'd considered and rejected the local *advertise for a roommate* habit as not being her choice. The house *could* use more company at times—again, there was an echo when she hit the bottom of the stairs in her traction boots—but even with Cheever's potential agreement she doubted she was ready yet to add a child to this place, hollow as it could sometimes be.

Sealing the coat as she hit the entry hall, she glanced to the vidscreen, unsurprised to find the local walks devoid of pedestrians; only a glimmer of vehicle lights, and a blue glow coming down a side street.

Vertu paused, checking her coat seals, glaring into the sky, and its promise of messy driving. There was noise behind the clouds— a rumble she thought wasn't thunder but the latest passenger arrival that meant her afternoon was likely to be busy, snow or rain.

She closed the door behind her as Tommy turned the corner, prompt as always on the one wake-the-day shift he covered every ten days. It was good to have commonplace comforts, and she smiled as he vacated the driver's seat, bowing her in.

Scene Two

In Vertu's Taxicab
Enter Yulie, Mary, Anna, Rascal

VERTU'S MORNING SHIFT had been busy, what with the increased mercenary traffic onworld, and much of it carried about town in their cabs—Jemmie's having Tommy Lee as just one of their merc connections, and Vertu herself another—they would need more cars and drivers soon if the merc presence was going to continue increasing. Jemmie had taken to leasing such spare local vehicles as there were, at day rate, but it hadn't taken long for a half dozen more cab services to start up, most of them not much more than a car that sort of moved and an idea that there was money to be made.

Twice before lunch, Vertu had seen fare jumpers at work; that, with the weather, infusing the day with more tension than necessary. At times like these, it was good to see the Tree waving in a breeze, but not much chance of that today. She reported the fare jumps to Jemmie's office via com-link when it worked, but the low-power system the Scouts had introduced them to was still highly variable—possibly because it was built with "borrowed" end-of-life equipment, possibly because of Surebleak's own odd planetary makeup.

The problem with Surebleak, she thought, was that it lacked taxi guilds, and even traffic laws. The result was unsafe cars, and incompetent drivers, with no sense of . . . Balance. Denying so Liaden a concept still left the problem of drivers like the ones who drove the garishly red-and-blue-striped cars—she thought there were two of them, both usually hatless, a stupidity in a Surebleak winter. One of them had several times in the last few days followed her, and tried to arrive before she did at groups standing near the road. A guild, an association, a club—*something* would need to be done. She shook her head, Terran-style then—perhaps she should bring it to one of the Road Bosses. Well . . . maybe she should talk to Jemmie first.

Vertu's breakfast at Flourpower was a distant memory and the carry-away grab-lunch was hours gone by the time she stopped at

Reski's to drop off a pair of fares and take on more coffee. The house specialty was a decent bean-based scrapple handwich if she had time to order one!—and not being waved down immediately for another ride, she took an actual break, calling in as off-duty despite the com unit's buzz, side-parking the cab a half block away, and stretching her legs while she leaned into the sudden fine snowmizzle that seemed incongruous coming from clouds *that* dark.

Well, they promised *some*thing, those clouds, and, as warm as it was at the moment, the mizzle might actually turn to rain. Her fares had all been concerned about the weather, since it had been cold enough lately that rain might slick into ice on the slightest excuse. On Liad, of course, rain had always meant an uptick in her business, but here? Here she was too straight out to have rain be anything more than a bother. Ice would be another matter entire.

The precipitation hid the Tree on the hill from sight; even so, she *felt* its location, just like she had when she'd been driving her taxi in Solcintra, port and city. The Tree was a magnet; part of her landscape, visible or hidden.

Reski's was packed with hungry people, but she got noticed quick and probably ahead of others—with a "Jemmie's Taxi" hat on her head she was recognized as much as a public service as a business—and she was glad not to be trying to pack herself into the grid of crowded tables. The cab had more room than one of Reski's tables, so long as she didn't fill it with passengers.

She was back to the taxi in less than a half hour, carrying two full coffee cups and a triple handwich pack. There were two people waiting near the cab, tucked into the slight protection of a leather shop's overhanging sill, a number of bags at their feet. There was a dog nearby, too, and a youth. Vertu sighed. This was one of the more difficult parts of her job, sorting out who got to go first and who had to be left behind.

She hurried past, opened the cab, and showed the "On Break" card. One of those in the doorway—wearing an orange cap—nodded, and leaned in closer under the overhang.

Vertu sealed the door, and grabbed half a handwich. She played music over the speaker while she ate, and drank some coffee.

She closed her eyes, and counted to twelve twelve times.

Opening her eyes, she turned the "On Break" card face down on the dashboard, brushing crumbs to the road as she opened.

The kid and the dog circled in from their explorations down the walk while the two in the doorway stepped out, each grabbing a couple of bags. The one in the orange hat, Vertu saw, was Yulie Shaper, and his coat looked like it might be new. She'd seen him not long ago, having gone as Cheever's guest to Lady yo'Lanna's arrival reception, and he'd been wearing what looked like new there, too. Good on him, as they said here, things must be picking up!

"Where do we go?" Vertu asked. "Who arrived first?"

Yulie laughed, and it was a good laugh for someone with a reputation of being distant if not entirely elsewhere most of the time.

"All got here at once, that's how it is, since we come down together we're all going to the same place."

Now Vertu recognized the dog and the kid—Anna, that was the kid, connected to Boss Nova's place—she didn't remember the dog's name but the kid was hardly around without it, and the woman with them someone else she'd seen around, always walking at her own pace and not usually a cab user that Vertu knew of. Yes. She had been at the reception, too; and the source of some merriment, too. Her name, Vertu thought, was Mary—another one of the folks who had been living quietly come suddenly to light. Odd that it took an influx of strangers from outworld to make the locals stand forward.

"All together, then," she said with what she hoped was an encompassing nod.

"Load up."

This they did with swift efficiency. Vertu, seeing all in hand, slid into her seat, and keyed the heater for more warm air.

"Where do we go?" she asked again, unlocking the doors all around.

The girl jumped into the front seat, calling out.

"Rascal, here!"

But the dog had run ahead of the cab, ears perked, sniffing, looking—up.

"Haysum!"

That was Yulie, looking in the same direction as Rascal, where barely a block away the world looked like it was being closed behind a sudden curtain of heavy snow. The snow engulfed them with an audible susurration, the flakes as big as tea saucers.

The adults got into the back seat, tucking themselves around the bags, wiping snow from faces and gloves.

"Rascal!"

The dog turned and jumped through the door into the girl's lap. The door sealed, and the girl cuddled the dog—whether for the dog or herself was difficult to tell, Vertu thought, upping the heat again.

"We're going to my place—our place," said Yulie Shaper. "All the way up Undertree Hill—Port Road's your best route, in this. Just go left right before you get to the gate that locks the Tree in. . . ."

Vertu tapped on the steering wheel for several moments, considering the route, and reflecting on the phrase, "the gate that locks the Tree . . . " before she put the cab into driving mode.

"Do you think," she said, as she waited for a truck to pass them slowly before she pulled out into traffic, "that the Tree minds being locked in? What of the Road Bosses? I never thought about it like that before."

Beside her Anna pursed her lips in consideration, and from the back a couple of noncommittal hems and haws happened.

Yulie finally ventured a word. . . .

"It was me said it, and I never really thought about it that way, either, truthtelled. It's not like the Bosses or the Tree is *really* locked in, at least not for long; I figure they're all where they wanna be, don't you? I mean, I like where I growed up and I'm still there, and that's kind of what they have, isn't it, give or take a thousand light-years or so. But the Bosses and the Tree, they got things they hafta do to keep the world right. . . ."

Yulie let his pensive consideration stall while Vertu avoided one of the striped taxis that was barely making headway in the opposite direction. The windscreen on that one was showing an ice buildup already, making Vertu pleased that she and Jemmie agreed on maintenance rules and schedules. Difficult to drive when the windscreen was full of snow.

They drove in silence, Rascal's tail ticking a happy rhythm on Anna's coat sleeve, accepting the belly scritches the girl lavished while peering through their own spotless windscreen, the cones of oncoming lights and the sudden looming of passing cars bringing ears to alert.

"A traveler, your dog," Vertu offered, "likes to be on point!"

Anna nodded, scritched the top of the dog's muzzle teasingly.

"Also, lazy a little, maybe. Rascal does not often get to travel this way, and being in front is a treat for both of us—right, Rascal?"

For her trouble Anna got her chin licked and some dog-breathy ear sniffs as Vertu slowed the vehicle to a walking pace behind several wind-whipped pedestrians leaning into the snow as they crossed the street at an oblique angle.

Snow muffled the wind just as it muffled the road noise, a gritty squealing vibration permeating the car as Vertu ducked their path close to the sidewalk and behind the walkers. The windshield's air jets weren't sufficient to the task now so she activated the wipers in the gloom. Dusk was still over an hour away but this—this would take concentration.

"Hush, Rascal," Anna said then, low and serious. "We all need to listen and watch in case there's a problem going up the hill. Watch hard. Might be a problem on the hill. You too, Mary, watch hard!"

A flutter of concern tightened Vertu's gut now, an edge of nerves down the back of her neck, a touch of extra speed to her eye motions. She didn't often feel these things, but she had learned to pay attention to them, despite that her delm had put her youthful mention of such tensions aside with a terse, *You're no Healer, girl*.

"Quiet," the girl whispered, and her head moved . . . ah, looking for the driver info on the dashboard. . . .

"Oh, no,—Miss Vertu—not you, you're watching good already. And Yulie sees a lot more than anyone knows, 'cept maybe Mary. But we should *all* pay attention, in weather like this."

"Anna?"

That was Mary, and clearly the question had levels within levels.

Anna glanced over her shoulder, shrugged, made a quick hand motion, said a word that slid past Vertu's ears, and continued.

"Probably nothing for us. For us we have Miss Vertu, who is a very good driver. But this snow, it—the situation is unsettled."

The girl had the right of it; the situation was unsettled. Vertu got them to the outskirts at Port Edge and then into the jumble of traffic at Grady's Crossroads, a jumble made harder to sort by the number of pedestrians and their uniform unwillingness to give way before anything on wheels. They waited at one point for five minutes until Yulie had her pull over while he and Mary enlisted as volunteers, joining half a dozen others. They finally managed to untangle a three-car confusion where one car had gotten wedged between two others.

Vertu restarted the clock when her passengers returned to her, brushing snow off each other, and laughing.

At last, they were through the intersection and on the Port Road itself, headed out of town, and up the hill.

Scene Three

In Vertu's Taxicab, on the Port Road. Outside, a Blizzard.

PROGRESS WAS SLOW; Jemmie called on the radio to make sure the car was in motion, at least, and Vertu's confirmation of a fare in progress to a known destination was welcome.

"You call in when you get to the top, hear me? We got folks wanting a ride, but I'm thinking we're all best just staying put. This is a wallop of a storm all of a sudden; couple the old-timers say we'll be lucky to move anything much on the road tomorrow, much less tonight. So you *call me*, Vertu, before you head back down. Promise."

"I promise," Vertu said mildly, as if Jemmie wasn't younger than her youngest daughter.

"That's all right, then. You drive careful."

Vertu had already driven through a Surebleak winter, and seen two storms that the locals had grudgingly awarded the accolade *bad 'un*. This storm, though, this was, in Vertu's opinion, shaping up to be something other than a mere *bad 'un*. This one was *a worrier*.

She got them through a small intersection where two cars had been pushed to the side, quiescent. Periodically the vibration transmitted from the road to the taxi changed . . . oddly.

"Graupel," said Yulie, "in layers with some sleet and then with fling-snow. Slick as"—and here he paused, considering, perhaps, the ears of the girl, before continuing—"slick like skin ice from a rain it can be. We're good, though; our Miss Vertu's got us on course, all good."

About that, Miss Vertu herself was less confident—and in the next moment realized what exactly was wrong with the light approaching them.

"Wrong side!" Yulie said sharply.

Vertu slowed the cab to a stop while the other vehicle—a small panel truck—continued down what must have been the gravel edge of the wrong side of the road at a breathtakingly slow pace.

"Flo's Grocery Wagon?" Mary read the side of the truck as it passed. "They're city-based. What is it doing up here?"

"Musta been up to Lady yo'Lanna's place!" said Yulie. "Geez, ain't got no sense, city or else, 'noring oncoming traffic!"

By now dusk had edged into dark, with other traffic nonexistent. There were tracks in the road, but the snow and breeze were working together to fill them in, leaving vague ruts. Vertu wondered about the van's driver, seeing several places where it appeared the ruts wandered off the road entirely, but there—parallel ruts—must have been other traffic going one way or another.

Questioned, Vertu would have told anyone that she knew the Port Road well, but in the dark, with the snow blowing it wasn't clear to her exactly where she was, and with two major turns—surely she couldn't have negotiated those without knowing it!—she missed the Tree's presence as a guide and found herself peering into the snow's star field as if—

Hah! Likely that was. . . .

But she heard Anna give an intake of breath and then Yulie, who'd been leaning comfortably against Mary in the back, sat up straighter.

"Yanno," he said, "sometimes we get weather a little different on top the hill than at the bottom; I think we might not have that slick ice under us now—haven't heard that grind! We're not too far away from that turn at Chan's Pond, I'm thinking. See, there's the pointer rock for that slick twisty part—kinda looks different under snow, though, if you don't know it."

Vertu *didn't* know it, and barely made out a lump three times the size of the car lurking just by the right edge of the road. She tried to imagine the thing dry and unshrouded by snow, sunlit on an early fall day and—failed.

The snow and gathered darkness had her driving by instinct now. She recalled that there were more than a few twisty parts to the road, and if she remembered correctly, this part was twistier but not as steep and angled as the next, *very sharp*, turn.

Rascal mumbled a complaint on the seat next to her and Anna shifted him so that his shoulder leaned more against the side window. He peered at—and possibly through—it, vague trails of smoke rising from his nostrils.

Anna spoke then; another word again that Vertu missed hearing. Yulie didn't catch it either, and he said so.

"Anna, not thinking I got that clear . . . "

She looked over her shoulder briefly, then at Vertu.

"It was for Rascal. He's got fidgets and I asked him to stay still. I think he's been seeing the wavy tracks off on this side and he's worried."

"Might be. Can't see 'em so good, myself. You watch hard, then. Tell Rascal we're not letting a little snow get in the way of giving him his dinner!"

The girl whispered something to the dog; his fidgets grew quieter.

Vertu shrugged tension out of her shoulders. She'd been unconsciously using those very same tracks as a guide while avoiding them because they affected traction and also because they tended, in her estimation, to hug the edge far too closely.

Briefly, Vertu was sure she knew exactly where they were. The slow motion exaggerated the twists, and she knew this as one of the spots she enjoyed driving a little harder into on dry days, without snow. The acceleration here could be exhilarating, the car willing to grab at the road and allow the driver to fling it this way and that.

She smiled. *That* was the kind of driving she was required to deplore in her underlings, of course—officially; but there, a useful kind of training it was sometimes to know how the car might act at the edge of control.

Vertu allowed the taxi to slow now, the tracks before her an odd jumble.

"He's driving scared," Anna said with the kind of forcefulness that brooked no doubt. "See? He ran off the side of the road. The—"

She stopped as if she'd caught herself being a Seer. On Liad, Vertu had twice driven those in the throes of their Sight—and the girl sounded as if she might be on that route.

Hugging Rascal, Anna turned to speak to her.

"Liad does not have such weather?"

Vertu answered, wondering why this question *now*.

"There are parts of Liad that have snow in some seasons, but not so much—and in any wise, no such storms as we have here."

She might have said more, but she was startled into silence, as the scene beyond the windscreen grew momentarily bright as early dawn, the blowing snow drifting across their vision and sharing the light an eerie moment or two before thunder bounced about the cab. Rascal whined, the humans all gasped. The light lessened, came back twice, both times with the shock of nearby thunder, before the storm deepened and there was the sound of hail bouncing off the cab's roof and windshield before their world was again the small tunnel of light they carried with them.

"There's a problem," Anna said abruptly. "She's out of patience. They're all scared and she's ready!"

Rascal whined.

Mary asked, "Who, Anna? Where?"

Anna shrugged, the dog pushing his head against her shoulder.

"Where—ahead of us. I don't know who, but she is ahead of us—up!"

ACT TWO
Scene One

Beset in the Belly of the Storm
Enter Toragin, the blue-and-red driver, Chelada

"UNDERSTANDING the theory is not the same as understanding the fact."

The delm had uttered those words to the nadelm. The nadelm had discoursed upon them at length several times afterwards to *his* mother—the delm's sister, who had also been present—and several times more to the rest of the household, including the lesser children of his siblings, of which large group Toragin del'Pemridj was the least, in terms of both age and in the regard of the nadelm.

Toragin had herself been present when those words were uttered and had been permitted a second drink of the morning wine on that occasion, it having been the morning when the sky grew dark, the valley echoed and rumbled, the horizon changed—and, well, *every*thing had changed. Toragin was here, now, on Surebleak because—precisely because—of that morning when Clan Korval, and, more importantly, Clan Korval's Tree—had vanished from Liad.

The theory, back then, was simply that a space vehicle would approach Liad's surface and remove Korval's house. Of the family, perhaps the delm's sister, Toragin's grandmother, had the best idea of what that had *meant*, she having spent ten Standards as an orbital mining engineer before having been ordered home to produce multiple heirs for multiple contract husbands. Her skills running to administration, once home she'd not escaped into space again, nor had she found it easy to reenter society. So, she had spent more time in the company of cats than of people, achieving a certain serenity for herself and her like-minded assistants amidst the bustle and intrigues of an ambitious clan.

Being the closest clan house but one to Korval's Valley had always meant that a peculiar peace informed Lazmeln's clan house, for the city was kept at a distance by geography and the agreements made with the first captains. Then, with the changes, those ancient agreements fell. Tourists, spies, and opportunists traveled the local roads—serenity was broken for Clan Lazmeln's in-house overseer as well as for the delm.

Theory now—

But, no. This was *not* theory. This was reality. Toragin was hungry, colder than she'd ever been in her life, and more afraid than she would allow herself to know, much less Chelada.

Chelada the Determined, Toragin thought, but this time, in this reality, she did not smile. Chelada's determination had brought them here.

Chelada's determination might see them die here.

That, too, was reality—or, rather, a possible reality, looming much too close.

And in this reality that was not theory, Toragin considered that as afraid—terrified!—as she had been when Korval's clan house and Tree were scooped up from Liad and taken away, this was the first time that her life, and Chelada's, was actually in danger. To have come this far with so little trouble beyond that of convincing Lazmeln Herself that this journey was necessary to honor and to Lazmeln's continued peace—to have come so far, and so quickly, only to meet bleak disaster, lost in the snow within grasp of the goal!

Who could have imagined a world this wild? A world in which anti-collision devices were turned *off* on vehicles during a storm because the snow and ice registered as threat; a world where vehicles might ignore the road entire, or force each other off-route despite lights and flashing markers?

Their driver, Toragin thought, had done well to avoid the collision. Going over the event in her mind she again saw the lights loom out of the snow, saw those lights continuing to aim at them, as if they were a target. She felt the cab slide, grab, and turn away, handsbreadths separating them from the small road which was their proper route, and then on. She recalled the driver saying, "Best if we keep momentum here; I think this road comes back into Port Road a little way ahead, and we got good gravel!"

"We are going the wrong way!" she protested. "We are going *away* from the Tree!"

"All roads here gotta aim up that way," the driver countered. "The side roads connect back into the Port Road."

This sounded as if he knew his territory and Toragin was prepared to allow herself to be calmed, until he added, not quite under his breath:

"Pretty sure so, anyhoots."

It was too late by then, and Toragin sat in the front seat, Chelada snug in the back, her conveyance against a heat vent. They both sat, and allowed the driver to do his work, while they felt the presence of the Tree, not ahead of them anymore, but to the right of the cab's slippery route. Too far to the right.

Still, the driver had been doing well in keeping his vehicle on the snow-covered road. As the route began to turn, slowly, back to the right, Toragin had begun to relax in truth, thinking that it could not be so far, now—

Lightning ripped through the grey curtains of snow, startling, disorienting even before the thunder boomed.

The driver started, jerking the wheel in his astonishment. The tires were forced off of the safe gravel onto solid ice.

The taxi spun around, twice, the vaunted momentum giving way to a fading slide.

The slide was slow, nearly silent, ending in a lurch, and a crunch as the road edge turned to leafed-over mud covered by ice.

"Sleet! Crud! Graupel and sludge!"

The driver hit the dashboard with a mittened fist.

Using the shock webbing, Toragin dragged herself more or less upright, and stared into the back seat.

"Chelada!"

There came a *huff* from the blanket-covered resting place, and a touch along her inner senses, as if a pink tongue had licked her nose. Toragin relaxed. Chelada was not pleased—well, and who might blame her?—but she had not been hurt.

"Taxis!" the driver was continuing his rant. "Easy money, she says. How tough can it be to drive around all day?"

Toragin took a deep breath, and closed her eyes. She could feel the Tree, up the hill, still too far to the right. How far, she wondered? Could she walk to it from here? More to the point, could she walk to the Tree in the teeth of a lightning-laced snowstorm, with the snow already fallen perhaps to her knees, *and* carrying Chelada?

Well, no, she admitted to herself. Perhaps not.

Definitely not.

The driver had stopped cursing.

"Miss?" he said.

She opened her eyes and looked at him.

"Yes?"

"Will that thing live if you let it go? It has fur; I saw it. Don't know that the car's power packs are going to last long enough for this to stop and us to get found. If we gotta walk out, that's gonna be a long walk, and you don't wanna be carrying extra. Can you—"

Toragin recoiled in horror.

"Abandon Chelada! No!"

The driver sighed, nodded.

"I'm gonna go out and take a look at how we're in, Miss. Might be we can rock 'er out. If we can't get moving, we could all freeze, and in not too long!"

Toragin put a hand out as he turned toward his door.

"Comm?" she said. "Radio? Can we call for help?"

The driver smiled—perhaps it was a smile—and shook his head.

"Nah, no radio on this one. Cheap doin's, right? Who needs a radio?"

"I'm going out now. You watch me, okay? If I go down, I'd take it kindly if you tried to get me back into the cab."

The only light in the car was a vague red glow from the sparse instruments. The driver was pulling his stretch cap far down on his head, covering his ears, while he stared into the windscreen as if it were a mirror in truth and not simply covered in snow.

The wind screamed suddenly, and the cab rocked. Toragin held her breath; she thought the driver did, too.

"Right," he said, and looked to her. "Miss, I want you to use this shovel when I start to push on the door, and try to keep the snow away from the side I got to go through, so it don't fill up the car or freeze the lock. Can you do that?"

"Yes," Toragin said without conviction. She wasn't used to people—other than cats, of course—depending on her strength. Still, it wasn't as if she was weak, after all. She'd been almost strong enough to keep up with *all* the older children around the house, children who pushed and played secret nasty games of shoving, who risked being denounced to a half-distracted tutor because, after all, who would *believe* that the elders—the oh-so-well-behaved elders— would torment the clan's precious youngers?

"Pull the hood, Miss, your hood. When I open up you'll want it. Cover that cage up good, too, if that thing needs to be warm."

Toragin bristled.

That thing.

Cage.

It.

On Liad there would have been Balance due . . . except not really, for on Liad both Toragin and the cats were—among those who knew of them at all—just another of Clan Lazmeln's aberrations.

Chelada was ignoring everything. She was being patient. So *very* patient. She had nothing to say to the driver; he was beneath her notice. Toragin, she trusted to take everything in hand. That was Toragin's function, after all. In the meanwhile, she arranged herself against the heat vent, and slipped into a dream state. For a moment, Toragin thought wistfully of slipping into sleep, to awake when all inconveniences had been solved.

"Okay, here's how we work it," said the driver. "I'm gonna get out, like I said. Gonna clean off the windscreen, and take a walk around the cab, see where's the tires, zackly, and what's the best angle to rock 'er. You keep the snow outta the door and watch me. Right?"

"Right," said Toragin, so faintly she didn't even convince herself.

The shovel arrived to hand and the driver heaved against the door, fighting drifts and wind, until of a sudden, it was open, and he slipped out.

Cold and wind seeped in, and then all heat fled as the crystals of ice flowed around the opening, top and bottom.

Toragin dutifully used the shovel, pushing the snow away from the door, squinting against the blowing snow, the wind howling in her ears, awed by the power of the storm.

There were places on Liad where it snowed, but Liad's weather was well tracked and one needn't generally be where it might snow unless snow was the goal. Here weather was never so well behaved. It had said as much in the planetary guide, when she had researched Surebleak, but—understanding the theory is not the same as understanding the fact.

The driver leaned in at the top of the door, holding on with a gloved hand. Between the wind and the uncertain footing the position looked precarious. The driver's voice was strained as he pointed toward the back seat.

"Miss, if you can reach that broom and hand it out?"

Toragin turned, awkwardly seized the implement and dragged it over the seat, turning back in time to hear a muffled yell. She caught a glimpse of a gloved hand tracing a clear spot on the window glass as it slid, and there was another yell, this time of pain, as something thumped on the side of the taxi.

The car door fell back, closing with a dull thud.

Chelada complained.

"Out," she said quite clearly. "Toweeell."

"Oh, not now!" Toragin's voice carried a desperate overtone against the wind and clatter of snow.

"Help me, Miss, I'm under!"

Under? What could that mean?

Under?

What?

Chelada spoke again.

"Towellll!"

* * * ✧ * * *

TOWELS.

Fiber towels from the roll helped staunch the blood—Toragin had never seen so much blood in her life. The driver's legs were both scraped and bleeding. She thought that was all the trouble, and certainly enough, and dragged the driver out from beneath the vehicle by hauling on one arm, while he used the other in a swimming motion against the snow.

Then, with blood on her gloves and the driver's cold-weather undersuit struggling to keep temperature, they'd both tried to rise.

It was obvious instantly, as they'd held onto the door and pulled, that there was some kind of urgent damage to the driver's right leg. Or to the foot.

Toragin was no med-tech, though she had some training in identifying and treating veterinary issues like blocked urinary tracts, pregnancy, hairballs. She didn't *think* she was looking at a broken leg, but even light touches to the side of the leg, low down, and the top of the foot, showed serious swelling. There was bleeding, too, which she wrapped with a precious cleaning cloth meant for Chelada; the leg didn't feel right to her—might there be a splinter of bone *there*?

"Can you drive?" asked the driver, panting. "There's no autopilot in this thing."

"Aren't we stuck?" she countered.

A pause then, while the wind counterpointed the silence of the cab. There were clicks that matched the rhythm of the flashing yellow, green, and red lights outside the cab, and there was Chelada's breathing, getting louder like it did when she was going into a deep sleep.

Finally the driver spoke.

"We are stuck, but maybe not so bad. Might be able to pull it loose, if you can drive it. Else . . . "

From the back seat came Chelada's worried mutter. Yes, thought Toragin. First, they had to arrange the inside of the cab so that she could occupy the driver's seat.

The best bet, all things being what they were with that foot, was either for the driver to let Toragin climb over him, possibly dislodging the cab, or—

"I can try to walk around," Toragin said.

"Don't fall, but try. Very slick!"

With snow and wind flapping the hood of her coat she managed to walk around the front of the car, avoiding the slick streaks where the driver's worn boots had lost traction and carried them and their occupant well under the car.

Opening the door was harder—the driver having dragged himself into the other seat, there wasn't sufficient purchase for a one-legged push on the door to be much help. Chelada's voice from the back seat gave Toragin an extra urgency—she was afraid she'd heard *that* sound from an expectant cat-mother before.

"Point and shoot," the driver said. "You engage the car with this button and just aim it. Now, my plan was to go really really *really* slow to try to get some traction, and then aim, like I said, along this little ridge. Aim just to the right of the ridge at first, and then when we get purchase, you'll turn it, just a little, back toward the rest of the road. That ought to do it!"

Toragin's experience as a fair-weather driver was hard to translate to this spot, this *now*.

The doing, after a few minutes of effort, just didn't. Tires spun and the car chattered sidewise just the smallest bit, ending up, so Toragin thought, even deeper in the morass of snow and ice. The rest of the road was either across the ice ridge in front of them, if the turn-loop they'd used to avoid the oncoming lorry was traversable at all, or it was behind them by multiple car lengths.

Breathing was loud in the car, again. Toragin could see the driver dabbing at one gashed leg slightly.

"If I take the shovel and dig until I reach dirt, can I put that under the wheels and . . . "

The driver considered her briefly.

"Not snowbred, are you? I mean, you just about got me in the car, with us both working. You think you have snow-shifting muscles? Can you move gravel that's froze together? Gets hard fast."

There was more silence. In the back seat, Chelada's breathing was faster and louder.

The driver spoke again.

"How much did your boots cost? Where'd you get 'em? Did someone help you or did you just buy them off the rack?"

Toragin bristled. She doubted she'd ever talked about the cost of anything with a casual stranger and why now?

"That's not something I share!"

"Calm down, Miss. I can't go nowhere with this leg. Cab's stuck. I'm trying to figure if we can get you to walk out for help or not, and if you bought cheap or stupid, it ain't gonna work."

ACT THREE

In the Hall of the Mountain King
*Enter Talizea, Miri, Jeeves, Val Con, the Tree,
clowders of cats and kindles of kittens*

UPHILL THE WIND was stronger than on the roads below, the flattened plateau a leftover of Surebleak's early days, when the company used this spot to prove their claim and take the first modest dense-lode of timonium.

On one side of the road, not quite as exposed to the weather, due to being tucked back into a grove of small sturdy trees, Yulie Shaper's holding huddled against the storm. A goodly-sized property, with house and outbuildings above ground, most of the real holdings were subsurface. Long-dormant market gardens were coming into their own after generations of disuse.

Also aboveground, between house and subterranean gardens, a small, brave Tree—in fact, a planted branch of the larger Tree in whose shadow it lay in the evenings of the summer's brighter days— did not so much huddle as dare the winds that shook it.

If the larger Tree communicated with the smaller there was no sign of it amidst the fury of the storm. The large Tree stood shoulders above the rest of the plateau, dwarfing the vehicles parked on the outside of the small, fenced drive as well as the several more inside that were not garaged. For that matter the Tree dwarfed the house that circumscribed the Tree's ancient trunk. A walker outside the gates might have noticed the way the Tree absorbed the local winds, might have realized that the spirals and eddies carried snow that had not only been deflected from the house and Tree but from the nearby grounds, and to a lesser extent even the smaller Tree was spared the worst of the storm's abuses.

Outside, then, snow and wind, filling the air with energy.

Inside Jelaza Kazone, the house, the wind was distant, the fallen snow as much as the ancient stone serving to muffle the roar. The directed energies moderated by the Tree's gathering and dropping of snow, by the local wind patterns born under the branches and reaching out to the very edges of the plateau, were invisible inside, even to those with surveillance cameras available.

Though it was quieter inside the house than out, the storm's energies still made themselves felt to the inmates.

Talizea was particularly alert to the storm. She, like a number of the other residents, had never experienced a storm quite like this— indeed, the *house itself* in all of its many Standards had never seen so much snow in such a short time, so much wind burdened with so much precipitation all at once. The child was not quite comfortable with the wind sounds, muffled as they were, and her edge of alertness gathered around her and drifted onto others.

Talizea's cats—for usually she had an honor guard of two or three—were this evening increased by a half dozen, or perhaps more. The cats shifted position as if taking point when a particular blast of air from the northeast slammed the same windows twice.

The child's mother, Miri, was also alert to the wind. The other sounds she knew from her past, especially the sound of snow sliding, peeling from a wall or window ledge or branch, to fall with a slow *whomp*. Miri doubted she'd ever felt this safe or this warm in a storm like this as she did tonight, but—she'd never had her child in hand during a blizzard; so she, too, was alert.

The cook and other staff walked carefully, listening. They too, with decades of experience in-house, and generations of backstory, were new to this kind of storm, and this *much* storm. Even Jeeves— butler, security, and possibly the best military mind in the system—wandered the floor as if calculating and cataloging all the new sounds and all the potential dangers. His wheels played the floorboards like a xylophone, the ancient wood tuned by the feet of generations of clan members.

It was perhaps the robot's musical movements that brought Val Con yos'Phelium from the delm's office, where he had been called to speak with the so-called boss of Surebleak Transport. Mr. Mulvaney's plan was to consolidate several local small trucking operations under his company's name, and thus gain the benefits of numbers for all. It was a plan ill-suited to Surebleak and the current regulations governing the Port Road. Still, Mr. Mulvaney *kept in touch*, but never during the Road Bosses office hours.

Finishing the call with less than the abruptness it merited, Val Con stepped out of the office, aware of Jeeves' pacing, of the wind, and something...else. At first, it seemed to be Tree-touch; on consideration, though—not entirely so. Was the storm so desperate that it *concerned* the Tree?

Now, *there* was an unsettling thought.

Val Con tarried another moment, trying to remember the last time the Tree had seemed—concerned. Nothing came to mind.

Which was possibly *even more* unsettling.

Frowning slightly, he moved down the hall, silent in soft house shoes, heading for the room that had become Jelaza Kazone's center.

The ruckus room was quiet, where quiet encompassed the snoring of cats, the wrestling of kittens, the crackle of paper as Talizea fingered her book; and another, as Miri turned a page.

They sat together in the pillow corner, tucked comfortably under the same blanket. There were cats atop the blanket, curled next to the quiet readers, several purring.

Val Con dropped to the blanket beside Talizea, rescuing his own book from under the chin of Merekit, who found every object a pillow.

"I am released," he said.

"'Bout time," Miri commented, looking up at him with a lopsided grin. "Like to find who gave that *loobelli* the delm's comm number."

"That would be interesting," Val Con agreed. The sound of wheels rolling along wood caught his attention, and he called out.

"Jeeves, will you join us?"

"At once, Master Val Con."

Indeed, almost immediately the door opened silently and the robot's head-ball flashed blue-and-violet greetings to Talizea, who laughed and, lacking a head-ball with the appropriate capabilities, flapped her hands in reply.

More cats arrived in the wake of the butler. They, like Val Con, seemed to have ears lifted, trying to track a sound they could not quite hear.

"Jeeves, tell me if you might, is there something amiss? Are we forgetting something, overlooking a small thing that needs done? Have we already forgotten something? Is there a . . . a problem? Is the house—unsettled?"

Jeeves, who could instantaneously send pinbeams across space, who could directly read the planetary defense nets, who could communicate with intelligences far from human, flashed a subdued fog-green to the assembled.

"I understand the question to be: Is the house unsettled? Working."

Val Con and Miri, Road Boss, Delm of Korval, looked at each other.

"*Working*?" Miri repeated.

"Apparently so."

Val Con glanced about, taking in the sheer numbers of whiskers on display.

"Do we *have* this many cats, *cha'trez*?"

He swept his arm out, encompassing those in the room, and inferring as yet untold numbers in the halls.

One of the newcomers—a fluffy grey cat with large black feet—caught Val Con's eye.

"Is that not Yulie's favorite? Jeeves, have they all come to us for safety in the storm? Is there danger?"

Jeeves repeated the word, head-ball flashing. "Danger?"

"Working still?"

Val Con and Miri exchanged another glance, each feeling the other trying to shrug off unease.

At that moment came the sound of thunder—a distant rattle—then more, like cannon fire near the front gates. Val Con snapped to his feet as cat ears swiveled.

Silence followed, soft *whomps* were more felt than heard, as the thunder-shaken snow fell from the branches of the Tree, visible through the windows overlooking the inner garden.

Talizea looked around, an expression of grim concentration on her small face. Several cats detached themselves from nearby clowders and came over to her, draping themselves across her lap and tucking against her sides.

Jeeves gave what might be termed a *mutter* in a human, a small sound of frustration or disbelief.

"Sir," he said formally, head-ball a steady pale orange. "As usual, you have astutely assessed the situation. The cats—all of them—find the weather to be unusual. The cats from Liad, you understand, are not yet entirely acclimated—they have perhaps not assimilated all the tales and information shared by the local cat clans. The local cat clans are not yet fully synced, you might say, with the information shared by the cats who have lived undertree, and who of course bear the memories of the generations who went before."

"Among the cats, there is uncertainty. The Tree is uncertain as well."

Miri rose and leaned gently against Val Con's side, arms folded tightly across her chest.

"So," she said, "being uncertain makes the cats unsettled, which we feel, since the cats bring us so much news?"

She unfolded her arms—tapped Val Con on the shoulder—

"You been holding out on me, Tough Guy? Tree been slipping you inside information?"

"*Cha'trez*, I think the Tree has not been in touch with me today, certainly not to the point of passing coded messages via the cats!" He paused.

"Jeeves, I wonder if you might be able to tell me exactly how you and the Tree communicate, or you and the cats. How is it that you know that the Tree is unsettled if it has not shared this directly with me?"

The head-ball brightened momentarily.

"I believe that I cannot precisely explain that, sir," Jeeves said earnestly. "It does seem that certain of the—means—of sharing information among us all are less sharply defined than they might be, almost a matter of habit rather than content.

"But on the day, yes, the energy level has been strange in the lower atmosphere. That, combined with an unpredicted bomb cyclone, resulted in the storm growing much larger than expected. That led to a—revelation of error, and—forgetfulness, on the part of the Tree."

Miri put a hand on Val Con's shoulder, then settled her chin on it. With her other hand she made a rolling motion—

"Please go on," she said, "if there's more."

"Yes, thank you. It appears that something has been forgotten, or understood—incorrectly. Now that it has come clear to me, I must inform you that there are visitors on the way."

"Visitors," Miri repeated, and Val Con added:

"On the way from where, I wonder? I mean to ask after an arrival time."

"Ah," said Jeeves. "Tonight."

"*In that*?" Miri twisted her free hand overhead, perhaps miming the storm without.

"Yes," said Jeeves, head-ball losing a bit of brightness. "In fact, if you will permit, we—that is, the Tree and myself, with the cat clans, have a request to put before the House."

Val Con turned his head and caught Miri's eye over his shoulder. He raised an eyebrow. She wrinkled her nose.

He turned back to Jeeves.

"Please continue," he said politely.

"Yes," Jeeves said again. "It would be good—for the House and for projects undertaken by those of the House which date before, even well before, our removal to Surebleak—if we might welcome guests. Soon. Tonight, in fact. It would be good if a guesting suite, or several, might be made ready for use."

Once again, Val Con surveyed the room, and the cats therein. Inside his head, he heard Miri laughing wryly. He felt a bump against his knee, and looked down, to find that they were surrounded by cats, tails held high, purring, and bumping.

"Tonight?" Miri's voice did not hide her wonderment. Talizea shrieked laughter at the circling felines, and Val Con asked:

"How many, and who?"

"I believe at least two, but, given the weather, there may be more. As to who they are—I do not believe we have a permissive agreement to share that information. Formerly, we have had a coded arrangement. I speak of that pair of guests. The others, if there are others, will be with us as storm-wrack. Travelers in need."

Val Con was silent. Miri was silent. Talizea was purring at a cat.

"Of course," Jeeves said, somewhat desperately, "I would not expect the House to admit these persons without knowing who they are. Indeed, as House Security, I would advise strongly against it. I will secure permission to reveal their identities."

Val Con took a deep breath.

"Is this not a great muddle, Jeeves?" he asked.

"It is, sir," Jeeves acknowledged. "Without speaking out of turn, sir, I believe I've not seen such a comprehensive muddle for some time. If you like, I will prepare a list of the ten greatest Korval muddles. . . ."

Miri burst out laughing.

"Very good," Val Con said evenly. "You will send me the list at your leisure, perhaps with an explanation of the communication methods employed by yourself, the cats, and the Tree. What I wish to know, now, with storm guests approaching, is: What has produced *this particular* muddle now?"

"Again, sir, if I may be so bold—imminence is the problem, the *now* of *now* if you will. Imminence and commitment."

Miri straightened up, and stepped to Val Con's side, shaking her head.

"I've had dyed-in-sweater sad-sack troops who couldn't've done that good playing a delay," she said, possibly to Jeeves, possibly to her lifemate.

Possibly to the cats.

Or, Val Con thought with a shiver, to the Tree.

Jeeves rolled backward an inch or two—his sometimes approximation of a bow.

"Thank you," he said gravely. "Calculation suggested that a solution to this *particular muddle* might become clear during the course of our discussion. Sadly, it has not."

"As I mentioned, the difficulty is that between us, the Tree and myself have had to deal with a range of things that are, or might be, imminent. We have discovered that time scales sometimes translate badly—that things which are *soon* to a cat or a human may not be . . . *as soon* to a logic with a long history or a Tree with a vastly longer history."

He paused.

"In short form, the Tree and I have pursued, in addition to our primary commitments to Line yos'Phelium and to Clan Korval, commitments to other communities. Other . . . persons.

"As you are aware, I had been much involved in the welfare of cats on Liad, and developed a network there of people with similar interests and necessities. Indeed, I was, through my independent funds and investments, the backbone of several organizations devoted to the welfare of non-humans. When it became obvious that we would be relocating away from Liad I did my best to spin-off such funds and anonymous board positions as appropriate.

"Meanwhile, of course, and honestly, well begun long before I appeared on the scene, the Tree has had ongoing personal and support relationships with a variety of cat families and clans. In person the Tree has followed certain lines of cats . . . "

"Yes," Val Con said. "We had known as much. After all, there is Merlin—"

"Indeed, Merlin!" Jeeves said, perhaps too quickly. "But the Tree has not simply followed lines and clans of cats. It has also taken an interest in a line—that is one line—of humans."

Val Con stood suddenly taller; Miri shifted her weight as if centering herself.

"I don't mean to cause distress," Jeeves said suddenly. "But it should be clear that there are ripples to the Tree's effects, as ripples to my own, and then there are interference patterns of sorts where your influence, and mine, and the Tree's, add up to unanticipated entanglements, to anticipated events becoming imminent well before they are expected, and to commitments thus coming due in a . . . as you say, sir, in a great muddle."

There was another pause. The head-ball wavered between orange, and yellow, and the palest of pale rose.

"What fuels this muddle now is a commitment made—too lightly, on one side—and too firmly—perhaps too firmly—on the other."

Miri looked at the settled cats, at Lizzy, curled beneath the blanket, and an additional blanket of cats.

"It's a bad storm," she said, slowly. "Are you sure they're coming in? That they haven't sheltered in town until this blows out?"

"We are certain that they are traveling to us now," said Jeeves. "In addition to what they hold was our promise, they labor under a constraint of time."

"Hm. And what's the Tree doing, while you and us're taking care of the hard stuff?"

"The Tree's concentration is much divided," Jeeves began—and stopped.

A dozen or more cats shifted, sat up, stood and stared at one wall of the house as if hearing something beyond the ken of human ears just beyond.

"There is a problem," Jeeves said. "Lives may be in danger. Somewhere on the road. The Tree—"

But Val Con and Miri, and Talizea too, felt the green presence now, looming and concerned, no hint of amusement in the unease, no hint of surety. Images of dragons, struggling against some unknown problem, failing to take flight, wilting, collapsing, followed by anguish and despair.

Cats began to gather, to move toward the door, to move down the hall, alert. Val Con was sure he heard a cat's complaint, strangely distant—the memory, perhaps of such a complaint, voiced by no cat present.

"The Tree is a private person," said Jeeves, "and there are promises at risk."

The green glow suffusing human thoughts receded. From without the sound of the wind increased, and with it the intermittent rumble of snow arriving in great lumps at the base of the Tree, having collected and slid down the network of branches.

ACT FOUR
Scene One

Comes a Stranger from the Storm
Enter Boss Gotta

VERTU'S CONCENTRATION was threatening to bring on a headache, the snow was bright, nearly blue in the lights. There was something else at work, too, a kind of green undertone urging her to hurry, as if the top of the hill beckoned with promises of warmth, comfort, food, bed—

"Slow!"

There was command in the girl's voice. The dog whined, and the child said, "*Malda, malda,*" and other words in that language that slipped so easily by Vertu's ears.

However, she *had* slowed, in response to the tone of command, which had seemed also to speak to that green urging, which felt stronger now—closer, perhaps—but not nearly so focused on speed.

"Something happened here," Anna said, "something—look!"

Whatever *had* happened was a story told by patterns in the snow. Vertu had been following the path broken by some previous vehicle, and here *right here* there were mounds as if the wakes of two boats had solidified around some uncharted island.

The weaker track came from what may or may not have been the road to the top, the stronger veered around and . . .

"Fool grocery truck almost hit somebody else, right here," was Yulie's guess from the back seat. "They weren't so lucky as us—slid all over the place—maybe got kicked off course."

"Very slow, please. We must know . . ."

That was Anna again, her voice strong and sure.

"See, this track, not as wide as the truck, goes this way."

Wind buffeted them with renewed strength, snow pelted the side windows, offering the track Anna pointed to as a better choice.

Vertu reluctantly let the taxi come to a stop, lights flashing, trying to analyze what she saw on the road and then, closing her eyes and finding not the expected darkness but a kind of green glow beneath her eyelids. She peered through the flow with eyes closed, trying to *see* the Tree, to orient herself, and to make a plan— preferably a plan that would not further endanger her passengers, the taxi, or herself.

If she took the left track, she would be aiming to the left of where she felt the Tree stood. If she took the right, she would be too far to the right. In this new snowbound geography, there was no center road straight up the hill to Korval's house and Tree. Though there should be.

There should.

"We must go this way," Anna said, tapping the window insistently, and when Vertu opened her uncertain eyes she felt that perhaps *yes*, that track *might* be fresher. The certainty on the girl's tongue, though, that needed checking...

"Can you tell me if this is a wizard's call, or a guess? Are you *dramliza*?"

Anna turned her head, peering into the back seat as if for guidance.

Mary's voice was gentle.

"Anna, are you *very* sure?"

"This is the way," the girl insisted, "the Old One is worried, and—"

She turned suddenly to face Vertu.

"*You* see, Miss Vertu. *You see* the Old One, I can tell. *I see* the Old One, waiting and worried. Someone—somewhere nearby—is in pain, I see them, too. Another is filled with anticipation, I have some training... we need to go this way."

Vertu closed her eyes briefly, the green presence closer, insistent. The Old One. Korval's Tree. She saw it in her mind's eye, and felt it *return her regard*, know her warmly as a familiar watcher.

When she opened her eyes the taxi was already moving. Carefully she guided it along the narrow path, snow crunching under the tires, using the vague snow-filled ruts of the previous passage as a guide.

"Hurry," Anna said, but there was no *hurry* here, off the main road and with conditions uncertain. The green presence also demanded hurry—and abruptly acquiesced to Vertu's certainty that she must go slow, and be vigilant.

There!

A flash of something blue, gone in the snow, then another, ahead.

Vertu hit the horn in warning against a car coming their way, but there was only...

A red flash, this time, closer, wilder, maybe too high to be a car, though maybe...

Rascal barked a sharp warning.

Anna cried, "Watch out!"

And Yulie said, "She's frozen!"

How Yulie knew the figure in the bright orange wrap, holding lights over her head, was female, Vertu didn't ask. She was too much concerned with stopping the cab safely, and shoving the door open into the swirling snow.

"We see you! Safety is here!" she called out in Liaden—and had no time to wonder why *that* language *here* before she was answered in the same tongue.

"They're trapped! I need help, they're trapped! Follow me!"

The voice *was* female, the Liaden pure in Command mode.

The figure turned and fled away into the snow, flashing the light at them over her shoulder.

Swearing in Liaden, Vertu threw herself into the driver's seat, slammed the door, and put the cab into gear, following the high-definition boot tracks, and the occasional flash of a red or blue light through the sheeting snow.

"She says they're trapped," she told her passengers over the storm. "That they need help."

"Well, it's happenin' on our side of the tollbooth," Yulie said lightly. "Looks like we're Boss Gotta. Let's go fetch!"

Scene Two

On a Snow-Filled Road, Under a Snowy Sky

RASCAL BOUNDED INTO THE SNOW as soon as Anna pushed the door open, following the Liaden woman's trail up to a roadside where the tire ruts disappeared off the lighted edge and down a hill.

"There!"

Vertu, Anna, Mary and Rascal stood on that edge for a moment, peering into a snow-swirled scene confused by flashing lights beneath the still-accumulating crystalline surface. The woman was floundering down the hill in her light-reflecting coat—soon followed by Vertu.

The car—one of the blue-and-red-striped cabs prone to stealing fares—was on a steep incline, tail end lower than front, driver's side mostly in the clear, while the passenger's side was nearly buried in a snowdrift-covered pile of leafless brush.

Yulie arrived, and without preamble followed the trail the women had broken. He carried a bag in one hand and turned—

"Anna, you stay up there, this could be too deep for you. Mary— you come down and gimme a hand."

"You'll need me if someone's hurt!" Anna's voice barely made it through the racket of the snow and wind. She was holding two of Vertu's emergency lights. Rascal charged down the hill after Yulie, casting bounding shadows.

"We need the light from up there! Stay up there and hold 'em steady! If somebody's hurt, we'll bring 'em to you!"

Vertu caught up to the woman as they both reached the side of the snowbound car; she saw a determined red face under a hood. The woman spoke, her first words taken by the wind as its toll, then—

" . . . blood on the driver, which I wrapped, a leg injury," the woman said, the accent of Solcintra strong. "There is some damage to the foot, also. He cannot walk, I think. And Chelada—she is in the back, unharmed—but she is pregnant and ready tonight!"

The angle made getting the door open difficult, and the chaos of the interior was not what Vertu had expected.

In the back was *not* a woman with a fat belly, but a large multicolored cat in a travel wagon partly covered by a small rug, wide-eyed and panting. The driver's side front seat was empty, with the floor partly filled with legs stretched from the passenger's side. The passenger—or driver it must be!—was awkwardly placed, leaning half on the passenger door and half on the worn seat, bent in a way meant to take strain off of a leg but clearly uncomfortable.

"We stopped on the edge," the Liaden explained to Vertu, as the others gathered to see what could be done, "then the accident with the leg. When I got out to find help, the wind slammed the door shut; the car slipped off the edge. The snow kept it from sliding too far—but this is far enough!"

"Can't walk, I don't think," the driver was saying to Yulie. "Can't stay, either. Prolly only got half hour more heat—"

"Right. Gotta a notion to haul you outta there. That's first. Then we'll work out how to get you to the top. Here—"

There came the rustle of a bag being opened, and Yulie spoke again.

"Miss Vertu, you're smallest. We'll get you in there—"

"I'm smaller," the other woman said sharply in Terran.

"You already been in a wreck, saved this fella's life, I'm thinking, then went for a hike inna snowstorm, looking for help. Why not let the rest of us get some work in while you take a rest?"

The woman looked inclined to argue still. Mary touched her arm.

"You could do it, no one doubts," she said. "But we are fresher; the work will go quicker, and speed is important, for the cat, and the man."

The stiff shoulders relaxed somewhat.

"Yes."

"All right, then," said Yulie. "Miss Vertu, you climb on in. First thing is to get the cat into this bag. You hand her out to this lady, and then we'll have enough room to work this fella 'round so we can pull him out with these."

These were blankets pulled from the bag he'd been carrying, still bundled in their sales wrap. He shredded the thin strips in his rush, jammed them in his pocket and handed one to Vertu as she climbed over the door sill.

Rascal began barking, and jumped back from the car, barking again as snow fell from an overhead branch—and again as the car moved, threatening to slide between two of the snow-covered brush piles it leaned against.

"Right," said Yulie. "Best get to work."

Scene Three

A Rescue

IN THE END they stashed most of what Yulie, Mary, and Anna had brought with them into the stricken cab to make room for the rescued. With Yulie as center lead, Vertu on the right side, and Mary on the left, they managed to get the impromptu travois, and the driver, over the edge and into Vertu's cab.

The Liaden woman—Toragin, she named herself—carried a small bag in addition to the one with the quiet cat in it—led the way up the hill with Rascal a presence to her left, managing a steady pace despite the uncertain footing and wind. She accepted Anna's hand as an aid to getting over the edge and stood there, cuddling her cat and her bag.

Once over the edge, the travois team took a moment to rest. The wounded cab driver was swearing softly and constantly, and Vertu moved slightly away from him, so as to give him the privacy such a rendering of art deserved.

That put her close to Toragin, who was also speaking—not swearing, Vertu thought, but alternating between murmuring comforting phrases to the cat, and recriminating with someone else—or perhaps herself.

"You told her she would have her kittens under branch. A promise given, and cast away, with no word or care for her. As if you had forgotten!"

"All right," Yulie called. "All's we got left is the easy part!"

Mary laughed, and took hold of her side of the blanket. Vertu stepped up, and took hold of hers.

They reached Vertu's cab, all the worse for the weather, and the rescue. When the passenger's side front door was opened to urge Toragin and Chelada into the warmth, Rascal settled onto the floor at her feet.

The rest of them dealt with the driver, the final configuration being Yulie, Mary, and Anna sitting together on the back seat with the driver half reclining across their laps. His boots were in Anna's lap, and Vertu saw her nod with satisfaction as Mary twisted to pull the cab's first aid kit from the compartment under the seat.

Meanwhile, Toragin was next to Vertu, a blanket wrapped around her coat, barely looking up as the heavily burdened cab got cautiously underway. The bag was in her lap, open, and she was looking down at the cat curled there. Rascal sat very quietly, crowded against

Toragin's legs as if offering warmth, alert ears and face turned respectfully away from the cat, whose back was turned to him.

Vertu measured her turn, looking to the end of the road, as determined by the marks their boots and Rascal's wandering pace had left.

"If you see something outside I should know about," she said to her passengers at large, "please tell me. Elsewise talk as you need, but not to me, is that understood? I will need to concentrate."

Those in the back answered in the affirmative, while next to her the mumbling continued, low enough that it did not distract. From the back seat, Anna spoke low and with composure.

"I will unwrap these wet towels and inspect your hurts. Now, tell me—this part here?"

"It stings."

"If I do this . . . "

"Don't *touch* it, it already . . . "

"To help, I need to work in two ways. One way will hurt to start, since your muscles have tangled up their needs with your pain. Also, you have been pierced by something, but we'll need to have good light to see that. We will leave the wrap in place."

"I will touch the muscles and warm them some, and they will be able to relax, some. When they do the other muscles will fight—don't kick! If you need, Mary will hold your hand—squeeze that if you hurt, but don't twist away. So, open your hands and let Mary have one . . . "

Vertu followed the ruts back to the proper road where the ghost tracks of passed vehicles could barely be searched out in the lights.

"You want to go right just here," Yulie said from the backseat. "Not too sharp, 'cause it might be best to miss where the other tracks was. I'm thinking there'll be a rock pile kind of shining off the side in your lights, 'cause the snow's going cold and fine now so we can see better. Come summer there's a spring near that rock, so sometimes we get a squiggly slick spot in winter if the ditch catches free water."

He was right, of course, about missing the tracks, and the news about the potential ice was useful.

Vertu drove, saw the rock face, felt the small lurch as they traveled over one ice stream, and another, and another. She just let the cab find its own way through, and when they were through the worst of, she touched the accelerator gently.

"Relax that spot now," Anna said to her reluctant patient. "Yes, you can. I will touch you here and you'll feel the spot. I will rub it and we'll let the muscles relax, they are as tight as if you stood on tiptoe—and you do not. Yes, see, when I touch the warm will help you relax . . . very good. Now it doesn't hurt as bad, and it will hurt less soon."

"Going to hurt a while . . . " came the reply. "That's my driving foot, you know! If I don't drive I can't eat!"

"Tonight you'll eat, and tomorrow," came the soothing voice, "and after that, too, I'm sure. Driving is only delayed a few days . . . "

"Here then, hold your glove. I will try to see if there's anything more wrong—squeeze hard if you need . . . "

"Sleet, sleet, sleet!"

"Squeeze and be a little quiet—Miss Vertu needs to concentrate!"

Gloves made Vertu recall the other new passenger. She glanced to that side, noting that cat and bag had been tucked into the floor, between the woman's boots; Rascal sitting firmly on the door side of those same boots.

"Toragin, your name is?" Vertu murmured. "Toragin was a Lazmeln name some generations ago, if I recall my lineages properly."

"And is now," the woman admitted, "though for how long is a guess. I am Toragin del'Pemridj Clan Lazmeln."

"Whatever your line, Toragin, you might take your gloves off now, and open your coat. This car is not so cold as the other, and the gloves will be holding cold. Your boots may hold some cold, too, but I have the heat up—as well as I may and still see the road—on feet."

The young woman divested herself of her gloves, doing her best not to disturb the cat in the footwell.

"You sound of Solcintra," she ventured. "You are?"

Vertu glanced at the passenger wryly.

"The Council of Clans made it possible for me to find work on Surebleak—and on Surebleak I am Vertu Dysan."

"Ah," said the knowing tone. "And Vertu was at least twice a name in a line in Solcintra." After a short pause and a glance at Vertu she went on. "I cannot put my clan in debt for this rescue, I fear, but Chelada and I both See you, Vertu Dysan, and somewhere there will be Balance for your timely assistance."

Vertu made a short motion with her hand—a Surebleak usage of a pilot's shorthand—

"Call this neighbor-work, Toragin. You would have done the same for me . . ."

Neighbor-work—well, that was more properly a Surebleak thing than a Liaden one as well.

"I have no such connection," Toragin said. "Those I know here to recognize are some of Korval, and of course, the Tree beyond Korval's gate, and whoever else has shied away without formal notice, of whom there are many, I'm told. I *had been* neighbor to the Tree until it was chased away by the Council of Clans."

Vertu reconciled the map in her head now with the memory of fares delivered in years past, and indeed Lazmeln's clan house was—had been—in the physical shadow of the Tree.

Silence for a moment or two then, which Vertu was glad of as the cab skittered on some unseen unevenness below the snowy surface.

The silence gave way then to a cooing noise.

Toragin had taken the purring cat into her lap and was speaking in catlike tones, expertly petting and perhaps stroking a flank or belly. The purr fell into a breathy pant; Toragin's posture changed as she became more alert.

Vertu did an extra scan of the road, but saw nothing that might have claimed the other woman's attention. Instead Toragin carefully placed the cat into the bag at her feet, staring into the darkness there.

"Is it this close to your time then?" Toragin's voice was low. "I think I feel contractions, Chelada!"

"Here! Yulie, hand this up to the front! The cat has need!"

Anna was moving things and at that sound there was rustling behind Vertu's head and then:

"Toragin, that's right—take this."

This was a mostly dry blanket of bright green, threaded over the seat tops . . .

"She will not wait, or cannot," Anna said. "Help her make a better nest for her four."

"Let Rascal come back here with us," said Mary. "There's room on the floor, and another blanket."

Anna spoke in that other language. In the screen, Vertu saw the dog carefully jump to the seat top and then over, into Mary's arms. Anna reached out to tug an ear, and then down he went to the floor and his own blanket.

Vertu sped the cab up just a little, wishing she had a better idea of where they were.

ACT FIVE

In the Hall of the Mountain King

THE RUCKUS ROOM had the air now of a council of war, with Jeeves reporting on results of scans borrowed from ships in orbit and aircraft in flight, of radio waves interpreted and—

"There are two cabs thought to be on the road between here and the city proper: one driven by Vertu Dysan, carrying Yulie Shaper and other fares to his home. The other is a wild cab which may be carrying one or more passengers from *Finifter's Shave*," Jeeves said. "It seems that the passengers of both cabs have consolidated, and that the House may be called upon to host eight, of whom five are known. We have not yet received permission to reveal the names of the remaining three, though this is perhaps imminent, as one of the principals has taken up recriminations."

"Recriminations against the Tree?" Val Con murmured. "How could such a thing be so?"

"The Tree has erred, Master Val Con. It feels its error, keenly."

"Gotta admit, that's something new and innerestin," Miri said.

"Perhaps not entirely new, though I allow it to be a rarity," Val Con answered, and looked to Jeeves.

"The nature of these *recriminations* interests me. Do they presage violence against the Tree, or, indeed, the House? Is Korval considered a party to this—error?"

"The Tree is attempting to ascertain the answers to these very questions," Jeeves said.

"The travelers, as I understand, have been having an adventure, and the Tree is not acclimated to carrying on communications—conversations—with those not of Jela's Line, especially not at a distance, when the communicant is distraught. The Tree does not *know* this individual, merely is *aware* of them as a . . . closely affiliated ally."

"Or even as a one of a number of carefully engineered guard pets," Val Con murmured.

"You are unfair, sir," Jeeves said, chidingly. "Also, I would suggest that the Tree finds itself in a unique situation, which it is working to understand, and to resolve in such a manner that all parties are satisfied—and safe. This is perhaps not the time to distract it with more recrimination."

"You are quite correct," Val Con said. "I am insupportably rude. I withdraw my tasteless irony until such time as the Tree and myself are less dismayed by the imminent arrival of a stranger who may wish to visit harm on my lifemate and our child."

"Thank you, sir. Your understanding is appreciated."

Miri snorted. Val Con sighed, and reached over to take her hand. They were occupying the pillow corner, sitting cross-legged atop the blanket, cats in various attitudes of alertness and repose scattered about. Talizea had been sent up to the nursery, accompanied by a guard of six, Mrs. pel'Esla having been directed to allow the cats to sleep with the heir, if they, and she, so desired.

"I wonder," Val Con said now, "if you will hazard a guess as to the Tree's core problem with this recriminating individual? I understand that we are looking at approximation rather than exactitude."

"Yes," said Jeeves, head-ball glowing and pulsing in shades of orange. "It is my understanding that the Tree is dealing with the weight of . . . guilt."

"Guilt?" Miri's startled response beat Val Con's by a quarter second.

"Yes. It has lately been expressing concern over decisions made long ago. The severing of Tinsori Light's last link to the crystallized universe inspired a great deal of thought, of what might be called introspection, as if there had been a tension for centuries between the great resistance and the smaller deeds. Now that there is no great resistance to be concerned with, the importance of small deeds becomes magnified."

A pause. The head-ball flickered.

"Guilt. Remorse. Regret—I have only analogs to work from, you understand, because the Tree's sentience is not like yours, or mine, and it encompasses far more than we can comprehend. Simply put— now that the great resistance has collapsed, the Tree considers what it might have done—differently."

"So it's depressed," Miri said.

"Possibly," said Jeeves. "The analogs—"

"Yes," said Val Con. "We deal in approximations. It is not so uncommon, when a large, all-consuming project has finally seen completion, to experience a sense of—disorientation, even sadness. A sense, perhaps, that victory ought to have been something—*more*."

"Healer?" Miri murmured.

"If so, it would need to be one of us, who grew up under branch—and received the—pardon me, the *benefits* of the Tree's long interaction with our bloodlines."

Miri looked thoughtful.

"Tree's really old," she commented. "Maybe the Clutch could help?"

"That," said Jeeves, "is a useful thought. Collectively, the Clutch elders may be as old in this universe as the Tree was in the Crystal Universe. There is no adequate or useful comparison of age, but the Clutch sentience is far closer to the Tree's than to human sentience—or the sentience of an Independent Logic designed by humans."

"We ought also to consider the norbears, in that wise," said Val Con. "Perhaps we ought consult a council of elders."

"Clutch, norbears, Tree, Free Logics, humans." Miri was shaking her head. "Would that include Uncle?"

Val Con lifted his eyes to the ceiling as if seeking an answer to that question, then returned his gaze to Jeeves.

"*Do* we need a Healing? Or a council of elders?"

Jeeves' head-ball dimmed somewhat, signaling deep thought.

"I believe we do not, in the short term, need either. An *informal* council of elders is an idea deserving consideration. Such a council might have understood the problem of the Department much sooner. Given open information, such a council might have managed an answer to Tinsori Light as well, but such openness would not come easily."

Miri wrinkled her nose. Val Con shook his head.

"We shall place the council of elders aside just now. For the moment, what is required in order to honor the Tree's ambition to resolve the present situation in a manner that is both satisfactory and safe for all?"

"I—" Jeeves began, and stopped, head-ball flashing red, then returning to orange.

"Lord Pat Rin calls via relay," he announced. "He asks first for the Road Boss. May I put him through?"

"Of course. Here if you will."

Miri joined Val Con at the comm screen. Pat Rin was there before them, his smile wry.

"My immediate need is for the Road Boss, but I also have a brief question for the delm: The next time the clan requires rescue will you please find me a clement planet to suborn?"

"The delm," said Miri, "is sitting undertree in the puckerbrush in a stay-don't-move blizzard. The delm chooses to smile gently at your levity . . . "

"Yes, I suppose they do. I thank the delm, most sincerely, for their forbearance."

He gave a casual pilot's hand sign—*next order of business*—"I have news from Mr. McFarland that Vertu Dysan is in the midst of a rescue and wishes to stop, with her passengers, and shelter at Jelaza Kazone for the evening, given the difficulty of driving. I gather contact is intermittent in this storm. Also, I'm informed that at least one of the seven passengers insists the Tree itself has issued an invitation."

"Heard a rumor like that ourselves," Miri said. "Tree's not being all that communicative right now."

She heard Val Con's agreement inside her head before she saw his nod.

"Rooms are being prepared," he said. "Pass that along if you get contact back. Otherwise, we are forewarned, and the gate will be open for them."

"Excellent. I expect that we will speak again in the morning. Luck willing, we will not have to speak again, tonight."

The contact ended, screen now showing a view from the spaceport—the packet ship *Finifter's Shave* bathed in bright lights as snow drifted and blustered across the tarmac and receded into darkness.

Weather aside, there was a silence in the ruckus room as the humans looked one to another, and it appeared the cats as well. Then a cat made a brief sound, and shared it again, as did another, and soon there was an undercurrent of restless feline muttering— never quite so formal as *meow* nor as quiet as *prrt*—as the gathered cats mustered themselves into a company before splitting into tribes and leaving on their own business.

"Is it possible, Jeeves, that you might get the Tree's attention? I ask since Miri and I will shortly settle ourselves down and consider the Tree until it considers us. The Tree must understand that whatever its past misdeeds, we must talk, and talk now, before our guests arrive."

ACT SIX
Scene One

Exploring Inner Landscapes

TORAGIN WAS NOT FLUSTERED. Say rather that she was anxious. Or perhaps it was beyond that, to something more personal and more powerful. She was, in fact, bordering on that strange cliff between awe and frustration that breeds a righteous—well, she wasn't supposed to feel the stress that bordered on anger. Not. Supposed. To.

She'd felt Chelada's contractions, and was familiar enough with the process; getting the dog out of the way and the blanket down made things easier, but still, here she was having what must stand for an adventure, on a world she'd never heard of before Korval's Tree had gone away. She was not an adventurer. She did not *believe in* adventures.

But she *did* believe in promises.

Promises? Oh, she'd had promises from her grandmother, who knew that Toragin's barely socially acceptable "not of the usual-type" was something the Healers would not Heal and the matchmakers never bothered to challenge. The promise to "let the child do worthy work and have her cats"... oh, *that* promise had covered pregnant cats and feral, that promise had covered mystery organizations sending cat food and cat-vets around Liad and even to Low Port—but now? Here was the result of that promise to let the child be who she was... and Chelada's labor was within moments of producing her first kitten in the midst of dangerous weather on a dangerous world, when she had been promised the comfort and safety of birthing those kittens beneath the Tree's very branches.

Chelada had earned that promise. Toragin had earned the right to be taken seriously. Or so she had thought. Now it appeared that, yet again, she had no rights in the face of another's necessity. That—was such a constant in her life, she had scarcely noticed the slight.

But Chelada.

Chelada had been *promised*, and Toragin had stood witness to that promise.

So, when it came apparent that Chelada *would* have kittens, Toragin had done research—she was good at research—found the new location of the Tree, transit time, cost, and only then told her delm of the necessity of taking Chelada to the place where she might redeem her promise.

Her delm had asked a few perfunctory questions about the potential of a secret lover having gone to ground on Surebleak, and had authorized purchase of the tickets, one way, with the understanding that a return fare would come from Toragin's quartershare. She had also acquiesced to the demands of the nadelm, who had "grave misgivings" about Toragin's ability to travel alone, and called in the Healer who was most familiar with Toragin's case.

To him, Toragin had said, "Yes, Chelada is pregnant and bears a promise from the great Tree of Korval. Her kittens are to be born under—they *must be born under*—the Tree's protection."

The Healer had bowed. It was, he said, apparent that Toragin believed this to be true to the very base of her being. The cat's claim on the Tree was not as accessible as the cat's claim on Toragin, and Toragin's on the cat, but he allowed such claims, also, to be true, and strong. The Tree's claim on Toragin was a matter for some consideration. Was it a child's fascination grown into an obsession? Was it a child's fancy grown into compulsion? If it was either, ought it to be Healed?

The Healer thought not. The Healer, and the Hall, found the Tree disquieting. If Toragin were "Tree-mazed," said the Healer, best she was left to sort it out on her own. And if the method of sorting out was a trip to Surebleak and a confrontation, that was surely for the best.

And now, here she was—*not* under the branches of the Tree, and Chelada giving birth, not safe, but in appalling danger.

Though, they must be nearby. She could—well, *hear* was scarcely accurate. Not like she could *hear* the cats. But she felt attention on her, caught nuance, and she spoke to it, careful to keep her voice low, so as not to disturb the driver's concentration.

"I hear you hiding in the wind. Is this your storm? Is this to deny us? I am here. Chelada is here. We come to claim the boon you have promised since first I saw your glow! Show yourself!"

Chelada made a small sound, just then, a small sound. In the blanket, a form expanded into the strange world.

"Listen," said Toragin sharp and low, "your cats are coming. Show yourself!"

Yes. The fluster was gone, anxiety was gone, and now there was no boundary or border about it. Anger it was, and it flared.

"Think of something besides yourself. Think about those whose lives depend on your whim!"

In the dimness she felt the presence, felt a confused contrition. The presence receded slightly, returned, offering a sense of warmth, perhaps of hope, reminiscent of the first time she'd stared out her window into the silhouetted shadow of the Tree and demanded that it see her.

Patience, she felt she heard from the night. *You will be safe. You will be satisfied.*

And then, so understated that she suspected she had not heard it at all:

Please forgive me.

Scene Two

In the Shadow of the Tree

SNOW ON THE WINDSCREEN flashed with the bright glow of lightning inside the storm. Again and now, thunder rolled over the cab, echoing. A bolt of lightning struck close to the car, a weird green glow behind it all, the combination of flashes and sound so overwhelming that Vertu eased the cab to a halt.

Thunder died away, yet the wind-driven snow remained too thick to see through as the car shook. The passengers said nothing for several minutes, listening to Toragin's coos and the cat's undernoises when they could be heard over the storm's constant rumble.

Vertu, fearing for alertness, recalled the coffee and, with it, the food.

"I cannot see to drive at this moment. I can share some food, if you can take coffee—"

Toragin had water for her and the cat. She declined coffee but accepted a half handwich; the others were pleased to get something—the recumbent driver in the back being allowed to partially sit up to sip at one of the cups passed to the rear seat.

Amid thanks and sips it took a moment for Vertu to realize

that the cab's wind-inspired trembling had nearly stopped; indeed, the snow was no longer falling slantwise. Her cab's lights gained range, though how much was hard to gauge in the soft-edged whiteness.

"Might be over!" Yulie said, startling everyone else in the near silence.

Vertu let the windscreen clean itself; now only tiny flakes fell, the density and demeanor of the storm fallen to flurry that quickly.

"Guess the lightning blew it out," suggested the other cab driver. "Must've been one last huff of wind!"

Anna spoke then, sounding as certain as a priestess:

"We are in the Old One's shadow. It knows where we are and has sucked the storm into itself!"

Despite the outside temperature, now well below frost point, Vertu lowered her window briefly, allowing a few fine crystals of flurry to drift in on a lazy clean-smelling breeze. Peering forward, up the road, she felt that she knew exactly where the Tree was.

"Ten minutes it'd be from here in dry weather," Yulie volunteered, "might be eight if you was hurrying. Guessing two or three time that now, driving careful. Do that—drive careful, 'cause it's a heckuva walk in the snow. Even if the wind's gone."

Another brilliant crystal of snow flitted into the window before Vertu sealed it.

"Three," said Toragin. "Three kittens so far. They will want a warm place to sleep tonight."

The rest of the drive was not uneventful—there was the arrival of the fourth kitten to begin with, and then there was the moment when the cab's entire structure began to glow, starting with a light misty haze and then with a vivid bluish glow that slowly phased to green.

"Salmo's Fire!" Yulie said excitedly. "Salmo's Fire happens when them electrons gets all into a plasma and settles tight around something that can trade electrons around it. I've seen it on quiet nights hanging on 'quipment tips and stuff. My brother had it ball up at the end of his rifle one night when we was out . . . "

Yulie let the sentence die then, like the memory might be best if left unstirred, but everyone in the cab could feel the glow dancing across their skins. Chelada's fourth kitten was born then, enveloped along with her mother in the pulsing green. Vertu felt her hair standing away from her head, and saw motion in the "fire" itself, as if the kittens were, one by one, petted and soothed by the action of the plasma, the final kitten getting an extra helping.

"I don't do much dreaming but I could think I was dreaming this whole thing!" Again Yulie caught the mood of the cab, but the glow was real, reflecting back into the vehicle from the surrounding snow for several eerie minutes until it faded infinitesimally to normal.

Vertu's glance flitted from interior to exterior, the night's darkness gaining depth as clouds rapidly dissipated; now only the instrument lights lit the interior.

The darkness outside wasn't complete since the cab's lights played over the snow-covered road and the snow-covered vegetation. Vertu glanced up, sensing—

Yes! There, where that glow was—*that* was where the Tree waited!

Toragin laughed. Vertu caught sight of the nursery as the new mother dabbed at the kittens, adjusting herself for their comfort. Toragin's face was bright in the instrument lights. She gasped as the pinnacle of green was briefly visible between the line of vegetation that flanked the road before it hit another curve.

"There, that's the Tree!"

"Old One!" said Anna, then something in that other language to Rascal, and perhaps to Mary, while Yulie muttered.

"'Splains those pods right good. Darn thing's got eyes can see all the way to town and more, don't it?"

After a pause he went on—

"Prolly another three minutes, now, to my place. Me an' Mary, Anna an' Rascal'll just get out and walk in—no sense you going all the way in to the house, Miss Vertu, then havin' to come back out again. Been enough o'that recently. This fella here'll be better with the neighbors, and Miss Toragin and her family's got their invitation, and Miss Vertu'll do the smart thing, and let the neighbor take care of her tonight."

"Yes," said Vertu, thinking that the chances were very good, indeed, that *Clan Korval's* comms worked. She ought to call Cheever, and Jemmie...

"Here we're comin' up on it," Yulie said. "Just ease to a stop under that twisted tree there. Right, now—"

He stopped talking.

Vertu looked out the window, at the so-called driveway.

"That drift's taller than Anna," Mary commented. "I guess we could toss her and Rascal over it."

"Don't know how wide is it," Yulie said, sounding momentarily glum. "Not to say that leaves you an' me walking through up to our waists."

"We can do it."

"Well, sure, we *can* do it," said Yulie, rallying. "But do we *gotta* do it, that's the question."

There was a moment's silence.

"Well, no. We *ain't* gotta do it. We'll just all of us go on up the hill, if Miss Vertu'll still have us, and ask the neighbor do they have room."

He sniffed.

"Huh. Not sure where that come from. Like somebody whispered—welcome—inside my ear."

"An invitation," Toragin said surprisingly, "from the Tree. I have heard such whisperings myself."

"Guess that'll do until something official turns up," said Yulie.

Toragin gave a rueful laugh.

"Perhaps it will, at that," she said.

ACT SEVEN

In the Hall of the Mountain King
Enter Dragons

THE ROOM was full of dragons.

Given that the room in question was a small, intimate parlor off a side hall with quick access to an outside door, it might be said to have been overfull of dragons.

There were, for instance, the two curled together on the sofa near the fire. The room had been built to their scale.

There were, too, those other dragons—dozens and dozens of dragons undertaking an intricate, multileveled dance against a glittering sky. Wings brushed wings, dancers wheeling. Here, one or two folded and fell, wings snapping wide with a *boom* and they rocketed upward, into the dance and through it, seeking the limits of space.

Green warmth informed the dance—the Tree's regard for its dragons was true. It remembered them all, celebrated their lives and the frequent astonishment of their achievements. Mint scented the air, and saw a wash of green, like leaves between her and the dancers. Beside her Val Con shifted, and she felt him move, wings stirring, as if he would rise from the sofa and join the others in celebration.

There came the impression of an indulgent laugh; the idea of a kiss upon the cheek.

The Tree embraced them, and for a moment Miri's senses swam, as she stretched her wings, feeling the starwind fill them, bearing her further up, beyond branches and leaves. She looked to her right where Val Con flew at her very wingtip.

Above them, the dance was ending, dragons peeling away from the group, singly, or in small groups, fading into the glittering sky.

Miri folded her wings, saw Val Con do the same, and opened her eyes a moment later to the fire in the hearth, her head on Val Con's shoulder, and her legs curled beneath her.

She stretched, and sat up, looking into brilliant green eyes.

"Gotta say, you're a nice lookin' dragon," she told him.

He smiled.

"I return the compliment. We should fly together again—soon."

"Done," she said and tipped her head, considering. The impression of a vast, green regard remained present, and also an undercurrent of what might have been—apprehension.

"So," she said. "We're loved and respected and the first in the Tree's regard. I read that right?"

"I believe that is the message, yes," Val Con said. "It must of course be flattering to know that we stand at the pinnacle of the Tree's regard. However, the Tree fails to instruct us with regard to those others who are also held in its regard. It is the duty of those who stand high to care for those who stand lower. As delm, we know this."

The warm greenness lost some of its depth; Miri felt a little flutter, as if of confusion, and a quick flash of dragons, dancing. The feeling of close green attention faded, somewhat.

"If I may . . . " Jeeves spoke from the ceiling grid.

"Please," said Val Con. "We should like to offer the promise-bearer proper honor, and time, as I understand it, is short."

"Indeed, sir. The taxi has passed Yulie Shaper's house. Scans indicate that the drive is impassable. The House will be asked to guest twelve. I have updated staff."

"Twelve!" Miri repeated.

"To be precise, four of those are newly born, and will wish to stay with their mother, who will, I believe, wish to remain with the other promise-bearer. Of the six remaining, four are Yulie Shaper and his party of four—this including Rascal—one is Vertu Dysan, and the other is the driver of another taxi, who has taken injury. I calculate the car will be with us in seven minutes."

"Time is very short," Val Con said dryly. "Jeeves—sum up, if you will!"

"Yes, sir. In short: the recent opening of the Tree's horizons, including conversations with various members of the Clutch, access to the Surebleak gestalt, has resulted in the Tree reevaluating the way it communicates with all of us. As I said before, the Tree realizes that it has made errors in the past. Some—I would say, most—of those errors are so far in the past that the Tree can do nothing to rectify them. It has understood that it must Balance with the promise-bearers now approaching, that to do anything else would be to dishonor the long service of its dragons. This realization, combined with the broadening of its understanding, brought additional introspection. It has become aware that, while it has acted always for the good of Jela's heirs, that—occasionally—it may have worked with too much force, acted with, I will say, *hauteur*—"

The feeling of intense green attention was back, so dense Miri worried that the walls might crack.

"Yes," said Jeeves, "hauteur. The Tree will be making changes in the way it deals with Jela's get—that is a promise, a *considered promise*. It will also seek to modify and improve its way of dealing with those others who may assist, or serve it in capacity outside the care of dragons."

He paused; Miri caught the sense that he was listening.

"Yes. The Tree offers the idea that its dragons are—family, sir. And that the promise-bearers, and those others which assist it in the pursuit of its hobbies are—friends."

There was a strong sense of affirmation inside the little room— the flames fluttered, as if by a sudden draft. Then the sense of the Tree was gone entirely, and Jeeves spoke once more.

"The cab is here. I have opened the gate to them."

"Excellent," Val Con said, rising with Miri. "We will meet them at the side door. Please have Nelirikk attend us. If our wounded cabbie cannot walk, then he can be carried, and given medical attention."

ACT EIGHT
Scene One

The Gate
Enter Nelirikk and Jarome

SOMETHING GLITTERED in the headlights. The cab crept forward, out of deep snow into what felt like naked road surface beneath the wheels. The glitter resolved itself into a gate—*the* gate, wrought metal with leaves and dragons woven along the bars and arches.

Vertu sighed; heard it echoed by every one of her passengers, save, perhaps, the kittens.

"Made it," said Yulie. "Wasn't never any doubt, not with Miss Vertu drivin.'"

She felt laughter tighten her chest, rising, and deliberately swallowed. Perhaps it was wisest to not laugh *yet*, she thought.

For a long moment, they sat there, contemplating the gate, while the gate contemplated them.

Slowly, then, the sections separated, swinging back with a stately inevitability. Vertu nudged the cab forward, noting that the driveway beyond the gate was in fact clear of snow.

Carefully, she followed the drive, and when snow again appeared on the surface, she scrupulously kept the cab to the dry surface until the drive ended at a low wall, a lighted door beyond.

Standing between them and the door were three people in snow coats—two Liaden high, and one very tall—one of Korval's guards, she knew, but was uncertain as to which, with his face hidden in the shadow of his hood.

"There, now, driver," said Yulie, apparently to the wounded cabbie. "That big fella there, that's Nelirikk. He'll have you outta here and them legs looked at and fixed up before you can say *snowflakes are fallin' on my head*!"

"He a medic?" asked the cabbie, sounding nervous.

"He was a soldier, now security for the Road Bosses," Mary said surprisingly. "He is a field medic, and Anna has already done much of what was needful for you. I think you will find that you can drive, tomorrow."

"That'd be fine by me," said the cabbie. "S'long's I can get my cab out."

"You come on over to my place tomorrow, after we're all rested," Yulie said. "Get the snow tractor out and rustle up a couple o'my hands. Haver out in no time."

Vertu locked the wheel, opened the door, and got out of the cab.

The three walked forward, and Vertu recognized Korval Themselves.

She bowed, lesser to greater, and received bows of welcome to the guest in return.

"Boss," she said, in Terran so that all of her fares would understand what she asked for in their behalf. "The storm brought us to you. We ask shelter, and rest—"

"And Rascal wants his dinner!" Anna called out, opening the back door and coming to Vertu's side, dog at her heel.

"Good even, Miri. Good even, Val Con. Nelirikk, come and get Jarome out of the back. He's hurt, and needs to be looked at in good light."

"Good evening, Anna. Rascal," said Val Con yos'Phelium.

"Have you done first aid?" Nelirikk asked Anna.

"I'll show you, but first you need to get him out."

"Yes," he said, and walked around Vertu, heading for the back of the car.

"There's Yulie and Mary, too, we heard," said Miri Tiazan. "And someone with a cat and kittens."

"I am here, Korval."

The front passenger door opened, and Toragin stepped out. She advanced, and bowed as one who has been invited.

"Toragin del'Pemridj Clan Lazmeln; Chelada is with me, and her newborns. She was promised by the Tree itself that she would have her kittens safe beneath its branches."

"And so the Tree is forsworn," said Val Con yos'Phelium. "We may have you escorted directly to the Tree, with Chelada and the newborn, if that is your wish."

"Yes," said Toragin, and paused as a burst of cursing at the back of the cab told the progress of Cabbie Jarome's extraction.

"I will need a basket, or a box," Toragin said, turning back to Korval. "Right now, the kittens and Chelada are on the floor, in a blanket."

"Right," said Miri Tiazan, and tipped her head. "Jeeves, need us some kitten transport."

"Yes, Miri," a mellow voice spoke from the air. "I will bring it."

There came another burst of swearing, and a gasp. Rascal barked, once, and here came Nelirikk, Anna and the dog beside him, Jarome flung over one broad shoulder in a field carry.

The door opened as they approached, and they vanished within. A moment later, a man-high cylindrical object, with a bright orange ball where a man's head might have been exited by the same door, holding a basket in one gripper, and a blanket in the other.

It approached and extended the basket.

"Will these suffice?"

Toragin considered. The basket was deep and wide enough for all five cats. The blanket would make a soft nest.

"Thank you," she said. "I will be a moment."

She turned back to the cab.

From the back of the cab now came Yulie and Mary. They passed Toragin, and approached, Yulie with a grin on his face.

"Some kinda storm," he said affably. "Get 'em like that at the old home?"

"Nothing nearly so awe-inspiring," Val Con yos'Phelium said. "I see that you have come to no harm."

"Not the least bit," Yulie said. "We're a might peckish, though. I don't s'pose there's any of Mrs. ana'Tak's cookies 'round the kitchen?"

"In fact, there is an entire buffet in the breakfast room. Mrs. ana'Tak would have it no other way. I believe there are cookies, and also soup, and biscuits, wine and juice. If you will, let us show you the way."

He turned, sweeping an arm out toward the patio door, ushering the couple forward.

"Vertu?" Miri Tiazan gave her a grin. "That's you, too. Got rooms ready, too, 'cause if you don't mind my sayin' so, you're lookin' all done in."

Vertu managed a smile.

"It was a trying day," she murmured.

"All done now, though, right? This way—"

She turned, and Vertu followed, pausing just at the edge of the patio to look up—up into the now-cloudless dark sky, where a monumental shadow was silhouetted against the stars.

Scene Two

In the Hall of the Mountain King
Enter Joey

THERE WERE CATS. Many cats. Cats of all colors. Vertu walked carefully, unwilling to step on a vulnerable paw in her storm boots, until she saw that the cats displayed a fine understanding of where she and her boots were, and that they were not so much a random mob, as an—escort down the hall.

"Hoping to get some handouts from the buffet," Miri Tiazan said from beside her. "Hear them tell it, all they got here is empty bowls."

Vertu smiled. She had left her coat on the hook by the door, alongside her hosts' jackets, and those of Yulie and Mary. It was pleasantly warm in the hallway; she was glad to be walking, no matter the comfort of her driving seat, and the cats, seen as escort, began to amuse her.

Perhaps a little too much, she thought.

"I am grateful for the House's care," she said, in Liaden.

Miri Tiazan slanted a look at her face.

"The House is grateful to be able to extend its care," she answered, and her accent in the High Tongue was that of Solcintra. She jerked her chin slightly to the right.

"Here we are," she said, back in Terran.

Yulie and Mary were standing, struck, in the center of the room, while Val Con yos'Phelium was seen at the wine table, seeing to the filling of glasses.

"Driver Dysan," he said, not looking 'round. "Red or white?"

"Red, if you please," she answered, as their cat escort flowed around her feet, and one in particular—a large, fuzzy gray with black feet—marched forward with purpose.

"Joey!" shouted Yulie Shaper, and went down on one knee, arms wide. Vertu thought to glance at the wine table, but Val Con yos'Phelium's nerves were as steady as any Scout's might be. The glasses were intact, the wine unspilled.

The gray cat leapt, and landed in Yulie's arms. He rose, hugging it over his shoulder.

"But, Joey, what're you doin' here? Botherin' the Bosses?"

"Not at all," said the host, turning to offer Mary a glass of the white. "We believe that several of yours came up the hill when the storm became apparent, as support for our cats in-house."

"Well, that's a nice face to put on it," said Yulie, "an' I'm glad you kept 'em inside. But they start makin' a habit—or a nuisance—you send 'em packing."

"Sure we will," said Miri Tiazan. "You ever try to tell a cat what to do?"

Mary laughed.

"Yulie, your wine," she said.

"Hmm—oh, right. Thanks, Boss."

Joey slung over one shoulder like a furry towel, Yulie turned and took his glass.

Vertu stepped forward and received hers, with a bow of the head.

"My thanks," she murmured.

"My pleasure," he returned.

"I wonder," she said then, "if I might use the comm."

"Of course. I will show you."

Jemmie was pleased, though not surprised, to learn that Vertu was sheltering at the top of the hill.

"Road Boss knows their bidness, always said so," she said in sum-up.

"When I come back down," Vertu said, "we will need to talk about the rogue cabs. We nearly lost a man to his own incompetence, and a failure to maintain an adequate machine. It is our place as the professionals to do something."

"Yanno, I been thinking the same. We'll talk about it when you get back home. Might need to take it up with the Bosses—but that's later, Vertu. Right now, you call your big man an' let him know you're safe, fed, an' about to tuck up. Then you go and tuck up, hear me?"

"I hear you, Jemmie," Vertu said softly. "Thank you for your care."

"Funny to be thanked for something comes so nat'ral. Now, you hang up this call and get with that man o'yours."

• • • ✧ • • •

"**SO, YOU GOT UP TO THE HOUSE** all right, then. They taking good care of you?"

Someone who was not as familiar with Cheever McFarland's voice might have thought him unconcerned, even bored. Vertu heard otherwise, and smiled into the phone.

"Indeed, we have arrived safely, all twelve of us."

"*Twelve* of you! How'd that happen?"

She smiled, took a sip of her wine, and told him.

Sometime during the telling, she felt something soft land in her lap and glanced down to find one of the ubiquitous cats sitting on one knee and kneading the other, while purring. Loudly.

"What's that, a motor?"

"A cat," Vertu told him. "This house is full of cats, and apparently this one has seen an opportunity to claim a comfortable lap for itself."

"What color cat?" Cheever asked.

Vertu frowned.

"All the colors," she said, after a moment. "Brown, orange, grey, white, black . . . The two front feet are white; the two back feet are black."

"Got a real looker, there," Cheever said. "So, what're you gonna do about the wild cabs?"

Vertu laughed. He knew her so well.

"Jemmie and I will talk about it, when I am back home."

"Good idea. Let me know if you need any help putting together a presentation for the Bosses."

She shook her head. The cat continued to purr and knead.

"Jemmie also thought we'd have to get the Bosses involved," she said.

"Road Boss at least," said Cheever. "Might be best to bring it up to all of 'em, though. Surebleak's gonna be needing associations and formal rules sooner more'n later."

"I fear you are correct," she said, "though I would not want to see Surebleak become Liad."

"Nobody wants that!" Cheever said in mock horror. "Now, you get yourself something to eat and some downtime. I got the house covered. Snow clearin' crews are already out, so you should be able to get back down into the city tomorrow in time to meet me for lunch at the Emerald."

"Excellent," Vertu said cordially. "I will see you then, Cheever." She hesitated. "Thank you for your care," she added.

"You bet," he said after a small pause. "You take care now, hear?"

"I will," she said, and resolutely cut the connection.

The cat was curled tightly in her lap. She sighed, and carefully slipped her hands under its dense, furry body, and moved it carefully to the bench. She then stood, picked up her wine glass and went back to the breakfast room.

Anna and Rascal had joined Mary and Yulie. The hosts were not in sight.

"Left us to ourselfs," said Yulie, "so we don't feel we gotta do the polite. Once Anna's finished eating, we'll just say we're *ready to retire* an' somebody'll come along to show us the way. Got it all set up with Nelirikk for him to take us over to my place tomorrow morning, by snow machine. So, we'll be saying goodnight and bye-for-now, Miss Vertu."

"Thank you," she said. "You were wonderful passengers."

"And you were a wonderful driver," Mary said, smiling. "We were fortunate, that it was your cab that we saw, and decided to wait."

"Goodnight, Miss Vertu," said Anna, coming to stand at Mary's side, Rascal cuddled in her arms. "Good driving!"

"Thank you for your help," Vertu answered. "Without your Sight, we would have missed the other cab, which would have been very bad."

"Yes," Anna said, and yawned widely.

"I think that's our cue," said Yulie. He bent and picked the fuzzy grey cat from the chair where it was napping. "C'mon, Joey, you're worn right down to bones and claws. Best get to bed."

A shadow moved in the door, murmuring.

"This way, please. We have prepared rooms."

The three of them marched out, and Vertu turned to the buffet to make herself a plate.

She poured another glass of wine, carried it and the plate to a small table, and sat down. She felt something land in her lap, and looked down to see the same multicolored cat in her lap, looking up in to her face with wide green eyes.

Vertu smiled.

"I suppose you're hungry?" she said.

Scene Three

The Tree Court

IT WAS WARM in this place—the Tree Court, according to Jeeves, who had brought them here—and the air smelled of mint and green growing things. There were gloan-roses, just like those at home—on the side of the enclosure opposite the Tree. There was no snow on the short, velvety grass, though the ground was disturbed by humps and hillocks made by the roots closest to the surface.

Toragin hesitated at the edge of the space, basket of cats cuddled against her chest, shivering slightly.

Her anger—her anger on her own behalf—was gone. But for Chelada, and her kittens, she found she could yet be angry.

And so she hesitated, wondering of a sudden if a prudent person would bring anger into this place, or confront the presence that filled this place, like a—well, like a god was said to fill a place holy to her.

She received the idea of gentle laughter, and a sense of soft denial. The Tree was no god, though the Tree had met gods, years and universes gone.

She received the idea that she should come forward, to the Tree's massive trunk, and that she might present her companions.

Careful of her footing among the roots, Toragin did go forward, and knelt in a soft patch of grass at the Tree's base. She settled the basket, and lifted the blanket, glancing up into the leaves.

"This proud mother is Chelada," she said softly. "She gave birth to these four fine kits as we were on the final step of our journey to see your promise to her fulfilled today. They were born in the midst of adventure, but they seem none the worse for it. I have not yet had a chance to do a thorough examination . . . "

She received the thought that the kittens were beautiful, healthy and free of deformity. After a moment, another such thought inserted itself into her head, that Chelada was likewise beautiful and healthy, and also wise. It put Toragin in mind of one of the elder uncles, who depended upon compliments and charm to rescue him from any social faux pas he might make—and he made many.

"You failed to keep your promise," she said sternly.

What arrived this time was not so much a notion or a thought, but an emotion—dismay, thought Toragin, embarrassment.

Sorrow.

"If you will allow," said Jeeves, the robot who had escorted them to this place. "I am empowered to translate the Tree's—communications—into speech. I offer because the conversation will move more quickly, which you may find desirable, as you are—forgive me—hungry and weary after a very trying day. The Tree would by no means prevent you from enjoying the hospitality of the House, but it wishes to have this matter that lies between it, and yourselves . . . Balanced as quickly as may be."

"Yes," Toragin said, aware of a grittiness in her eyes, and a certain feeling of . . . uncertainty in her thoughts. "Let us by all means come into Balance. Chelada and I had treasured our connection on the homeworld. We had thought we had mattered to the network, that our work was of value. In particular, Chelada had valued the promise that her kittens would be born undertree. To find everything swept aside, without one word, with, so it seemed to me, no thought given to promises made . . . "

"Precisely," said Jeeves. "The Tree acknowledges its error. It wishes you to know that it is *sorry*—profoundly so—for failing to honor its promises, and also for its failure to properly appreciate work well done. It would make amends, but it does not know what would be appropriate.

"It asks if you would view some specific action or object as *being*—or perhaps *representing*—amends."

Toragin settled back on her heels, considering the kittens in the basket. She listened for Chelada's voice without very much hope—and thus was surprised.

"Chelada wishes the original promise honored in broad outline," she said slowly. "She would stay, with her kittens—these kittens—undertree and safe until I find a suitable establishment in the city for us. She would also have it that the last-born will remain as her representative to the Tree, to remind it to honor its promises."

There was a small silence before Jeeves spoke.

"The Tree will make these amends and so return to Balance with Chelada."

Toragin inclined her head, realized her eyes were drifting shut and sat up straighter.

"And you, Toragin del'Pemridj, what would you have as amends?"

"Consideration for a place in the cat welfare network the Tree has undoubtedly built here, on Surebleak." She squared her shoulders, shook her hair back and stared up into the branches.

"Understand me! I do not want to be given a position—I want fair consideration for a position. Neither I nor Chelada mean to return to Liad. I wish to be of use, which I will never be on Liad. If I cannot be of use to you, I will find something else!"

There was another silence, slightly longer than the first. Jeeves spoke again.

"If you are determined not to return to Liad," he said slowly, "the Tree has a proposition for you ... "

ACT NINE

In the Hall of the Mountain King

VERTU DRIFTED slowly toward wakefulness, there being no alarm to insist upon her arising. She smiled, sleepily, and turned her head on the pillow, seeking after the surety of the Tree—just there, on her left, its presence as strong as she had ever felt it.

More, she felt a steady return regard, amused, and oddly tender.

Vertu Dysan, the thought came into her head. *Good morn, neighbor.*

"Good morn," she murmured, and stretched, noting that her left foot was slightly stiff, which was odd. She would have understood it, had her driving foot been complaining, after yesterday's demands, but this was not her driving foot.

She stretched again—and heard a sneeze from that quadrant.

Carefully, she sat up.

The multicolored cat was lying half on her foot among the bedclothes. It opened its eyes as if it had felt Vertu's attention, then deliberately squinted them shut.

"I see," she said. "Good morn to you, also, cat. I will be rising in another moment, and dressing, and going to find some tea, and news of the road. It has been pleasant, sharing a bed with you, but all pleasures come to an end."

The cat yawned, showing a wide dainty mouth full of pointed teeth.

Vertu arrived at the breakfast room to find Toragin before her, sipping tea and eating an egg muffin.

"Good morn," she said. "Are the rest of us still abed?"

"Yulie, Mary, Anna, and Rascal left an hour ago, on a snow truck driven by the very large man who is a medic," Toragin said. "Jarome is resting still. The hosts were in, and promise a return after certain of their morning business has been resolved. In the meanwhile, there is news on the comm."

She used her chin to point.

Vertu poured a cup of tea, and approached the comm, being careful of the multicolored cat, weaving between her feet.

"If you trip me, we will neither escape injury," she said to it.

"She is trying to convince you of her devotion," Toragin said. "She is looking for a quieter place, with a convivial companion, and believes that you will do very well for each other."

Vertu eyed her.

"If you speak cat, please allow—her—to know that my house includes one other individual."

Toragin inclined her head, and murmured, "She does not find that objectionable. I am desired to say that she is a very good hunter, and knows all of the songs for sleeping, and healing, and heart's ease."

"That is an impressive list of accomplishments in one I believe to be quite young. Has she a name, I wonder?"

Toragin smiled slightly.

"She will accept a House name from you."

"Ah," said Vertu, and turned to the news.

"It would appear," she said after some study, "that I may safely return to the city this morning. May I offer you a ride? Or do you and Chelada guest with Korval?"

"Chelada and the kittens guest with the Tree," Toragin said. "I—I have been offered a position, which I am inclined to accept, it being work I enjoy, and which I do well. I will not live here, however, but will need my own establishment, in the city. Might you advise me?"

"I would be honored," said Vertu. "You should know that finding a suitable place may take some time." She hesitated; she remembered the many empty, echoing rooms in her own house.

"If you wish it, you may stay with me while you look for a more pleasing arrangement. I have recently purchased a house, which was once several apartments. There is, right now, myself and occasionally my lover, but that is not enough to keep the house happy."

"That is very generous," said Toragin. "I will accept, and thank you."

"We assist each other," said Vertu. "Neighbor-work, as Yulie would have it."

"Yes. I wonder—"

The comm buzzed, and Vertu turned back to it, even as a mellow voice spoke from the vicinity of the ceiling.

"Call for Vertu Dysan, routed to the screen in the breakfast room."

She touched the accept button, and Cheever's face snapped into sharp focus.

"I knew it," he said. "Sleeping in."

"Indeed," she answered with a smile. "Tell me you would do differently."

"Not me. Just callin' to let you know the roads are cleaning up fast. Temps are up and the sun's as bright as can be. You can come on down soon's you're awake."

"I'll do that," she told him, and tipped her head. "Cheever," she said.

"Yeah?"

"I wonder—do you like cats?"

✧ Preferred Seating ✧

PART OF THE ONGOING DISCUSSIONS about the existence of, and the problems caused by, luck. When the happenstance of having luck can be so fraught, being luck personified becomes life-altering. Preferred Seating is mirrored by Ambient Conditions.

✧✧✧

SAY WHAT YOU MIGHT about foolish valor—and Can Ith had said his share—the mission had provided an interesting piloting exercise, and fortunate it was that he had been home on leave, if one could conceive of such a thing.

They had made excellent time to this faraway port, three small tradeships, pod-stripped, one of Ixin's, showing the Moon and Rabbit with some reluctance—but what else could they do when Korval's two vessels flaunted the Tree-and-Dragon and never thought to do otherwise?

So, three small ships, as traders went, pelting through space as though pursued, which was only . . . somewhat . . . likely. Port was raised, and permission gained to off-load the cargo, which was done, shuttle-load by shuttle-load, none of the captains being quite so gallant as to risk the big ships at dock.

Can Ith had drawn shuttle duty, which would not have been so ill, had he not drawn second seat, and his cousin Sin Jin first. Still, it wasn't as if they needed to speak to one another, and the off-loading went quickly.

It wasn't until the last of the cargo was down and off, that the mission acquired a complication, and red tape tied the shuttles to the dock.

It seemed that there were tests to be administered to the cargo, and those found to fall short were to be returned to the ships. The number of those failing as of this port-morning had been three, which was not so high a percentage. Still, their contract had been to make delivery here, off-loading *safely and fully* before turning back to the homeworld.

Safely and fully had its own power, in contracts; and if it had not, even Sin Jin would have been hard put to justify simply abandoning the culls at the dock.

It was decided in consultation between the captains that the Rabbit's ship was best placed to take up the rejected, as there was another port open to them, which would not necessarily welcome a Dragon. The shuttle Firsts were dispatched as a group to place this plan before the portmaster. Assuming it found favor, Korval's ships would be free to return to the homeworld. In theory. Can Ith's faith in theory was . . . not nonexistent, and of no matter in any case. Scout captain he might be, but family, so the saying went, kept its own rank, and Sin Jin was his elder by two Standards, and was further favored by the delm, for the sake of his mother.

The Firsts had been away for some time. Rather longer, Can Ith considered, than they ought to have been, had the portmaster been inclined to the proposal. That was worrying, for personal reasons. Home-leave from the Scouts only *seemed* to last forever, and he was running close to time. Mission planning had not considered the possibility of a lengthy layover. If the proposal was accepted, and Korval's ships given leave to depart, and they flew home with the same vigor with which they had flown away . . .

. . . he would arrive on Liad in good time to make his bow to the delm, and report to Scout Headquarters.

If the proposal was not accepted, Can Ith would need to find his own way home, and that quickly.

He accessed star maps and trade routes—which only proved his fears. If they did not leave this port, *soon*, he would not raise Liad before his leave was over.

He might, of course, pinbeam Scout Commander and his team second, to apprise them of his projected tardiness. Neither would be pleased, but—

The hatch-open light flashed on his board; the security screen at the bottom right of his array came live. Sin Jin was back and not seeming particularly buoyant.

Can Ith was on his feet when his cousin hit the bridge.

"Are we free to fly?" he asked.

That earned him two raised eyebrows—he and his cousin were not friends, and scarcely spoke.

Can Ith raised his eyebrows in answer, and received a small, malicious smile.

"So eager to raise Liad? Cousin."

"Truly, my need for Liad is temporary; merely I must pass through on the way to Scout Headquarters. My leave is running out, and I would prefer not to have to explain a tardy arrival to the commander."

"Oh, is *that* what distresses you! I am pleased to be able to do proper duty of kin and relieve you of anxiety. You will not be tasked to give an accounting of yourself to the Scout commander—ever again. The delm has sent that you are required by your clan, and has removed you from the roster of active Scouts."

The deck moved—Can Ith thought so, but his cousin stood steady, so it had merely been the force of the information—which was *surely* false. So he told himself. He knew his cousin's malice of old; it would be like him to lie for the simple pleasure of causing consternation.

"I see that you don't wish to believe me!" said Sin Jin. "I assure you, it is so. You no longer owe duty to any but to Korval. The delm has found Lezina yos'Phelium unfit for the more strenuous duties attending the second speaker. You will assume those, as Lezina's assistant."

Can Ith stared, still not wanting to believe. *Assistant* to the second speaker, who had served, all honor to her, for forty years, before she fell into dotage? It was a paired cruelty to force her to continue in a position she could no longer understand, and to name the new second-speaker-in-fact a mere assistant.

Yet, Can Ith admitted, there was a certain terrible logic to it, from the viewpoint of a delm. Korval was the author of this current folly, robbing the Council of Clans of its scapegoats. The clan could not show weak, or in any way vulnerable. To replace so notable a personage as the second speaker at such a time . . .

No, Can Ith thought.

Sin Jin was not lying.

It was true.

The only wonder was that his cousin had managed to contain himself thus long before delivering the blow.

And even that was scarcely a wonder. Why blurt the thing out, when a little waiting would eventually produce a situation where the payoff in dismay would be so very much higher?

Numbly, Can Ith reached for his jacket.

"Where are you going?" his cousin asked.

"Out," he replied. "I'm overdue leave."

Can Ith didn't stay to hear what first chair might say, or even looked at him at all. He turned on his heel and walked down the hall to the hatchway.

* * * ✦ * * *

THE PORT was scarcely three streets deep, and no more than four long. For all of that, it was divided into lawful and less-lawful sections, with the less-lawful including those things most of interest to a spacer on leave—drink, gambling, companionship, and rough entertainments. The lawful side encompassed a casino, a restaurant, a luxury hotel, and a theater, those being both overpriced and chancy for persons new on port. Also, the restaurant at least, where the captains and the pilots had dined with the portmaster and the receiving committee, was perhaps not so fine as the locals believed.

It was instinct to turn away from the lawful port, where proctors waited to discover the unwary spacer in violation of a law—and to approach the less-lawful side, where a pilot might drink in peace, with only the occasional threat of footpads. In his present state, the opportunity to lesson footpads would only be a relief.

He had taken a heavy blow, but he was not entirely lost to good sense. He did not seek the downright dangerous streets off of the port proper; indeed, he made for the bar his opposite number on the Rabbit shuttle had recommended as a decent and quiet place to have a glass or two of tolerable wine, and a tray of the local breads and cheeses, which she represented as excellent. She had warned him that there was live music, adding that it had been easy to ignore, and that apparent attention to the musicians had not been interpreted by the locals as a desire for company.

So it was that he turned into the well-lit doorway of an establishment styling itself the Dancing Colors, entering a room slightly less well lit, and moderately full of patrons. There *was* music; he traced its source to a back corner, where two persons sat on a low dais, one holding a stringed instrument across her lap; the other playing a pipe.

The result of their efforts was moderately pleasing, certainly nothing that would intrude upon his thoughts.

He decided against a stool at the crowded bar. Rather, he took a table near the musicians and sat with his back against the wall, and most of the room before him—his preferred seating in such situations—and smiled up at the server.

* * * ⟡ * * *

THE MUSICIANS left the stage for their break, and Can Ith was considering calling for a second glass of very tolerable wine. He had ordered the bread and cheese plate, which arrived with a separate small bowl of "*akashi*, sir," which he was given to know was a local fruit, and this its season.

He sampled the small loaf of crusty brown bread—still warm inside, and tasting of malt. It paired well with the hard yellow cheese, and he made a mental note to thank the Rabbit co-pilot for her information.

Despite the good flavor, it was not food—nor even wine—that he wanted. What he *wanted* was Sin Jin's throat between his hands—which, unhappily, was no new desire.

Can Ith sighed. It was not done, to murder one's cousin. Nor was it done to disobey the delm, though he was less rigorous on that point. He was, after all, a Scout, trained to think outside of Liad's customs and the strict clan hierarchies. No, he might *easily* disobey his delm—if he could realize a profit.

Can Ith accepted as truth that the Recall Clause had been invoked. Even if it were possible to manipulate Korval into declaring him dead, he could not return to the Scouts. Once recalled, a Scout was dead to the service.

He sighed, and looked down at his folded hands, the Jump Pilot's Ring a glittering chaos on his second finger.

Taking a deep breath, he cleared his mind, put aside distress and considered the future his delm had chosen for him.

Second speaker—that was a position of some consequence with the hierarchy of the clan. He was not to be second speaker, however; but assistant, and no guarantee that he would rise to her honors when she gave up her soul to the stars.

He laughed, softly, in self-ridicule. *Rise to her honors, indeed!* he jeered inwardly. *Will you give the rest of your life over to organizing seating charts?*

He might, he thought, go *eklykt'i*—fade away into the city, or the outback. Everything he needed was in his jacket; he might go at once.

Despair lifted as he realized that choice existed. Indeed, a very generous choice existed. If Sin Jin had possessed anything like an imagination, he would have tried to keep Can Ith from leaving the ship. No; he was unjust; Sin Jin possessed a very fine imagination, else his mischiefs would not be half so effective.

But Sin Jin had not had the benefit of Scout training.

Sin Jin believed that one must—always—obey the delm.

So, Can Ith thought, finishing the last of his glass. He would call for the check and go.

Let Sin Jin search, if he cared to—and, *here* was a jest! Of *course* he would search! To return to the delm with news that he had exposed her plans to Can Ith beforetime, whereupon he was vanished?

Oh, Sin Jin would search.

Much good it might do him, Can Ith thought, suddenly feeling quite cheerful. It was trivial for a Scout to remain unfound. Sin Jin must at last go home and face Korval, while Can Ith would return to port the moment it was safe to do so, and search about him for a ship—Terran, by necessity—in need of a pilot, or a mechanic, or a cargo master.

Yes. It would do.

Having taken his decision, he looked up—and met the thoughtful dark gaze of a brown-haired Liaden woman. To Scout eyes, she looked worn with long care and too little food. At the same time, there was an excitement in her that drew him, who had only just taken an exhilarating decision of his own.

"Captain yos'Phelium," she said.

"No," he answered gently. "Merely Pilot yos'Phelium."

"But a yos'Phelium is never *merely* a pilot," she said.

He laughed, and intercepted her glance at the bread-and-cheese tray. Hungry, yes. And her jest suggested that she was one of the culls.

Well, he could afford to be generous.

"Sit," he invited her, "if you have a taste for chancy company. I was about to call for more wine. Will you join me?"

"Thank you," she said, and took the chair at his left, which put her back to the wall, the room open to her gaze.

He glanced 'round—and the server was there immediately, receiving his order and the coins that paid for all. There was a stir at the back of the room; an over-shoulder glance discovered the musicians mounting the small stage once again.

"If you were not here for the previous set, you may find the music of interest," he said, playing the host with what charm he could muster. It was the least he might do for his sudden guest. Gods knew what she had endured on Liad, and her good luck that she had made it to the relief ships.

There came a tootling from the pipe, and some plucking of the strings. He looked again, seeing the woman slowly winding pegs on her instrument's neck, plucking, twisting, plucking—until her face blossomed into a smile.

A shift of shadow warned him, and he turned back as their glasses were placed on the table, and more bread, too.

"Cook's gift," the server said to his uplifted brow. "Crowd's thinner than her baking tonight."

"Our thanks to the cook," his companion said with fervor.

The server nodded and swept away.

"The bread is very good," Can Ith said, "and the cheese even better. I did not much care for the *akashi* fruit, but you may find otherwise. Please, make yourself free."

She smiled at him then—fully, as would a comrade, or a friend, or a lover—and raised her glass.

"To the fullness of fortune," she said.

He raised his own glass, pleased to find a toast he could meet.

"To the luck," he answered.

They drank. His companion helped herself to cheese and bread, tasted of the fruits, head tipped consideringly to one side—and returned to bread and cheese.

The musicians began to play, quietly. He listened with half an ear, as he watched the room, and also his tablemate.

Eventually, he spoke.

"You were looking for me—*specifically*, for me."

Dark eyes met his straightly.

"Yes," she said.

"Ah." He sipped wine. "I don't wish to be rude, but if there is something you wish to say, you must speak. I'm soon away."

"Yes," she said again, and then—"You have very strong shields."

"So I am told. I hope you will not ask me to lower them, for I haven't the least notion how to do so. The shields came with me into this life."

She smiled.

"My name is Kishara jit'Luso, Pilot. I am lucky, so my delm cast me out, in order that the clan take no damage from sheltering faulty genes."

Sipping his wine, he considered her.

"Forgive me if I am impertinent," he said, "but, being as I am I know little of those who are gifted. It is true that my entire clan is lucky—and risky. I wonder if you put yourself in danger by seeking me out."

Amusement crossed her face, and he saw that she was younger than he had at first thought.

"As the moth is endangered by the candleflame?" she asked. "You are kind to regard it, but no. I think in this moment, our lucks reinforce each other, to the betterment of both."

"Ah?" he murmured politely.

"Yes," she said, taking up another slice of bread with cheese. "You see, there's about to be a pirate raid."

He blinked at her.

"A pirate raid?" he repeated, as the front door smashed open.

* * * ✧ * * *

THREE BRAVOS rushed in and split up, each overseeing a third of the room, weapons leveled, faces grim.

There was a brief hurrah from the clientele, voices raised, chairs and stools noisily overturned as people leapt to their feet. Can Ith stood silently, keeping his hand deliberately away from his weapon, and watched the scene unfold.

From the side of his eye, he saw that Kishara jit'Luso had risen as well, moving somewhat closer to his side. Possibly, she wished to partake of his luck, he thought, and snorted lightly.

From the center of the room, a chair came flying, and another. The barkeeper ducked beneath the bar, coming up with what looked to be a laser rifle left over from the AI wars.

She got off one shot, burning a gash into the floor a whisker's width from the boots of the nearest bravo, who spun, weapon dropping into line, finger tightening.

Can Ith twitched forward, felt his arm caught in a surprisingly tight grip, just as a shadow moved in the doorway, and one of the most astonishing figures Can Ith had ever seen, outside of a *melant'i* play, strolled into the bar.

He was, at a hazard, Liaden, wearing a space leather jacket over sweater and pants. His boots were new; a multitude of gleaming necklaces festooned him; his hands were a-glitter with rings. He held a halfling Terran girl negligently by her wrist. Her eyes were fixed and flat, and Can Ith wondered if she might be blind.

"Friends, friends!" the new arrival cried in an oddly resonant voice. He held his free hand up, showing it empty, and looked mildly around the room.

"There is no reason for dispute. We are here to pick up supplies and funds, and perhaps personnel. Please, all be calm."

Everyone froze. Can Ith took a breath, felt the hold on his arm tighten, and drop away.

The new arrival pointed a finger at the bartender.

"Put that down," he said chidingly. "You will do someone a hurt."

The bartender put the rifle on the bar.

"Very good," said the Liaden coolly. "Now, if you please—go to the storeroom, and pack up three cases of your best liquor and wine. Bring them here." He pointed at the near end of the bar.

Without a word, the bartender turned, and walked down the bar to a door that must lead to the stockroom.

The Liaden shook the halfling sharply.

"How is that weapon disarmed?"

"Push...red...button...stock."

He pointed at the nearest patron, sitting blank-faced on her barstool.

"You—disarm the rifle."

The woman leaned forward, pushed the red button on the rifle's stock, and sat back.

"Good."

He raised his voice.

"We will now accept donations," he said, his voice washing against the back of the room.

"You—you—you!" He pointed at three frozen patrons, one from each third of the room. "Take a plate or a bowl from the table. Empty it."

He waited while this order was obeyed, food and liquids dumped onto tabletops.

"Now, go to every person in your section. They will give you all their valuable items."

The three turned, and Can Ith watched as every person at every table reached into pockets and pouches, dropping rings, necklets, coins, arm-clasps and other precious things into the proffered container. No one protested. No one appeared to be aware that they were being robbed.

The collector for their section was approaching. Can Ith deliberately held himself still, and made his expression flat. It would appear that the entire room was ensorcelled, under some compulsion that left him, and, seemingly, his companion untouched. He assumed his natural shielding was the cause of his continued liberty. Perhaps Kishara's faulty genes granted her immunity.

The collector was before them. Kishara surrendered half a dozen small coins and a silver ring. Can Ith gave the money from his public pocket, and, with a pang he did not allow to inform his movements, pulled the Jump Pilot's Ring from his finger.

The collector passed on, face blank, movements precise and unnatural, pausing to take the stringed instrument, the flute, and the bowl of coins from the frozen musicians.

"Bring everything to the bar," said the compelling voice, and this, too, was done.

"Go back to your places," he told the collectors, and they did. He stepped to the bar, dragging the halfling with him, and ran his fingers through those things that had been gathered.

"Wait—what is this?"

He turned, Can Ith's ring in his hand. Frowning, he subjected it to a long moment of scrutiny before holding it high.

"Who gave this? Raise a hand!"

Teeth grit, Can Ith raised his hand.

The Liaden strolled down the room, pulling the halfling with him. He stopped before Can Ith, looking him up and down, his smile growing wide.

"Well! Pilot, is it? *Jump*-pilot, in fact? *You* will be coming with me. And who is this—ah . . . lady? What is your relationship with this pilot? Speak true!"

"We are partners," Kishara lied, her voice flat.

"Very good. You also will take employment with me. What is your name?"

"Pelli azSulo."

"What is your name, Pilot? Speak true!"

"Sin Jin Isfelm," Can Ith replied, keeping his face and his tone flat.

"They now belong to me, as you do. Follow."

There seemed to be no choice, here and now. Perhaps an opportunity would arise. Perhaps—well, thought Can Ith—perhaps he would get lucky. Though the reason that Kishara had tied herself to him—partners, indeed!—eluded him. He could wish for a private moment to find what her scheme was, but—

They had arrived at the bar. Their captor pulled a sack from an inside pocket and threw it into Kishara's face. She made no move to catch it, and it settled across her shoulder.

"Pelli! Gather all the donations into the sack."

She plucked the sack up, shook it open and did as she had been ordered, her movements wooden, her face blank. Can Ith observed her as he could—plainly, she was an expert at this game.

"Sin Jin!" his supposed master snapped. "Pick up that case from the bar and stand aside."

"You and you!" A finger indicated two patrons seated placidly at the bar. "Pick up the other cases, and stand aside."

This was done, and Pelli—Kishara—stood forward, holding the sack, and also the two instruments. Their captor frowned, grabbed the stringed instrument in his free hand, lifted it, and smashed it against the bar. Can Ith stiffened, expecting a scream from the musician, but none came. Grinning, the man dropped the pipe to the floor and slammed his boot heel down, the sound of splintering wood perfectly audible.

"Carry the sack," he told Kishara, and turned to face the room.

"We are done here," he said coolly, and Can Ith saw the captive halfling shudder.

"All of you!" He pointed out over the room. "Forget our faces. Forget what happened."

He turned, striding to the door, the halfling stumbling in his wake, then turned, pointing deliberately at Can Ith, Kishara, and the two nameless patrons.

"Follow me!" he ordered, and perforce, they did.

. . .⟡. . .

THEY ARRIVED AT A SHUTTLE. Those who had carried were dismissed with a command to forget. The Liaden looked at his bravos, and said a single word: "Go."

They went, taking their weapons with them.

Can Ith considered his options. If the man would release the halfling, he thought, and felt pressure against his side. Kishara, warning him to be still. He considered that. How if she were, herself, part of this pirate raid? He shifted slightly, centering himself—but the moment was past.

The Liaden jerked the halfling forward, pushing her palm flat against the plate, forcing her chin up with his other hand, so that the scanner got her face and eyes.

The hatch slid open. The Liaden snatched the halfling back against the shuttle's side and pointed at Can Ith and Kishara.

"Stow the goods."

Almost, Can Ith balked, but it came to him that the odds of his survival, Kishara's, and the halfling's, rose significantly, once he was aboard a ship. He carried the case within, as ordered, stowing it.

Kishara brought in the second box of alcohol, and he bent close to her ear.

"I'll want an explanation," he breathed.

"No time," came the answering breath. "Trust me."

Snorting, he turned and went back for the last case, reflecting ruefully on the unlikely fact that he *did* trust her.

The Liaden watched, leaning against the hull, the halfling in one hand, the sack in the other.

When Can Ith stepped back into the shuttle, the Liaden came after, shoving the halfling before him.

"Sin Jin will pilot. Pelli will take the jump-seat. I will have the co-pilot's chair. My carte blanche will kneel, so."

He shoved the halfling down to her knees on the decking, wasting no gentleness. It must have hurt her, yet she gave no cry, nor even blinked, her blind eyes staring.

Can Ith sat in First Seat, and glanced down at the board. The pilot had properly cleared and taken the key. He could, of course, fly the shuttle without a ship's key, though it would require him to do some work behind the board, which would take initiative. He was in receipt of the notion that their captor supposed him dead to initiative.

A full minute passed—two—while he wondered if he would betray his unensorcelled state if he asked—

Beside him, the Liaden made a little purring sound.

"You will want this," he said, reaching to his belt. He held out a ship's key, recognizable, though coated with a brown substance that Can Ith greatly feared was blood.

"Take it," the Liaden snapped. "Dock us with the ship *Merry Mushroom*. Do not contact them."

Can Ith took the key and slotted it. It was sticky, and left red-brown smudges on his fingers.

The board came live. He located the *Merry Mushroom*, and filed intent to lift with the port. The ack came back as he was making sure of his webbing; and they were away.

• • •✧• • •

THE HALFLING SPOKE to the ship, her voice thin and expressionless. The shuttle docked, and they disembarked.

The Liaden went first, shoving the halfling ahead, and it seemed to Can Ith that she dragged her feet somewhat. He heard a definite whimper when she was pushed hard against the wall as the Liaden put her palm to the plate.

The door slid open to a common room. The Liaden threw the halfling in; she hit the floor with a cry, rolling, as crew started up, alarm dawning on their faces.

"Sit down and be calm!" the Liaden said, firmly, in just such a tone as had gotten results down below.

The crew hesitated, looking from one to the other, and from the floor, the halfling screamed, "Kill him! He killed Father and Sinda!"

• • •✧• • •

AFTER, Can Ith and Kishara sat with the crew, and the halfling Jaim Evrit, daughter of Trader Ban Evrit and Pilot Sinda Mark, and told over what had happened.

"The field is peculiar to the planet," Kishara said. "I felt it ebb, as we lifted."

She threw a conscious look at Can Ith.

"I was in the same test group. We had all felt the effects as soon as we hit planet, but he"—she waved toward the airlock hatch, beyond which the body rested—"he understood the possibilities more quickly than the rest of us, and did not hesitate to act for his own advantage."

Can Ith inclined his head.

"All well and good," said the first mate, a grey-haired woman called Vina Greiz. "My question is what we're to do now. Trader's gone, pilot, too. Young Jaim—" She threw a worried look at the halfling slumped in her chair.

"I'm not certified," Jaim said, her voice considerably stronger than Can Ith would have supposed. "Can't run the trade."

"We'll have to marry *Shroom* to the Mikancy Family," said another of the crew from the back.

"No." Young Jaim's face set.

"What else then?" came yet a third voice. "Sell out and stay downside?"

"Not that either." She took a hard breath and gave Can Ith the full force of her eyes—not blind, after all—determined.

"You're a Jump-pilot."

He glanced down at the gaudy ring, rescued from the sack and back on his finger.

"That is so."

"Are you at liberty?"

"I am," he admitted.

"I," Kishara said from beside him, "was raised in a trading house. I can advise, as required, and you need not marry to your disadvantage."

Jaim's smile was grim.

"I'm family," she said. "I *can* offer contract."

Kishara bowed, and, Can Ith did.

"I think we might manage," Jaim said to her crew. "And not impossible to borrow a Second Trader from one of our friendlies, if we gotta."

"We trust *them*?" asked the first mate.

"You'd rather the Mikancy? You know their style. We'll be lucky to be set down on a backworld alive."

The crew was silent. The first mate threw up her hands.

"We trust 'em, then. What's next?"

"Gotta cover the route," Jaim said. "Need to get goin'."

"In that wise," Can Ith said slowly. "Let us first make up a pod, with the stolen goods, our late friend, and a locator. We will inform the port authority before we Jump out."

"Yes," said Jaim, and looked to the first mate.

"Vina, show Pilot Can Ith to his seat, please."

✧ Ambient Conditions ✧

PART OF THE ONGOING DISCUSSIONS about the existence of, and the problems caused by, luck. When the happenstance of having luck can be so fraught, being luck personified becomes life-altering. Ambient Conditions is mirrored by Preferred Seating.

✧✧✧✧

"OH," Kishara's younger sister Troodi said as she opened the door and beheld her elder sitting in the chair by the window, a book on her knee.

"Oh," Troodi said again, her eyes filling with tears. "Shara, I thought that—I'd *hoped that*—you'd—gone ahead."

"As you see, I am here," Kishara said gently, putting the book aside and rising. That she'd leave clan and kin ahead of this, her delm's summons to a banishment—but where would she have gone? She might, perhaps, have fled to *Maplekai*, had it been in port, but such a move would have endangered Clan Monfit entire. The Council in its current mood was perfectly capable of seizing her family's tradeship in Balance of an attempt to escape its instructions. And to hide on Liad—well, there was only the Low Port, and no one's dreams survived there.

She did not say these things to her sister, who was not yet

halfling, and could only see their uncle's betrayal. Later, when she was older, and, one hoped, her life less imperiled—then she would see that this had been the only course that would have preserved the clan, which was the duty of a delm. To Troodi, at twelve, it must seem there were no limits on the delm's power.

Kishara, her elder by a dozen Standards, had no fault to find with the delm's actions to preserve the clan, though she might have wished for a small sign or token to demonstrate an uncle's regard for the niece he must sacrifice, but there, Uncle Bry Sen had scarcely emerged from the delm, or the delm from his office, since the decision had at last been taken.

"This," Troodi said abruptly, her voice warm with hope, "Kishara, *surely* this proves them wrong? How is this moment lucky for you? How, therefore, are you *lucky beyond nature*?"

Her gift—the talent that made her a despised outcast—was at the best of times too strange to explain to one not similarly burdened. Still, one could not leave a young sister utterly without comfort. Kishara folded Troodi into an embrace.

"Sometimes," she murmured, her dry cheek pressed against her sister's damp one. "Sometimes, what seems at first to be the blackest bad luck is found, after a passage of time, and a re-examination of circumstance, to have been the best luck possible."

Her sister sniffled.

"Is this one of those times?" she asked, her tone, rightly, doubtful.

Kishara held her at arm's length, and produced a smile that was not wholly false.

"That we cannot know, until we allow time to pass."

She bent and kissed her sister's cheek.

"I must go," she said. "Try to forgive Uncle Bry Sen, sweeting; he's never so fierce as you are. And the delm—why, the delm has no choice in this at all, if he would protect the greater part of Monfit's treasures. This is not over, I'll wager. Your ferocity will be needed on behalf of the clan, yet."

Her sister considered her, face bearing an expression between wariness and hope.

"Do you—do you *know* that?" she asked.

Kishara thought about those things that had produced this moment, when all of those in possession of small talents were held away from joining with the Healers in their guildhall, were declared dangers to society and to the homeworld, and ordered to submit to sterilization, execution, or banishment.

There had been a certain amount of genuine fear in the discovery that there were *so many* "unregulated talents" present in the general population, for there are always those who fear what they fail to understand. But there had also been greed—for some clans would lose too many, and they would be easy meat for those who were ruled by avarice.

So, then, thought Kishara; the truth for Troodi, so that she might stand strong and vigilant for the clan.

"Yes," said Kishara firmly. "I *know* that you will be needed."

There were footsteps heard then, down the end of the hall, moving rapidly closer. Kishara turned to pick up her jacket.

She kissed her sister's cheek again before opening the door to reveal her cousin Ern Din's frowning face.

"Come," she said briskly, stepping 'round him. "It is time for me to go."

* * * ✧ * * *

PERHAPS IT WAS SPITE. Perhaps it was expediency. Perhaps it was, as they said, honest horror to find a dire threat to the purity of Liaden society living, all unrecognized, among them.

However it became known, and for whatever reason it was pursued, the Council of Clans had, by majority vote—Korval and Ixin, Justus and Deshnol the four clans who stood against—decreed that all clans give up such members who exhibited abilities which were known to be out of the common way, whether the delm deemed them dangerous or not.

The penalty for withholding such persons was to be written out of the Book of Clans, which threat was immediately implemented, to the sorrow of Clan-Natis-that-was, which had long been a thorn in the side of the Council. It had been a thorough breaking, with the delm, both thodelms, and their heirs sent to outworlds as bonded laborers, while those others of Natis who were deemed "untainted" were acquired by such houses that had need to boost their numbers. The two found to possess abilities out of the common way were put to death, the Council disallowing the delm her right to perform the act herself.

Though she had been required to watch.

Having administered this terrible lesson, the Council may have been confident that delms would act as delms must—to preserve the greater good, and the greater numbers, of their clans.

But even frightened delms could not bring themselves to surrender their children—innocent of any wrongdoing save being odd—to death. Delm spoke to delm, there was talk—much talk— regarding what *melant'i* required, and more talk yet regarding the Code, and what might fall outside of civilized behavior.

There had been consternation in the halls of the Council. There had been shouting and threats. The Council offered a compromise—the odd ones would not be murdered, but merely sterilized so their abnormal genes died with them.

Into this second wave of outrage stepped Clan Korval, who had been instrumental in creating the Healers Guild, some years gone by. Korval suggested that the abnormal—which in gentle courtesy they named "small talents"—be brought into the Healers Guild, and trained in the forms of that House. Thus affiliated, they would be neither surprise nor threat.

The Council ordered the Accountants Guild, who had drawn up the charter for the Healers, to find if Korval's suggested solution had merit.

It was said that the *qe'andra* who stood before the Council to report the results of research wept openly as he gave the opinion of the experts: none but those who displayed the talents detailed in the charter, those talents acknowledged as being on the Healer Spectrum, might join the Guild. No provision had been made in the charter for other, or different, styles of talent. The advice of the Accountants Guild was that the Healers Guild amend their charter, or that another charter be drawn up, forming a guild which would protect those talents not found to be on the Healer Spectrum. He had added, into the silence that greeted this report, that the Accountants Guild would be pleased to assist in either project, pro bono.

Speaker for Council ruled the discussion of amended charters and new Guilds off-topic, and was on the edge of calling for a vote on the issue of nullifying the threat posed by the abnormal, but Korval was up again, demanding that each and all of the small talents be tested by the Healers, so that those who were found to be on the Healer Spectrum could properly be brought into the Guild.

The demand was reasonable; the Council could not gainsay it, though it could and did set a tight deadline.

So, the small talents were tested.

Kishara herself had come close—quite *improbably* close, to her mind—to achieving the Healer Spectrum on the strength of her second small talent. The testing Healer, all honor to him, had insisted on a second examination, by a master of the Guild. The master found her gift too erratic to be of use to the House. Even then, the testing Healer had asserted that she might well improve with training; that they were none of them born in perfect control of their gifts, that—

He had been silenced then by the Council-appointed witness, even as Kishara had whispered to *let be*, lest he suddenly be discovered to have no aptitude for Healing, and was in addition a danger to the general population.

It was said that three of the many tested were found to be on the Healer Spectrum. The rest—were once again championed by Clan Korval and their allies.

They offered those small talents who did not wish to remain on the homeworld at the price of their future children the opportunity to emigrate to a world seeking colonists, well away from Liad, and far from the oversight of the Council of Clans. Clan Korval and Clan Ixin between them would supply transport.

* * * ✧ * * *

THEY WERE COUNTED OFF in twelves as they came aboard, the twelfth given a tablet, which displayed orders and information. The tablet-holder of Kishara's group was a woman who gave her name simply as Pritti, with neither Line nor clan to distinguish her further, who asked their names, and ticked them off on the screen. That done, she guided them to a pod of twelve acceleration couches placed kin-close near the end of a short hallway.

They settled in their own order, with Kishara on Pritti's left, which earned her a smile and a question.

"What is your talent?"

"I am found to be too fortunate," she said promptly. "And you?"

"I can tell who has touched an object only by touching it myself."

Kishara frowned.

"That sounds—rather useful," she said, then caught herself up. "Your pardon."

"No need." Pritti smiled. "It *is* rather useful, as it happens, merely it is not on the Healer Spectrum. Also, my cousin Ihana has secrets to keep, and has long wished me away."

She glanced beyond Kishara, and spoke to the elder reclining on the next couch.

"And your talent, sir?"

"I can weave rainbows." He moved a wrinkled hand in an arc above his face, as he lay there.

Colors glowed against the air, following the pattern his hand described. He made a fist, and the dainty thing lingered for a moment before fading coyly away.

"Where is the harm in that?" demanded Kishara.

The elder laughed softly and said, "Not on the Healer Spectrum."

"Indeed." Pritti turned to the couch on her right, where a man of no particular distinction sat, feet firmly on the decking.

"What is your talent, Mor Gan?"

"I?" He lifted a shoulder, and let it fall. "I—make suggestions."

It was said easily enough, but Kishara shivered where she lay, propped on one elbow.

"Suggest *what sort* of things?" Pritti asked, sharp enough that Kishara knew she was not alone in being discomfited.

"Well, I might suggest that you give me that silver ring on your finger," he said, and there was *some*thing there, in the cadence of his words. Pritti raised a hand on which silver flashed brightly. She raised her other hand, as if she would have the ornament off. Kishara held her breath even as the other woman hesitated.

"No," Pritti said, firmly, and folded her hands together in her lap.

The man—Mor Gan—laughed.

"And there you have it," he said, his voice easy again, "perfectly useless. However, it *is* disquieting, which is why my delm cast me out before even the Council's recent start."

"Cast you out?" said the elder. "Where did you go, then?"

"Oh, to Low Port," said Mor Gan, and there, again, was *that* note in his voice. "A man might profit there, if he takes good counsel and aligns himself well."

"And yet," Pritti said, "you did not choose to stay on Liad, though you were so well situated."

There was a smile in his voice this time.

"I had always wished to see other worlds, and it scarcely seemed that a like offer would come my way again."

There was an uneasy silence. Pritti had raised her head to address the couch beyond, when there came a loud click, which might have been, Kishara thought, from the all-ship comm. In another moment, this theory was confirmed by a voice speaking in the mode of pilot to passengers.

"All passengers, this is Grasa ven'Deelin Clan Ixin, pilot and first board. We will be lifting within the next hour. Allow me to regret the conditions in which you are constrained to undertake this journey. Our purpose was to accommodate as many as we might without endangering either the ship or its passengers. In keeping with these goals, we will be introducing a soporific into the air supply. The journey will pass more quickly for you, and you will consume less supplies. By reducing the amount of rations we must carry, we were able to accommodate three more passengers.

"Those who were given tablets upon boarding are the leaders of your twelve-group. Each group will be waked according to the schedule now on the screen. Leaders will at those times check on the well-being of the group, and see that each partakes of the nutrients provided. Again, allow me to regret these conditions. The pilots swear that we will go as quickly as possible, and will deliver you safely into circumstances far better than those you are leaving."

There was some exclamation, and a very modest amount of disturbance, due, Kishara thought, lying back on her couch, to the drug that had doubtless been introduced into the air supply some time ago.

She sighed, and closed her eyes, and deliberately took deep breaths until sleep swept her away.

• • • ◇ • • •

IT WAS A STRANGE SLEEP, full with chaotic events and odd people, and her brief wakings scarcely more sensible. She was given a hard bar to eat and something thick and vile-tasting to drink, marched to the necessary, and back to the couch, where the dreams took her again between one blink and another.

There was, she thought, at one waking, an empty couch, which had been the elder's. She had stopped there, struck with something that might have been sorrow, had she been awake enough to process the emotion.

"It was only a pretty thing he did, and no harm to it," she'd said, and Pritti—perhaps it was Pritti—made some answer that she forgot as soon as she'd heard it.

The dreams became ever more mysterious, salted with a sense of danger, and one face, seen often—a hard face, set in displeasure, well-marked brows pulled tight over dark eyes, mouth straight and tight.

There was something attached to that face—some sort of urgency that tasted of her gift. She sought that face, tried to tarry nearby when she found it, but she had no control, no technique, and the other images crowded her away, confusing her with their multitudes.

Then, the dreams stopped.

"Kishara," someone said. "Kishara, wake now. We are arrived."

• • • ◇ • • •

THEY WERE A MOTLEY CROWD of supplicants, to be sure, thin and pale and not a little anxious. Kishara might have found it in her to think hardly of their supposed rescuers, saving that the pilots came on-screen to explain procedures going forward, and it could be seen that they were not one whit less worn than their passengers.

"The Office of Colonization has long expected our arrival," Pilot ven'Deelin said. "There are certain examinations which must be made before applicants receive certification and are allowed the freedom of the planet. It has been requested that you be told—not all will be accepted. Those who are not will be returned to the ship."

Kishara shivered, and there was a general mutter of dismay and one question, shouted from elsewhere on the ship.

"What then, Pilots? Are we returned to the mercies of the homeworld?"

Pilot ven'Deelin raised a hand, and Kishara marked that it was not entirely steady.

"The pilots—by which I mean myself and my co-pilot, and the pilot-sets from the other transports—will be discussing our options. I believe that we may still do better for you than the homeworld, but we have not the details, having only been made aware of this within the last hour ourselves."

She paused, perhaps ready to receive other questions. None came. She inclined her head and continued.

"We have received a protocol from the Colonization Office. Tablet holders will find this on their screens. Please share it with your group. The first call for this ship is expected within the next hour, local."

She sighed and closed her eyes briefly.

"Are there other questions?"

There were none. The pilot inclined her head.

"Tablet holders, please choose one of yours to pick up rations for the groups at the distribution point."

The screen went dark. Pritti used her chin to point at the man sitting two seats to her left.

"Tai Lor, of your goodness, fetch our rations."

* * * ✧ * * *

THEIR GROUP was among the last to be called to the shuttle to go down to the planet surface.

The ten that remained of their original pod of twelve sat in their designated area. Once they were strapped in Pritti, tablet in hand, read out their personal names one by one: Kishara, Mor Gan, Elasa, Tai Lor, Peiaza, Jas Min, Wilcee, Bri And, Kanni, ending with her own.

"What sort of examinations do you think we will be given?" asked Elasa, who looked the veriest child.

"Physical, certainly," said Bri And.

"Will they take note of our gifts?" asked Wilcee. "Have they even been told of our gifts?"

"Surely so," said Jas Min. "How could *that* have been hidden?"

"Very easily," answered Wilcee. "One need only fail of mentioning it."

"That would be unscrupulous," Jas Min objected, which drew a laugh from Peiaza.

"Recall who made these pleasant arrangements on our behalf," she said.

"Certainly, the Dragon is honorable, in its way," Jas Min said, "but if you would have it otherwise, what do you say of the Rabbit?"

"That they lend credence to the Dragon's actions," came the response. "And that it is entirely possible that *they* have not been given the whole, no more than we were."

"Well, if you—" Jas Min began, but Pritti waved a hand, cutting his comment short.

"The information included here"—she raised her tablet so that all might see it—"is that the Colonization Office is fully informed regarding our situation and our abilities. They have no objection to talents of any sort. It is stated that some number of the existing population are likewise gifted."

She lowered the tablet and frowned.

"If I read this aright," she continued, "we comprise a second wave of colonists, the first having lost many due to the *unusual environment which favors a particular sensitivity, and also the complete absence of sensitivity.*"

"So some of us," said Tai Lor lightly, "may be found too little in tune—or too much in tune—with this unusual environment? Which is it, I wonder?"

"That will be made known to us soon enough, I'll wager," said Peiaza, in a tone that predicted such knowledge to be dire.

The rest of them exchanged glances.

"I, for one, will put off worry until we are landed, tested, and presented with real information," Bri And said sensibly. "In the meanwhile, I shall be taking a nap."

Despite they passed the entire journey unaware, that state had been more exhausting than restful. Kishara found that she might also welcome a nap. She disposed herself more comfortably in her chair, leaned her head back into the rest, and closed her eyes.

• • •✧• • •

KISHARA SHIVERED in the damp breeze that teased them as they moved slowly, one by one, down the ramp to the omnibus at the far end. For all it was damp, and cooler than her jacket allowed for, Kishara approved of the breeze. Its freshness woke her senses, and sharpened her thoughts. There was a quality to it—a sort of sparkle, as one might have in a glass of mineral water.

The port beyond the bus—was meager. One of course had not expected Solcintra, but had envisioned something nearer to one of the modest outworld ports that *Maplekai* served.

From her vantage near the top of the ramp, she saw that she had been optimistic in her imaginings. The port was possibly three streets deep, and three long. Most of the buildings were low, only one rising above four stories, and that so much higher that it must be the portmaster's office.

Well, she said to herself, it is a colony world. You did *know* that.

The breeze buffeted her once more, and she wished for a heavier jacket. Pritti, ahead of her in line, shivered, and hunched her shoulders, as if that might protect her from the wind.

Kishara looked down the ramp toward the bus—and frowned.

A woman wearing a green tunic, and holding a clipboard, stood at the door of the bus. Each person had to speak with her before they were allowed to board the bus. And, as Kishara watched, here came Pritti, tablet in hand.

Kishara frowned, and tried to look away, to look at Pritti just ahead of her in line, but her eyes would not move; she was wholly concentrated on the scene at the door.

The woman in the green tunic held out her hand. Pritti, clutching the tablet tight, spoke—sharply, so it seemed to Kishara. The official spoke again, extending her hand more fully, and after a moment's hesitation, Pritti surrendered the tablet.

Kishara, watching, leaned forward even as Pritti turned to board the bus. In that instant, her eyesight blurred, she stumbled—and felt her arm caught, steadying her.

"Here now!" a voice said sharply. "What's amiss?"

Kishara drew a shaky breath, and turned her head. It was grim-faced Bri And who was her rescuer.

"I came a bit dizzy," she said, trying to ignore the phantoms obscuring her vision. It was as if she was trying to focus on his face from a distance, with a bright, busy crowd between them. She took another breath.

"Perhaps there's something in the air," she said.

Bri And sniffed.

"The more likely cause is too little food. Even entranced, we burn calories, and we burned more than were replenished by ration bars and that wretched drink. Haven't you noticed that we're all thin as needles?"

The line moved forward a few paces. Bri And stepped to her side, still holding her arm, keeping her steady. It was impertinence, perhaps, but she was grateful for his support.

Kishara took another breath and closed her eyes briefly, to no avail. The busy crowd still bustled behind her eyelids, sharper now that reality did not distract her.

"Mind your step," Bri And said from that distant reality. "We are going more quickly now."

She opened her eyes and moved at his urging, allowing him still to support her, while she kept her head bent and concentrated on seeing the ramp through the phantom crowds.

At last, they stood on hard 'crete behind Pritti, who had just reached the guard in her green tunic.

"Name," she stated, and Pritti murmured a reply, shoulders hunched.

Kishara's vision cleared, the scene in front of her taking on more weight. Surely, she had seen this—only very recently? Frowning, she inched closer, and Bri And came with her, firm hand under her elbow.

The woman in the green tunic had made her note on the clipboard, and held out a broad hand, palm up.

"Tablet," she said.

Pritti stiffened, and clutched the tablet closer.

"I am the guide for the remaining ten of us. The pilots entrusted me with the duty, to care for the group and impart such information as the tablet provides."

"Yes," the guard said, barely patient. "That duty has come to an end. All of you are equally under the care and protection of the Office of Colonization Services. The tablets are to be returned to the ship. The pilots have said it."

Yes, Kishara thought. This was precisely what she had seen from the top of the ramp, replaying now, in real time. She recalled the Healer who had tried so hard to argue her a Seer. Had he been right, after all? But what had increased her gift to the point where the future overwrote her present? Was this what it was like for Seers—no. She brought herself up. No, the Healer had said something, had *shown* her something, that she had scarcely been able to grasp at the time. She groped for the memory while Pritti bowed her head, and placed the tablet into the guard's waiting hand.

The guard jerked her head toward the bus, and Pritti, shoulders drooping, turned and climbed the stairs.

The guard turned aside to place the tablet into a box.

"You now," Bri And murmured, and supported Kishara as she stepped forward, concentrating on her surroundings—the carpeted stairs into the bus, the red exterior, the guard's green tunic, and the emblems on each shoulder. The ghosts of the future still crowded at the edge of her sight, but if she held her attention firm, they did not, much, disrupt reality.

The guard turned back, hefting her clipboard, a frown forming on her angular face.

"What's this, then?"

Kishara swallowed, but no words came, all of her resources concentrated on holding the ghosts at bay.

"She feels unwell," Bri And said after a moment. "Rations were short."

The guard's face softened somewhat.

"Understood," she said. "Name?"

Kishara found her tongue, "Kishara jit'Luso."

The guard made a tick-mark on her clipboard, and raised her eyes to Bri And.

"Name?"

"Bri And bel'Vester," he said.

The guard again had recourse to her clipboard, and jerked her head toward the bus.

"Please board. There will be food and a physician at the examination hall."

They passed on, Kishara more than glad of Bri And's support on the stairs. Inside, there were only a few seats left open. He saw her situated on the first they found, near the center of the bus.

"Sit and be easy," he murmured. "If you wish it, I will be your support when we debark."

"Thank you," she answered, and managed a polite inclination of her head. "I am steadier than I was."

That earned her a sharp look, but there was another passenger moving up the aisle, and perforce Bri And moved on, to a seat in the back of the bus.

Kishara sighed, leaned back in her seat, and closed her eyes.

This was a mistake. The ghosts of might-be assaulted her. She saw, in an ever-increasing cascade, the bus exploding, bodies falling to the street, blood bright against the stones, windows smashed, and ships lifting willy-nilly from port. She saw a body in an airlock, a catch-net floating against a backdrop of stars, a plate of bread and cheese, the sharp-faced individual she had seen in shipboard dreaming, and another explosion as glass flew and pierced her.

She cried out at that, but the visions flowed on. She saw Pritti lift her hand, and have her silver ring off; she saw the guard in the green tunic pulling a sidearm from her belt, and offering it, butt-first, across her arm. She saw people, a busload of people, fall and lie still. She saw—she saw—

A stinging slap to her cheek shocked her eyes open. The guard, without her clipboard now, was bending over, her bulk shielding Kishara from the rest of the bus.

"What is it?" the woman demanded.

"I see—disaster, murder, and mayhem," Kishara heard herself say, well aware that it was babble and the guard would think her mad. "The bus explodes, there are bodies in the street. I am struck, and we are robbed—"

The guard placed a hand on Kishara's shoulder and pressed, not unkindly. Kishara's voice died, and she felt considerably calmer. The guard inclined her head, looking both wise and sad.

"I see," she said. "You will be going back to the ships, my dear. The world is too much for you."

Kishara blinked up at her.

"*Is* it the air?" she asked.

"In a manner of speaking. It takes some harder than others, and the lesson we have from the first wave is that those it takes hardest cannot survive. The ambient conditions will tear your mind apart, and you'll become a danger to yourself and your neighbors. Best for all and everyone, to go back where you came from."

"Never that," Kishara snapped, and the woman lifted a shoulder.

"Go someplace else, then, but the Office won't let you stay here. For this moment, I can offer you a drug that will put you to sleep—"

But Kishara had had enough of being put to sleep for her own good.

"I thank you," she said coldly, "but no. I seem calm enough now."

"That's because I'm shielding you," the guard told her. "Once I take my hand away, those sights will come back again. Unless you shield yourself."

Kishara took a breath.

"I have seen danger to this bus and passengers," she said as calmly as she could manage. "I know that this may not come to pass, but equally it may."

The guard sighed lightly, patted her shoulder and removed her hand. "I'll just fetch my kit," she said, and left.

Kishara squinted after her, ignoring the ghosts rioting at the edge of her vision. She thought she saw—no, she *did* see!—a shimmer as of bright metal or reinforced glass.

She looked across the aisle at her fellow refugees, startled to find many displaying a similar effect.

Was this, Kishara wondered, something natural that she lacked, or was it—

She almost closed her eyes, but managed to avoid that error. Instead, she concentrated on the Healer who had tried so hard to save her for the homeworld. He had hurriedly attempted to teach her something that she had not been able to grasp, or even imagine. Blind and ignorant, she had tried to follow his instructions, and had failed.

Now, however, with the ambient conditions assisting her, she understood. In memory, she could even hear the Healer's voice, patiently telling over the steps for building a shield around her core.

Concentrating, Kishara used her new understanding to follow those careful, remembered instructions.

She felt heat at the base of her spine, which the Healer had mentioned as a sign that she was engaged with her gifts. The ghosts at the edge of her vision went into a frenzy, but she forced herself to concentrate on the shadow that was building about her, which was becoming more solid, despite the shadow's attempts to distract and dismay—

There was a *click*, surely audible to the rest of the bus. The ghosts were gone. It was—quiet inside her head, though she had not been aware of any noise until it had stopped.

"You might have done that first," said a familiar voice, and Kishara looked up into the face of the guard, who had a small medkit in her hand.

The woman smiled slightly.

"That's what you want, though I'll tell you right now that, shielded or open, the Office still isn't likely to let you stay."

Kishara sighed, thinking of those possible futures that had come to her attention, and inclined her head.

"Perhaps I will be able to convince them otherwise," she said, and the guard gave her a thoughtful look.

"Perhaps you will," she said, and went away toward the front of the bus.

• • •✧• • •

KISHARA SAT QUIETLY inside her shields, and thought about those other things the Healer had tried to teach her in their short time together. Shields, she recalled, were vital, a protection and also a secure situation to rest behind. That said, the Healer had not recommended staying entirely behind shields. The information her gifts brought to her was valuable—uniquely valuable—and she should therefore allow her shields to be somewhat open, balancing the needs for protection and information.

Resting behind her shields, she sighed and considered what else the Healer might have told her.

"Stop the bus," a clear and absolutely certain voice stated. "Everyone else, be entirely still."

The bus slowed, and stopped.

Kishara opened her eyes.

At the driver's station stood—Mor Gan, from her group, now draped in necklaces, his fingers glittering with rings. His pockets visibly bulged.

"Good," he said to the bus driver. "Give me all of your money."

The driver reached beneath the seat and produced a pouch, which he handed to Mor Gan. No one else in her sight moved. Cautiously, she turned her head very slightly to the right, seeing more passengers frozen in place.

"Give me your weapon," Mor Gan directed the bus driver, and received what seemed to be a small firearm.

"Open the door," Mor Gan said, then, having disposed pouch and gun about his person.

The driver touched something on his board and the bus door sighed open.

"Keep absolutely still," Mor Gan said and stepped into the aisle, looking over the motionless passengers with such an expression on his face, that Kishara feared for their lives.

Whatever thought had passed through his mind, Kishara saw him reject it. When he spoke, that note she had marked before was in his voice, only much clearer, issuing not suggestions but *commands*.

"All of you," he said, "go to sleep for ten minutes. When you awake, you will have forgotten me entirely."

He turned and leapt down the stairs into the street.

Kishara jumped to her feet, rushed down the aisle, and leapt the stairs in his wake. Mor Gan was racing toward a small street just beyond the back of the bus. She gave chase, thinking only that he had robbed the driver, and many passengers—and that he must be stopped. She had reached the top of the street he had vanished into before she also recalled that he had taken a gun.

She leaned into a doorway, and tried to reason her way to the path she ought to take. Going to the Office of Colonization would be fruitless; she had to believe that Mor Gan, whose gift had been the ability to *suggest* things, had found that gift enhanced. She must believe, therefore, that his suggestion that he be forgotten had taken hold, and no one on the bus, or even from their group, would recall him, never mind be alarmed by a description of his alleged crimes. Especially, she thought wryly, when that description came from the weak-minded woman who was to be sent away before the planet broke her mind.

She recalled the visions she had experienced—the bus exploding, people dying—but none of that had happened. Recall, she told herself, the Healer had said that the future is not immutable. What she had seen on the bus had been *possible* futures. Mor Gan's actions had put them onto a path where bus and passengers survived; they were past that point; it could not be chosen again.

Every subsequent choice Mor Gan made limited the number of choices he *could* make, until he was locked into one line, all his future actions forced.

At the moment, she supposed him dazzled, perhaps slightly mad, with the sudden scope of his gift. Perhaps she *should* follow him, and bring him into hand before he did someone a grievous hurt. She thought she could trust her luck to keep her safe from . . . too much harm. She—no.

She was a fool.

Mor Gan had come from Low Port. He was no innocent. He was a man who profited from the pain of others. Perhaps he had chosen to emigrate because he desired a wider field for his efforts. Perhaps Low Port had become . . . inhospitable to him. Why did not matter.

What did matter was that Mor Gan *meant* to do mischief, and very possibly worse. He had intended this robbery, or something like it, from the first. It was only a bonus that his power of suggestion had increased under the ambient conditions.

The question for her, however—that remained the same: How was she to stop him? Surely, it fell to her to stop him, as the only person on-planet who remembered him.

Kishara bit her lip, thinking, taking stock of her gifts, both of them. Then she nodded once. Mor Gan sealed his future as he ran, decision by decision. *She* had the advantage, there. *She* could see ahead of him, and choose the path that would allow her to stop him. Her luck—she still trusted that her luck would keep her safe in the doing of it.

She smiled slightly. All that was required of her was to choose the correct path. Now that she had the way of it, that should not be so difficult a task.

Still smiling, she opened her shields, and let the ghosts of the future take her.

* * * ⟡ * * *

SHE CAME TO HERSELF standing at the side of a table in what appeared to be a tavern. It was a noisy room, but the table her gifts had chosen for her was occupied only by a dark-haired man wearing a pilot's jacket, wineglass in hand, gaze directed at some landscape only he could see. He wore a great, glittering gaud of a ring on his unencumbered hand, and Kishara, still in thrall to her gifts, thought that he looked familiar.

He looked up, as if he had suddenly become aware that he was not alone—black eyes under strong black brows, a hard face and a secretive mouth. Kishara realized that she *had* seen him, and more than once. In her dreams, and more recently, in her plans.

One of those strong brows lifted, and Kishara bent in a slight bow. Her lips parted, and she waited with interest to hear what she might say.

"Captain yos'Phelium." Her voice was not precisely steady, her tone too low for the loud room, but he heard her. His hard mouth softened slightly.

"No," he said, his voice not hard at all. "Merely Pilot yos'Phelium."

"But a yos'Phelium is never *merely* a pilot," she returned saucily.

His laugh put the lie to the grim face and stern eyes. She glanced down, lest he see the relief in her eyes—and discovered a plate of cheese, somewhat depleted, and half a small loaf of bread. It was then that she realized that she was very hungry, indeed.

"Sit," Pilot yos'Phelium said, his voice cordial. "If you have a taste for chancy company. I was about to call for more wine. Will you join me?"

"Thank you," she said, and took the chair at his left, which put her back against the wall, the room, and especially the entry door, full in her gaze.

The server arrived in answer to the pilot's glance, received the order for two glasses of wine, and the coins that paid for all.

There was a stir behind her, and he glanced in that direction before looking to her again.

"If you were not here for the previous set, you may find the music of interest," he said courteously, as if they had been partnered at a public entertainment, on the homeworld.

There came a tootling sound, and some plucking of strings as the musicians bent to their task, and here was the server again, bearing wine and a new loaf of bread.

"Cook's gift," he said. "Crowd's thinner than her baking tonight."

"Our thanks to the cook," Kishara said with fervor, though it was scarcely her place to say it.

The server swept away, and Pilot yos'Phelium tipped his head toward the plates.

"The bread is very good," he said, "and the cheese better. I did not much care for the *akashi* fruit, but you may find otherwise. Please, make yourself free."

She smiled at him, then, with no restraint at all, and reached out to raise the glass the server had set by her hand.

"To the fullness of fortune," she proposed.

Both eyebrows quirked, but he lifted his glass willingly enough, and answered her.

"To the luck."

They drank. Kishara set her glass aside and reached to the plates. The cheese was excellent, and the bread delightful. The fruit—no, the fruit was not to her taste, either. She made another selection from among the cheeses.

Behind them, the musicians played, quietly. Kishara ate, conscious of the passage of time, as well as the warmth at the base of her spine. Mindful of the abbreviated teachings of the Healer, she had made shift to examine the futures her gift had spun from the ambient conditions, and she had—she was almost entirely certain that she had—chosen that future which provided the best chance of her continued survival with her mind intact, and provided the quickest end to Mor Gan's career.

Once she had chosen, it seemed her tendency to be fortunate had leapt into operation, moving her through the port on a mission of its own. There was some confusion at the beginning of this part of her adventure, until she realized that her part was to utterly surrender her own will and submit to being moved by the force of her gift. She had achieved the knack of it eventually, and so her feet had brought her here, to this place, to this man, and to the confrontation that would provide the solution she had chosen.

It would be soon, now, she thought. She sipped her wine, and took up another piece of bread.

She looked up to find Pilot yos'Phelium's sharp eyes on her.

"You were looking for me," he said. "*Specifically* for me."

She met his gaze calmly.

"Yes."

"Ah." He sipped wine. "I don't wish to be rude, but if there is something you need to say to me, you must speak. I'm soon away."

"Yes," she said again, and then, because in her current state she could not fail to remark them—"You have very strong shields."

"So I am told. I hope you will not ask me to lower them, for I haven't the least notion how to do so. The shields came with me into this life."

Ah, she thought, her gifts were canny, indeed.

Smiling, she inclined her head.

"My name is Kishara jit'Luso, Pilot. I am lucky, so my delm cast me out, in order that the clan take no damage from sheltering faulty genes."

He sipped his wine and considered her.

"Forgive me if I am impertinent," he said eventually, "but, being as I am, I know little of those who are gifted. It is true that my entire clan is lucky—and risky. I wonder if you put yourself in danger by seeking me out."

Danger, Kishara thought, amused.

"As the moth is endangered by the candle flame?" she asked lightly. "You are kind to regard it, but no. I think, in this moment, that our lucks reinforce each other, to the betterment of both."

"Ah?" he murmured politely.

"Yes," she said, reaching for another slice of bread with cheese. "You see, there's about to be a pirate raid."

He blinked and put his glass carefully on the table.

"A pirate raid?" he repeated.

Just then, the front door smashed open.

* * * ✧ * * *

KISHARA DRANK the last of her wine and put the glass down. It was begun; she felt the warmth at the base grow warmer still, and was content. From here . . . from this moment, all was forced.

A shout went up from among the diners and drinkers; chairs and stools were noisily overturned as people leapt to their feet. Pilot yos'Phelium also rose, silently, hands loose at his sides as he observed the unfolding scene.

Kishara likewise rose, and put herself a few steps closer to his side, into the shadow of his shields.

There came another shout. A chair was thrown, a bravo ducked. Rifles were raised. Without turning around, she knew that the musicians had leapt up behind her, while, forward, the 'tender swung below the bar and came up with a long arm, oddly made, and glowing weirdly—

Pilot yos'Phelium moved, as if he would introduce himself into the situation, and put all into order. Kishara extended her hand to grip his arm tightly. He paused, and she removed her hand, for here came Mor Gan now, strolling in all unconcerned, dragging a halfling girl by her wrist.

Mor Gan had, Kishara saw, made other suggestions before his arrival into the snare of her chosen future. He now wore a space leather jacket, and at least a dozen necklaces. His hands were ablaze with rings. She felt . . . something tighten around her, as if her gifts sought to protect her.

There came a sharp *fssstt!* from the weapon in the bartender's hands. The shot burned the floor near the boot of the nearest bravo, who spun, weapon up.

"Friends, friends!" Mor Gan called, his voice compelling attention. "There is no reason for dispute. We are here to pick up supplies, funds, and perhaps personnel. Please all be calm."

Even tucked inside the influence of the pilot's shields, Kishara felt drawn—a quick glance around the room showed that the bar's customers were thoroughly caught, beguiled by his voice, and entranced in a moment.

Mor Gan turned and pointed a finger at the gape-mouthed bartender.

"Put that down," he said chidingly, "you will do someone a hurt."

The bartender put the rifle on the bar.

"Very good," Mor Gan said. "Now, if you please—go to the storeroom and pack up three cases of your best liquor and wine and bring them here."

The bartender left on this mission, and Mor Gan shook the girl by the wrist, demanding to know how the weapon was disarmed.

She told him, her voice flat, her face blank. Kishara frowned. The girl—surely, she had not chosen to endanger a halfling?

Mor Gan pointed to a customer seated at the bar.

"You," he said, "do as she said."

The customer rose to approach the weapon, and Mor Gan turned his attention to the room at large.

In short order, he had the entranced working for him, directing three to go among the many, who were instructed to give over all their money and precious things. This, they willingly did.

When it came their turn to donate, Kishara reached into her pocket and fingered out her entire wealth of coins. She also gave the ring she wore, looking into the collector's eyes as she did so.

His eyes were blank, as if blind. Receiving Kishara's offering, he thrust his collection tray at Pilot yos'Phelium, who deposited a few coins from an outside jacket pocket, and with not the least hesitation, drew the big gaudy ring from his finger, and placed it among the rest of the items gathered.

The collector moved past. The musicians gave their instruments, and the coins in their cup.

"Bring all that you have collected to the bar," said the compelling voice, and this, too, was done.

Kishara took a breath as Mor Gan went to the bar to inspect his takings, dragging the halfling with him. There came the subtle sound of metal ringing, loud in the silence of the room. Suddenly, he paused, and turned, holding the pilot's gaudy ring high.

"Who gave this? Raise a hand!"

Her pilot did so, blank-faced and slow, and Mor Gan came down the room toward them, ring in one hand, halfling dragged, half-stumbling in his wake.

Kishara took another breath, and tried to take comfort from the warm emanations of her gifts. This was a danger point. If Mor Gan should recognize her—

But his glance passed over her and settled on the pilot.

"Well! Pilot, is it? Jump-pilot, in fact? You will be coming with me. And who is this—ah . . . lady?"

He looked directly at her, no recognition in his face. Kishara, daring to look into his eyes, saw that, even as he entranced others, he was himself entranced. The guard had warned her that those who responded too well to the ambient conditions were in danger of their minds, if not their lives, and in Mor Gan's eyes Kishara saw the truth of that.

"What is your relationship with this pilot?" he asked her. "Speak true!"

"We are partners," Kishara heard herself say, flat-voiced.

"Very good. You will also be taking employment with me. What is your name?"

Her gift spoke again. "Pelli azSulo."

Mor Gan accepted the name without question.

"What is your name, Pilot? Speak true!"

"Sin Jin Isfelm," the pilot replied, lying in his turn.

"They now belong to me, as you do. Follow."

They followed, and Kishara rejoiced. They had passed a point, the quarry was trapped, and her safety assured. They *could not* vary now.

· · ·✧· · ·

MOR GAN HAD DESIGNATED two others besides herself and the pilot to carry his goods. He had instructed the room to forget all that had happened, and Kishara did have some curiosity as to how that would play, once they were no longer in thrall.

That, however, was not her business. Her business was to escape this planet before the ambient conditions broke her mind, and to do so in company of the Korval pilot, who was also unnaturally lucky, and safely isolated from such madness as threatened her.

Their group arrived at a shuttle, and the two extra carriers were instructed to put down their burdens. They were dismissed with a curt command to forget the events of this night.

Mor Gan then looked at his three bravos, with their blank faces and their weapons at ready, and said, "Leave me."

They went, taking their weapons with them, and Kishara spared a thought for the damage they might do on-port. Beside her, the pilot shifted, as if he were weighing this moment as an opportunity to act. She took a careful breath, and *felt* him take the decision to wait.

Excellent, she thought, he has a cool head.

Mor Gan moved then, dragging the halfling to the hatch, slapping her open palm against the plate with one hand, and with the other pushing her chin up so that the scanner registered her face and eyes.

The hatch slid open. Mor Gan snatched the halfling roughly back, slamming her into the side of the shuttle. It must have hurt, but the girl didn't cry out, nor did her expression change. She might have been a doll, Kishara thought, or a puppet. She blinked at that last thought, and wondered how deeply Mor Gan had attached the girl. If matters fell as she, Kishara, had ordered them, she would have blood on her hands if the girl were damaged, though she had not—she was certain that she had not agreed to anything that endangered an innocent.

"Stow the goods," Mor Gan snapped, and the pilot moved to do so, neither quick nor slow, face blank. Kishara picked up another case and followed him into the shuttle.

The pilot was waiting for her at the bin. He bent and breathed into her ear.

"I will want an explanation."

"No time," she answered. "Trust me."

He snorted lightly, for which she blamed him not at all, and went back out onto the dock, returning a moment later, carrying the last case. Mor Gan came after, carrying his sack of loot and shoving the halfling before him.

He slapped the switch as he passed, and the hatch came down. Kishara moved further into the shuttle to make room, which she hoped did not show too much initiative for one supposedly under Mor Gan's control. The pilot finished stowing the last crate, got the bin locked, and came after, stopping at her side. Kishara saw him give one sharp look at the piloting board before Mor Gan arrived, striding past them toward the pilot's station.

"Sin Jin will pilot, Pelli will take the jump-seat. I will have the co-pilot's chair. My carte blanche will kneel, so."

He shoved the girl roughly to the decking. She made no protest, nor even blinked, her eyes staring blindly ahead.

Kishara sank into the jump-seat, as directed. Pilot yos'Phelium went to his appointed station, sat, and stared down at the board. For a long moment, he did nothing at all, and Kishara caught her breath. If he were to openly resist, now—well, but he couldn't, could he? They were all caught and moving toward her chosen future.

Mor Gan made a small sound, slipped a hand into his belt and withdrew a flat rectangle, which he held out. It was a ship's key, Kishara saw, though there was something odd about it—as if it had been dipped in chocolate, or—

"You will want this," Mor Gan said.

The pilot turned his head, eyes dropping to the key, but he made no other move.

"Take it," Mor Gan snapped, and Kishara felt the force of that order act on her own muscles. Her hand twitched, and she pressed it firmly against her knee.

"Dock us with the ship *Merry Mushroom*," Mor Gan said. "Do not contact them."

The pilot's hand moved slowly, but he did take the key, and pushed it into the slot. The board came live. Kishara could see that his fingers bore dark stains, and looked to the halfling, the hostage, who knelt motionless on the deck. Whose blood is on that key? she asked herself, and the pilot gave the shuttle leave to lift.

• • •◇• • •

KISHARA FELT HER GIFTS begin to cool as the shuttle rose, and she breathed a careful sigh of relief, though it was far too soon, much could still go wrong. Perhaps, now, *even more* could go wrong. She had made her decisions, and chosen her future while bathed in the planet's ambient conditions. If they were now leaving the field's influence, then—she was safe, surely, from the two dark futures that had been hers?

"This is *Merry Mushroom*," a voice came out of the comm. "Aincha talking to me, Sinda?"

Mor Gan shoved the girl toward the board, snarling, "Talk to them. There is a situation which the pilot must attend. Say it!"

The halfling leaned forward.

"This is Jaim, Vina," she said, her voice flat. "Sinda's got a glitch to ride. We're coming in to dock."

Hesitation, then a gruff, "Come on, then."

The pilot reached to his board.

• • • ✧ • • •

"DOCKING complete."

The brilliant burn of her gift was embers now, leaving Kishara cold. She could remember—she could remember what she had decided, she recalled making choices, but the manner of choosing and deciding—that was lost to her. She looked to Mor Gan, but if he was experiencing the same sort of loss, there was no outward sign of it.

The halfling had wilted, her shoulders hunched, and she directed her sightless gaze now at the decking on which she knelt.

Mor Gan unsnapped his webbing, stood, and yanked the girl to her feet.

"Follow us!" he snapped, pushing ahead, and shoving the halfling before him. "Go!"

The girl went, though too slowly to please her captor. He shoved her again, and when she reached the hatch, slammed her forcefully against the wall, grabbing her wrist and jerking her hand to the plate as if he intended to rip the arm from the socket.

Kishara heard a gasp—the first the girl had made, and looked sharply. She felt a hand on her shoulder, and glanced up, to see the pilot frowning at her. He meant her to stay back, she thought, and stepped out of his way.

The hatch opened into a common room. Mor Gan threw the girl in ahead of him. She hit the deck with a cry, rolling. Crew started up with shouts, alarm showing on their faces.

"Sit down and be calm!" Mor Gan said firmly, and Kishara with a sinking heart heard that *particular* note still in his voice. She had been a fool, playing with what she did not understand. Was she a goddess, to pick and choose the future she preferred? The planet's ambient conditions did more, and worse, than magnify such gifts one possessed. It overset one's reason, and—

"Kill him!" screamed the girl on the floor. "Kill him! He killed Father and Sinda!"

It was the pilot who moved first, fast and sure. There was a snap, loud even above the shouting of the crew. The pilot took Mor Gan's weight and sank to one knee, seeing him gently to the deck, and closed his empty, staring eyes.

• • • ✧ • • •

"I AM," the pilot said to the question put by Jaim Evrit, daughter of Trader Ban Evrit and Pilot Sinda Mark, "Can Ith yos'Phelium."

Like the refugees, he omitted his clan affiliation, possibly, Kishara thought, because he was conversing with the clanless.

"And you, ma'am?" Jaim Evrit asked.

"Kishara jit'Luso," she answered.

The halfling nodded.

"Do either of *you* know what happened, that I could finally act on my own?"

It was well that the question was put in such a fashion, Kishara thought. She need not lie, nor confess her part in the ruin of this girl's life. Though she would have to explain herself more fully to Pilot yos'Phelium. Later. In private.

"The field is particular to the planet," Kishara said. "I felt it ebb, as we lifted."

She bit her lip, and cast a conscious look at Can Ith yos'Phelium.

"I was in the same test group," she said. "We all felt the effects as soon as we hit planet, but he"—she waved toward the air lock hatch, beyond which the body rested—"he understood the possibilities more quickly than the others of us, and did not hesitate to act for his own advantage."

Can Ith inclined his head, and Kishara awaited the next reasonable question, from him, or from some one of the crew, but the first mate—a gray-haired woman called Vina Greiz—spoke then, and at a tangent.

"All well and good," she said. "*My* question is what we're gonna do now. Trader's gone, pilot, too. Young Jaim—" She threw a worried look at the halfling slumped in her chair.

"I'm not certified," Jaim said, and her voice was stronger. She straightened. "Can't run the trade."

"We'll have to marry *Shroom* to the Mikancy Family," said another of the crew from the back.

"No." Young Jaim's face was set.

"What else, then?" came yet a third voice. "Sell out and stay downside?"

"Not that either." Jaim took a hard breath and gave Can Ith a stare.

"You're a Jump-pilot."

He glanced down at the gaudy ring, rescued from the sack of stolen goods and back on his finger.

"That is so," he admitted.

"Are you at liberty?" she asked then, and he smiled.

"Very much so."

"I was raised in a trading house," Kishara said, for the ship had lost two skills this day. Both must be replaced, if Jaim was determined to keep her independence. "I can advise, as required. I think that you will not need to marry to your disadvantage."

Jaim's smile was grim as she looked over her crew.

"I'm family," she said. "I *can* offer contract."

Kishara bowed, and so did Pilot Can Ith.

"I think we might manage," Jaim said to her crew. "And not impossible to borrow a Second Trader from one of our friendlies, if we gotta."

"We trust *them*?" the first mate demanded, jerking her head in the direction of themselves.

"You'd rather the Mikancy?" Jaim asked, sharp and strong. "You know their style. We'll be lucky to be set down on a backworld alive. These two gentles have done more good for this ship an' crew in one day than the Mikancy in all the decades we've known 'em."

The crew was silent. The first mate threw up her hands.

"We trust 'em, then. What's next?"

"Gotta cover the route," Jaim said, and stood. "Need to get goin.'"

"In that wise," Can Ith said slowly. "Let us first make up a pod, with the stolen goods, and our late friend, and a locator. We will inform the port authority before we Jump out."

"Yes," said Jaim, and looked again to the first mate.

"Vina, show Pilot Can Ith to his seat, please. Trader Kishara and me'll go over the route and the inventory."

"Right," Vina said, and turned to the rest of the crew.

"Well?" she demanded, "I don't guess you lot have stations to man, do you?"

There was a general bustle at that, and Can Ith leaned over to speak into Kishara's ear.

"And when will you tell me—only me—the rest of the truth, Kishara?"

"Soon," she told him, and smiled. "We'll have some amount of time together."

Mobile eyebrows rose.

"Will we?" he said, his head went up at the sound of his name. "A moment," he told the first mate, and looked again to Kishara.

"I look forward to our continued association," he said, politely. "Until soon."

Kishara closed her eyes in relief, feeling only tired, her gifts quiescent or dead, it mattered not one whit to her.

"Yes," she murmured. "Until soon."

* * * ✧ * * *

THEY WERE BOTH due leave on Fussbudget, and had agreed to share a meal at a town-side tavern not much frequented by their shipmates.

It was there that she finally told him the tale entire, stinting her part not at all.

" . . . so they were right—the Council," Kishara concluded, putting down her glass. "We *are* an unpredictable menace, and a danger to the innocent."

Can Ith did not immediately answer, but she was used to his ways by now, and did not suppose his silence signaled either condemnation or approval. He was thinking, that was all. In a moment—or a day—he would come forth with what thought had produced.

The product of thought came just after he set his own glass on the table.

"The Council was wrong," he stated, his voice allowing no room for doubt. "No one of the small talents, saving those who had already set themselves up to be a danger and a menace, were a threat to society or to the homeworld. Some few may have been dangers to themselves, and might have harmed an innocent through inexperience, or error."

He glanced at her. She motioned him to go on.

"The Council would have done better for all and everyone had they allowed the Healers to amend their charter, and enlarge their House. They would have done no particular harm, had they granted the small talents their own Guild. From there, the Guilds might have assisted each other, to the betterment of both, and to have a Talent in the clan would have been a matter of pride."

He met her eyes.

"Ambient conditions came into play when the game was removed from Liad, and untrained persons were left to fend for themselves. Then and *only then* did some few of the small talents become dangerous, and that not from their own desires." He moved his shoulders and raised a hand to call for more wine.

"Well. We must allow the account to show that one was not so well intentioned as he might have been."

"Two," Kishara said. "I abetted murder and mind control, stole your life—"

Can Ith blinked.

"Is this pride?" he interrupted, black eyes well opened.

"It is not, and you well know it!"

"Will you strip Mor Gan's honors from him? I do assure you, he *meant* to rob, and to kill, and to control. Do not imagine, my friend, that he was a good man made bad by your meddling with futures."

"No, of course he was not—" Kishara began, and paused as the server came to refresh their glasses.

"As for having stolen my life—" Can Ith said, as soon as the server had left them, "that attempt had been made, and I decided upon my answer before ever you stopped at my table." He raised his glass, black eyes quizzing her over the rim.

"Now, answer me this. Can you be certain that *your* luck was ascendant?"

She blinked.

"What do you mean?"

He grinned.

"Korval is lucky—that is well known. Does it not make sense to suppose that ambient conditions acted upon my own gift, as well as yours? Who, in fact, meddled with whom, and for what gain?"

He sipped, and put the glass down. Kishara continued to stare.

"But your shields—"

He snorted. "My shields have never protected me from the action of Korval's luck before. I see no reason why it should have been otherwise under ambient conditions."

He leaned forward, catching her gaze with his.

"Do you not see how *neat* it all is? That a ship should discover an urgent need for a Jump-pilot just as I had decided to walk away from my clan and make my own future? *That* is how my luck works, Kishara. *I* think that your luck operated to preserve you by placing you into the shadow of mine, which was already engaged. There was risk; your life might have been forfeit, but we chanced upon a best case for both."

He leaned back, picked up his glass, and waited.

She took a hard breath.

"That's—eerie," she said at last.

"Yes," he agreed, smiling. He raised his glass. "A toast."

She lifted her glass.

"To ambient conditions," Can Ith said, "and to our very good fortunes."

⋄ Dead Men Dream ⋄

WE WERE ASKED to write a story no longer than six thousand words for a theme anthology. The problem was that in every iteration of the story—and there were several!—the characters needed more time and space to properly address their situation, and kept drifting from the editor's assignment toward their own particular problems. Finally, we simply wrote another story for the anthology, and allowed these characters room to work. It took them a whole novella, but they got there.

⋄⋄⋄⋄

ONE

EVEN DEAD MEN have to eat.

It fell to Khana to forage for two such, and he was pleased to do so, for the necessity put him out among people, allowed him opportunity for exercise, and to improve his language.

This morning's foraging was nearly done. He had eaten his breakfast, and had the second in hand, needing only to show the ID to the lad behind the counter and be on his way. However, he had another mission, aside food, and he asked about Malvern's continued absence.

A smile was his first answer, and Khana was once more surprised to find that this open betrayal of emotion was a . . . comfort.

"Don't you worry," the boy—Miki, according to the badge on his shirt—said cheerfully, "she'll be back after she finishes her tour. She's a Reservist, and they call her up now and then."

Khana moved his head slowly side to side—this was a new gesture for him, and he feared that this was one of the times when he had failed of accurately displaying nuance, for the boy reached out and patted his arm, as one offering comfort.

"Oh no, it's not a sad thing! She did the work for twenty years and plus, but even once you're done, you're not *really* done, if you know what I mean?"

The boy was—yes, a boy; surely younger than Bar Jan, though much larger. He was Terran of the type the InfoBooklet claimed as "Port Chavvy Born," his hair dark and long, and dark hair also on the lower part of his pale face.

"I mean," Khana said slowly in his careful new-learned Terran, "that I do *not* know what you mean. As you know"—here he waved his *ticket* that was at once ID, room key, permission to eat on *Chavvy's cred*, and entrée to those places he was permitted to go on-station, including this kitchen—"I am not from around here, myself."

"Oh, oh, right, I forgot! Sorry! You're a reg'lar and always glad to see you, and I just—well. Been here my whole life, is what. I forget things is different elseplace. Someday, maybe, I'll land on a planet!"

There came a chime from a piece of equipment behind him.

"Be a sec," he said, turning to open a small baking unit, and using the paddle to slide out a pan of cheese muffins.

"There, let those cool a bit," he said, coming back to the counter, and bestowing another smile on Khana.

"See, when you're born here, or if you take the course and go for Port Resident—gotta swear to do that—but it's the same thing, really, 'cause that means you're took care of if you die here, and Port Chavvy admits you live here if you go off-station and get in trouble Out There." He snapped his fingers, a gesture to which Khana could attach no ready meaning.

"I remember! It's called *citizen*, Out There. So being a *citizen* of the Port means you got responsibilities, and you gotta do service for three years wherever the Port needs you. After you're done your three years, though, you're on Reserve—a Reservist. That means you get called up in every little while, so somebody else can have a break, or to keep what you know fresh. So here's Chief Malvern, she served for seven turns—she wears those little pins, you might've seen 'em. Officially, she can't be made to serve again full-time, so now they just call her up whenever they need her. An' that's where she is now—called up to fix something. I mean, Malvern knows it all—*done all the spots*, is what we say—and knows Port Chavvy inside out."

"I see," Khana said, bowing slightly in thanks. It was not done on Port Chavvy, the nuanced bow; there was none to read them, after all. However, it was allowed, the small inclination, as a thanks.

"Is it permitted to ask the nature of your own service?"

Miki's pale face reddened, but there, he was a comely lad for all his size and it went well on him.

"Oh, well—I mean—me, I'm training on the fuel supply systems and such, but part-time dock help for the A Deck, that's my official service spot. We don't have all that many big ones come in, I mean the last was that Liaden . . . oh."

Miki stopped, took a breath, glanced over his shoulder at the pan of cooling muffins, and looked back to Khana, cheeks still becomingly pink.

"So *eny-how*, yeah, we're trying to work out a service option that'll let me combine the fuel system stuff with the A Deck stuff. But, see, Chief Malvern, she has so much time in grade . . . you know what that means?"

Khana thought of Malvern, her modest uniform impeccably presented, always alert. She had the bearing of a commander, even if it was only a commander of pastry and hot food. That she had been a leader, he did not doubt.

"I think," Khana said, careful of his pronunciation, "that this is related to the concept I was taught as *melant'i*."

"Might be, might be," Miki allowed, "but yeah, so she gets the call 'cause even though she's not in the chain of command these days, she's the one who knows it all—all the systems, I mean, and how they work together, and—"

"Hey, Miki!" came a voice from behind. Startled, Khana turned to see a woman in a Port Chavvy volunteer duty vest waving an ID card. She gave him a nod, which was mannerly, here. Khana returned it.

"Them cheese muffins ready to be 'preciated?"

"Sure are!" The boy snatched a carry box, and turned to the tray he had put to cool. "How many?"

"Just the one today; they got me workin' solo, inventoryin' the aid closets. I'll be grabbing a cup of caf on the way out, too."

"You got it." Miki handed the box over, the worker slid the card through the reader, and that quick was gone, stopping briefly at the entrance to draw a cup of the hot, bitter drink that on Port Chavvy served as "work tea."

Khana turned back to the counter, thinking that he had taken up enough of the lad's time, but Miki wasn't done yet.

"So yeah, Malvern, she knows Port Chavvy inside out, like they say. An' she was right here behind this counter, doin' the dinner prep, setting the breads up to rise and all, when her comm buzzes. She listens for maybe two minutes, puts it away in her pocket and says to Baydee, 'I been attached for a few days, Hon. Keep the griddles in tune for me, right? And call upstairs to ask himself to tend to my breads.'

"So yeah, it was sudden." Miki frowned, and leaned forward a little. "If this is rude, you just tell me so, all right, and no offense to me, nor meant to you, but I wonder—your friend. Ain't seen him for a while again. He doin' right fine? No troubles? Malvern worried, him bein' so broke up like he was."

This, Khana reminded himself, was not the seeking of advantage that it most certainly would have been in the society he had moved in before his summary death. No, this was kindness, very nearly kin-care, and was properly answered as such.

So.

"My . . . friend," Khana said carefully. "He grows stronger, though there is still pain. He was made sad when we last came here together, to find that Malvern was absent." He hesitated, wondering if he had said enough to satisfy—and it appeared that he had.

Miki nodded. "Yeah, everybody misses her. You tell 'im—your friend—that we miss him, too, and we're lookin' to see him again, when he's ready. An' you know what? I noticed he favors that dark loaf that none of us can get quite the way Malvern gets it. You tell your friend there's only one other baker on all Port Chavvy has Malvern's touch with that loaf. He's a top chef, an' it's hard to get him down here, but he'll be comin' to give us a hand alt-shift, and we'll be havin' the dark on hand, startin' tomorrow." He paused, and added. "Me 'n' Baydee are gonna be standin' by as helpers, so might be we'll catch the way of it, this time."

That they had noticed so much, Khana told himself severely, was not dangerous. It was kindness, again, and he schooled himself to receive it as it was given.

"Thank you," he said. "I will tell him." He stopped short of saying that his friend would be pleased, and was saved from trying to introduce another question by a noisy bustle at the entrance to the Cantina.

Khana turned his head, espying a full work crew of ten, and looked back to Miki.

"Yeah, looks like I'm on," the lad said with a grin. "You take care now."

He turned down-counter, raising a hand and calling out a greeting to "Reeves."

Khana took his carry box, and went out into the corridor.

* * * ◇ * * *

IT HAD BECOME KHANA'S HABIT to take the long way home. Even on those infrequent occasions when Bar Jan accompanied him, they took the back hallways, his companion pronouncing them *interesting* with such sincerity that it had taken Khana two trips to realize that the most interesting thing about them was the scarcity of other travelers.

The benefit that Khana took from walking the back hallways arose from the fact that the route between Cantina and wayroom encompassed very nearly eight thousand of his short steps. The literature provided by the Port had suggested that the planet-born achieve ten thousand steps a day in order to retain a modicum of physical fitness while on-station. Given the circumstances of their residence on Port Chavvy, it was unlikely that Khana would ever walk on a planet again. However, he dreamed—of flowers, and of Liad's green-blue day-sky, the taste of fresh air. He had visited the E Deck Atrium, once, and there had been flowers, trees, grass. At the time, he had been distressed by the lack of a sky, and the taste, still, of station air. Lately, he had been thinking that he might visit the atrium again.

Though not today.

There was an unusual amount of traffic in the back halls today, groups of people wearing gray overalls with the Port Chavvy logo on them. Some were inspecting doors and locks, others were occupied with the various cabinets and closets. He passed one worker who was staring into a closet lavishly decorated with the outlines of what must, Khana thought, be tools, masks, flasks. While some of the silhouettes were filled by the objects they represented, most—were not. The worker shook her head, and pulled a note-taker out of her pocket as he went by.

"Good thing we ain't *had* an emergency, 's'all I can say," he heard her mutter.

At the intersection of hallways where his necessity took him to the right, there was a cluster of workers around several open closets, note-takers in some hands while others stood at ease, talking. Khana paused, looking for the best route through the crowd. One man looked up, saw him, and waved cheerfully.

"You come on ahead!" he called, and to his comrades, "Hey, make some room, why not? Commerce has gotta go forth!"

This was apparently a pleasantry, for those of the group laughed, or grinned, all in good humor, and arranged themselves so that Khana had a clear path through.

"Thank you," he said, loud enough, he hoped, to be heard by all.

"No problem," returned the man who had first noticed him. "We ain't paid to block the halls."

One of the inconveniences of traveling the back corridors was the lack of public newsfeeds. There was only one on the route between the wayrooms and the Cantina. Despite that, there were rarely more than three or four people paused to read the news, so Khana could be assured of finding a place where the screen was not blocked by tall Terrans.

Today, he was the only one attending the news at this hour. He put his box on the floor at his feet and looked up at the screen. Most often, the news had nothing to do with him, but it gave him practice reading Terran, and also gave him something of real life to take to Bar Jan on those frequent days when he did not venture beyond the wayroom.

The background news-view today was of starry space, courtesy of the top-class restaurant he'd never been to up in the high decks. He glimpsed *Oncoming trouble?* as a brief headline, but the colors changed then, and he saw he was fortunate to have arrived just as the scroll was finishing. There came a space of blank screen, followed by the Port Chavvy logo, and the scroll began again, from the top.

First was General Port News: there were corridor closures in the business section, a part of the station Khana had never seen. The five-year inspection and repair of the water delivery system to the Administrative Level was scheduled for tonight alt-shift; offices were to be closed during the work.

Next came an announcement from Port Administration, and this—so seldom did the news impact his life that Khana read the announcement, and the next item was scrolling up before he realized that something—*advantageous*—was about to happen.

The next item summarized the findings of the recent audit of the station's shielding; the next, a list of Amended Departures; and, last, the daily update on the comet.

Khana scanned them all impatiently, waiting for the scroll to repeat, so he could read that interesting item again, to be certain that he had read correctly, and that—there!

Allotment Increases for Awaiting Rescue, Transport, or Skillful Habitation: Eight percent base rate; four percent volunteer rate; one percent facilitator rate. Medical stipend increase six percent. All increases effective next pay-in.

Khana's breath caught. He drew at base rate. Bar Jan received the medical stipend through his next appointment at the clinic. If he was declared "fit" then he also would draw at base rate.

Once Bar Jan was "fit," Khana would be free to apply himself to the volunteer listings, something that had been beyond his reach, and that rate had also increased. Combining those resources, they might move into larger quarters in the ARTS hallways where their current wayroom was located. The potential to improve their situation was unexpectedly exciting.

Khana's gaze had still been on the screen, though he had seen nothing but his own excited thoughts until the word UPDATE in bright red letters caught his attention.

The same image he'd seen before courtesy of the Long View restaurant appeared.

The trajectory of the inbound comet has changed. Attempts are being made to push it further from Port Chavvy. There is no danger to the station; the adjustments are being made merely to increase the distance between the comet and the station during its passage.

Khana stared at the screen as the image magnification picked up. Comets, asteroids, meteors—he'd not had much to do with space objects while caring for his master's needs, and before that, as a youth training to care for his master, he'd had only Liad's quiet skies overhead and his delm's admonition to always watch the skies, that the weather never show Rinork's heir to disadvantage.

Khana shook himself from the hypnotic image and the news scrolls. If all was well, all was well, and Bar Jan was waiting for his breakfast and his news.

• • • ✧ • • •

SHANNA was late returning with the meal.

In the downtime between the fifth and sixth *sets* of exercise, he weighed whether Shanna was late *enough* that he must begin to fear himself abandoned.

Again.

Not that there was any fault to find, if Shanna had decided to leave. The only question that might be asked was why he had waited so long. Well. There was also the question of why he had remained at all.

Surely, it would have been the better plan to have departed when Delm Rinork had declared Shanna's master dead, and ordered the body stripped of everything of value. Rinork by contract was bound to return servants of the clan to Liad, should their service end while off-world. Not even Rinork could lay blame on *Shanna*. She had been displeased with him, but Shanna knew the way around her anger. If he had exerted himself, abased himself, only a little—Rinork would have honored the contract, and taken Shanna home to Liad, where his own delm would most assuredly have been angry, though not so angry that Shanna need fear for his life.

The timer declared his rest interval done. He stood once more, made sure of the weights on his wrists, and began the next set.

Six sets of six was the rule, three times a day, until he felt that had become too easy. Tomorrow, he would promote himself to seven sets of seven. His goal was to achieve ten sets of ten by the time he was to return to the clinic for his next evaluation.

It was, by any accounting, a modest enough goal.

If Shanna were gone, he would need to do better.

Fear interrupted the working of the weights.

If Shanna were gone, he, himself, had no ID—Shanna had needed both in order to collect two meals. He, who had stayed in the room they shared, had nothing to prove his status with regard to the station, which fed him, and clothed him, and provided his medical care.

Swallowing, he forced himself to take up the interrupted rhythm of the weight work. There was no advantage to Shanna in keeping his ID, he told himself. The assertion did little to soothe him. Perhaps if he had known less about unscrupulous means, and the justifications for using them . . .

He worked through the prescribed routine, counting meticulously. When he had done, he sat down and removed the weights. Then he closed his eyes.

Shanna's absence, he told himself, had been longer than average, but not worrisomely so. He was hungry; that was what fretted him. Hunger made him impatient.

As did so many other things.

He opened his eyes and he brought his hands up for inspection. One was well shaped and seemly, the fingers long and straight, the skin gold toned and supple. The other—was a nightmare, wizened, with blotched pink skin. The reconstructed fingers were long and straight, but the merest pegs, all but strengthless muscles not yet fully reconstituted.

Which reminded him that he had yet to work with the pressure ball. Usually, he did his first session after breakfast was eaten. Today, with breakfast late—no.

No, he corrected himself. The book; recall the book—*change is opportunity*, so the book had it, a curiously Liaden sentiment, given a special poignancy by circumstances.

He rose and crossed the small room, opened the drawer where he kept the pressure ball when it was not in use, and took it up in his ruined—no, he caught himself up once more. Not ruined. Rebuilt. His hand had been rebuilt, even now it was useful for some small tasks. It would become more so, did he continue with his exercises.

So. Today, he had been given the opportunity to have an extra session with the pressure ball, thus speeding his healing.

There, that was positive. The book also taught the importance of a positive viewpoint. See the *benefit* of the situation, then work to improve it; that was the book's advice. This placed one in a position of strength and allowed a survey of circumstance through eyes untainted by anger or fear.

He worked the ball, and turned to consider the place in which he found himself.

It was a small room—which was, he reminded himself, good, for there was less for Shanna to maintain. The space was orderly, neat, and clean, for Shanna would never tolerate a room that was at sixes and twelves. Everything must be where he could immediately lay hand on it, to best to serve his master.

So, a small room, two beds that folded into the walls during waking hours; a table and two chairs; an upholstered chair; the set of drawers. An alcove next to the table held a cool-box, a tap into the station's water supply, and a single heating coil so that they might make tea, or warm leftover food without having to go out into the common area.

Next to the drawers was a discreet door which opened onto a basic accommodation, with a sonic shower.

How had he, once the named heir to the delm of Clan Rinork, come to occupy this tidy, tiny space, and stand grateful for it?

Ah, but that had to do with his—*error*.

In the realm of errors, his had been—spectacular. There, that followed the book's advice.

He had goaded a trader—a lad scarcely past halfling, his junior by several Standards, adopted son to one of the most well-connected and canny of the masters of trade—he had pursued and goaded this young trader into a duel.

Had all gone his way, he would have killed the young trader, the dueling set he had proposed to use having been tuned to guarantee such a result. But the young trader, as the challenged, had the right to choose the weapons of Balance, and he *had* chosen . . .

Wisely. A canny lad, that one. He would do excellently—well. ven'Deelin's very apprentice. How could it be otherwise?

Stinks hammers and starbars, seven paces and closing! We shall have a smash to remember!

Wryly, he looked at his hand, moved his rebuilt arm.

Smash. An apt descriptor, *smash*.

The error then compounded itself, for he might have cried off before ever it came to smashing—his seconds had argued for it, and the boy's second, as well. But, no. By then, he had crossed into that state past anger, long lost to reason. Everything he had wanted in those moments was to kill Jethri Gobelyn ven'Deelin. He had been so enraged that it did not seem possible that he would fail in that goal.

He realized that he had stopped squeezing the ball, and resumed.

Well, he *had* failed. And if he had succeeded, he had no doubt—*now*—that the witnessing crowd would have carried him to the nearest airlock and spaced him. Odd, that the price of both failure and success was the same.

He might have died in truth from failure, had Port Chavvy not proved efficient. There was a wounded man on the docks? Port Chavvy gathered the injured to itself.

Meanwhile, his erstwhile victim, now victor—did not pursue Balance and call the minions of law down upon him. No, the victor, and those who had witnessed the affair—Terrans, very nearly all!— declared that there had been *an accident*, which had left the victor with a head wound, ably doctored by a medic from one of the docked ships, and himself, *smashed*. Questioned, not one deviated from this interpretation of the event, and so did Port Chavvy administration record it.

An accident.

The victim of an accident, he had lived some little while longer, until his mother and his delm had arrived to declare him dead.

He paused, having lost his count, looked down at the ball gripped in his fingers, and began again.

Port Chavvy was situated deep in a backwater spiral arm. It was near to trade lanes menaced by pirates and worlds of chancy circumstance, far from Liad. Liaden culture, tradition—*Liaden law*—meant nothing to Port Chavvy. The notion that a single person might create a death merely by announcing that it was so—that was not a notion to which Port Chavvy subscribed.

Of travelers and crew abandoned by their ships, Port Chavvy was well versed, and being so far from Liad, and not in the least Liaden, Port Chavvy had fashioned its response to those unfortunates not out of Liaden Balance and questions of *melant'i*, but from the cloth of Terran hospitality.

Port Chavvy, confronted with someone who might bleed to death, stopped the bleeding.

Port Chavvy, confronted with someone who might suicide while despondent and under medication, mounted a watch comprised of volunteers and medics.

Port Chavvy, having seen someone on the path to recovery and judged to no longer present a threat to themselves, provided sleep-learning courses in Terran. Once proficiency was established, Port Chavvy released him to the lower decks and the ARTS halls, first providing ID, a packet including clothing, toiletries, the book, and the number of the wayroom that he would now be pleased to call his home.

When he had been alive, he would have laughed at the idea, but death—death, he discovered, provided a clarifying influence. In fact, he *was* pleased to call this compact and orderly space his home, and—

The door made the high-pitched squeak that meant someone had shown it their ID. It opened to admit Shanna, balancing boxes between hands, and looking practically disheveled.

* * * ✧ * * *

TURNING INTO THEIR CORRIDOR, Khana saw he was later than he'd thought—the color of the wall was shading subtly from blue to green. When the color was solid, it would be Green Shift. The ARTS—that was, those Awaiting Rescue, Transport or Skilled Habitation—were housed in the older section of Port Chavvy's under-warrens. Five of their nineteen cohabitants were gathered in a wide space designated as "the lounge." It was a gathering place for those who then departed for a group activity, as well as a place to socialize, and the place where the Session was convened.

He had a time or two lingered at the lounge when returning from the Cantina while Bar Jan slept off his pain meds in the early days of their time here, finding it a place where, all being in the ARTS community after all, there was a type of collegiality one might find backstairs at a delm's home, an assumption of being in the same struggle, day by day. His fellow residents had gently corrected his pronunciations, the sleep learner apparently being academic on some words and phrases, not having the local accent, timing, or diction.

There was a corner near the intersection of halls where singers often gathered. This hour, there were five, four engaged in a complex round robin song-sing. All Terran, they nodded, smiled, and allowed him to pass without offering a place to stand. Khana felt a pang. They had used to offer, but he had not once in the twenty-nine days since Bar Jan had been freed from the med wards accepted this extension of that backstairs feeling. Why should the singers continue to open themselves to rebuff?

He continued across the lounge, hurrying now that he realized the time.

"There's the man himself," came a voice from his left, and here was Femta approaching, a meal box in his hand. Khana paused.

Femta rarely spoke, and, having caught Khana's attention, apparently felt no need to speak further. He offered the box, and when Khana did not reach out a hand to accept it, committed himself to a smile.

"Forgive me," Khana said. "I do not . . . understand."

Femta nodded and produced more words.

"Extras from last night. Kitchen help had them boxed, a little care because your friend's been distant. Time they came looking, you'd left, so they asked me to bring them, if you would not mind." The voice was oddly without accent, subdued, unobtrusive, like the person.

"Ah," Khana said, and took a breath. More kindness, he told himself, and offered a smile in return, as he took the additional box.

"Thank you for your care," he said, and added, perhaps not truthfully, "My friend will be grateful."

"No trouble for me," Femta said. "Hope to see your friend out and around soon."

With that, he turned and moved away into the lounge.

Khana shifted his various burdens cautiously. They were a little unwieldy, but it wasn't far now. He continued on his way.

· · · ✧ · · ·

A SLIGHT FIGURE was turning away from the door to their room as Khana arrived at the top of the hall. Fear spiked, for bounty hunters were not to be discounted, though it had not yet been a relumma, and—

The figure raised her head, and fear evaporated, for it was Joolia, another of their group, so slim and small she appeared Liaden.

The smile she gave him was pure Terran, delight writ large on her pointed face, and touching her dark eyes with warmth.

"There you are!" she said. "I came looking for you, then I didn't want to press the bell, in case your friend was resting."

"Here I am," Khana agreed, smiling in his turn. "Why are you looking for me?"

That was, perhaps, unfortunately phrased. Joolia's face grew solemn.

"I need you—or, well! I need *your help* organizing the common supply room, if you have time? Ferlandy asked me to do it, and I *can* do it, but it'll take some time, it's that messy. So, I need a helper, and I'd seen you that time sorting the lounge closet into order, so quick I don't think anybody else noticed—and I thought—that's who I need for this!"

She looked doubtfully at the boxes in his arms.

"Unless you're busy?"

Khana bowed his head. This, too, reminded of the backstairs, the acknowledgment that one's duty came first but that the sharing of burdens made all lives easier, all more worthy. It was an equality he was amazed to find offered, and was happy to accept.

"I am pleased to assist," he said, "but I must bring my friend his breakfast. I have gotten behind time."

"No worries," Joolia said. "I've got some things to take care of myself. Say we meet at the supply room in an hour, will that do for you? Give us time to do the job and still get to the Session."

"Yes," said Khana, unaccountably warmed. "That will do for me. Thank you."

He moved toward the door, fumbling for the ID card in his jacket pocket. The boxes shifted, and he twisted, making a recover, but—

"Here, let me," said Joolia, dipping a slender hand into his pocket and pulling the ID out. "I'll open the door for you."

She waved the card at the reader, and stepped back as the door began to open. Dropping the card back in his pocket, she turned away.

"I'll see you soon," she said.

• • • ✧ • •

WITHIN, Bar Jan stood dressed, his good arm visible to what might be a public view, his day slacks on as well as his socks and mocs.

This was good, Khana thought, as he carried the boxes to the table. Occupational Therapy Tech Salmoa had assigned Bar Jan an occupation: to take care of his own needs. True, he should also have been coming to breakfast these last seven days and more, but balanced against that lack was the fact that Bar Jan dressed himself every day, and was meticulous in the exercises meant to strengthen his shattered arm and hand.

That it was difficult for Bar Jan to do these things, Khana had no doubt, for he had seen the sweat on the other man's face.

The exercise was also difficult for Khana, and he had to restrain himself from merely taking the task over. It had been part of his duty, to dress his lord, and to arrange matters, so far as he was able, that his master was in no way impeded in his business.

As he opened the boxes, he recalled his father, who had trained him in his duty, many Standards past: "You must take daily exercise, in order to properly serve. You must be strong, stronger than your lord, though you will never allow him to know it."

There was no doubt who was stronger, now, and that Bar Jan was aware. And how strange it was, that he must now use his strength in support of his master's struggles, and encourage him to do for himself.

"What is all this, Shanna?" Bar Jan was at the table, staring down, the exercise ball held in his spindly fingers. The rest of the arm from shoulder to wrist was still enmeshed in the healing shroud. In public, he wore a white secondhand lab jacket, the front sealed to his throat. In the privacy of their room, he wore a long-sleeved shirt, likewise sealed tightly. Khana pinned both unneeded sleeves neatly out of the way, which was certainly beyond Bar Jan's abilities, no matter his determination, and they both felt the better for it.

"The dinner staff made a box for you. Out of care," he added, because care had not been often present in Bar Jan's life, even between kin.

"Do they think we are desperate?" It seemed that the question was posed in simple curiosity, rather than anger, or insult. Khana was pleased to encourage this mood, so he did not mention that, compared to many on Port Chavvy, they *were* desperate. Instead, he focused on the lesson Miki had given him.

"The kitchen staff, they marked your absence from recent meals, and they felt concern, that your wound was paining you, or that you were unwell, or unhappy. Look, they have sent five of the cheese rolls you favor. The gift is thoughtful."

It was also practical, Khana saw. Each of the cheese rolls was individually wrapped, as were the two dense fiber rolls, with attending jars of jells. The food would keep for days in the carry box.

"So," he finished, looking up to Bar Jan. "These are extra, so that you may follow the tech's advice to *feed yourself up!*"

That of course was said in Terran, the Liaden—even in flexible Low Liaden—being nonsensical.

"I of course strive to follow all of the med tech's excellent advice," Bar Jan said, in a curious flat tone that was neither irony nor pique.

Khana looked at him carefully, before attending the table again. He placed the breakfast box next to the book that Bar Jan kept to hand—the book provided by Port Chavvy to all of its dependents, *Crisis Survivorship: Managing Massive Life Changes*, by Professor Linda Jeef Marteen. The volume was dual-language—Trade and Terran. Khana had read it, but Bar Jan—Bar Jan was *studying* it, performing the various closed- and open-eyed meditations from its pages, and sometimes checking a dictionary tablet, that usually with a scowl.

"What is a *jeef*, after all?" he had demanded on one occasion, before putting the book irritably aside.

"You are behind on your meal," Khana said. "Eat now, and I will tell you the news before I must go to an—" He paused, unsure of how to describe the task for which Joolia had requested his assistance. "An appointment."

"An appointment." Still that odd, uninflected tone. Bar Jan put the ball aside, and sat to table. Spork in hand, he looked up.

"Shanna, may I have my ID card?"

"Certainly!" He pulled it from his pocket and placed it atop the book.

"My thanks." Bar Jan murmured. "So, there is news?"

"The comet continues our way," Khana began. "The station is attempting a protocol to increase our margin of safety. This from the newsboard. The audit of the meteor shields has been completed. It seems that they are more vulnerable than anticipated to the unique threat of this comet, which has both density and mass as well as velocity and rotation. The combination of these might breach the shields."

Khana paused, but Bar Jan seemed utterly intent on his meal.

"A number of ships at dock have filed for early departure, one assumes from concerns regarding the comet's pass."

"They will be safer undocked, if the station is struck," Bar Jan said, with something like his old authority. Khana blinked, and then recalled that he had been fascinated by the practical business of ships, which his mother and delm had deplored.

"Is there other news?" Bar Jan asked, glancing up from his meal.

"Ah! There is indeed. The Port has increased the ARTS allotments. Base rate increases eight percent; medical stipend increases six percent; the volunteer rate increases by four percent; facilitators will receive a one percent increase."

"Eight percent—" Bar Jan had always been good at his numbers. Now, he lifted his eyebrows, doing, so Khana supposed, sums in his head.

"You might achieve your own suite, Shanna."

He had not thought of that, and he paused to do so before shrugging it aside.

"What I had thought," he said, as Bar Jan finished his meal and closed the box, "is that we might together achieve a larger space. I daresay that will be best for both of us."

"Yes, you *do* dare say," Bar Jan answered—angry words, but there was no heat in his voice. "Always planning, Shanna, and giving direction."

Seated as he was, Khana bowed, his temper engaged by this flat-voiced accusation. In all the years he had served Bar Jan chel'Gaibin, he had never felt such anger as this. It would have been inappropriate, given their *melant'is*.

But here, where there was no *melant'i*, no *Code*—

"Indeed, yes, I gave direction, and was sometimes fortunate to see you accept it!" The voice was hard—*angry*. It was a moment before Khana realized that it was *his* voice, and by that time he was sweeping on.

"When you bothered to take my direction, you wore the proper suit at the proper time, the proper shoes, and boots. When you bothered to take my direction, your mother noticed you with more favor and less anger. I directed your choices, from hair shine to socks, for that was my duty! As for planning—only see the success of *your* planning! You might have died in truth, save for *my* planning, *my* direction, *my* appeal—"

He stopped, his breath caught in horror. Bar Jan was standing, he saw, and realized that he was, as well.

There was a way to heal this, Khana thought rapidly. He need only admit his error, abase himself, and speak mildly.

He took a careful breath, averting his eyes.

"Master—" he began—and stopped, because Bar Jan had raised his good hand.

He was in pain, Khana saw, marking the damp forehead, the tight mouth, the narrowed eyes. He was too frail for . . .

Bar Jan sighed softly. "I have waited too long for this," he said. "It must be acknowledged, and it is mine to do."

He took a deep, deliberate breath, and in that moment the cheap station clothes were the business attire of a lord; a man of substance and *melant'i*.

Then, he bowed.

It was . . . a simple bow, carefully flensed of years of hauteur. It was a bow Khana had never in his years of duty seen from one of Rinork, much less from the heir himself.

It was the bow between equals, with an additional careful tip of the head, which acknowledged that a debt was owed.

Face grim, Bar Jan straightened, waiting.

"Yes," Khana managed against a tight throat.

His bow was simple as well. The bow between equals, with the hand sign that conveyed all debts were paid.

He paused, resisting another bow, and instead closed on Bar Jan, clapping him on his good shoulder, as an equal might after a game of *piket*.

"Come, let me check your wrappings, and then I must to my appointment. Will you come to the Session today?"

Bar Jan hesitated as he turned to the chair.

"I—will be reading," he said after a moment.

Khana paused with his hand on med box, wondering if he dared to push again.

Well, and why not?

"The boy at the Cantina—Miki—asked after your health and professes that he will be pleased to see you again. Our . . . neighbors here, as well. They ask of you, of your health. They care for you."

Improbably, Bar Jan's face relaxed into a smile.

"No, Shanna," he said gently. "They care for *you*."

TWO

JOOLIA WAS ALREADY AT WORK when Khana arrived, having made a start of clearing the counters on the right side of the room. She had removed the hooded over-garment she wore in the hallways and the lounge, and rolled the sleeves of the sweater beneath. There was a look of grim determination on her pointed face that reminded him of Bar Jan.

She turned as he entered the room, grimness melting into a faint smile.

"You came!"

"Of course I came," he answered, remembering to answer her smile. "Did I not say so?"

"Well, you did, but I wouldn't've much blamed you, if you'd taken one look at this mess and just backed out."

Khana looked about him.

Yes, he thought, *mess* would cover it.

"What happened?" he asked. He had been in the common supply room many times, to draw clean towels, recyclable dishes, cutlery—and while it always had the slightly disheveled look of a space that was used briefly by many individuals, it had never been this . . . chaotic.

Joolia sighed.

"Cazzy had the Scareds come on her over sleep-shift. Hasn't

happened for a long time, Windy said. I've never seen it, but I haven't been here so long. Anyhow, the Scareds make her think there's something hiding and waiting to get her, an' last night I guess she s'posed whatever it was, it was hiding in here."

She blew out a breath, turning in place to survey the carnage.

"Anyway, Ferlandy an' Windy caught her at it, only not too soon, as you can see, and took her up to the clinic. Windy came back with Ferlandy's word could I set things to right, so here *I* am. Then I got a good look, figured I needed help, and here *you* are."

"I am," Khana agreed, "and the two of us will soon put it right."

She smiled again. "You sound like somebody who knows what he's doing. Since I don't, that makes you lead. Tell me what and how and I'll do it."

Khana saw what she had done so far and what needed done.

"First, we will separate those things which must go into the recycler and those that are still whole and useful."

"Right you are," Joolia said. "I'll take this side."

Joolia was a determined worker, and Khana had Standards of experience in sorting out messes of all kinds. Between them, the first step was quickly accomplished.

"Whew," Joolia said, as they paused for a moment to survey their progress. "I'd never have gotten this far, this fast, without you, Khana."

"Why did Ferlandy give you the task? If asking does not offend."

She laughed.

"Well, see, I'm a research librarian, and in Ferlandy's thinking, a librarian is somebody who keeps things in order so other people can find them."

Khana blinked, wondering—

"Ah," he said, enlightened. "Ferlandy makes no difference between righting chaos and keeping order."

"That's it." She gave him an approving nod. "But you—where'd you learn to find order in a mess?"

"A subset of my training," he said, surveying what remained for them. Cazzy had been thorough, and most of what had been in the cabinets now—was not. Fortunately, the closets were labeled, which would make the next stage of their operation much easier. There was a system in place, even if it was a system that Khana itched to adjust; they would not be slowed down by having to invent their own.

"Training in what? If it's not an insult to ask," Joolia said.

He turned to face her.

"I . . . was," he said slowly, "a *kie'floran*, which required me to care for the personal belongings of . . . the one I served; to pack, unpack, to always know where everything was, and put it away into its proper place when it was no longer needed. As much as possible also to be sure of the timing of things, to aid with the meeting of appointments and necessities."

"And your friend?" she asked, then quickly brought her hand to her lips. "I'm sorry, that's prying. Only, I was thinking, if Ferlandy knew what his training was, maybe there was something he—your friend—could be set to do. Which would help him feel better." Color stained her cheekbones, and he realized that she, like Miki before her, had been discomfited by her own boldness.

"Of course," she said, her voice strained. "He might not be well enough . . ."

Khana glanced at the wall. They were approaching time for the Session. If they wished to be done ordering the room by then, they had best move on.

"The next step," he said, stretching his arms out to encompass the room, "is to create piles of like and like." He looked around. Cazzy had not been dainty in her search for assassins. "I suggest we use the table."

"All right," Joolia said, sounding somewhat subdued. She bent and gathered an armful of miscellaneous items to carry to the worktable.

Khana brought his armful to the opposite end, and began to work. The song from the group at the intersection of the hallways was suddenly very loud. He looked up from his sorting, and his glance crossed Joolia's. Sighing somewhat, he answered her question as best he was able.

"My friend," he said, slowly. "He was trained to be the center—unchanging, fixed—and to also seek advantage—for himself, and for those who were aligned with him. He had not a trade, such as you have, or I, but a *position*."

He glanced up. Joolia's head was down, watching her own hands. He left the table to gather more items for sorting, and fell into the rhythm of the work.

When Joolia spoke again, he started, and looked up to meet her eyes.

"So," she said. "He doesn't know who he is, anymore, with all that gone—all those people and systems that he was center for."

Khana cleared his throat.

"Yes," he said. "Exactly that. It is—hard for him."

"I'm guessing so," said Joolia, giving him a faint smile. "But he looks sharp, yanno? He'll figure himself out."

"Yes," said Khana, his throat unaccountably tight. "I am certain that he will."

A thought occurred then, and he raised a hand.

"You are a research librarian," he said.

"That's right." The smile was broader this time. "Got something you need researched? I owe you for your help, after all."

He had previously noticed that some Terrans practiced an informal sort of Balance, and it pleased him that Joolia was one of them.

"Yes, if you please," he said. "I wonder if you could find for me what the word *jeef* means."

· · · ✦ · · ·

BAR JAN REREAD THE CHAPTERS on decision-making and self-management. The book would have one select for personal happiness, rather than advantage, which was not at all a Liaden concept, but one he thought he might adopt. Considering happiness, he made a cup of tea, and unwrapped one of the cheese rolls.

His happiness had never been of much importance to anyone, including himself. He was the son of Rinork, heir to her honors and her duties. If he had thought of the matter in the terms provided by the book, he would have realized that those things did not make him happy; that his duties weighed heavily on him; that the constant seeking of advantage made him—angry.

He had been happy, he realized now, when the pilots and mechanics would speak to him of ship lore and the mysteries of piloting, though he had gained no advantage from their lessons. In fact, the opposite, for his mother had despised him for his interest. Why did he bother himself? she had asked. He was plainly no pilot, nor ever would be. Perhaps, she had suggested caustically, he proposed to be a mechanic?

But no. It was unthinkable that one of Rinork, never mind the heir, might study to become a spaceship mechanic.

No matter; his current situation also put that . . . potential . . . happiness out of reach.

Sipping tea, he stared through the wall and into the past.

What else, then, he asked himself.

Had it made him happy to ruin livelihoods, and tarnish reputations? Would he have been *happy*, if he had killed Jethri Gobelyn ven'Deelin?

He suspected not, even if he had managed to survive the act.

Well, then. Was he so poor a thing that he had no happiness in him?

There must, he thought, feeling his chest tighten in something like the old panic—there must be *some*thing since his death that had caused him to feel, if not happiness, then—contentment?

Malvern. The thought rose so sudden and so certain that he sat, amazed, until his mind began to work again. Then, he followed the steps outlined in the book, to discover whether it was Malvern herself—her person, her demeanor—which gave him ease; some aspect of the environment in which she operated, or—

It came in a flash: The first time Shanna had bullied him into walking to the Cantina to claim and eat his breakfast. There had been Malvern, clearly in command of the enterprise. She had taken note of them—of him in particular as he stood puzzling over the breads and sweet things on offer. She had taken time to go over every item with him, making certain he understood the nature of each, correcting his faltering Terran with neither mockery nor patronage. He had been happy—in her company, in the lore she had shared, and especially in her parting comment, that, once his arm was healed, he might if he wished take up an apprenticeship, and learn how to bake.

He had regarded that pleasantry as a *promise*, he realized now. He had kept it close, giving himself something to look forward to that was not the pills he had hidden away against a time when surcease from pain was all he had left.

Bar Jan finished the roll, and the tea, considering his next step. The book would have him make a list of things that stood between him and his happiness, and another list, of how he would surmount each.

To make that list, he needed the assistance of an expert. He would, he thought, standing, go to the Cantina and find Malvern, else her second, and learn what he needed to do in order to become a baker.

He would go. Now.

* * * ◇ * * *

JOOLIA CLOSED THE LAST CABINET and stood with her palms against the door as if she expected the towels inside to come rushing out at her.

"Done," she said, after a moment, and turned around to give Khana a grin.

"Done," he agreed, "and in good time. Listen. The singing has stopped."

"Well, then, it's us for the Session, my friend! We can make a report of progress."

She pushed the sleeves of her sweater down, took up her hooded jacket and slipped it on.

Khana turned slowly on his heel, surveying the room. All was seemly. Good. He smiled, pleased.

"It does feel good, doesn't it," Joolia said from beside him. "Looking at it now, and remembering how it had been?"

"Yes," he said, turning his head to smile at her. "You worked well."

"I just did what I was told. Couldn't've gone nearly as well without you breaking it all down into steps for me." She jerked her head toward the door. "C'mon, let's grab some good seats."

She turned and went out into the hall, Khana one step behind her. At the entrance to the lounge, he paused, and turned toward their room—

And found his arm caught in a surprisingly firm grip.

"Hey," said Joolia, "the Session's this way."

Khana opened his mouth, and she shook her head.

"He'll be okay," she said. "If he wants to come to the Session, he will. Right?"

Khana considered her with something like wonder.

"Right," he said, and followed her into the lounge.

• • •✧• • •

THE SESSION WAS UNLIKE any other event Khana had attended in his previous life. The first meeting had been horrifying; the second bewildering, but by the end of the third, he'd become accustomed. It was the one dependable marker in days that were sometimes too much alike. Attendance was not compulsory, but most ARTS did attend. Khana made it a point to come to every meeting, bringing Bar Jan when he could manage it, which had not been often.

A Liaden would say that the purpose of the Session was to publicly display one's vulnerabilities, surely a risky endeavor.

Now at this, his tenth Session, Khana was comfortable with— and comforted by—the Progress Report, and hoped one day to have something to share, himself.

Chairs were arranged in the lounge in a semicircle facing a table at which the leader stood. Everyone took turns as leader, and Khana realized with a start that *he* would have a turn, if he attended eight out of the next ten Sessions.

Today, Femta stood at the table, waiting while seats filled.

"Got only one item of general bidness today," he said when the talk had subsided. "Cazzy's at clinic. Ferlandy's with her. He sends she'll be took down to the planet for treatment, if the clinic techs can't figure out a new good dose for to keep her easy. Anybody wants to stop by and catch up, now's the time."

He paused for a slow count of ten. When no one stood, or spoke, he nodded.

"This Session is a joint meeting of Travelers Awaiting Rescue,

Transport or Skilled Habitation and Port Chavvy Residents Accepting Aid. We convene every two days to report our efforts to improve Port Chavvy however we may, and to fortify our own lives and well-being by sharing our searches for increased prosperity for all."

That was the formal start of every Session, followed by, "Success and failure may be equally discussed, because as we all know—progress is a history of failures gone right."

Femta looked at those assembled, took one step back from the table and opened his arms, as if he would embrace all who were gathered.

"Who's seen progress or caught a success?"

"I have!" A plump woman in overalls embroidered with strange flowers stood up. Khana recognized her as one of the singers.

"Boradeen," she said, at Femta's nod. "Four and a half Standards ART. Just got the confirm—tomorrow I'm reporting to Air Filtration Nine, to start training for backup tech."

There was a whistle from the back row of chairs. Somebody upfront clapped.

Boradeen grinned.

"Really," she said, grinning, "pretty much what I did on Sylvester's cruise ships, 'cept there I was running a whole stinks crew—pretty much ASO—All Shifts On! Here it'll be a five-hour shift every five days, working on units I'm half familiar with. Chance to move up. Gimme a Standard and I'll be off the hall."

"Don't you go too far, too fast, Bordy, we need you on the quartets!"

There was laughter—and a sudden solemn look on the singer's face.

"True," she said. "I just got some of you trained right. Prolly they'll keep me alt-shift for awhile, so I won't be missing practs too soon."

There was a smattering of claps as she sat down, still smiling.

"Right, then," Femta said. "Who else?"

Windy stood. In Khana's experience, Windy spoke second at every meeting, and he always had a piece of hardcopy in his hand, which he would look at, rather than at those gathered.

The last time Khana had seen Windy at the Session, he had wept during his entire presentation, as had several other members of the meeting.

Today, Windy was dressed in a light blue lab coat, kin to Bar Jan's white one. Not new, either garment, but not shabby.

"Windy VinHalin, two Standards and nine-tens on Port. My aunt Mithes, she's back in 'hab for too much 'stim, but she got my news to her youngest sister. That's Cindra, some of you might recall. Cindra, she sent some credit toward clothes—" He caught his sleeve in his free hand and raised his arms, showing off his finery.

When he lowered his arms, he stared at the hardcopy for a long time, then looked up, at Femta, who nodded.

"Right," Windy said, sounding breathless. "So Cindra, she—it says in her letter she's going to court to force the Chaendle Line trustees to make good on my ticket."

Someone cheered, but Windy waved him down.

"First date she's got is for a circuit court—judge comes in start of next Standard. Meantime, the advocate, she thinks they might raise me a ticket if the funds ain't spooled by then. That'd be two Standards, with the orbits all running together."

He looked back at the hardcopy, and told it, "So, I'm here for a bit yet, even with best luck."

The groan was universal, accompanied by shaking heads, muttered curses, and frustrated sighs.

"That's progress," Windy said, voice firm, and sat down.

Khana felt a light pressure against his arm. He turned his head, but Joolia was already rising.

"Joolia Tenuta. One Standard even, come tomorrow blue shift. I've got pickup work at Port Admin, doing law and precedent research. Might go somewhere interesting, though I'm still hoping for a ship."

She paused to look down at him, and tugged on his arm. Belatedly understanding, Khana stood.

"Ferlandy asked me to clean up the mess that overtook the common supply area. I realized it was too big for me, so I asked Khana for an assist. He took lead, and the result is the room's back in good order."

She looked at him. He looked at her.

"You got anything to add, Khana?" Femta asked, kindly.

Khana touched tongue to lips.

"It was a pleasure to assist," he said, faintly. And the room erupted into whistles and claps.

* * * ✧ * * *

HE HAD TAKEN a wrong turn, and then another in an attempt to correct his course. Still, he eventually came to his intended location, if somewhat later into the Port-day than he had supposed he would. This was, he reminded himself, as he rested on a bench outside the Cantina's entrance, not a failure, but a success. He had achieved Step One of his Action Plan: Arrive at the Cantina.

Step Two was: Enter the Cantina and speak with Malvern about his Goal, asking her advice in how best to achieve it. If Malvern was not present, he would identify the next most knowledgeable person on staff and speak with them. He would proceed to that step as soon as he was rested. It would not help his case if he arrived breathless and disordered. A calm face was necessary.

As he sat, resting, he reviewed his Plan in its entirety, especially the necessity to thank whomever he found to advise him, even if they had not been useful to his Goal. *Immediately useful*, he corrected himself, to *this* Goal. He might, after all, have a new Goal, later, and again require advice.

Also, he thought, he should make another Plan, which was to have something to eat and drink while he was in the Cantina, so that the walk . . . home . . . would be easier.

He took a breath, assessing himself, finding that he was rested and calm. Excellent. On to Step Two.

* * * ✧ * * *

THERE WERE NO DINERS in the Cantina. Behind the counter was someone he had never seen before.

"Help you?" she asked, smiling.

He smiled, and came to the counter. "Thank you," he said, in Terran, because that was courtesy. "Is Malvern here?"

She shook her head. "She's been called up, hon. We're doing the best we can without her."

He was not clear on *called up*, though he grasped the general message was that Malvern was not present—but for how long?

"She will return?" he asked.

Her face altered, though he wasn't sure of the meaning of this new expression.

"Sure, she'll be back, don't you worry about that! We just don't know when. Hoping for soon. Is there somebody else can help you now?"

He had thought of this, and prepared his next question.

"The one who performs Malvern's duties, in absence? Is that one here?" He paused, thought, and added, "I need advice."

The smile was back.

"Well, we all kinda split Malvern's job stuff between us, 'cause it's four of us to one of her. The second-key-holder, though—Acting Manager—that's Baydee, and she's right in the back. I'll go get her for you. Wait right there."

She vanished through the door that he supposed led to the kitchens, and he stood where he was. He heard voices, faint, then footsteps. The door swung open, and a woman he recalled from his few previous visits to the Cantina emerged. She was younger than Malvern, shorter, and rounder. Her hair was bundled under a white cap, and she wore an apron. There was a smear of pale dust— perhaps flour—on one dark cheek.

"Hey," she said, with a nod. She came to the counter and leaned her arms on it. "I'm Baydee. You're Khana's friend, right? I remember you were in a couple times. What can I do for you?"

"I wish to become a—baker, or, more. A chef. Like yourself. I hoped you could give me advice . . . how I would achieve this."

She considered him, eyes inevitably going to his damaged arm. He recruited himself to wait.

"I'm taking this is a long-term goal," Baydee said finally.

He was pleased. She understood.

"Yes, thank you. If there is study, or work that I could begin now, as I heal, or—" He moved his good hand in the gesture he had seen others use to signify the depth of their ignorance.

"Gotcha. Can I see your ticket?"

He hesitated, which was foolish. He had asked for advice, and Baydee was the current expert willing to give him advice. She was not going to rob him of his ID.

He took it from his pocket and offered it across the palm of his undamaged hand.

"'Kay, now . . ." Baydee squinted slightly as she read the card, then nodded and handed it back.

"So, there's some details you need to tend to before you can start working on your goal." She gave him a smile. "Stuff that you can work on while you're waiting for your arm to finish healing."

Ah, this was excellent! He inclined his head, recalled himself, and said, "Please go on."

"Right. Now, first thing is you still got a Port Chavvy general ticket—what I mean to say is that it's coded with your number, but there's no name. You wanna start contributing to the station's welfare, you gotta do it under your name." He stirred and she held up a hand.

"Hear me out. It don't have to be whatever your name is, Out from here, but it does have to be a name you'll answer to, and that you'll care enough about to keep it outta trouble. So, first thing's to line up what you want people to call you, and file that with the Port right now, if you're so minded." She nodded toward something that was apparently over his shoulder. He turned, looked, and saw the public terminal in the corner.

"Thank you," he said. "It is a fact that my . . . former name must give way to another." And soon, he reminded himself silently; before the grace period was run and Rinork sent bounty hunters to deal with nameless rogues posing as chel'Gaibin.

Baydee gave him an approving nod. "That's right. New beginnings. You can get the new name set up while you're still on medical, but you can't volunteer or 'prentice 'til you're off medical." She raised a hand again, though he had not been about to speak.

"You be sensible and wait 'til the medics let you go. There'll be hungry people to feed when you got two good arms to feed 'em with, and you don't wanna stop once you start, so make sure the medics *clear you*, right?"

"Right," he said, seriously.

"Once you're cleared, you can apply for volunteer, and even 'prentice. You'll prolly hafta wait for something to come open, so you work at general volunteer, like we all do, and you hook yourself into the Port's vocational library and start educating yourself, and maybe fine-tune your goal. What you said right at first? You wanted to be a baker—a chef? Those are two different things, so you'll want to get clear about which is it, or—" Another smile. "Might turn out that it's something else—that's okay, too. Goals change."

"I am—grateful," he said, and that was honest. "You have given me—"

"Be aware and awake, Cantina! Klyken is here!"

Following the shout came a tall, extremely thin man wearing a bouffant white hat, and spotless white tunic, trousers, and shoes.

"Baydee!" he cried. "I will inform myself, and then we will bake!"

"Yessir," Baydee said, but Klyken had already swept through the door into the kitchen. He could be heard calling for station reports. Baydee smiled.

"Looks like I'm on. You need anything else before I go?"

"I should eat . . . " he began, and stopped as the door came open at Baydee's back and Klyken stepped up to the counter.

"I met you," he said pointing at the damaged arm with his first finger—a rudeness to Liadens, but he reminded himself that he was no longer Liaden.

"Yes," Klyken continued, "before this thing happened with your arm. You came to my restaurant with a large party from *Wynhael*. You had the three-cheese soup, the hunion bread, and a stripe of beefsta, rare. Also, my nillon crisp-crust stuffed with whirled berry spread. It appeared you enjoyed it very much."

It was so very distant, that memory, but he *did* remember the meal, even as he chose not to recall why his mother had gathered those particular people to dine with them.

"It was a fine meal, one of the best I recall enjoying," he said to Klyken, and it wasn't a lie. "You are the chef at the Long View Restaurant?"

"Chef-owner," Klyken said, and there was pride—justified—in his voice and face.

He shook his head then.

"It would be good to talk with you, about memorable meals, hey? But I am here to bake Malvern's special dark, and train Baydee and Miki in the way of it. If you are here to find a meal, please continue, and we will send out to finish the—"

"I am here," he heard himself say, "because I wished to learn what I must do to become a baker, or a chef. Baydee has given me much good advice. But, I would—is it possible to watch you at work?"

There was silence. He swallowed, wondering if—knowing that—he had overstepped.

Baydee spoke. "He's on medical."

"Hah. So, he is disallowed from volunteering or standing as a 'prentice." Klyken looked him in the eye. "Have you ever seen bread made? Have you made bread, or any other foodstuff for others to eat?"

"No," he said, his mouth dry.

"So. What you know is that you like to eat. What you need to discover is whether you like to cook."

"Yes," he said, very nearly voiceless.

"You may watch," Klyken said. He looked at Baydee. "We all understand that he is neither volunteer nor 'prentice. He is allowed to watch because I have said it."

"Right," Baydee said.

Klyken turned and vanished through the door into the kitchens. Baydee waved him down-counter, and opened the pass-through.

"Come on back, and let's find you a good spot for to watch."

• • ◇ • •

"WELL, BUT SEE, there's where your math's gone off. If it was a simple *comet*, you'd be solid, not sayin' not, but that thing ain't no more a wild comet than I am. That's runaway mining, that's what that is—a broke-off piece of that planetary mining op they just up and left—you remember that! That's why Chavvy Admin thought they could steer it away, 'cause they was sending 'structions to the rigs still attached. Not a bad idea, but no word if it worked, an' if it don't work—"

Khana sat between Bordy and the person introduced as Malc, with whom Bordy was speaking. Loudly. Joolia was across the table and three places to the right, in earnest conversation with a man in a bright green volunteers vest.

He wasn't quite sure how he had gotten caught up into the group, but here he was in a public diner near station center, many halls removed from the wayrooms, having ordered his food, and presented his ID, which was accepted with neither comment nor smile.

"Well, it din't work," a new voice said, as a thump sounded just behind and to Khana's left. He turned his head and saw a man in a Port Chavvy foreman's uniform straddling a chair, his arms folded on the back. His face was damp, and drawn.

"Hey, Reg," Bordy said, not so loudly.

On Khana's other side, Malc turned his head. He paused, then lifted his arm.

"Reg needs a beer, here, mate! Put 'er 'gainst the mercy fund!"

"Comin' up!" came an answering shout.

"What din't work?" Bordy asked.

"Contacting the machinery on that hunk o'asteroid bearing down on us—'preciate it"—this last to the woman who delivered a bulb of dark liquid to his hand. He took a moment to drink, sighed, and shook his head.

"Well, we got the machine's attention, all right. Then we sent that it should move itself to the coords the pilots'd worked out. An' it tried. Looked like it was gonna work for a couple minutes, there."

He paused for another gulp from the bulb.

"Problem wasn't the idea, or the machine. Problem was the rock being unstable. Protoplanets are like that, half random and all. Enough frozen gas, mixed salts, and wannabe ocean to make things interesting. Enough to spout off like a comet, dense enough to hit hard if it hits something. They'd had the rig all tied and gridded in for the long haul, but the machine moved, and it—blooie!— fragmented."

Silence.

Out of the corner of his eye, Khana saw Joolia rise from her place and leave the table, apparently headed for the screen in the back corner of the room.

"Soooo," Bordy extended the word as if she were singing it, "what's that mean, zackly?"

Reg finished what was left in the bulb. Somebody reached over his shoulder and took it out of his hand. There were, Khana saw, quite a number of people gathered 'round, listening with worry plain on their faces.

"What it means, zackly, is that we got some luck, but not too much." Reg straightened and looked around him, noting those listening, and nodding his head.

"See, the big rock, it broke into three pieces, mostly, with some odd crumbs here and there. The biggest piece, with the machine attached, looks like that's gonna fly on by, big miss, now that all other stuff got flung off by rotation.

"Second piece is small enough, it'll prolly stick with the big one, even though they ain't connected any more. If it does separate, it'll still miss us."

"An' the third piece?" Malc asked.

Reg sighed.

"Well, now the third piece—no machinery attached, but it's a sizeable rock all on its own, with some gas and ice to boot. Really pretty when you look at it through a lens, yanno? Just like a regular comet!"

He shook his head.

"The third piece—buncha that's gonna hit us, friends. Real soon now."

• • •✧• • •

HE STOOD OUTSIDE of the Cantina, trying to pull his dazzled wits together. What he had witnessed—it had been . . . enthralling. The discipline, the grace, the inevitability of the loaves. It had been an honor, to observe. It had been . . . a great happiness, to eat a slice of the first loaf, still warm from the oven.

While the baking went forward, he had been allowed to assist in the inventory of supplies, so that Baydee could place her order with Supply. His attendance upon Baydee had allowed Miki to do the day's accounting and file receipts with Finance. Therefore, he had been useful.

There at last being nothing else for him to do, he had taken his leave, and now stood by the bench, recruiting himself.

"Well, my friend," a lately familiar voice said from near at hand, "and how do you find the making of food?"

He turned, his body inclining by itself into a small bow of respect.

"I find it compelling and good," he said. "I will wish to pursue this, I think."

"Do you? It is not an easy trade, but it has compensations." There was a pause as Klyken came beside him.

"I don't want to offend, but, why do you stand here?"

"I am trying to recall the route home," he said, though admitting his uncertainty would give Klyken an advantage over him. "I became confused on my way here, and I would avoid making the same error."

"No, better by far to make new errors," Klyken said, with a smile. "You are in the ARTS halls?"

"Yes."

"If you like, we can walk together for a while, and I will point you the rest of the way to your halls when we part."

He had just given Klyken an advantage over him, old habit said. Would he now put himself into his hands?

This had been covered in the book, that old habits might arise and lead to action inappropriate to a new situation. It took time to form new, more appropriate habits, thus mindfulness was suggested.

He took a deep breath, and smiled at Klyken.

"That would be most kind of you," he said.

· · · ✧ · · ·

KLYKEN SPOKE, after they turned the first corner.

"Your ship left you, I heard. Family emergency they said. Always sad, such things."

He continued to walk, and said nothing, ignoring the clamoring of old habit in the back of his head.

"They left me, too," said the chef without rancor, "with bills for five banquets unpaid."

"I . . . regret," he said, when Klyken paused.

"Eh." The other man shrugged. "I filed a claim with the Port. If *Wynhael* comes back, she must pay my bill, and interest, before she can dock." A pause. "Do you know if *Wynhael* will come back? For you, maybe?"

Almost, he laughed, but Klyken was Terran, and would not understand his reasons. He said, gently, "No, Master Klyken, *Wynhael* will *not* come back for me."

Klyken made a soft sound, and spoke again.

"I heard that you were the son of the trader, and that she threw you away."

He said nothing. What was there to say? After a few steps Klyken continued.

"It isn't a good thing, to throw a child away. I know that I have been sorry, for a long time now."

They walked on, turning another corner, and continuing down a hallway that seemed to him familiar.

"I regret," he said again, and indeed he felt sadness for the master's obvious sorrow.

"Eh." Klyken shrugged again. "The Long View—my restaurant. That is my child, now."

They turned another corner, and Klyken stopped. He did, too, turning to look at the chef.

"This is where we part," Klyken said, and raised his arm to point. "You—you walk straight down this hall until that intersection, where the news screen is, eh? At that intersection, you turn right, then continue straight ahead. Another two hall crossings and you will be home."

"Thank you," he said. "I hope to see you again."

"For that, I hope you will come up to the Long View when the medics free you. I often need an extra worker, and I've seen tonight that you know how to work."

He felt tears prick his eyes.

"I will come," he said.

"I'll look forward to that," said Klyken, and with that turned, walking back to the intersection, and taking the left-hand hall.

He stood another moment to compose himself, and began to

smile, recalling again the Cantina, the bread, the inventory! Smiling, he walked down the familiar hallway, toward home.

• • • ◇ • • •

THE WALLS WERE PURPLE when Khana returned to the wayrooms with Bordy and Windy and Joolia. Malc had come along, too, though he wasn't a resident. Bordy had asked Reg to come with them, but he'd shaken his head, and said something about telling Ferlandy to expect a call up.

Khana hadn't noted the passage of time, but, now they were home, and the wall was purple, and Bar Jan—

He gasped.

"Khana?" Joolia said. "Something wrong?"

"My . . . friend . . . I should not have left him so long."

She looked serious. "He that frail he can't be left? I mean, I know he's still on medical, but—"

"Who's up for a game of Corners?" Bordy called. "Khana?"

"No, I thank you," he managed. "It is late, and I must . . . go home."

Bordy grinned. "Did get a little long, din't it? Well, some time other, then."

Khana smiled, but he was already moving toward his corridor, their small room. Bar Jan . . . There was a hoard of pills, he was certain of it, though he had never found them. If Bar Jan had thought himself abandoned—abandoned *again* . . .

It was then that he realized Joolia was still with him.

He looked at her in surprise. She shrugged.

"In case you need help," she said. "'Less you'd rather I leave?"

"No . . . " he said, which was the truth, as he reached into his pocket, pulled out the ID, and waved it at the reader.

The door slid out of the way. He stepped through, leaving Joolia behind as he went swiftly through the tiny 'fresher, returning to the main room to stare around the painfully neat space.

The painfully neat and *empty* space.

There on the table was Bar Jan's book, the medical supplies, and a note-taker. The extra rolls from the morning were not on the table, but they might have equally been placed in the cool box, or taken as wander-food.

"Wander-food," he repeated aloud, mocking himself. Where was there to wander, on a space station?

"Problem?" Joolia asked.

He blinked at her.

"He is not here, and that is not like him. He does not . . . care to leave the room."

"Might've gone out to get something to eat?" Joolia suggested. "It's late, but if he's not used to goin' about by himself, he might've got lost. Where would he most likely go?"

"The Cantina," Khana said, and felt a shudder of guilt. In the other events of the day, he had forgotten to tell Bar Jan that Malvern had been marked by the Port for duty. He forced himself to think. What Joolia suggested made sense. Bar Jan was not accustomed to going about by himself, and there were several sections between home and the Cantina where the confluence of the hallways required interpretation.

Khana started toward the door.

"I will go and see if I can find him," he said to Joolia, as he opened the door, and started back up the corridor. "Thank you."

"No worries. I'll go with you, if you want."

He looked at her again.

"Yes," he said. "Thank you."

Together they crossed the lounge, ignoring the card players in the far corner, and came out into the public hall at the intersection where the singers gathered during day-shifts.

Khana turned left, which was the only choice, from the wayrooms. At the next intersection, however, he would have to decide if Bar Jan would have attempted the twisty back halls, or kept to the more public ways.

They were only steps away from that intersection, when a thin man with bright golden hair, one sleeve of his white coat pinned up, turned the corner.

"Shanna!" cried Bar Jan, flinging up his good arm.

He stopped, staring, thinking for a moment that Bar Jan was . . . glowing. But no, he was standing in the subtle spill of light from a night dim, that was all.

"Where have you been?" he asked. "I came back and you were gone."

"Then we are both keeping late hours," Bar Jan said jovially—*jovially*. "Shanna, I hope your adventure was as amazing as mine."

"It was—very pleasant," Khana said, and felt his stomach clench as Bar Jan turned toward Joolia.

"Hello," he said. "I have seen you, but it is my error that I do not know your name."

"Joolia Tenuta," she said. "I'm glad you're home. Khana was—" She broke off, and turned.

"He calls you Shanna?"

"Yes," said Bar Jan before he could speak. "I was a small boy when I . . . met Khana, and could not say his name properly. It is his kindness that he has never corrected me."

Joolia smiled. "It's a nickname. I get it. You've known each other a long time, then?"

"Yes," Bar Jan said. "When we met, I had not quite eight Standards."

"I had fourteen," Khana said, and added, for what reason he could not have said, "I now have twenty-nine."

Joolia's eyes widened.

"All that time together, you're practically brothers," she said, and touched Khana lightly on the sleeve. "Hey, that word you wanted to know what it means—*jeef*?"

Bar Jan went still.

"Yes?" said Khana.

"So I took a minute while everybody was being noisy at the meal, and put a search in to the central library through the public terminal. Picked it up when we were leaving." He'd seen her get up and leave the group table, Khana recalled.

"Turns out that *jeef*? It don't mean anything in Terran, Trade, or Liaden. Prolly a name-word."

"Professor Linda Jeef Marteen," Bar Jan said quietly. "Joolia Tenuta, please explain about names. Is it permitted that I . . . use a name of an admired person as my own? Or do I . . . steal from them?"

"Oh, *you* wanted to know!" Joolia turned to him. "So long's you're only using a piece—you're not planning on setting up as Professor Linda Jeef Marteen, are you? Pretending to be her, is what I mean."

There was a small pause, which Khana knew was Bar Jan deciphering Joolia's question.

"No," he said at last. "I wish to call myself Jeef before the Port. I was advised to choose a name that I care enough about to *keep it out of trouble*." That was said very carefully—a quote, Khana thought, from Bar Jan's advisor. "I have admiration for Professor Marteen—her book, the process of her thought. I would honor her, and remind myself of . . . who I am, now."

"Don't see any problem with that," Joolia said. "You're still on medical?"

"Yes. I was advised that I could register a name while on medical."

"That's right, you can. There's a form. You want somebody to stand by while you're filling it out, in case you got a question, I'll volunteer for that. I'm a librarian, so I pretty much got forms down."

Another pause before Bar Jan gave a measured nod of his head, not quite a bow.

"Thank you," he said. "I will be . . . glad of your help."

There was another pause before Joolia cleared her throat.

"When do you think you'll be ready to make the change?"

Bar Jan's eyebrows went up. "Now," he said, definitely, and glanced aside. "Shanna? You also, I—if you will allow me to advise you."

"I allow, and I agree," Khana said, thinking that there should be no thread left to tie them to the dead past, and that the sooner those last remaining threads were severed, the sooner they would be . . . free.

He looked at Joolia.

"*Can* it be now?" he asked.

She smiled. "Sure can. There's an Admin Portal right at the Green Line Mall."

Khana blinked, trying to recall the station map.

Joolia's smile became a grin. She stepped forward, and tucked one hand around his arm, and the other around Bar Jan's good arm.

"I'll show you," she said. "Might as well get it done."

• • •◇• • •

GREEN LINE MALL was a shopping area, up two levels from the ARTS halls. While Bar Jan and Joolia were inside, filing the necessary forms, Khana went for a walk around the mall.

Despite it being well into alt-shift, there were people about, shopping, eating, walking together. No one seemed panicked, or, indeed, worried, and he supposed that the news of the upcoming comet strike had not yet been shared by Port Admin.

Well, and nor had Khana shared the news with Bar Jan, though it would have been difficult to stem the enthusiastic flow of his conversation.

For it would seem that Bar—no. It would seem that *Jeef* had found a new course for himself. He had entertained them with tales of the kitchens behind the Cantina, and the wonders of baking bread. Chef Klyken had invited Jeef to come and observe at his own restaurant, once he was no longer a medical dependent of the Port. That, Khana thought, was promising. If Jeef's interest was constant, perhaps he would earn a position in this Klyken's kitchen, while Khana . . .

While Khana what? he asked himself, half-amused. He, who had planned for them both for so long, had not planned for himself beyond a certain yearning to be of use. He would of course place himself on the volunteer roster, but he had yet to consider anything long-term. For half his lifetime, he had cared for the heir of Rinork, and he had assumed that the tale of his life would hold very little change, save that which occurred when the heir ascended to delm.

But now, his life was upended, and it would seem that his charge, neither heir nor delm, would not for much longer require, or, indeed, want his care.

It was an odd thought—that all his care might be for . . . himself.

Whatever, he thought with sudden wryness, he might choose to call himself.

He finished his arc through the shops, and was strolling back to the Admin Portal, when the door opened, and . . . Jeef came out. He was smiling broadly, like a Terran, and there was an ID card in his good hand.

Behind him came Joolia, looking tired, but also smiling.

Khana stretched his legs to meet them.

"All's well?" he asked.

"Well and more than well!" Jeef declared, holding up the card so Khana could read that it was coded to Jeef Baker.

"Baker?" Khana asked.

"Joolia tells me that it is a well-used Terran name. As it is also the profession I hope to follow, it seemed . . . a good choice."

"A good choice, indeed," Khana said, producing his own smile.

"Your turn," Joolia said.

He looked up to meet her eyes; nodded.

"Jeef—"

"Go, I will be well," Jeef said, using his chin to point to the public screen. "When you are done, find me reading the news."

* * * ◆ * * *

"HERE," Joolia said, pointing at the screen. "This is where you input your name. It's got be no less than two words and no more than five. Okay?"

"Yes," he breathed, and stared at the place where he was to put his . . . name. Khana vo'Daran Clan Baling was dead by his own will, so Rinork would inform Baling. The life-price would likely already have been paid, Rinork being meticulous in such things. While it was unlikely that Baling would set a bounty on him, Rinork assuredly would, on Bar Jan. For Rinork's purpose, Khana was nothing other than a loose thread to be cut.

"If you're not ready," Joolia said, softly. "We can come back later."

"Sooner is better," he said, and looked down to the input pad.

In the space labeled "Call-name" he placed *Shanna*. It was a thread that tied him, past to present, honoring the choices he had made. He looked at it on the screen—Shanna. Yes. It was correct.

"One more," Joolia said next to his ear. "The Port has a list you can pick from, if you don't have something particular in mind."

"Yes, please," he said.

She reached past him to tap the screen, and a list unfurled down the right side.

He scrolled, frowning—and used his finger to arrest the scroll.

"Newman," he said. "That is apt."

"Then make it your own," Joolia said, and he placed the name in the appropriate space.

"All right, now there's some questions," Joolia said. "Won't take long."

* * * ◇ * * *

THEY EXITED THE PORTAL and found Jeef sitting on a bench across from the door. He was not smiling.

Shanna went forward.

"What has happened?" he asked.

Jeef jerked his head, and it was then that Shanna saw that there was a crowd around the public screen. A silent and strangely tense crowd.

"The comet," Jeef said. "No, I mistake. A piece of the comet. It will strike the station. So." He looked back to Shanna, and it seemed he tried to smile.

"There is something said in Terran," he said then. "About living joy, no matter how short a time?"

"A short life," Joolia said, "but a merry one."

"Yes," said Jeef, "that is it."

"The Port has shields," Joolia said, extending a hand to help him to his feet. "It's survived strikes before. There are several reports in the library. I wouldn't figure this comet's going to win, just yet."

Shanna felt the muscles of his stomach loosen, even as he offered his arm to Joolia.

"What, then, should we do?"

"Honestly? We should go back home and get some rest before day-shift catches us asleep on our feet."

THREE

THEY WERE WOKEN by a bell, loud and unaccustomed, followed by Ferlandy's voice over the little-used intercom.

"Special Session for ARTS in an hour," he said. "Attendance mandatory."

• • •✧• • •

SHANNA AND JEEF broke their fast with cheese muffins and tea, and arrived at the lounge to find it already awash in ARTS residents. They took two chairs together at the end of a row near the front, settling just as Ferlandy strode in and took his place behind the front table.

"We're having a guest today, so no sharing," he said briskly. "She should be—"

He paused, and Shanna heard the brisk step in the hallway. Heads turned as the tall woman in a Port Admin uniform strode into the room. There was a sudden uproar, as some residents clapped hands, others whistled, and many came to their feet.

"Residents and Travelers, I see most of you know our guest already," Ferlandy said, his voice raised over the racket, "so I'll just step back and let Chief Operator Malvern have the floor for as long as she needs it."

Malvern came to the front table and paused, looking at them, as they looked at her. There was, Shanna thought, a fell energy to her that had never been apparent when they had met at the Cantina. This woman was a delm, a commander, practical and hard.

"So." She greeted them all with a single nod, and began to speak.

"Some of you might not've heard that the Port's attempt to nudge the incoming comet away from us by directing the mining equipment trapped on the surface to move wasn't our most notable success. The comet broke apart, and while two big pieces are gonna give us some room, the third's likely gonna hit. That's better than the whole thing hits us, but it's still not good.

"You also might not've heard that Chas Debiro and his entire shift of Port Controllers left on the Veddy Line's big freighter a couple days ago. His backup left with most of her shift next ship out, same day—that was *Ozwall*, which had filed for quick departure.

"Seems the upgraded shielding and brand-new comet-capturing protocol you'll remember we had done couple Standards back, that project headed by Chief Debiro, isn't so robust as the contractor and the chief would have had Admin believe."

She paused to look out over the room, but no one spoke, nor moved. It was possible, Shanna thought, remembering to do it himself, that no one breathed.

Malvern nodded.

"Yeah, there's crimes, and malfeasance, and criminal intent, but that's not my problem, nor yours. *Our* problem is keeping Port Chavvy's people safe."

Her mouth moved, a smile, Shanna thought, wry and wistful.

"I retired as Chief Operator nineteen Standards back, but before I did that, I thought of, designed, tested, and put into place the Port Chavvy Structural Emergency Response Protocols. According to that document, in an emergency like we have now, the Port Controllers implement the protocols and procedures. Since we seem to be out of Port Controllers, I got called up from Reserve to sit back down in Ops Seat One, in charge of implementing the protocols and procedures.

"Which brings me to why I'm here, talking to you."

She paused again, but her audience sat rapt.

"Right. Short tell is this: Step three in the protocols, subhead long-term emergency, is *take stock of human potential*. That's everybody on this station, including you, including me."

Windy stood up. "You're counting *us*? What for?"

Malvern smiled at him.

"Good question, and put straight. 'Preciate that. What's your name?"

"Wi-Wallace VinHalin, ma'am. Awaitin' Transport."

"Pleased to meet you, Mr. VinHalin. Now the reason I'm *counting you* is that the Station's gotta run, and we need a certain number of people to make sure that all the necessary jobs are covered at least twice. By necessary jobs I mean stinks, and maintenance, food service, engineering, life support, communications—all of it, saving Port Admin because for the duration of the emergency that particular seat belongs to me."

She raised a hand.

"So, before anybody says that we already got triple redundancy on almost all jobs on-station, I'll say, that's *now*, before we evacuate."

She stopped talking then because the word *evacuate* had elicited a response from the group, a sort of a startled murmur, Shanna thought, folding his hands tightly together on his knee.

The murmur having died, Malvern spoke again.

"Yeah, we're evacuating. Kids, olds, med-cases, those'll go first, each with one caregiver. Then we'll move down to those who don't wanna stay in harm's way. Outstation Quince isn't even gonna see the comet go past, so we're putting as many as we can under the dome. Ships in port can take the overflow. Planetary Admin is talking about sending shuttles up, taking anybody who don't mind dirt downside. We could get everybody out, and would, if the situation was more dangerous than what we got."

She paused, as if struck by what she had just said, then smiled slightly and shook her head.

"What we got is dangerous enough for me. But there'll still be a station to come home to, even if that rock with our name on it strikes truer than projections. So what I'm looking for is people who will stay, and keep Port Chavvy running, and do whatever needs doing during and after the collision.

"Here's what I can guarantee: things will be confusing; there'll be more work than hands, which is a new kind of problem; and it'll be dangerous. We're looking at dealing with anything from a major breach—in which case people will die—to watching a couple antennas get ripped out of our array."

There came a rumble of voices. Malvern continued to talk, louder, asserting her precedence.

"The other things I can guarantee: everybody who stays and helps keep Port Chavvy up and running, will get three meals a day, bunk space, training as necessary, and, when the emergency is over and Admin takes back its damn chair—all the emergency volunteers will be recognized as having fulfilled their residency requirements."

Silence overflowed the lounge, as if those present utterly disbelieved what they had just heard. Shanna felt his blood quicken. Residency! He could do more than volunteer, he could learn a trade, he could—

"In just a few minutes, I'll ask those who are volunteering to come up here and talk to Mr. Ferlandy. There's some questions to be answered, and so forth. Before we do that, though, we need to get the med-cases on their way to safety. There are two, I think, Mr. Ferlandy?"

"Yes'm. Cazzy's still under clinic-care, but—" He glanced out over the lounge.

Shanna felt a movement in the seat beside him, as Jeef rose to his full meager height, the empty sleeve of his lab coat pinned neatly out of the way.

"Jeef Baker," he said. "I volunteer to stay and work for the safety of the Port."

Malvern frowned at him.

"Medics let you go?" she asked.

"They have not yet. Will there be no medics among those who remain?"

The frown eased.

"We'll have medics. Tell me what you can do for me, Jeef Baker."

He inclined his head, very Liaden in that gesture.

"I can read. I can do inventory. I can cipher. I can—"

"Follow orders?" Malvern interrupted.

Jeef took a breath, and this time inclined from the waist.

"Yes," he said.

"Then get yourself up to the clinic, right now. Tell 'em I sent you for a work eval. Tell 'em you volunteered for Comet Utility Crew. You bring whatever the medics give you back to Mr. Ferlandy, here. Got that?"

"Yes," Jeef said again. He stepped out of the row, walking out of the lounge without a backward glance.

Shanna thought about going after him, took a breath and remained seated.

When he looked up, Malvern gave him a nod and a smile.

• • •✧• • •

THEY WERE ISSUED Port volunteer vests, protective gloves, goggles, and a utility belt. Every sixth of them, by count-off, was issued a comm unit, and that person became a team leader. As a group, they were known as Uties, and their first duty was to assist in the evacuation, keeping order among those moving to the docks and the ships that would take them to safety. As each apt was cleared, it was entered by a Utie, who verified that no one had been left behind before using their Admin-issued general key to trigger the inflation of air bags that would keep furniture in place, should—when—the comet struck the station.

As Uties were rotated out of escort-and-lockdown, they were given tours of vents, stink-pots, utility cabinets, wiring and plumbing closets, tool-bins, and emergency hatches.

The tool-bin proved unexpectedly exhilarating for Shanna, as the tools within were handed around and named as a primer to their duties.

"Bashbar," said their tutor, handing it to the first of the group, who obediently repeated the phrase and passed it to the Utie on her right.

"Life-pry," the tutor continued, "stinks hammer, starbar..."

Shanna flinched as that came to hand, sagging with the weight of it. He had not seen the instrument of his master's maiming, and had imagined something...powered and smooth. But this object was evidently meant to be used violently, and was clearly capable of damaging the fabric of Port Chavvy itself, much less the fabric of a Liaden lordling's expensive port-side coat sleeve, and the arm it embraced.

Jeef, separated from him by several of their team members, his wounded arm now enclosed in a flexible cast that allowed him to fully occupy his shirt and vest, received the starbar in his good hand, and went to one knee, bearing the weight of the thing to the deck.

"Yeah, starbar'll getcher attention, all right!" said the Utie on his right, reaching down and hefting the thing as if it were a twig.

Jeef regained his feet, caught Shanna's worried eye and bowed with subtle irony.

* * * ✧ * * *

THE EVACUEES DEPARTED; the Uties' work shifts grew longer and more frantic. The images of the onrushing comet were on all the news screens, the constant beauty of them dimmed by the other information that they absorbed as they worked: the protoplanet had been being mined for metals and ice; and among the metals nickel and iron were common, with a smattering of the heavier elements. Shanna found Jeef's interest in the technical side of things imposing but not surprising; he seemed more at home among real things than the fripperies of etiquette and dominance that had been so commonplace in their *melant'i*-ridden past.

Word came that the station's maneuvering jets and pocket engine were useless in the present emergency. Port Chavvy could, indeed, be relocated, but not quickly enough to avoid its oncoming doom. The question of tugs pulling the station out of the way was dismissed by the engineers as likely to cause more structural damage than the comet's kiss.

The Uties worked on.

Most of the store fronts of the various malls and shopping districts were no longer airtight, despite the maintenance rules requiring it. Rumors went through the decks that certain owners had paid bribes to be excused from higher levels of compliance, with Malvern promising damnation and worse to anyone she might prove it against. The Uties condensed the goods in the stores around the known pipes, conduits, and air vents in an attempt to allay the potential damage from objects traveling at the rate of a kilometer or more a second.

And then the comet broke again, becoming ash and dense cores, spinning madly.

Aghast, an on-break team stood watching the streaming, nearly foaming mass of hurtling objects split away from the larger masses in a view from a probe. Some parts appeared to adhere to the pockmarked centers, others spewed away as if under power. Portions, at least, were still on course for the station.

"But why?" Shanna asked while shaking his head. "Why this chaos now, why like this?"

He'd expected no answer, but Jeef's quiet voice came, as if trying to soothe with explanation.

"Transition phases, Shanna, change of state. The coma—the comet-head—is not an atmosphere, has almost no pressure whatsoever and with the approach to the inner system the ices become gas without being liquid—they boil. Then in the starlight they look like they burn into smoke or turn to ribbons, but there's no flame. Just a change of state."

Around them a mix of nodding and shaking heads, and an echo: "Just a change of state, that's all."

* * * ✧ * * *

MALVERN HAD ORDERED everyone who remained into the core safe lounges, where they strapped in, fresh batteries in their comms, food and water packs to hand, with pressure masks and breathers. They had done everything they could, all they had been asked to do, and more. Now, they waited for the impact. Any other duty lay on the far side of that event.

The all-station intercom snapped, and here came Malvern's voice.

"Strapped in and waiting," she said. "You got what I got. There's maybe a chance these things are gonna rush by and we won't have to worry about 'em 'til we hit this section of the orbit again in five Standards. But that's a *maybe* chance, and I don't think we're gonna get that lucky. So, stay strapped in, be ready to call your leaders. *Zanzo's Flitter* is standing off, observing. They sent a radar image of a mess of stuff—the rocks and what they've attracted—coming through our intersection in fifty-eight minutes. There may be rapid accelerations. Strap down. Stay strapped down until I send all clear!"

* * * ✧ * * *

SCARCELY TEN MINUTES had elapsed when the comm blared again.

"Movement in the Long View! Chef Klyken, acknowledge!"

There was a pause, then again, more urgently: "Long View, acknowledge!"

There was a grunt in his ear, and Jeef was up, unstrapped, in danger.

"Stay!" Shanna cried. "What are you—"

"Klyken," Jeef snapped. "I will get him!"

And he was gone, running.

Shanna repeated several of the useful new words he had learned as a Utie, released his own webbing, and ran after.

* * * ✧ * * *

THE WINDOW—it was the window that gave the Long View Restaurant its name. Jeef remembered that it was said to be tougher than hull-plate. He remembered the view, the long swell of stars, against the black of space.

Now, the window opened on mud and dust. Objects struck it, audibly.

And Klyken was nowhere to be seen.

Jeef turned on his heel, straining to see in the meager light of the emergency dims.

"Klyken?" he called.

There was no answer.

No, Jeef thought suddenly. Klyken would not be *here* where other people ate what he had made for them.

Klyken would be in the kitchen.

He spun and bolted through the pass-door.

The kitchen was locked down, pristine, and empty.

The door worked at his back, and Shanna was there. He spun. "Go!"

"Come with me! Jeef, this is too dangerous!"

"Yes!" he shouted. "It is dangerous! Shanna—go! You already died of me once! I will find Chef Klyken—he must be here!"

"Perhaps he is tied down," Shanna suggested, not leaving.

"Here?" Jeef said, with a shudder, imagining the damage. "Malvern wants everyone in the core lounges. Shanna—"

"Yes, I will go. Let us find the chef, first."

There was no more time to argue, if they were, indeed, to find Klyken and bring them all safely to the core.

Jeef moved down the aisle, came to the freezer, the bread safe, the—

The bread safe.

He put his hand on the latch, but it was locked.

"Klyken?" he called.

There was no answer.

"Jeef, he is not here, or he does not want to be rescued." Shanna came down the other aisle. "Come, we must save ourselves."

"Go," he said. "I—" He bit his lip, as memory rose.

It isn't a good thing, to throw a child away. The Long View—that is my child now.

He took a breath. It was dishonest, what he was about to do, and the book made a strong case for honesty in all things, even as it also instructed one to care for those in need.

Surely, Jeef thought, here is need.

"Father!" he called, sharply. "Father, I am here!"

For a long moment, nothing happened. The clicking against the window was loud in the silence. Shanna extended a hand.

The latch of the bread safe moved. Klyken stepped out, holding a stasis box.

He paused on the threshold of the room, and Jeef had a momentary fear that he would bolt back inside.

Then, the chef nodded.

"Yes," he said, quietly. "I had only wanted my bread-heart."

FOUR

THE LARGEST ROCK destroyed much of the comm and power array in a single jolting strike that took an hour of Malvern's superb piloting of station resources to quell.

The ashen remains of the smaller rock smashed into dust on the Long View's window.

The middle-sized rock passed through the shattered remains of Port Chavvy's array, flew by the dusty detritus splattered by the small rock, and left no additional trace to add to the confusion already spawned.

• • • ✧ • • •

THE LAST OF THE EVACUEES was home, joining forces with the Uties, as they repaired the damage the comet, and neglect, had done.

The station had paid each Utie a "stake," and issued each a new card, declaring them to be Residents of Port Chavvy Station. They still lived in the ARTS halls, as apts were being repaired and made ready for them.

Shanna was now full-time leader of a Utie team. He'd kept the tool set he'd been assigned for the duration of the emergency in their rooms for eleven days, for quick response in case one more lump of the comet managed to find the Port, but it hadn't happened and both he and Jeef were relieved once the set that included starbars and stinks hammers went back to their emergency closets rather than bulking large just inside their own door. Jeef was Klyken's apprentice, certified and formal, and most of his hours were spent in the Long View, repairing and cleaning with the rest of Klyken's workers—and also learning somewhat of baking.

At the Admin level, investigations were underway, and a team of auditors had come up from the planet to assist.

Shanna was crossing the lounge, thinking of a shower before he joined the usual group to go in search of supper. This was a better habit than backstairs at the delm's residence, with none of the tension of those rule-bound precincts. Joolia and he had taken to walking apart from the group after the meal was done, going up to the Atrium on E Deck, which had taken only a little damage from the comet.

"Shanna!" a voice came, sharp and unexpected from the right. He stopped, and turned to face Femta; a talkative Femta, as it happened.

"Just the man I wanted to see! A friend of mine got in today, first time on port. I wonder if you'd be willing to meet him and me at the Atrium on E Deck, at purple. There's a couple others coming, too. We've got an offer to put in front of you."

Shanna frowned slightly.

"A job?"

"A job?" Femta nodded. "You could call it that, sure."

Uties did worthy work, but Shanna had lately been thinking about what he might prefer to do, as his service to the port and to people.

"I would be interested," he said, and Femta grinned.

"Good, then. See you at purple."

• • • ✧ • • •

HE LET THE DINNER GROUP get ahead of him, and realized that he was not alone.

"Going up to the garden again?" Joolia asked.

"Yes, but tonight I am to meet Femta and his friend, to hear about a job."

Joolia grinned.

"Funny thing—me, too."

Shanna tipped his head, not liking to think of Joolia as . . . competition. However—

"I figure it can't hurt to listen to what they got to say," Joolia continued. "Might be inneresting; might not."

"Yes," he said, and offered his arm. "Let us go together."

"Great idea," she said, and slipped her arm through his.

· · · ✧ · · ·

IT HAD JUST COME PURPLE when they strolled into the Atrium, to find Femta and another person awaiting them at the first grouping of benches.

"Just on time," Femta said, and urged his companion forward. "This is my colleague of many years, Jemmon Fairkin, who has come to fetch me away! Jemmon, this is Joolia Tenuta and Shanna Newman."

The man was bulky and bald. A long fine silver chain depended from his left ear. He bowed in the Terran style, one hand over his heart, the other held loose at his side.

"Joolia Tenuta, Shanna Newman, I am happy to see you."

"We invited one more to speak with us this evening. He did warn that he might be a little behind the—"

There came the sharp sound of bootheels on decking, and 'round the curve of the path came a figure dressed in white, carrying a tray in two hands.

"Here I am," Jeef said, "late as promised! I bring my first batch of *cupcakes*, to balance my tardiness."

He came up with them, and smiled, a scent of citrus and sugar wafting in with him.

"Joolia. Shanna. Good evening."

"Good evening," Joolia said, adding, "cupcakes?"

"Do not expect very much," Jeef said, stepping forward to place the tray on one of the benches. "I am told that they are misshapen and mis-decorated, which is true, and my fault for jostling them too much for curiosity while baking. But they taste very good, if I say it myself."

"Then I'll close my eyes when I eat one," Joolia said solemnly, and Jeef smiled.

"A perfect solution."

Each chose a sweet and a seat, and for a few minutes there was silence, while they gave the food its due. Jeef had not misrepresented his efforts. The little cakes were very lopsided and the icing unevenly spread, faults that did not detract at all from the pleasing taste.

"Very good!" Joolia pronounced. "Thank you."

"You are welcome," Jeef said.

Femta shifted subtly on the bench, and all attention was immediately on him.

"Now, Jemmon needs to be brought up to the present, so I'll just tell him real quick that all three of you earned Port Chavvy Resident status during the recent comet emergency. These folks have the right to call Port Chavvy their home, to use it as a home port, and receive care and food, if needed. They've gotten a bonus for their work during the emergency—and they'll receive the Resident Basic Allotment, plus whatever they earn by working for the Port. All clear?"

"Clear," Jemmon said with a nod.

"Right." Femta turned to them. "Now, I'll ask you—what do you intend to do with the rest of your lives? You're secure here. Will you stay on and be busy for the Port?

"Will you look up legal references, and mine the archives for Admin for the rest of your life, Joolia? Do you think it will take that long to wind up affairs against the runaways?

"What will you do, Jeef, with your background in trade—be a buyer for a shop on a rebuilt C Deck?

"And you, Shanna, you have experience running a household and in dealing with fashion and grooming needs for another. Both of you have impeccable Liaden form and language and both of you will find it hard to make use of your knowledge of Liaden culture here, where *Wynhael* is a rare visitor at best."

A pause as Femta looked hard at each of them, and then to his colleague, who nodded agreement with the questions.

"We have no interest in *Wynhael*," Jeef said quietly. "And she has no interest in us. I hope you have not built plans on the profit you hope to gain by selling us back to her, friend Femta, for you will go broke."

Femta raised both hands, fingers spread. "Nothing like that, friend Jeef. Will you let me follow my questions with my offer?"

Jeef nodded.

"I feel that the three of you have more scope than Port Chavvy. Consider what your lives will be, if you remain in a world encompassed by seven levels. Walking the same halls, waiting for the same ships to come back, on the same schedules, and of course the construction, interruption, and inconveniences of the repair and rebuild. It would be, understand, a good life—or not a bad one. Security is a powerful draw.

"What we offer—Jemmon and me—is an option that is less secure, that has the potential to help thinking people, and to demonstrate to the numberless cultures across space that we are the same more than we are different.

"What we suggest, is that you join us, to help us explore, and learn, and share what we've learned. We will accomplish our goal by—traveling. Being travelers. We will take ship, arrive, explore places—planets, stations, ships—using what we know to entertain ourselves and enlighten others, learning from them the things— food, music and songs—the customs that are unique and the customs that beneath things echo other places."

"What's your funding?" Joolia asked. "Who's your sponsor? I like the notion of traveling, but I don't want to be stranded. Never again."

Jemmon nodded this time, and cleared his throat.

"Femta and I hold tenured university positions as traveling professors of civil culture. We are funded by a revolving grant from Crystal Energy Systems. Among the things we do is study business practices, cultures, custom. We give presentations and reports to librarians, universities, teaching colleagues. Our methods are varied. We can stand in a bar and trade stories with the locals, if that is what we wish to do. What we must not do—is argue the superiority of one culture over another. What we must understand—and by experiencing things first hand we *shall* understand!—is how best to let the worlds of thinking people behave well toward each other.

"We have funding for the first five Standards of travel, which will be distributed among the first of us, whether that be two or five. We expect in seven years to be joined by two more colleagues and have the option of adding one or two along the way, should we find like minds. We shall be a happy tour group, learning, enjoying, witnessing . . . and if we can make worlds work better by quietly insinuating information, by pointing to successes without demanding they be followed, by locating people who are mis-cultured and ought to be elsewhere, as you may have been, Jeef . . . "

Jemmon leaned back, and exchanged a look with Femta.

"So. In three days, Jemmon and I will depart Port Chavvy with tickets to three planets over the next two Standards in hand. We ask you to join us, that we be useful to the universe. You don't have to decide now, but—soon."

"This offer, this opportunity now? This would be a major change of state, I think," said Jeef, glancing to Shanna and back to Femta.

Shanna nodded, allowing himself to wonderingly exhale.

"Change of state, indeed," he murmured.

Shanna was aware that he was shivering. To visit a planet again? To be of use? To travel under his own direction, and for himself? His nodding had never stopped, and he smiled.

"Yes," he said, his voice mingling with Joolia's, "Yes!"

Jeef shook his head, a Terran habit he'd grown to admire. His face was thoughtful, perhaps wistful.

"No."

He paused, looked into the faces of his friends.

"Shanna, Joolia. I have a place here, and the smallness of the world I live in pleases me. I have chosen a trade, and I will learn to be something other than I was. Jeef Baker is the man I wish to be!"

He smiled at Shanna.

"And I will be pleased to see you, brother, when you come home again."